Crossing the Witchline

T.L. Brown

Praise for A Thin Witchline Between Love & Hate

"This is definitely a dark paranormal fantasy read with mature themes, but certainly not a case of the author shocking for shock's sake. The darkness Brown brings is the marrow within the bones of this tale..."
- Julie Embleton, author of the Turning Moon Series and the Coveted Power Series

"...Lucie Bellerose is a brilliant character — she oozes with intellect, magic and a burning passion that's downright combustible."
- Shari T. Mitchell, author of the Marnie Reilly Mysteries

"...I love that the author pushed boundaries. Leaving child's play at the door, we are pulled into a new adventure, more dark, more twisted, more sexy!"

- Jessica Cantwell, author of the young adult series, The Realm Saga

Praise for Crossing the Witchline

"With the latest installment in her Bellerose Witchline series, Brown has amped up everything — the emotions, the stakes, the world-building, and the twists are all on overdrive. It's a ride you don't want to miss!"
- Book review site Jill-Elizabeth.com

"Brown packs a ton into this second of a trilogy, but the story never feels like too much to consume. It is the perfect thrill with just the right level of heat."
- Jennifer Brasington-Crowley, author of the Raven Song Series and the Stillwaters Series

"*Crossing the Witchline* picks up from the dramatic conclusion at the end of the first book in the series, and continues with the same mix of drama, romance, and heartache that readers already know and love from this author."

- Saffron Amatti, author of the Lucas Rathbone Mysteries

Books by This Author

Bellerose Witchline Series

A Thin Witchline Between Love & Hate (Book 1)
Crossing the Witchline (Book 2)
Walking a Fine Witchline (Book 3, coming in 2023)

Door to Door Paranormal Mystery Series

Looking for something lighter? Meet Emily Swift, Templeton, and Rabbit BEFORE they cross paths with fiery witch Lucie Bellerose in the *Door to Door Paranormal Mystery Series* — also by T.L. Brown! Find the series on Amazon.

Door to Door (Book 1)
Through the Door (Book 2)
Doors Wide Open (Book 3)

Copyright © 2022 Tracy Brown-Simmons

All rights reserved.

The characters and events portrayed in this book are fictitious. Any similarity to real persons, living or dead, business establishments, events, or locales is coincidental and not intended by the author.

No part of this book may be reproduced, or stored in a retrieval system, or transmitted in any form or by any means, electronic, mechanical, photocopying, recording, or otherwise, without express written permission of the publisher.

ISBN: 979-8-9859503-3-5

First Edition: September 2022

Created / printed in the United States of America

to second chances...

Saffron,
Open your heart
+ Shine on!
XO,
Tracy
T.L. Brown

Contents

Title Page
Praise for A Thin Witchline Between Love & Hate
Praise for Crossing the Witchline
Books by This Author
Copyright
Dedication

Prologue	1
Chapter 1	7
Chapter 2	32
Chapter 3	55
Chapter 4	81
Chapter 5	105
Chapter 6	128

Chapter 7	148
Chapter 8	169
Chapter 9	192
Chapter 10	216
Chapter 11	236
Chapter 12	262
Chapter 13	291
Chapter 14	314
Chapter 15	341
Chapter 16	362
Chapter 17	386
Chapter 18	412
Chapter 19	439
Chapter 20	464
Chapter 21	497
Chapter 22	525
Chapter 23	545
Chapter 24	574
Chapter 25	606
Epilogue	617
Resources	621
Acknowledgments	623
Find the Author Online	627
About the Author	629

Prologue

*From: The Ending, Empire
Tales for Children*

"...Each door leads to its own imagined place or reality. One door opens into your land in the Between. These doors blend into the Above. The Beams of Light from Above live there. It is a hard space for other creatures to endure. Most do not stay. Some get trapped," the bird finished.

"What happens when they get trapped?" asked the girl.

"They disappear into the bright white of the Above. They cease to be..."

- Source: Chapter 22, *A Thin Witchline Between Love & Hate*, by T.L. Brown

That April

In my living room, I didn't bother to light the fireplace insert. The weather was turning warmer. The snow had melted. The world outside was coming back to life after a hard winter.

I curled up on the couch and opened Templeton's book. I traced his handwriting with my fingertip. Oh, how I missed him.

I missed the damn infuriating man who set me on fire, who made my skin glow.

I missed my knight.

Reaching inside my shirt, I pulled out the necklace I wore against my heart. I'd put the three pieces of the Crimson Stone on a thick silver chain. It was my way of watching over the Stone and keeping Templeton close to me. I ran my fingers over the gemstones.

"Someday, I'll figure out how to put you back together," I whispered. "Then I'll wake you up. We'll open the fifth door. Then we'll go get him."

Flame stalked into the living room. He sat and spent a moment licking his paw and rubbing it over his face. He froze mid-swipe. His beautiful cat eyes blinked once as he peered up at me. In a flash, he'd jumped up on the sofa and put his front paws on my thigh. I lowered my head, and he bopped my forehead with his.

I scratched under his chin with my fingernails. "What do you think, buddy? Want to help me figure out how to get this damn thing working again?"

Flame meowed and lifted his right paw. His claws flexed in the air, and he gently patted my cheek. He lowered his furry foot, tapping one of the pieces of the Crimson Stone with a pointed nail.

A tongue of fire appeared.

Startled, I leapt from the couch, dumping Flame from my lap and grabbing at the gemstones hanging from my necklace.

Flame hopped to the floor.

The other two pieces of the Crimson Stone lit up and began to hum. The three pieces started talking to one another, pulsing and eventually finding the same rhythm.

I gaped at Flame. He sat in the middle of my living room.

"How?" I breathed. "Flame, what have you done?"

Flame stood again on his four legs, spinning

sweetly in a compact circle. Dumbfounded, I watched as the orange tabby cat's body twisted and his muscles rippled under the fur. He grew, raising up gracefully, shapeshifting from a handsome feline into a very pretty man with tousled strawberry-blond hair and striking amber eyes.

His tan body was lean, without an ounce of fat. His muscles flexed gently under his human skin. He rolled his shoulders, giving his young body a shake.

And he was naked. Completely and utterly naked.

His hands rested on his narrow hips, his fingers stretching like a cat flexing its claws. My eyes shot up to his upturned, almond-shaped ones.

Flame smiled broadly, white teeth gleaming behind a set of perfectly pink lips. He tossed his head proudly.

"Hello, Lucie."

> \- Source: Chapter 25, *A Thin Witchline Between Love & Hate*, by T.L. Brown

And the prophecy said...

A traveler is born.
The knight protects the light.
Their successor sets fire to the stone.
A shadow is cast out.

Emily Swift is the traveler. John Templeton is the knight.

And I, Lucie Bellerose, am the light.

I put the Crimson Stone to sleep, but now I need it to wake up.

I believe the successor has appeared. I call him Flame.

Shadows fill my heart.

And the book of fairy tales revealed...

North, East, West, South.
So as Above, moreso Below.

The fifth and sixth directional doors, the

Above and the Below, remain closed to me.

Behind the Above door, my magic man, *my knight*, is trapped.

Behind the Below door, my former lover, *now a demon*, is imprisoned.

Chapter 1

Each time I caught a hint of a human expression on the furry face of my cat should've been a clue: Flame was not your average feline. An orange mackerel tabby, he sported bright white stripes throughout his sleek coat. Over the classic 'M' pattern found on his forehead appeared a reddish tuft of fur in the shape of a flame.

Hence the name.

Flame was also a shapeshifter; his present form was a well-tanned half-dressed 20-year-old raiding my refrigerator.

I sat on a barstool, resting my elbows on the top of my kitchen counter and watching him through my fingers as he rambled on about having nothing to eat and how maybe he should be in charge of the grocery list moving forward.

Only six days had passed since he made his true nature known to me, but already he was eating me out of house and home. I was not prepared to have a shameless man-child-shapeshifter living under my roof – especially one with a bottomless pit for a stomach. I watched as he finally stood up to gulp down several large swallows of whole milk from the carton.

As he straightened, my gaze wandered to the waistband of his shorts. It was resting far lower than appropriate.

It was a battle to convince him to wear clothing. We'd compromised – he agreed to wear a pair of secondhand basketball shorts when in the house and in his human form. But it was all he'd put on when he was 'home.'

We needed to have a talk.

I had no idea what to do about this predicament.

And, of course, the timing wasn't good. But seriously, was there ever an ideal time to learn your cat was a shapeshifter with boundary issues? I glanced at the clock on the stove. I was meeting Loren Heatherworth for lunch in the northern part of Matar in 30 minutes. I needed to get going.

"Flame," I began. "Use a glass."

He lowered the carton, his lips splitting into a cheeky grin after wiping his wide mouth with the back of his hand – twice. "You don't even like whole milk."

"Yes, I know," I grumbled. I'd purchased the full-fat milk at his insistence. "Listen, I'm joining my friend Loren for lunch. I'll be back this afternoon by 3 o'clock. Maybe you can talk to David while I'm gone about getting the rest of your clothes?"

Flame's shoulders lifted. "He's at work."

I tried again. "Maybe you can get with him later tonight. In the meantime, speaking of work…"

"Right." He pointed a steady finger at me. "There are a couple of places I'm checking out this week. Some cool venues advertising for talent buyers. Positions opening up."

"Great." My teeth pressed together as my lips pulled into a crazed smile. Flame's grand dream was to become a concert promoter. He'd laid out his multi-step plan over the past weekend while he ate half a lasagna I'd baked. He'd decided talent buyer was the place for him to start. I'd suggested an education in the music business or maybe even marketing in general, but he was confident his plan was the way to go. Snag the job, get the experience.

He assessed me with a sweet face. "Relax, Lucie. You're too high-strung. Life always works out for the best. Trust me."

Flame's innocent words set off a searing pain in my chest. I swallowed and lowered my chin. His experience was clearly different from my own. I touched the tiny top hat hanging from the silver charm bracelet my friend Anne gave me when Templeton first disappeared. 'Hope' had been engraved on the surface of the hat. The other charms included a two-handled jar, a fly, a skull, a split heart, and a headstone. The jar was Pandora's box, and 'Hope' had been let out. Anne told me to have hope.

But I was losing it.

Taking a deep breath, I nodded, sliding from the barstool and reaching for my purse. I spared a look for him and hesitated.

He regarded me thoughtfully. The carefree expression disappeared from his face. "You're thinking about that guy again."

"Maybe," I replied. "I've got to go. See if you can get a message to your David. I'll drive you over tonight, and you can get the rest of your clothes. Or we'll get you more at *Second Act*." The consignment shop was within walking distance of my brownstone and where I'd purchased the shorts he wore now.

Flame rolled his eyes. "You are such a prude, Lucie."

I lifted my eyebrows as I dug my keys from my purse. "You might be the only person who's ever called me that."

The weather was lovely. A particularly sunshiny day for the end of April, there was no need for a coat. The khaki-colored blazer I'd pulled on over a long sleeve fitted tee in white was all I needed to be comfortable. I'd dressed up the combo by wrapping a navy silk scarf patterned with white polka dots around my neck. Below the scarf and under the white top, the three gemstones of the Crimson Stone hung safely from a silver chain and rested against my skin. Occasionally I'd feel the slight flicker of soothing fire as the gemstones communicated dreamily with one another.

I'd decided on jeans but compensated for the

casual look by tucking in my shirt and pairing the pants with tan sandals in a low heel. The sidewalks were dry after a wet winter. I knew my feet would be chilled, but the pleasant weather seduced me. With Flame somewhat waylaying me earlier, I only had enough time to pull my hair up into a messy bun. I hung thin silver hoops from my ears.

Before I made it down my front steps, the phone I'd stuffed deep into the front pocket of my jeans grew warm. Phones don't work in the Empire – no cell towers – but I'd been given a device used by the technologically-advanced Rabbit network. I fished it out quickly, ever hopeful to hear from my lost friend, Rabbit. Instead, I found a text from Big Rabbit, the massive man with a messy mop of black curls who'd unknowingly brought a shapeshifter into my life. I pressed my fingertip against the reader.

TODAY is someone's birthday! Big Rabbit had typed.

Be ready at 10am TOMORROW! I'm coming to get ya! We're going someplace SPECIAL!

Oh, boy – this would be interesting.

∞∞∞

When Flame abruptly morphed from a handsome feline into a cute boy – *yes, a boy, I don't care if he's 20* – in the middle of my living room, my already turned upside-down life took another tumble. The last thing I expected was for my new pet to turn into an unconventional roommate.

And I did not want a roommate – conventional or otherwise.

I drove out of the parking garage and headed east on Autumn Avenue. The clock on the dashboard told me I'd be late. Hopefully, I'd find a spot near the bistro where I'd lunch with Loren. I knew the older witch would've preferred the dining room at the Congress of Empire Witches, but since my membership was suspended, I was not allowed inside the building.

My thoughts ping-ponged back to Flame. The formerly skinny kitty had been a well-meaning gift from Big Rabbit. My mouth twisted to the side. Gift, indeed.

Flame didn't reveal himself as a shapeshifter

as he popped out of the cardboard box transporting him into my life. I'd agreed to adopt the sneaky feline under a small amount of duress – my friend had brought the stray to me since the 'little fella' needed someone to love and take care of him.

Plus, Big Rabbit already had five cats.

I'd reluctantly agreed, and frankly, it was good to have someone – well, something – to love inside my home again.

Since losing Templeton to the Above and Rabbit to life-changing injuries, my heart was not only broken, it was also achingly empty.

And then the unbelievable happened. As I sat on my couch trying to make sense of the archaic language in Templeton's book of magic, Flame, in his cat form, set off a tongue of fire inside one of the pieces of the Crimson Stone.

As the shock of what he'd done washed over me, the spark of hope I'd carried in my chest for almost three months burst into a...Well, into a *flame*.

As Flame-the-cat spun and transformed into a naked version of Flame-the-man, the other two pieces of the Crimson Stone came to life. The gemstones, hanging from a necklace, pulsed repeatedly, essentially 'talking' to one another. Awestruck, I held the pieces in the palm of my hand and wept.

With my eyes tightly closed, I'd felt a finger with a slightly pointed fingernail tuck under my chin. As he lifted my face up toward his, he'd cocked his head to the side. "Don't cry, Lucie. Whatever it is, we can fix it."

What Flame doesn't know is in that moment, he secured a firm hold on my heart – and my spare bedroom – with those innocent words. Flame might behave like an overgrown teenager on a good day, but he was especially kindhearted.

And kindness was something I valued.

We had a serious conversation after he changed into his human form – and after I made him put on one of my bathrobes. It was too short and didn't quite close in the way I would've liked, but it was better than averting my eyes or staring intently at his face while he remained in the buff. The conversation went something like this:

"Why didn't you tell me you were a shifter?"

"Would you have let me stay here?"

"No."

"Well then, it's obvious, isn't it?"

"Big Rabbit said you were a stray. A stray cat."

"Is he the mountain of muscles with all the curls?"

"Yes."

"Oh, well, he was sort of right. I hung out at this shop where all these people were working on wires and electronic stuff. It was only a matter of time. I'm very pretty and irresistible. Someone was bound to take me home."

I'd stared at him.

"Right?" He'd prompted.

"Right, pretty and irresistible. Um, what about before?"

"Before what?" He'd taken a seat on the couch. The robe gaped open when he stretched.

I'd raised a hand, wincing. "Please cover that."

After a dramatic sigh, he'd pulled a pillow onto his lap. "It's just a penis."

"Yes. Yes, it is, Flame. And I don't need to see it."

"It's a nice one." He'd lifted his end of the pillow and peeked at himself.

"I need you to focus," I'd told him. "Where did you live before coming here?"

Flame then fixed me with the unblinking gaze

that only could be held so confidently by a cat. "I lived with David. He's having issues, and we decided to take a break."

"What kind of 'issues' might David have?"

He'd shrugged and started to bite his thumbnail. He wasn't making eye contact any longer. "He wouldn't introduce me to his friends."

And so it went. I'd learned Flame moved to Matar early in the year and into this mystery man's home. He'd met David at a New Year's Eve party in Vue – an artsy city in the southern part of the Empire. David was 30, a lawyer, and not particularly open with his sexuality. He didn't only keep his private life...*private*. He'd lied and kept Flame a secret while he pretended to be someone else in public.

Flame himself was 'not into labels.' He liked 'all people' equally. He promised me he was not interested in me in any inappropriate way. Before I could laugh, he added because I was 'what, his mother's age? Forty? Maybe older?'

That is when I'd excused myself and got a big glass of wine.

This David apparently got in over his head. In Vue, he'd relaxed and invited Flame to come to Matar to visit for a while. Once Flame was here, living in a trendy neighborhood in an exciting new city, he decided to stay. Sometimes he stayed out all night – without David. Flame assured me he always asked David to go, but he was unwilling to be seen with his boyfriend in his home city.

"And he kicked you out? Without your clothes?" I'd asked. Flame nibbled on the corner of the pillow he held. I'd leaned over to pull it away, then remembered the ill-fitting robe.

"Not quite."

Following a big blowup, Flame stormed out of the house and shifted. David, who at that point was not aware his secret boyfriend was also a shapeshifter, witnessed the transformation and flipped out. By the time Flame came back, David had changed the locks and thrown the rest of the young man's clothing out into the yard.

Angry, Flame spent the night running around in cat form. When he returned for his clothes, he learned David had gathered them back up after realizing the neighbors might become curious. Flame assumed the clothes were inside the house. He hadn't talked to David in several weeks.

But, he had assured me, things always worked out. He had a place to stay – with me – until he found a place of his own.

Uh-huh.

I turned north onto High Street and navigated through traffic.

So why didn't I throw him out?

Because Flame set fire to the Crimson Stone.

∞∞∞

I'm part of a prophecy I don't fully understand. I learned of this last fall on a rainy afternoon before my entire world fell apart.

A traveler is born.
The knight protects the light.
Their successor sets fire to the stone.
A shadow is cast out.

I am 'the light' in this prophecy. John Templeton, an extraordinary man with door-traveling abilities, is 'the knight.' Together we've tried to understand our roles. We've struggled to figure out how we feel about each other – our magic blends together seamlessly.

His touch can control the fire coasting under my skin. He's exasperated me, excited me, and brought my battered heart back to life.

And then he was stolen from me.

A monster, a Beam of Light from Above, took him during a violent battle almost three months ago. He's missing, lost somewhere on the other side of the fifth door – a door leading into the Above. The Crimson Stone, rendered powerless during the battle, is the only key I have to open it. It's my only hope to save him.

The Crimson Stone is formed when three separate gemstones are magically connected. It was knocked from my hand during that wretched day in the Walled Zone. It 'broke' into the three individual pieces. They can only be reunited with a specific set of words – a spell only Templeton knows.

I have one of Templeton's handwritten books of magic, and it must be in there – *I hold onto hope it is written in there.* But he wrote much of the book in a language I don't recognize. The letters are unfamiliar, but my instincts tell me they're from one of the ancient languages of the Empire. It's possible I could find the key to these letters and what they mean in one of the archives in the library at the Congress of Empire Witches.

The problem is I'm not allowed in the library while my membership is suspended. I'm hoping to find a way to get access with help from Loren, an elder in the Congress. His influence is not as great as some of the other witches, but Loren is crafty. Loren is resourceful.

I'd planned on making the request for help over lunch even before I knew about Flame. Now I was doubly driven. The Stone had been awakened – *it was set on fire* – and this had to be a sign. Plus, the prophecy seemed to be moving forward. I needed Templeton by my side more than ever.

I needed my knight.

I hadn't told Flame about any of this. Well, I specifically didn't tell Flame about the prophecy. I did ask him how he was able to cause fire to appear in one of the gemstones. He blinked his amber eyes slowly and told me sometimes he could do 'things' when he was a cat.

I'd pressed him on that. Shapeshifters do not practice magic. Their power is simply that: shapeshifting into a particular animal.

Some, when human, had heightened strength, or speed, or improved senses based upon the animal they became. It was possible one of his parents was not a shapeshifter, or maybe there was another kind of magical being in his ancestral line.

Flame wasn't forthcoming. With additional prodding, he admitted his mother was a shifter. She was also a cat – another orange tabby, which was rare for female shifter-cats. Unlike Flame, however, she was not a mackerel tabby but bore the classic pattern of vivid orange swirls on a lighter ginger coat. I'd yet to meet her.

He didn't know his father, though. He laughed as he explained his mother was a free spirit like him in her younger years. He was conceived during a party at a musical venue. Flame grinned, shrugging. His mother had since settled down and was happily married to someone else.

The unknown father could be the connection. If not him, then perhaps someone from the father's family tree. Either way, Flame had the magic touch. The fact it manifested with the Crimson Stone threw me.

And until I figured out what Flame was – and

why he could set fire to the Crimson Stone – I was keeping him close.

But I'd still like him to put on some clothes and find a job.

∞∞∞

I managed to snag a parking spot about a block from *Ruby's*, a busy bistro in a section of Matar where many witch-related interests were concentrated. Inside, I provided my name to the hostess, and she led me toward a booth framed by a large window overlooking the sidewalk's foot traffic.

Loren stood as I approached, pausing to kiss my cheek. Ever the dapper dresser, he sported a pin-striped charcoal three-piece suit. Under the vest, he wore a starched snow-white dress shirt. A striking gold and black striped tie gave the suit a somewhat regal energy. He kept his hand on my shoulder until I sat, sliding onto the padded bench. Our server appeared and poured a glass of French rosé, placing it by my water. I noted Loren had the same.

"You must try the rigatoni with fennel and anchovies. This rosé is a perfect match," he explained. Loren had a habit of picking out my lunch for me. Fortunately, he had an excellent palette. I was never disappointed.

"I guess we're both having the rigatoni," I told the server.

"To you and your birthday!" Loren announced over the din. He lifted his wine, and we touched glasses. *Ruby's* was not known for its quiet atmosphere, but the noise from the hustle and bustle would allow us to enjoy a relatively private conversation.

"Thank you," I smiled. Today I turned 38. I sipped the wine and nodded. Crisp, but not too sweet.

"Michelle sends her best wishes." He dabbed at his lips with a napkin after setting his wine down. "She would have joined us, but she's visiting a granddaughter in Vue. Lizzie. Lovely girl. She's in college, and as part of her finals for the semester, she's performing in a dance recital."

"That's nice," I said politely.

"Yes," his small eyes twinkled. "Nice that I didn't need to attend."

"Loren!" I laughed.

"It's interpretative dance, Lucie. It's elder

abuse to force grandparents to watch such a confusing exhibition." Loren chuckled. "My wife has more patience than I do."

I shook my head at him. "I'm sure Michelle will enjoy seeing her granddaughter no matter what."

"Hmm." He took another sip of wine, studying me over his glass. "And how are you?"

I tapped the tabletop with a fingernail, pressing my lips together once before answering. "I'm okay."

"Still no word from...?" His voice trailed off.

"No," I answered quietly. Loren didn't know the details of Templeton's disappearance. He only knew there was a 'battle' and we didn't win. I'd told him we lost Templeton as a result.

"Hmm," he hummed again. "I'm sorry, Lucie. I know he meant a lot to you."

"The longer he's gone..." I lifted a hand. "Even Templeton has a limit to his powers."

"Yes, I'm sure," Loren agreed. "Have you exhausted all possibilities on helping him return?"

This was the opening I'd been hoping for. "I haven't. But last week, I think I got a lucky break. I need your help."

Loren sat back against the booth's cushion. "What happened?"

I wasn't going to tell him about accidentally adopting a shapeshifter – I was still wrapping my head around that one. Plus, as much as I trusted Loren, I felt this was something to keep to myself – for now. "I have a gemstone that belongs to Templeton's family. It's a key of sorts. Last week it kind of powered up. It's still not ready to be used, but I'm making progress."

Loren pursed his lips. "Intriguing. And you think I can help you?"

"Maybe." My hand absently strayed to the front of my scarf where I touched a piece of the Crimson Stone hidden under my clothing. I tried so hard to protect Templeton's privacy because he was such a secretive man. I wanted to honor his nature, but I was also desperate to bring him home. "I have a book. It's one of Templeton's."

The silence coming from the other side of the table caused me to look up. Loren's eyes had narrowed. "A book of Templeton's? A book of *his* magic?"

I nodded solemnly. "Yes."

"Did he give it to you before he disappeared?"

Loren shrewdly evaluated me.

"No," I said. "After he was lost, I took it from his home. My hope is I'll find the spell to prepare the gemstone somewhere in this book."

"Interesting." Loren paused as the server stopped at our table to tell us our lunch would be delivered soon. When we were alone again, he continued. "What is holding you back?"

"Most of the book is written in a language I don't recognize and cannot decipher. It's archaic."

My lunch date understood where the conversation was going. "You need the library."

"Yes. It's my only hope."

"Lucie, your membership with the Congress is suspended." He paused. "Perhaps after the three-month review, you'll be able to reestablish it and regain access to the library."

Following a disastrous demonstration where I was to show how I strengthened my thinning witchline, the Congress of Empire Witches suspended my membership. Readmittance to the Congress was pending as they investigated my 'behavior and activities' following my return to Matar after a year in France studying with Guillaume. Templeton's membership had been terminated without the benefit of a review. The Congress had been anxious to ban the powerful man. He'd violated several rules to save me from Guillaume's sadism during the presentation in front of the elders. Templeton, although a member of the Congress, was not a witch. They could easily expel him.

For the record, during the same demonstration that earned me the label of *persona non grata,* I more than proved my witchline was made stronger through the work I did with Guillaume.

"Every passing day makes it that much harder to safely bring back Templeton," I argued. "Loren, you and Templeton both indicated I have a powerful 'friend' inside the circle of elders at the Congress. Is it possible to appeal to him for help? One day's access to the library – that's all I'm requesting. Could you...Could you ask this elder on my behalf?"

Loren sighed. "I'm not sure I can –"

"My heart's dying," I blurted out. I hastily covered my mouth with a hand before any other declarations could escape.

"Oh, Lucie." Loren reached across the table and claimed my free hand. "I'll see what I can do. But

I can't promise anything. You've made strong enemies."

I nodded. "I know. But I've got to try. If this man, this elder, can grant me some mercy, I'll do my best to repay him."

Loren tilted his head to the side. "Should you get access while you're still suspended, be careful what you promise in return."

"Should I be worried about this elder?" I asked.

"You should be worried about any witch in the Congress who is willing to do you a favor."

∞∞∞

Our server brought our lunch, and as expected, I enjoyed the rigatoni. Loren made a good choice. He also surprised me with a cute two-person birthday cake. I was spared a *Happy Birthday* rendition by the staff, but Loren pulled a solitary white candle from the inside pocket of his suit coat.

"Wish candle," he beamed. He pressed it into the center of the decadent buttercream frosting and snapped his fingers. The small candle lit, the fire rising in a slender flame before retracting.

"Did Michelle make this?" I teased.

He feigned a scandalized look. "Of course not! I prepared it myself. But keep your wish lighthearted. I didn't create anything too complex."

"Fair enough," I laughed. My gaze drifted to the candle. A teeny voice inside my brain spoke up. *He said to keep it lighthearted,* it whispered. *You could…lighten your heart with the right wish.* I watched the flame bob and weave. *Lighten my heart,* I mused. *The right wish.* I glanced back up at Loren. He nodded encouragingly. I lowered my eyes to the candle again, then closed them. I pictured the cold day in the Walled Zone nearly three months ago when Templeton and Rabbit, two men I cared so deeply for, were wrenched from my life.

I wish…I wish for the men I love and lost in the Walled Zone to return safely to me.

Pursing my lips, I opened my eyes and blew out the candle's flame, triggering my wish. Three sparks zipped up into the air and burst into three mini fireworks. The celebratory display caught the attention of the other diners. A smattering of applause rippled through the bistro as friendly witches called out their happy birthday wishes to me.

Loren nodded at the candle's reaction. "Now that seems like a good sign. I expect your wish will be coming true sooner than you think."

Chapter 2

Time spent with Loren passed swiftly. After asking him to help me get permission to do research in the library, the conversation turned lighter, and I thoroughly enjoyed his company. The rich birthday cake and wish candle were thoughtful bonuses.

Outside, we said our goodbyes. I offered to drive him to wherever he planned to go next, but he declined. He lifted his hand, and a private car pulled up, double-parking near us. Loren slipped between the bumpers of the vehicles parked along the curb, waving as he climbed into the back seat.

I watched the car pull away before turning in the other direction and beginning the walk to my RAV4. It was out of my hands now. I needed to let Loren work his own magic. Well, the magic of witch politics, anyway.

As I strolled, I noted a young-looking woman with black curls pulled up into a ponytail. She leaned against the corner of a brick building. Her jeans were tucked into a pair of Doc Martens, and a red and black flannel shirt was tied around her waist. A worn concert tee stretched over her thin shoulders. She looked up from her texting, the phone swiftly disappearing into her pocket. The rich brown eyes scanning me up and down were warm. A Rabbit.

Oh, how she reminded me of *my Rabbit*. I offered a cautious smile as I passed. She grinned, bobbing her head once before rolling over the corner's edge and shuffling off down the block. I watched her go.

I wondered what Big Rabbit planned for tomorrow.

∞∞∞

Flame wasn't home by the time I returned. I hoped it meant he was looking for a job, but since his wardrobe consisted of a handful of loose shorts and tee shirts I found at *Second Act*, I wasn't going to count on it.

I'd stopped at the market and picked up two ahi tuna steaks for my birthday dinner. I figured Flame would also enjoy the treat if he wanted to dine with me. The thought of dining at home alone lodged itself in the middle of my chest, squeezing my heart. I slid the paper packages onto the top shelf in the refrigerator. *Stop it, Lucie,* I thought. *It's not like you don't have people who care about you.*

My throat grew tight. But I was lonely.

Bone-achingly lonely.

In the past three months, I'd withdrawn even deeper into my own world. After losing Templeton and Rabbit, I'd thrown myself into researching spells to reunite the Crimson Stone. When I wasn't obsessed with trying to find a way to 'fix' the one thing that could help me get Templeton back, I was replaying horrifying memories.

How I allowed myself to be separated from Rabbit in the warehouse.

How he was lost to me after being ripped into by those soulless, eyeless dog-like monsters.

How I turned my back on Templeton and allowed the Beam of Light to grab him, then watched as it drained him of his power, standing helplessly as it took him away from me.

How my fire was useless.

I used these miserable memories in a gloomy corner of my basement to pour a fresh stream of pain into my witchline. It grew stronger with each feeding but left my physical body weak. In particularly vulnerable moments, I allowed myself to remember how Templeton could see my witchline and how he touched it with his magic. I ached when I remembered his promise to find a way other than pain as a method to keep strengthening it.

As spring progressed, I turned even further inward. I never went back to offering Tarot readings at *Coffee Cove*. I couldn't trust myself to provide accurate interpretations to those who came to me for guidance. My words and explanations were worth nothing. After loading my car with boxes filled with books, Tarot decks, and various odds and ends, I'd wiped tears from my cheeks and surrendered my keys to Rick Manning, *Coffee Cove's* kind owner. Rick wrapped me in a bear hug and promised there'd always be a place for me at the shop if I ever changed my mind.

During this time, some members of the method coven were kind enough to continue to reach out to me, but I didn't have the energy to follow through and meet up with them. What would I say when they asked me how I was doing, where I'd been?

I still kept in contact with Emily Swift, the Salesman who most understood what I was going through and what I'd lost, but she had a life of her own and a wedding coming up. The last thing I wanted to do was color her joy with my heartache.

And now, I stood alone in my kitchen on my birthday, half-heartedly contemplating the contents inside my refrigerator.

"Alright, the pity party has *got* to stop," I chided myself as I gave my shoulders a shake.

I bent, pulling the crisper open. I'd put together a salad with ginger dressing to go with the seared tuna.

∞∞∞

"Voila!" That evening, as I pulled a frying pan from the bottom cupboard, Flame revealed a bottle of champagne.

I read the label. It was a top-shelf sparkling wine. "Flame, where did you get this?"

He suppressed a mischievous smile. "It's your birthday present, don't be rude."

"Do I want to know?"

"Well..." Flame let his unblinking cat-like stare roam to a distant spot over my right shoulder. "Some stories are best told years later."

I bit the corner of my lip. He was right.

"Besides, we should celebrate your milestone!" He set the bottle on the counter and rummaged through the cupboards by the sink.

"Milestone?"

"Forty!"

Oh, he would be the death of me. "I'm 38, Flame."

He found two champagne flutes on a high shelf and handed the glasses to me. "And you still look fantastic. I mean it. You do."

I died a little on the inside. "Thanks."

"Commencing popping." Flame angled the bottle toward the ceiling and twisted the metal cage off the cork. A moment later, he worked it out of the bottle with a pair of practiced thumbs. The *Pop!* bounced off the walls, but the champagne did not spurt out. He winked at me.

"It's all about control. You don't want it to shoot out before you're ready."

"I hope we're still talking about the champagne," I replied dryly, holding out the two flutes. Flame filled both glasses.

"To Lucie Bellerose!" Flame took a glass and clinked it against mine. "May the next year bring you lots of fun and excitement!"

"I'd settle for peace and love," I laughed, then immediately sobered when I realized what I'd said. I backtracked. "I just want good things. That's all. Quiet things."

My young friend observed me over his glass of champagne. The kind shimmer in his eyes almost did me in. "You'll get those good things, Lucie. I'll help you."

I watched the bubbles explode out of my champagne flute. "I think you already are."

∞∞∞

My celebration consisted of one flute of champagne. I was happy to let Flame enjoy the rest. The ahi tuna – rare on the inside, seared to perfection on the outside – was delicious. I'm sure I heard Flame purring lightly while he ate.

"Want to go out?" he asked out of nowhere.

"What do you mean?" I spread a thin sheen of wasabi on a bite of my fish.

"To a few clubs? We could milk your birthday with the bartenders. Free drinks!" Holding the stem of the champagne flute between his thumb and index finger, he waggled the empty glass at me. "I'm seeing...gin and tonics – no, Moscow mules! Go put on a sexy shirt. The jeans are fine. But skip those sandals. This is a boots night."

"I've got a better idea," I said. "How about we make a visit to David's? Get the rest of your clothes so you have more choices than secondhand tees and basketball shorts? I'll even go to the door for you if you don't want to deal with your friend."

His eyes bugged out. "This is how you want to celebrate your four decades?"

"I'm not 40!" I exclaimed. I held up a hand. "Tell you what. We'll stop off at a nice quiet pub if you want – *after* we go to David's. I'm buying. How about it? It's either that or staying in and renting a movie."

One dramatic sigh later, and my shapeshifter agreed. He went upstairs to 'revitalize' his hair, and I finished my salad. We were making headway on getting Flame properly clothed.

∞∞∞

David Mattison's house was located in a gentrified section of Matar. To be fair, Matar didn't have many low-income areas in the city. Still, there were a couple of old neighborhoods near the warehouse district to the west that had seen better days. About five years ago, city planners conspired with elected officials to dump money into these deteriorating precincts for development with the long-term goal of building a wealthier tax base. Their speculation was successful. Incentives for small businesses and restaurants to populate these hot 'new' neighborhoods produced highly desirable real estate for home buyers and renters alike.

The young and hungry upper class swarmed in. And the taxes went up.

According to Flame, David bought a narrow two-storied home with a modest yard when the renovated houses hit the market. A corporate lawyer with a sizable bank account, David was the target audience for the city's trendy initiative.

Flame sulked in the passenger seat as I rounded the block a second time, searching for a parking spot. "Can't you use your magic?"

"And do what?" I frowned, stopping and waving a couple along. They crossed in front of my RAV4.

"Make a car disappear and free up a space?"

"Yeah, that's not really what I can do," I answered. "And even if I could, I – *oh!* Hold on." I braked when I saw a turn signal appear on a parked car to my right.

Flame pitched forward in his seat, his nails tapping the dashboard as he watched the car pull away and free up the space. "I think that car belongs to one of David's friends."

"Doesn't matter. They're leaving," I replied, swinging my vehicle into the abandoned spot and shutting the car off. "Well, which house is it?"

Flame gestured in the direction of three houses nestled together. "There."

"Which one?" I opened my door after peeking into the side mirror.

"That one." Again, the unenthusiastic hand wave.

"Flame, maybe try being more specific?"

"The stupid gray one."

I shook my head. "We've got two gray houses sitting next to one another. You don't have to go with me, but you do have to help me out here."

"Red trim," he grumbled.

"Thank you." I climbed out of the driver's seat before looking back inside the car. Flame had slid lower in his seat. He pulled at a thread hanging from the hem of his shorts. "You okay to stay here?"

"Yes." A sizable pout.

"I'll be right back." I shut the car door and rounded the front of my vehicle. Front yards were narrow strips of grass between houses and the sidewalk but orderly. Ceramic containers boasting newly planted flowers dotted porches that had never seen peeling paint. Several short lawn signs thanked canine-loving neighbors for picking up doggie 'deposits.'

David's house wasn't any different. I climbed up the two steps and onto a front porch only wide enough for two wicker chairs, each sitting to a side of the door. Evening drinks would have to perch on knees – or maybe the low porch walls.

A simple brass knocker with an engraved 'M' sat in the center of a red front door. I raised the curved bar and tapped it several times. Since it was 8 o'clock on a Tuesday, I assumed Flame's friend would be home.

Off to the right, I saw a flutter of movement as someone brushed a window curtain aside to check the porch. I gave a wave and tried to appear non-threatening. I heard the door unlock, and I watched the doorknob turn.

A sharply dressed man appeared. I stifled an eye roll. He was the universal 'chiseled features' bachelor – clean-shaven, with kissable lips and a mass of jet-black lashes stretching out over ocean blue eyes. Chestnut-colored hair was styled in gentle waves and kept short. He was of average build and height – maybe 5'9" – but you could tell by how his clothing fit that he carried a gym membership. Tailored black trousers were paired with a plain white dress shirt left unbuttoned at the top. He'd pushed up the shirt sleeves to his elbows. Over his office attire, he wore an olive green apron, but I didn't detect any telltale kitchen smells. Instead, I noted his cologne. It was still fresh – or maybe recently reapplied – its crisp citrus scent slipping off his skin and poking up my nose.

It reminded me of freshly peeled oranges, and I've never been a fan.

"May I help you?" He swayed to the side to look past me.

I cut straight to it. "David Mattison? My name is Lucie Bellerose. I'm sorry to intrude, but I'm here to pick up, ah, some clothing for a friend."

"Marcus."

"Um, no. Flame," I corrected.

"No, Marcus." He lifted a soft hand and pointed.

I peered over my shoulder. Flame stood on the sidewalk with his hands on his narrow hips. His name was really Marcus? I'd wondered. He'd changed the subject when I'd questioned him after witnessing his first shift in my home, telling me it was fate that I'd named him Flame, and it was what he wanted to be called.

Standing there, I realized he'd foregone the plain secondhand sneakers for a pair of neon green flip-flops. They glowed at the bottom of his athletic legs. I looked up in time to catch him giving his head an impatient toss. He engaged in a slow cat-like blink before he glared in our direction.

I turned back to David. "Yeah, Marcus. Is it possible to get his clothes and go?"

"No."

"No?" I wasn't prepared for a challenge. I mean, they *were* Flame's clothes.

"I donated them to a shelter."

I grimaced. "Everything?"

David nodded. His eyes never left Flame.

"Well, that makes this visit short. I'm sorry to have bothered you," I said as I turned to leave.

"Wait." David's manicured hand grazed my shoulder.

I hesitated. "Yes?"

"Does he have a place to stay?"

"For now," I replied.

"Does he need money?" David mouthed.

I sighed. "What he needs is proper clothing. No clothes, no job."

"He's staying in Matar?" Was that a hopeful note I detected in David's voice?

"For the time being."

"One minute." David withdrew behind the door and disappeared into his house.

"Is he getting my clothes?" Flame called.

I shushed him with my hands.

David reappeared, pulling the door open. He

handed me a piece of paper. "You can get in touch with me here if he needs anything. Send the message through the Empire service line."

I glanced down at the slip of paper in my hand. David's contact information was written in a neat row. "Don't you want to speak to him yourself? Ask him what he needs? Maybe talk to him about…your relationship?"

David gave his handsome head a firm shake as his gaze skittered over the neighborhood as if I'd yelled: YOUR SECRET SEXUAL RELATIONSHIP WITH FLAME!

I blew out another breath. "I'm not going to get involved beyond this. I just want him to wear clothes when he's in my house."

That drew a tiny smile from David.

"And I know you were surprised to find out what he is," I continued.

The smile vanished.

"But you know now, and honestly, who cares?" I could understand David was upset that Flame, er, Marcus, wasn't forthcoming about his true nature, but I also understood Flame's desire to keep his ability private. Shapeshifters are notoriously secretive because people can get weird. Case in point.

"I care. He should have told me before...Before he..." David sniffed, and he searched out Flame.

"Are you sure you don't want to talk to him now?" It was obvious David had leftover feelings for Flame. I wasn't sure to what level, but...I let a slip of my energy reach out and bump into his. The barely perceptible twitch at the corner of his left eye revealed he'd sensed my touch only tangentially. His preoccupation remained locked on the young man behind me. The sad vibration I felt when I magically poked him told me he was hurting, but he was also building a wall around himself. He shook his head no.

I drew my energy away. "Okay, David, that's fine. Relationships can be complicated. Listen, I live in the Clover District. 1106 Autumn Avenue. Repeat that."

David spared me an amused look, one well-shaped eyebrow lifting. "1106 Autumn Avenue. Got it."

"We're leaving now," I told him. "But if you need to talk to him, that's where you'll find him." I left David standing in the doorway of his tidy house and met Flame on the sidewalk.

"My clothes?" Flame asked. Gone was the

haughty cat-like contempt. Instead, his gaze begged longingly over my shoulder. A beat later, I heard the distinct *click!* of David turning the lock behind me.

"Gracing the backs of the less fortunate," I answered Flame. I placed a hand on his elbow, spinning him away. "Come on. Let's go get those Moscow mules."

∞∞∞

The quiet Tuesday night pub within walking distance of my townhouse was not going to appease my young friend, but the karaoke bar located one block farther drew Flame in like a moth to a...*Oh.* Never mind.

I didn't remember the line *'and then you gave away my clothes and changed the locks on me'* in a popular 1970s song, but while onstage, Flame was determined to let everyone know he would survive.

We were offered free drinks – not for my birthday, but if Flame would swear to never take the microphone again. I now understood the meaning of caterwauling.

Our server recognized me from visits I'd made

with Rabbit in happier times. She paused to say hi between dropping off drinks at a crowded table of professionals blowing off steam and ferrying empties back to the bar.

"Hey!" She raised her voice to be heard over the latest bathroom shower singing sensation sashaying across the stage. "Haven't seen you in ages. Where's your friend?"

I lifted a finger and motioned to Flame. He was trying to charm the KJ into letting him sing another song.

"No, the cute guy with all those sexy black curls. Dark eyes. Kind of..." The woman waved her hand in front of her chest. "You know...tight shirts, snuggable chest. Good arms. Um, I think he was one of those Rabbits, maybe? They don't come in here much."

One of 'those' Rabbits. *My Rabbit.*

I took a sip of my mule. "He moved away."

"Oh, that's too bad. You know, I've never seen a man stare at someone as hard as he did when you were singing. His eyes would get...glittery. Does that make sense?"

It did. I nodded. "We were good friends."

"You sure about that?"

I startled. "Yes, very good friends."

She laughed, squeezing my shoulder. "Men don't look at their friends like he looked at you, honey." The server scowled in the direction of the bar. "I have orders backing up. It was good catching up with you, though. Make sure you hit the stage before you go. Singers like you keep customers in their seats."

The woman lifted her tray over the heads of seated partiers as she danced her way around the tables.

Rabbit. I stared at my drink. I missed him as much as I pined for Templeton. But at least I knew Rabbit was alive. Hopefully healing. I wished he'd reach out to me. I knew I'd failed him, too. I should never have left him alone in the warehouse. It was my fault he was so brutally –

I stopped the thought before the tuna from earlier made a reappearance. The mule was kicking at my insides.

My head still bowed, I heard Flame's voice streaming through the speakers once again. I should've known the KJ would break down and give Flame what he wanted. After all, he was very pretty and irresistible.

"And this goes out to my new bestie, my

witchy roomie, the birthday girl celebrating four decades!" Flame's arm swept through the air with a majestic flourish before a spotlight found me and clapping almost drowned out the first verse of Flame's next song.

I squinted blindly toward the stage. I was going to kill him.

"Happy is our family, lonely is the ward," Flame sang another 70s tune, the patrons eventually joining in with a chorus of *da-da-da-da-da-da, da-da-da-da-da's.*

∞∞∞

The rowdy table of professionals celebrating at the karaoke bar sent another round of drinks – plus shots of cinnamon whiskey – our way. Twice. Before we left, Flame also insisted we order Flaming Dr. Poppers – amaretto and rum shots set afire and dropped into beer.

The walk home was beginning to look longer. I contemplated hailing a taxi when we stepped outside.

"Ooh," Flame cooed. "If you take a cab, Luscious, I'll shift and have some fun before heading home."

Soon after the first set of shots, my name had migrated from Lucie to Luscious. I wanted to be annoyed, but honestly, I kind of liked it.

"Are you sure that's a safe idea?" I questioned. "Um, you're a little drunk."

"Pleasantly intoxicated," he corrected, lifting a finger. The streetlamp caught a claw protruding from the tip.

"Exactly," I said.

Flame placed a hand on each of my shoulders. He touched his forehead to mine once, then spun me around and gave me a friendly push. "There's an empty cab."

I waved toward the taxi and eyeballed Flame. "What about your clothes?"

He ran a hand over his shirt. "Right. Grab them for me, Luscious." With that, he slunk back into a shaded doorway leading into a closed storefront. Thirty seconds later, an orange mackerel tabby cat zoomed out, wound through my ankles once, and then strutted off down the sidewalk, tail held high.

I watched with one part fascination and one part worry before scooping up his discarded tee shirt and shorts from the shadows. I'd convinced him to leave the flip-flops at home and picked up the canvas sneakers, wincing when I caught the smell of man feet wafting up from the shoes. "Gah," I stuck my tongue out.

Arms full, I turned and realized the taxi was gone. Someone had been faster on the uptake.

I guessed I was hoofing it after all. The neighborhoods surrounding the Clover District were fairly safe, and it wasn't too late, but I'd flag down a cab if I saw one. I was tired.

On the way home, I passed what looked like an older teen. He leaned against a corner streetlamp, his right ankle crossed over his left. A gray knit hat was pulled firmly down over his ears, and glossy black hair peeked out, framing his pale face. He wore a ripped tee over a red shirt with long sleeves – the shirt on top bearing the logo of a local band. His busy thumbs glided swiftly over the device held in front of his chest. He pocketed the phone as he raised his head. Our eyes met, and he gave me a friendly nod before pushing off the pole and sauntering away in the opposite direction.

I watched him go, a familiar lump forming in my throat. I wondered where Rabbit was staying these days. I wondered if he was okay. I hoped his body was healed.

The loneliness found me again.

Chapter 3

The walk did me good. By the time I arrived home – noting an empty cab driving down my street as I climbed my stairs – the combination of mules, shots, and the strange Dr. Popper concoction had less of an effect on me.

At the top of the stairs, I turned and offered a slight wave toward the corner at the end of my block. Last year when I'd fled the Empire without telling my friends, Rabbit had hacked a security camera in my neighborhood and trained it on my front door, so he'd know when I returned home. Whenever there was activity on my front stoop, he'd get a text and a screenshot. To my knowledge, he never shut down this benign spy cam. In fact, I hoped it was still working, and he received images of me waving to him.

I checked my wards before entering. Nothing

unusual or menacing was indicated. They continued to hold long after Templeton worked with me to strengthen them against unwanted visitors. My magic, combined with his, was long-lasting.

Shutting my door, I kicked off my low-heeled boots, dropped Flame's clothes on the bottom stair, and tossed my purse on the hall table. I'd stuffed a sizable ponytail palm against the wall near the kitchen entrance. It wasn't ideal, but it hid one of the two handprints Templeton had 'helped' me burn into the wall one steamy night. The hall table hid the other. I didn't want to hire a woodworker to buff them out, but I couldn't look at them either.

After getting myself a tall glass of water, I went through the pantry and checked the back door. Now that I knew Flame was a shapeshifter, I didn't worry about him not being able to get in after I'd gone to bed. I simply cast a spell on the doorknob. Whenever Flame touched the back door in his human form, it would unlock and he would be able to get in. He did, however, have a bad habit of leaving it unlocked afterward. I compulsively checked it.

I returned to my kitchen and stood over the

sink, contemplating the lonely night through the window. I pulled the small device Rabbit had given to me from my pants pocket. When Big Rabbit reprogrammed my phone after Rabbit was hurt, he also removed my connection to my missing friend. I squinted at it now, wishing I had at least old messages to read.

I remembered how even though Templeton shouldn't have been able to send me a message, he somehow managed.

I didn't have any leftover texts from him either.

Blinking back the tears of self-pity, I did pull up the last message I'd received from Big Rabbit.

Be ready at 10am TOMORROW! I'm coming to get ya! We're going someplace SPECIAL!

Special. I could use something special.

∞∞∞

The next morning, I peeked into Flame's room – *I mean, the spare bedroom* – and saw that my shapeshifter had made it home in one piece. He was buried under the covers, with the exception of one stinky foot thrust out of the bundle of blankets and hanging over the side of the bed. I realized, somewhat anxiously, that I hadn't even heard him come home during the night. I was not a light sleeper, but someone on the stairs should get my attention. I shut the door quietly and let him be.

This was the last weekday morning I planned to let him sleep in. When I finished my outing with Big Rabbit, Flame and I were going shopping. I was buying him clothes appropriate for job hunting and interviewing.

Then it would be up at the ass crack of dawn every weekday for him until he landed something. I didn't care what it was.

My phone was charging on the kitchen counter, but I sensed when it grew warm. Big Rabbit was checking in.

10am! Be ready! We're taking your car!

I shook my head at my phone and replied with my own text. *We are?*

Yes! I'll grab it from the garage.

I had to laugh. I'd learned to roll with the Rabbit world. No one but me had a key to my car. Didn't matter. Big Rabbit would show up in front of my townhouse in it.

I'll be ready, I texted.

What in the world was Big Rabbit up to?

∞∞∞

Flame was still sleeping by the time Big Rabbit arrived. I'd been watching from the front stoop, my fingers fluttering over a water bottle while I sat and waited. I had no idea what to dress for, but I kept an extra pair of sneakers in my RAV4. If we had to walk, I'd be prepared. I'd tucked a pair of socks into my purse.

The sun was out again, and I hoped this warm spring would continue. It wouldn't be unlike Matar to wake up one morning in late April and see snow flurries in the air. The flowering pears lining my street were full of buds. Soon the trees would be filled with delicate bunches of white flowers and half-drunk buzzing bees.

I chose jeans and a plain sleeveless royal blue blouse for our outing. I felt dressed up enough for my invitation to do something 'special,' yet plenty casual to spend time with Big Rabbit. I wore a pair of canvas loafers in white, sans socks. The sunshine hitting my bare shoulders told me I would be able to throw my jean jacket into the back seat.

Right on time, Big Rabbit pulled up in front

of my house. He waved as I bounced down the steps. My passenger window lowered, and he leaned across the seat.

"I'm at the wheel today," he announced before cheerfully adding, "I have anxiety when women drive."

I paused halfway through opening the passenger door. "Seriously?"

He turned scarlet. "I didn't mean to say that out loud."

"Oh, that makes it better," I replied, climbing into the car. "But, since I don't know where we're going, I'll *let* you drive."

Big Rabbit grinned. "It's a perfect day for a road trip." Then. "Did you go to the bathroom first?"

Again I paused, this time while buckling my seatbelt. My head swiveled to the left, and I raised my eyebrows. "Why are we talking about my bathroom needs?"

"We're going to be in the car for the next three hours." He shrugged as he put the vehicle in drive. "You went, right? I don't like to stop once I'm going. Women always need to find a bathroom."

"I'm good," I assured him. "Moving on."

"Moving on!" Big Rabbit's voice boomed. He

reached over and gave my knee a squeeze before returning his large paw to the steering wheel. "Happy birthday, Lucie."

"Thank you," I said, tossing my jacket into the back seat. "Have I dressed appropriately for whatever it is you have planned?"

He contemplated my shirt and jeans, nodding his approval. "You look great. You always look nice in blue."

The man was so genuinely sweet and honest, the compliment made me feel good. "Thanks again. Hey, what about gas?"

He treated me to a super-sized smile. "I filled the tank before I picked you up."

I was astonished but also humbled. Rabbits, for all their resources, tend to be low on cash. Yet, they always got by. Culturally, they were incredibly communal. Their tech network was only eclipsed by the support system extended to every Rabbit. I wanted to recognize such a gift, but I didn't want to embarrass the gentle man either.

"Big Rabbit, I'm grateful for your friendship," I said. "You're one of the best men I've ever met." I offered a third round of gratitude. "Thank you."

The pleased expression on his face told me my

response was the right one. "You're welcome."

"Are you going to tell me where we're going?" I studied the side of his face. Like all Rabbits, he was fair-skinned, with eyes so brown they were almost black. His hair, again like other Rabbits, was pitch-black and wavy. Some Rabbits have curlier hair than others. Big Rabbit tended to let his hair grow longer than most. The curls were loose and plentiful.

"Nope," he answered.

"You're sure you're comfortable driving? I mean, I think you might have an inch of headroom if you're lucky." At 6'5", Big Rabbit had earned his nickname. He had to be at least 250 pounds of muscle. His biceps? It looked like someone shoved basketballs under his skin. Okay, maybe they weren't quite that big, but words often used to describe Big Rabbit included 'mammoth,' 'massive,' and 'giant.'

"All good!"

I squinted at the space above his head, focusing on the section where my RAV4 ceiling met the top of the windshield. "Um, did you detach my sun visor?"

Big Rabbit blushed again. "Even raised it was in my line of vision. I'll put it back."

"Alrighty." I settled in my seat. It was fun to pick on him, though. "You know, if you let me drive, you could slide the passenger seat way back and recline."

Big Rabbit gripped the wheel. "I...I don't like it when women have to drive." He reached over and fiddled with the radio. "I know you think I'm sexist, but honestly, that's not it."

"Are you sure about that?" I teased.

"No, really! It's...Well, we're very protective of our women."

"Female Rabbits," I stated.

"Yeah." He glanced over at me. "But you, too."

I beamed. "I'm honored to be included."

"It's because you're willing to fight by our side," he added. "Like our women do."

His explanation confused me. "What do you mean?"

Big Rabbit zipped up the on-ramp to the highway circling the city. When he said we were in for a three-hour drive, I assumed we'd be leaving Matar. It appeared we were heading southeast.

"I mean, our women will fight tooth and nail at our sides, never complaining and taking the full brunt of whatever we face in battle." He grew quiet, and I allowed the silence to linger as he gathered his thoughts. "Our mothers, sisters, wives, daughters...They never complain. When we can treat them better, take care of them, and do things for them, we do. They deserve it."

Paying close attention to the words Big Rabbit used was essential to understanding the dynamics in Rabbit culture. People on the outside might not understand, but I think I had an inkling as to what Big Rabbit was trying to say. I thought of my own Rabbit – how he was always making sure things were being taken care of for me, asking me what I needed, and looking for ways to make my life *easier*. How he *used* to do all that for me before he was gone.

These were all sincere expressions of love.

"I think I understand," I said. "But I want you to know if you ever need something from me, anything I can do to help you, you only need to let me know. It's more than owing you for how you've cared for me, especially since Rabbit is no longer around..." My voice faltered for a beat. "What I'm trying to say is I'd want to help you no matter what."

"I know you would, Lucie. Everyone knows what a special witch you are. That's why the network is always on board to help you."

Rabbits and witches don't always get along. The Empire is fairly diverse with its magical and non-magical beings. Each group tends to stick to its own community and views the others through their own suspicious lenses. But I've never been treated poorly by Rabbit's friends, and Big Rabbit was in the same camp. And truthfully, I owed their community much more than I could ever repay.

I watched as Rabbit signaled and coasted the car from one highway to the next. We were driving in the direction of Anwat, one of the three larger cities in the Empire. "Are we going to Anwat?"

"No, but we are heading that way. We'll reach our destination long before the city, though."

"And that is?"

"A surprise."

∞∞∞

Since Big Rabbit was in a sharing mood, I thought I'd press for more details about the mysterious world of Rabbits. And why not? We had a long drive, and I could find out all sorts of interesting things.

All Rabbits are called Rabbit. They always refer to each other as Rabbit. When I talk to Big Rabbit, he knows exactly to whom I'm referring when I say 'Rabbit.' We only called him Big Rabbit because Emily gave him the nickname when Rabbit assigned him to be her bodyguard for a while last year.

I opened with: "You know how we all call you Big Rabbit?"

His face lit up. "I like that."

"I bet," I laughed. "But you know we do that to distinguish between you and Rabbit when we're talking about you, right? Non-Rabbits have a hard time discussing multiple Rabbits who are all called...*Rabbit*."

"I can see where it might be difficult." He nodded thoughtfully as he switched lanes.

"What do you do when you're talking to another Rabbit, and he references several others? How do you figure it out?"

"There's no figuring out. It's part of the connectivity."

My forehead furrowed. "Wait, like a metaphysical network?"

Big Rabbit popped his lips. "I suppose you

could look at it that way. We just *know*. We recognize each other."

"Interesting," I replied, refocusing on the highway zipping under my car on the other side of the windshield. "And here I thought you all had a bunch of secret names you hid from non-Rabbits."

Big Rabbit didn't answer. His silence seemed to balloon in the air around us.

My head pivoted toward him. "Or do you?"

He gripped the steering wheel. "Let's talk about your cat. How's Flame fitting in?"

"It's like he's always lived there," I deadpanned. Oh, no. Big Rabbit wasn't going to change the subject. He was stuck in the car with me – there was no escape. "Come on, what's your secret name, Big Rabbit?"

"I don't have a secret name!" His cheeks puffed out.

"I don't believe you. Tell me," I prodded. "I mean, it's my birthday."

"Yesterday was your birthday," he corrected.

"But we're celebrating it today with this road trip. Think about it, it could be a special present. Tell me your Rabbit name. You know you want to," I teased.

Big Rabbit's brown eyes flicked in my direction once. His face softened. "It *would* be a special present, Lucie. And that's why I'm giving it to someone else." His fingers tapped absently on the steering wheel.

I considered his words. "Wait, you truly have another name – something other than Rabbit, don't you?"

He lifted a shoulder, but the tender expression he wore remained.

"Do other Rabbits know your real name?" I paused. "Wait, is this related to…?" I wasn't sure how to word what I wanted to ask. I didn't know much about pairings in the Rabbit community.

He sighed, but it wasn't an exasperated gush of air rushing from his lungs. Instead, it was a happy noise. "Yes. And as much as I love you, Lucie, you are not the woman I want to claim as my life mate."

"I see." And I did. I thought about the female Rabbit with the thin scar on her face. I'd seen Big Rabbit interact with her in the past. It was clear he had a mad crush on her. "But there *is* someone you'd like to reveal your name to, right?"

He worried his lower lip between his teeth,

then nodded. "Yes."

"Okay, you can't tell me your name – I understand. But tell me more. Tell me how you have a name, and yet no one knows it. Do you choose your own?"

"Oh, no. And..." Big Rabbit gave his head a shake, then a full toss. He was getting ready to give in. "Are you using magic on me? Are you making me tell you things?"

I held up a hand. "I'd never do that to you – and I'm not sure I could compel you to tell me things you didn't want to share. I'm simply using my... *feminine wiles*."

Big Rabbit pinned me with a sideways look. "Women."

"Come on, it's for my birthday. Tell me how it works with names in the Rabbit community."

"Fine!" He spent a moment grumbling under his breath about 'females' before he caved. "I'll tell you."

I rested my head against the seat. "All ears."

"Rabbits are named by their mothers. There is a private ceremony shortly after birth. They don't tell anyone – not even our fathers – what they've chosen for us. It's an intimate bond formed between mother and child. When the

Rabbit is old enough to select his own life mate, he reveals his true name," Big Rabbit finished.

This was fascinating. "This ritual is only between sons and their mothers?"

"Oh, no. All children. Females have their own names as well."

"And when you find a life mate, you tell that Rabbit your name?"

"If the other Rabbit wants to take you as a life mate as well, yes. You reveal your names to one another." Here Big Rabbit developed an unusually devilish grin. "It's not like we suddenly blurt it out during sex."

"I wouldn't think," I laughed. "But in all seriousness, I think it's beautiful. At this point in your life, only your mother knows your true name?"

"Yes," Big Rabbit nodded. "Mothers are special."

"Indeed," I agreed. For a quick moment, I allowed an image of my own mother to flit across the wall inside my brain. It'd been 35 years since she'd died. Clear memories were in short supply. Most faded as time passed. An unhappy thought crossed my mind. "What happens if the mother dies before she can name her child? I'm not trying to be gruesome, but I'm curious."

The corners of Big Rabbit's mouth turned down. "Female Rabbits are incredibly strong – and pregnancy has almost a reverse effect on them compared to non-Rabbits. They grow tougher, heartier. But occasionally, yes, a female will die in childbirth or shortly after and before the naming ceremony can take place. In those cases, a close female relative – the baby's aunt or grandmother – will step forward and name the child."

"It's a beautiful tradition," I told him. "Thank you for telling me about it. There's so much about your world I don't know, but I like to learn more when I can."

"Rabbits prefer to keep our community private," he said.

"I understand," I answered. "My lips are sealed."

He gave me the side-eye again.

I ignored him. "Now tell me, when are you going to reveal your name to the Rabbit you've been crushing on since last year?"

∞∞∞

The rest of the trip was spent discussing lighter topics – the beautiful spring we were having, Emily's upcoming wedding, Big Rabbit's upcoming family reunion...When I asked him who would be there, he answered: *Everyone.*

When the time came to let the conversation rest, he dialed through the few radio stations the Empire allowed, settling on one trending toward middle-of-the-road radio hits. As Big Rabbit raced down the highway, he sang merrily along with several pop tunes I never would've associated with a Rabbit.

They tended to like the harder stuff.

Eventually, we left the highway behind, taking secondary roads and driving patiently through small towns and minuscule villages. I'd lowered the window, and the warm air rushed in, blowing through my hair – and Big Rabbit's. I extended my arm out the window, my fingers wide as the wind buffeted my palm and slipped through my fingers. I felt free from all my moody thoughts. I felt...*happy.*

The scenery turned from short main streets to unending farm fields. A fresh green tinted the trees and the land. Where farmers had plugged the soil with seeds, uniform rows were defined when the first sprouts broke through the confines of the dirt and reached for the brightening sky.

Nature's rebirth was everywhere. It was impossible not to get caught up in its celebration.

Big Rabbit lowered the music, and I noted he'd begun to text one-handed while he steered.

"That's a dangerous habit," I noted.

He quickly slipped the device into a tee shirt pocket. "All done." He snuck a guilty look in my direction. "I had to send off a message. I won't do it again."

I nodded, letting him off the hook. In all fairness, I should be congratulating him on not checking his phone every five minutes. Rabbits were hardly ever offline.

I'd been reading the signs as we rode along, and the last one indicated we were several miles outside of a town called Becket. Before we reached it, however, Big Rabbit slowed and made a left turn. At first, I thought we'd pulled into a driveway, but as the narrow route continued to wind through the woods, I realized we'd turned onto a dirt road.

"You've definitely piqued my curiosity," I told

my chauffeur. "Are you going to tell me where we're going?"

"Almost there!" Big Rabbit sang out. "Maybe another 10 minutes."

My RAV4 bounced along as he slowed, navigating the tricky course. I tipped my head out the window, sucking in deep mouthfuls of the awakening forest after a long winter. I could smell the wet soil. It made my fingers tingle. I wanted to stick them into it.

Another dogleg curve revealed a cabin nestled back against the tree line on the other side of a grassy expanse. This time when Big Rabbit turned, it was into a driveway. He edged my vehicle over the bumps.

"What is this?" My eyes roamed over the woodland paradise. I zeroed in on the cabin with a porch running the length of the front. Someone was sitting at the top of the steps. A man.

Rabbit.

"Oh," I exhaled, blinking furiously. "Oh…"

"Yeah," Big Rabbit said quietly as he parked. He turned the keys, cutting the engine.

I gawked through the windshield. "Did he know we were coming?" I whispered. My heart rate shot up, causing an excited pulsing to course through my body. *It was Rabbit!* For a moment, I was overwhelmed.

"No." Big Rabbit unhooked his seatbelt and opened the driver's side door. "I hope he doesn't fuck this up," he mumbled. "Come on, Lucie."

With a shaking hand, I released my seatbelt and climbed out of the car. My body automatically twisted out of the way so I could shut the door, but every inch of my concentration was on Rabbit. I didn't want to even blink. I was afraid he'd vanish into the fresh forest air.

Disbelief first contorted his features, but then I saw his expression harden. Angry eyes swept from me to Big Rabbit. When he said nothing, I cautiously walked toward him, my loafers pressing a path into the soft earth.

Rabbit was thinner, and lines that hadn't been there before appeared at the corners of his eyes. His skin was pale, but the fact it didn't still carry the yellowish tinge I'd noted before gave me hope he truly was healing. I'd worried whatever had made him ill months ago would make it impossible for him to recover from the attack he'd miraculously survived.

His hair was much shorter than I'd ever seen it; the thick waves cut close to his head. He was minus his ubiquitous knit hat, but stray curls pressed damply and darkly against his forehead – perhaps from a recent shower. His right hand balled into a fist several times, but he wouldn't look at me. Instead, he focused on Big Rabbit. As his head turned, I saw the ragged scar stretching along his jawline and disappearing down the side of his neck. "Why did you bring her here?" His voice was strong and gruff.

"Because yesterday was her birthday, and I wanted to give her something to make her happy." Big Rabbit spoke from somewhere behind me. "Because she's so unhappy. She's missing you, and she's hurting a lot. Because you can help her stop hurting. Because you care about her but are too stupid to reach out to her – don't even deny it, Rabbit. I know things, too. I see what you've been doing these past two weeks."

I pried my attention away from Rabbit. "What do you mean?" I asked the determined man behind me. "What's he been doing?"

He shook his head, staring at his stoic friend. "Not my tale to tell."

Before I could press him for more, another vehicle crept up the road, slowing and pulling into the opening of the driveway where it stopped. Big Rabbit reached for my hand, placing the RAV4 keys into my palm.

"What's going on?" I asked, my fingers closing around the keys.

"My ride's here." Big Rabbit leaned over, dropping his voice. "Don't let him push you away."

"I...Um, okay." Confused, I watched as Big Rabbit gave Rabbit one last grim look before spinning on his heel and picking his way down the narrow driveway to the waiting van. He waved at us before cramming his hulking frame into its passenger seat. The driver ground the gears noisily into reverse and eased the beat-up vehicle onto the road, the wheels crunching against the stones and gravel as they turned and began to roll.

"You should leave." Rabbit's frosty voice crawled up my back. I stiffened. "I don't want you here, Lucie."

"Well, I'm here," I replied as I faced him. The tears threatening to fall broke free. I awkwardly wiped them away with my fingertips. "Rabbit, you have no idea how much I've missed you. How much I've wanted to see you."

Our eyes met. Where I'd once seen kindness and warmth, I now saw emptiness. "I don't think this is a good idea."

I shortened the space between us, my right hand lifting and settling over my crashing heart. My shame leaked out of my mouth. "It's because I wasn't there when...Isn't it? In the Walled Zone..." I stumbled, searching for the words I didn't want to hear myself say.

He didn't look away at first, but eventually, he let his gaze slide off into the distance. His eyes never swirled completely black, which gave me hope. I moved cautiously, lowering myself onto the second step and sitting on the edge. His bare arms revealed the scars left behind from the attack. Each one stole a breath from me as the image of Rabbit's limp body hanging helplessly from the monster dog's mouth came to life in my brain. My stomach churned when I imagined what he went through.

As much as I wanted to reach out and touch his energy with mine to get a sense of the damage done to his body, I didn't dare invade his space any more than I already had.

"I know I let you down. I shouldn't have left you in the warehouse when we knew something bad was in there. Your men..." My voice hitched, and again I couldn't finish.

Rabbit stared at me with dull eyes.

I tried again, desperate to bridge this horrible chasm separating us. "I'm so sorry, Rabbit. About everything. I am so damn sorry."

Still no response, just the empty stare.

When he said nothing, I gestured feebly to the picturesque scenery surrounding the cabin, then to Rabbit. "It's peaceful. I'm glad you're staying here. It's got a good vibe." An eager smile trembled on my lips.

Rabbit noticed, his attention dropping to my mouth. He still said nothing.

"I'm glad you have this place." I fumbled through my pitiful attempt to get him to talk to me. "It's good you're well enough now –"

Rabbit's snort cut me off. He swayed backward, clumsily reaching behind himself and retrieving two worn crutches. He shifted, using the pair to help him stand and shuffling to maneuver a crutch under each arm. He winced, a shadow of pain crossing his face.

Shocked, I craned my neck, watching him

sway as he established his balance. Dark red colored his cheeks.

"Who says I'm well enough?" Gritting his teeth, he twisted away, using the crutches to assist his labored progress up onto the porch. He lumbered across the worn wood, the slats groaning under his weight. Rabbit jerked the screen door open and swung his battered body into the cabin.

The door banged shut behind him.

Chapter 4

I remained seated on the porch steps processing the last five minutes, allowing myself time to calm down. The *smack-smack-smack* of my heart settled, and the energy zipping through my nerves quieted.

I couldn't leave – not now, not after seeing Rabbit after all these months. I rose to my feet, brushing my hands off on the front of my jeans. The old steps creaked under my feet as I climbed. On the top stair, I paused, surveying the porch. Two wooden rocking chairs flanked a short, square table off to one side. A bench swing hung at the other, swaying when a welcome breeze floated in from the west. In front of me was the door Rabbit had disappeared through. I didn't even bother to knock, pulling the screen door open and entering the tidy cabin even though I knew I was not invited.

As my vision adjusted, the open floor plan revealed an unfussy kitchen to the left and a couch and two chairs in the cozy living space to the right. Another rocker sat near the unlit fireplace. Braided rugs dotted the floor here and there and probably kept out the cold in winter. Past the fireplace, a door in the wall likely opened to a set of stairs leading to the second floor. Opposite it, on the kitchen side of the abode, I noted another door – to a closet perhaps, or maybe even a bathroom. Plain, light-colored curtains fluttered in all the windows as the breeze trickled in. The cabin was simple, unadorned, and clean.

Rabbit stood in the kitchen facing away, his head down and his hands on the counter. The crutches were wedged underneath both arms. I marveled how his back was solid and strong even though he'd lost weight and was obviously still healing. His plain black tee shirt had seen enough washings to turn dingy. The jeans he wore, also black, were missing a back pocket. On his feet were a pair of old gray sneakers minus the shoelaces. I'd never seen him wear anything but his Doc Martens. *The sneakers would be easier to put on,* I realized. I waited, wondering if he'd demand that I leave. When he said nothing, I tried again.

"I'm sorry my coming here was unexpected. I didn't know where Big Rabbit was taking me, and this is as much of a surprise to me as it is to you. I honestly didn't know until we pulled off the road and I saw you."

Rabbit muttered a few words, his shoulders rising and falling.

I moved into the kitchen, my hand landing on the back of one of three chairs sitting around a table placed against the wall. "I didn't catch that, Rabbit."

"Lunch?" The question caught me off guard. He didn't turn around.

"Sure," I answered. "Do you want me to –?"

"No." He looked over his shoulder. "Sit down."

I pulled out the kitchen chair, sinking into it and resting my elbows on the table's surface. I laced my fingers together and watched as Rabbit stretched to the left and retrieved one of the hanging cast iron pans from the wall. He shuffled to the stove, lighting the burner and setting the flame to low. Next, he pulled a loaf of sandwich bread from the counter breadbox before pivoting and opening the refrigerator.

I studied his profile. His lips were pressed together, and the tension in his face was evident. He ignored my scrutiny as he pulled a package of sliced cheese and yellow mustard from a shelf. Before shutting the door, he paused. Rabbit inclined his head toward me for a beat but didn't look at me. Instead, he returned his attention to the refrigerator's contents and swapped the plain yellow mustard for Dijon. Again, he turned his back to me.

After assembling the sandwiches and spreading butter on each slice of bread, he placed them in the warm pan to toast. Not even a minute passed before the smell of our lunch wafted from the stove to my nose.

While the frying pan worked its magic, Rabbit stretched and pulled two lunch plates from a cupboard. Before the final flip of the toasted cheese, he filled two glasses with tap water and ferried them one at a time to the table. After plating our sandwiches, he used the crutch again and brought my lunch to me first.

I managed to catch his eye as he set the plate in front of me. "Thanks, Rabbit."

He gave a nod, his eyes darting away quickly.

He maneuvered his body back to the counter, where he tucked a couple of napkins under his plate so he could carry them and his lunch in one go. He returned to the table, setting his plate down first. Grimacing, he eased himself into a chair. The crutches he leaned against the wall.

I waited for Rabbit to settle in before I motioned to the napkins balled in his hand. "May I have one?"

He realized he'd crumpled them and made as if to get up. I reached across the table and covered his hand with mine, stilling him. It was warm under my skin, and it gave me such joy. The last time I touched Rabbit, his unconscious body was frighteningly cold.

"These are fine," I spoke softly.

Rabbit didn't pull away – for that, I was grateful. But he didn't speak. He only nodded and opened his hand so I could pull one of the napkins from his palm. I drew back and left the napkin by my plate.

There were so many things I needed to say and even more things I wanted to ask. But the icy welcome from Rabbit confirmed my fears. I'd worried the radio silence I'd experienced from him meant he didn't want to speak to me after the nightmare we'd lived through in the Walled Zone. While I'd emerged virtually unscathed – a faint burn scar remained on my cheek – his body had been brutalized. It was clear he was recovering, but it was also obvious the attack had made a lasting impact. I desperately wanted to ask about the extent of his injuries and his long-term prognosis. I also knew this was not the time.

Understatement.

I picked up half of my toasted cheese sandwich and took a bite. Rabbit focused on his plate, but he didn't touch his food. His jaw worked slowly.

"It's good," I said. "Thank you."

Every time Rabbit raised his head and looked at me, I saw the steady anger living in his once friendly face. Again, he didn't answer but gave a tiny nod. He finally took a bite of his sandwich. The breeze blowing in through the windows had died, and the fresh air seemed to grow oppressive. Somewhere in the trees surrounding the cabin, the twittering of two birds mating – or maybe fighting – could be heard. Rabbit cleared his throat. "Who's the blond guy living with you?"

Of all the questions I thought Rabbit might

throw out there, this was not one of them. "What do you mean?" I demurred.

Frustrated, Rabbit dropped his sandwich on his plate and sat back abruptly. I saw the brief flash of pain skitter across his face following the sudden movement. "See? This is the problem, Lucie. This is why Rabbits don't like witches. You lie and keep secrets," he scoffed. "It's tiring. It's unfair."

His outburst startled me, but although his accusation wasn't completely true, I had withheld the truth from him more than once, and yes, I'd kept secrets. I had secrets then. I still did, and they were mine to keep. But I also understood he was fed up with wondering what I wasn't telling him. We'd been such close friends, and I'd kept a lot from him.

"Alright," I conceded. "That's sort of true."

His upper lip curled. "Sort of true? Wanna try again?"

I set my sandwich down. Well, I was dreading a silent lunch – it looked like that was about to change. "Yes, I do have a guest staying with me. His name is…" I faltered. Shit. *Shit shit shit!* I couldn't reveal Flame's secret.

Rabbit was already shaking his head and

taking a bite. "Yeah. That's about right. Let me know when you think up a good story to tell me."

If things weren't so bad between us, I would've told Rabbit to shove it. But I needed to repair our fractured friendship. I lifted a shoulder. "You're right. I'm holding back. But here's the truth, here's what I can tell you. His name is Marcus, and he's not from Matar. He went through a breakup with his significant other and needed a place to stay. He's been sleeping in the spare bedroom."

Rabbit eyeballed me. "Is he a witch?"

"No." Even though I suspected Flame – Marcus, *whatever* – had some sort of magical connection in his family tree, I knew it wasn't from a natural witch. As a witch, I would've sensed a traditional lineage if he had one.

"How do you know him?"

"A friend introduced us." Again, this was true.

I could see Rabbit was wary of my explanation. "How long is he staying?"

It was my turn to sit back in my chair. "I have no idea. He's looking for a job. When he's in a good spot financially, I expect he'll want to get into a place of his own rather quickly." This may or may not have been a slight exaggeration.

"I'm sure there's more you're not telling me," Rabbit sighed. He squished the edge of his sandwich between a thumb and a forefinger, watching the Dijon ooze out from between the slices of bread.

"How did you know he was staying with me?" I asked. Before he could reply, I answered my own question. "Oh, right. The corner camera and the network. You have Rabbits watching me."

This time when Rabbit's cheeks grew darker, they were pink from embarrassment. He delayed his answer by taking a bite of his toasted cheese and chewing slowly. He decided to skip answering me and shrugged, brushing off my question altogether.

I'd made peace with the fact Rabbit used surveillance more than once to determine my whereabouts or ensure my safety. At times, I was annoyed because it pushed a line with respecting my privacy, but right now I was happy to learn about this recent shadowing. Maybe he wasn't ready to let our friendship go. Maybe he still cared.

Last night, during my trek home, I'd seen a Rabbit leaning up against a lamppost. Earlier, a young female Rabbit was on the same block where I'd had lunch with Loren. Seeing a Rabbit in the city wasn't unusual – they're everywhere. But these two Rabbits...I now understood they were there for a reason.

Me.

I wondered how many Rabbits I hadn't noticed in recent weeks. I regarded Rabbit as he drew a corner of his sandwich through the mustard on his plate. This is what Big Rabbit was referring to before he left. He knew Rabbit had activated the network to keep an eye on me.

To protect me? To watch over me? To learn what I was doing?

To spy on me?

"You could've texted if you wanted to check up on me," I told him. "I still have the network phone you gave me. Big Rabbit reprogrammed it so I could text him if I needed something." I hesitated. "He removed the connection to your phone."

"I know."

When he didn't add anything more, another pang of pain targeted my heart. "Oh."

We ate what was left of our sandwiches in silence. I knew he wanted me to go, but everything felt unfinished between us. I didn't want to push him – especially since he was still healing, but I feared saying goodbye would turn into a permanent separation.

"I'm sorry I abandoned you in the warehouse," I said quietly.

Another long stretch of silence. I took a sip from my glass, for a moment distracted by the purity of the well water feeding the cabin. It was cool, soothing my dry mouth as I waited for Rabbit's condemnation.

"Is that what you believe? You think you abandoned me?" Rabbit held my gaze.

I lifted a hand, my palm facing the ceiling. "That's what happened."

"I told you to run, Lucie. I told you to run and hide."

"But then, Sebastian...And I left..." I faltered. I didn't know for sure what Rabbit already knew. I'd told Big Rabbit everything, and I assumed he eventually passed the blow-by-blow account on to Rabbit.

Rabbit's eyes slipped into a full black when I mentioned Sebastian. "You're lucky that fucker didn't drag you back to whatever hole he's been living in."

"He had the chance, but he didn't." I knew Rabbit wasn't going to like my answer. "And he tried to keep the Beams of Light away from me." Why was I telling him this? Defending Sebastian was not going to win me any prizes.

Incredulous, Rabbit shook his head. "After all this time, you are still rationalizing his behavior. Holy shit."

This time I raised both palms in surrender and tried to find the right words. "I don't want to talk about him. What I was trying to say... I left...I left you in the warehouse. I knew there were Beams in there, and I ran."

Rabbit reached for a crutch.

"Please don't walk away!" My palms slapped the table in frustration. Fat tears formed along the edge of my lower eyelids.

His irises were returning to a rich brown, the glossy black dropping away. "I'm just getting more water."

I made to rise, intending to save him the effort.

"Lucie, sit," Rabbit barked. "I don't need you."

I dropped my chin, picking up my napkin. I tore off a strip and nodded.

"I don't need you to wait on me," he said, his voice softer.

"Okay." The conversation was crushing me.

"I can't keep doing this." Rabbit grabbed the second crutch, spinning carefully and maneuvering back to the sink with his glass. He filled it with water and stood looking out the kitchen window while he drank. I watched his Adam's apple lift and lower under his skin as he swallowed. The prominent scar running along his jawline trailed down his neck in a shiny, jagged band.

"What are you saying?" There were so many things he could've meant.

Rabbit set the empty glass down on the counter. His brow lowered in anger when he faced me. "I lost two men that day. Then... *fucking this*." He made a noise of disgust as he gestured to himself, his face contorting in revulsion when he looked down at his body. "Pathetic."

Feeling the despair spill out of him, I wanted nothing more than to go to my friend and wrap my arms around his battered body. But I knew he wouldn't let me. He didn't want me here. He certainly didn't want any pity.

And then I was standing in front of him.

"Don't. Don't touch me," he warned, curving

backward.

I closed the remaining inches between us, wrapping my arms gingerly around his waist and bowing my head. I pressed my forehead to his shoulder.

He stiffened but didn't push me away.

"I'm not asking for your forgiveness – I don't deserve it," I said into his shirt. "But please don't shut me out. I can't handle losing you again."

I felt his body sigh and peeked up at him. He looked exhausted. One of Rabbit's arms awkwardly wrapped around my back as he managed his crutches. The sweet breeze returned and flowed over us from the kitchen window. Stray locks of my hair caught the wind and fluttered across his neck. His chin dipped, barely touching my forehead. The tiniest trace of stubble scraped over my skin, and I reluctantly drew away so I could look at him. Rabbit's hand slid down my arm and over my wrist. His thumb traced a circle on my palm before he gave my fingers a reassuring squeeze.

"What happened in the Walled Zone was not your fault." His lips pressed together for a beat. "But my men were my responsibility. And my failure to protect myself put you in danger."

"Rabbit –" I began.

"Listen to me," he interrupted. "My decisions cost people their lives, almost got me killed, and you could've..." Rabbit faltered, and he released my hand. He nervously swiped his tongue across his bottom lip. "You could've been..."

"Rabbit," I tried again, shaking my head at him.

"You were in danger from the moment we arrived, and I ignored my instincts. Everything was telling me to get you out of there. But I was overconfident. I made horrible choices. When I think what those dogs could've done to you..." Rabbit froze, closing his eyes.

The same hand he'd so tenderly held I now placed on his chest, letting a slip of my energy coast down my arm and into his body. I pushed as much love as I could into him, being careful not to let that same energy explore too deeply. He'd lowered a portion of the wall he'd built around himself, and I didn't want to jeopardize the progress we made. "Everything was out of control for all of us, Rabbit. You couldn't have stopped anything from happening. I know it in my heart. I want you to understand that, too."

Rabbit covered my hand with one of his,

pressing it firmly against his body. A ghost of a smile raised one corner of his mouth. "I can feel it when you do things like this."

"Good," I whispered, watching his face relax, the stress living there fading.

His eyelids fluttered, and he reluctantly peeled my hand away when he opened his eyes. "Okay, you should stop now. We probably shouldn't overwhelm this old man's heart."

His words tripped me up. "Rabbit, will you tell me if you're still sick? Before we went into the Walled Zone, I knew something wasn't right. I could sense it." I searched his face.

He didn't answer.

"Will you tell me –"

"Stop, Lucie."

"Maybe I could help if you told me –"

He shook his head. "Let's go sit outside on the porch before you leave. You should get going soon, and I need to rest."

∞∞∞

We sat together on the porch swing. I bit my tongue when I saw the pain crawl across his face when he lowered himself to the bench. The crutches he kept within easy reach. We didn't swing as much as drifted an inch or two back and forth. I very much wanted to cuddle into his side like I'd done so many times before when seeking solace. But not only might I hurt him physically, it wasn't fair for me to take any more comfort from this man.

"Did Big Rabbit tell you all he knew about what happened that day?" I asked, picking at a spot of white paint on the arm of the swing.

"Everything you told him plus what the Rabbits who rescued us reported."

"You know the Beam took Templeton then," I said, my voice hushed.

"I do." Rabbit's right hand flexed into a fist before relaxing on his leg again. "I'm sorry. I should've been there to help him."

"I had the Crimson Stone, but I couldn't figure out how to use it to stop them. And then..." I kept to the shortest version of the story so I wouldn't lose it. "And then the Beam carried him through the fifth door and into the Above. I dropped the Stone...I dropped the Stone, and it separated into the three pieces. The door to the Above disappeared, and with the Stone broken, I couldn't reopen it. I couldn't follow him."

"I'm glad you couldn't go after him. You could've died, too," he replied.

"You think he's dead." I turned to look at him. His expression was grim.

Rabbit didn't answer right away. When he did, he offered little comfort. "It's been months now. In my experience, when someone powerful disappears and doesn't return, they're either dead, or they don't want to come back."

"He wouldn't choose to leave me," I told him. "He must be trapped."

Rabbit's expression indicated he didn't agree, but he didn't argue.

"When I find the spell to reunite the three gemstones, I'm going to go after him. I'll be able to open the fifth door."

He nodded, fixing his attention on the porch boards under our feet. "I'm not surprised to hear you say that."

"I can't leave him to *them*." My voice hitched.

"I'm not going to lie to you, Lucie. I hope you never get the door open." Rabbit turned his head and searched my face. "And I'm not going to help you either. It's a suicide mission. I'm sorry. I know you…I know how you feel about him."

"I understand." I returned to fidgeting with

the paint spot. "And I'm not even asking you to help. This is something I need to do on my own. I have one of Templeton's books. The spell to put the Crimson Stone back together is in there. I'm sure of it. As soon as I can translate it, I'm going."

Rabbit grew silent again.

"Do you want to know before I go?" The paint spot fractured, and flakes fell from the swing's arm.

"No," he answered. "But tell Big Rabbit."

"Okay." I scanned the clearing in front of the cabin. It was such a peaceful place. Rabbit choosing to recover in this space was a good thing. The woods surrounding us were coming alive with the warmer weather. I could even smell the rich, heady scent of springtime emanating from the damp forest floor. He would heal here.

"You should probably hit the road. You have a three-hour drive."

"Yeah." I glanced at my RAV4 parked in the driveway. "My network phone is in the car. Do you want me to get it so you can connect it to yours?" I already knew the answer.

"No. Keep it the way you have it," he replied. I

heard the sadness in his voice. "But you have Big Rabbit if you need help. He'll come to you."

My heart twisted up into my throat, and I nodded. "I understand."

I stood, waiting until Rabbit was situated with his crutches. The swing made it difficult to rise, and I steadied it with my hand. I saw the fury lining his face as he labored to his feet.

He didn't want to look at me.

"You know where to find me," I said, trying for a lighter goodbye.

He gave his head a nod. I raised up on my toes and kissed his cheek. I paused, again noting the new lines at the corners of his eyes. The last time I'd seen Rabbit, he looked like he was in his mid-20s. Like all Rabbits, aging progressed at a snail's pace for him. But in the last few months, he'd aged by a decade – maybe more. Whether it was the attack or his illness, I didn't know. It was probably both.

"Okay, then." I backed away, turning and stepping down porch stairs, my hand skimming the wooden railing. When my feet touched the ground, I gave a tiny wave over my shoulder.

I retraced my earlier steps to my vehicle, pulling my keys from my pants pocket as I opened the door. I waved again before climbing into the car.

Rabbit's face was an unreadable mask as he watched me leave.

I started the engine, shifted into reverse, and backed down the short driveway to the road. I wanted to have the strength to not look toward the cabin as I put the car into drive, but I didn't.

Rabbit remained on the porch, his worn body propped up by his crutches. I touched the three pieces of the Crimson Stone hanging from the chain under my shirt. I knew in my heart his body would heal.

But his spirit?

Only time would tell.

∞∞∞

The road home seemed much longer as I traveled this leg of my 'birthday road trip' alone. I cried, made a pit stop at a roadside gas station, flipped off several shitty drivers, and pushed my speedometer past a reasonable limit.

By the time I arrived home, I was exhausted. After leaving my car in the garage where I rented a parking spot, I hustled the block to my house as the air turned chillier. The sunshine blessing the beginning of my day was long gone.

Once home, I hesitated at the top of the stairs leading up to my brownstone. This was when I'd typically turn and wave toward the corner of my block, hoping Rabbit was still hacked into the security camera there and would reach out to let me know he was okay. But times had changed. After today, I questioned whether Rabbit even bothered to keep the odd connection alive. For the first time in months, I simply unlocked my door and went inside.

Flame appeared to be out already – I had my home to myself for the evening. I threw my purse across the kitchen counter before stalking into the pantry and retrieving the bottle of vodka I kept for Rabbit on those nights when he'd come by for a nightcap.

When he *used* to come by – his fingers tapping on my front door, his friendly face lighting up my doorway.

I unscrewed the cap, forgoing a glass and drinking straight from the bottle. The smooth alcohol burned a beautiful trail as it crested my tongue and slid down my throat. My chest warmed, and I relished the thought of the blind drunkenness I would chase over the next hour. I'd make the events of the day go away for a while.

Chirping from a kitchen cupboard indicated I had a message waiting for me through the Empire service. I yanked the cupboard open, grabbing the phone's tan handset and purposefully bouncing the cradle up and down twice. Ticking and chimes sounded in my ear, and a recording revealed that I had a message and to 'please hold for an operator.'

"This is the award-winning Empire messaging service," a mechanical voice came on the line. "I have a message for one Ms. Lucie Bellerose from a Mr. Loren Heatherworth. Am I speaking to Ms. Bellerose?"

"You are," I answered, taking another swig from the bottle. I grimaced.

"Ms. Bellerose, Mr. Heatherworth has directed you to appear at the Congress of Empire Witches at 10 o'clock tomorrow morning. You are to wait in the lobby until you receive an official escort to the library. This is the end of the message from Mr. Heatherworth."

Loren had come through for me. I was one step closer to translating the spell that would reunite the pieces of the Crimson Stone. I was one step closer to opening the fifth door and going after Templeton.

"Ms. Bellerose? That is the end of the message."

"Yes," I automatically replied, checking the amount of vodka left in the bottle. "Thank you."

"Thank you for using the Empire messaging service. Have a good evening." The call ended.

I returned the handset to the cupboard and lifted the bottle of vodka high into the air. "To Loren."

I knocked back another mouthful of alcohol, swiping my fingers across my lips afterward.

I was feeling better already.

Chapter 5

"Oh, my god," I whimpered. My cheek rested against the cool porcelain of the toilet seat. "I am so damn stupid."

Flame petted my head. He'd heard the marvelous cacophony of sick from the spare bedroom and came to check on me as merciless dawn cut in through the windows. As humiliated as I was, I was pathetically grateful to him for holding my hair during the last 10 minutes.

"You shouldn't drink like this at your age," the shapeshifter tsked. "Recovery takes much longer."

I was too nauseous to reprimand him for the dig about my age.

"I mean, what were you thinking?" Flame continued. "You really put the vodka away. Did you take the bottle to bed with you? It's sitting on your nightstand."

"Please stop," I croaked before convulsing in another dry heave.

"There you go," he chirped, letting my lank locks drop down my back. "You're empty. What you need now is toast. I'll make you tea, too."

I lifted my head and squinted. "Flame?"

He stopped at the door. "Yeah?"

"Thank you. I appreciate it."

"No problem." He started to turn again.

"Flame?"

"Yes?" He spun in a compact circle like the half-feline he was.

I sat back on my haunches. "Put some clothes on."

∞∞∞

An hour later, I perched on a barstool in the kitchen, nursing my second cup of ginger tea. I'd managed to eat a piece of buttered toast and was feeling more human. Flame doted on me like I was a sick child, asking if he should go to the store for ginger ale, or order chicken soup from *Coffee Cove* – soup was a year-round staple at the café. I reminded him I wasn't ill, just stupid.

Flame pestered me as to why I'd jumped on the train to oblivion all by myself, but the last thing I wanted to do was talk about the sad reunion I'd experienced with Rabbit. Instead, I bribed him with a credit card, directing him to hit up *Second Act* for clothes appropriate for job hunting. I sweetened the pot by saying he could also buy an outfit for going out on the town. He talked me into money for a cab 'to bring it all home' and we had a deal.

I wasn't sure how I benefited from our transaction except for gaining some peace and quiet. Maybe this would give Flame the boost he needed to find a job and get a place of his own.

A witch can dream.

Flame went upstairs to shower while I popped a pill for my headache. The peppermint oil I'd been sniffing took the edge off the pounding in my skull, but it was clear it would linger. My eyes rolled toward the clock on my kitchen stove. I'd need to get a move on. My 10 o'clock appointment at the Congress of Empire Witches was one I did not want to miss. The CEW was a good 30 minutes from my house. I'd call for a cab so parking wouldn't be an issue.

The day was going to be an expensive one.

∞∞∞

After Flame took off on his shopping spree – *I had to give him credit for not whining about being limited to a secondhand clothing shop* – I dragged myself upstairs to shower and dress.

The shower helped wash away the rest of my nasty hangover, but the missing shampoo bottle told me Flame had raided my bathroom again. He had a thing for berry-scented toiletries.

While I got ready, I wondered what kind of 'official escort' awaited me at the Congress. I was somewhat bothered that Loren wouldn't be meeting me there, but perhaps he had another appointment. I also worried my time in the library would be limited. Would they have someone looking over my shoulder?

I certainly didn't plan to bring Templeton's book of magic with me. I wouldn't risk bringing any of his magical belongings into the CEW. Something could be lost or even confiscated.

This meant I'd leave the Crimson Stone at home as well. I placed the gemstones and the silver chain into a box I kept inside my jewelry armoire. After securing them safely inside, I paused, my fingers tracing the outside of the drawer containing not necklaces or rings but the dried blood of a demon. Sebastian's blood.

Sebastian, too, was gone from my life. Compelled to return to the Below, he hadn't resurfaced. Whatever kept him in the Below exercised a formidable power over him. A part of me wondered if he still lived.

I shoved thoughts of him far from my head as I closed the door to the armoire and recast the spell to guard its contents. It wasn't a terribly complex spell, but the wards erected to protect my home were designed to keep unwanted visitors out. I realized how dynamic they were when I wondered how Flame had so easily entered my house. Then again, he'd come in as a cat in a box – in Big Rabbit's arms.

Templeton and I had crafted the protection spell guarding my house to allow those I 'invited in' to enter. This magical invitation of sorts also considered the intentions of the visitor. Only those I'd *want* inside were allowed to enter. The protection spell, thus, was adaptive.

One of the reasons I let Flame stay with me was that the spell wouldn't have allowed him in if his intentions were not in my interest. The spell, working on my behalf, judged him as someone I'd invite in.

Templeton and I made beautiful magic together.

I stood in front of the cheval mirror as the thought wandered through my brain and ripped through my heart. Why was fate cruel to us? I put my hand to my chest and attempted a smile. I was getting somewhere, though. I needed to keep things in perspective. Gaining access to the library today was a huge step.

After covering the shadowy circles under my eyes with a smidgeon of makeup, I pulled my auburn hair up into a loose bun and secured it with a dozen pins. I gave up on trying to capture all the flyaway stray hairs and let them slip out if they were determined to remain free.

My outfit was simple: bootcut blue jeans with a fitted long sleeve heather gray tee shirt that I tucked in. On my feet, a pair of cherry red heeled loafers with a charcoal polish. I looped a handful of silver and black necklaces over my head and around my neck before pulling on a single-button black blazer. The leather belt matched my shoes and was twisted in a chain pattern. The blazer was cut well for my hips. I pushed its sleeves up to just below my elbows and fished an inch of the shirt out on each arm. Silver hoops adorned my earlobes. I added several black and silver bracelets to my right wrist, along with the charm bracelet Anne gave me. After a swish of mascara and a daub of red lipstick, I was ready to go.

I'd called for a cab through the Empire service line and met the car at the curb. The driver held the door for me and confirmed my destination. As we traveled, I pulled the notebook from my purse and reviewed the phrases and letters I'd copied from Templeton's book. The phrases might give me something to go on. The single letters would round out the possibility of a successful translation. Once I deciphered the words I'd written in my notebook, I hoped to have enough to find the right spell when back at home with the frustrating book of magic.

A new worry cropped up when I copied the lines from Templeton's book. He once mentioned not being able to utilize some of the spells he'd sourced from the CEW's library because of the inability to determine the correct pronunciation of the words when spoken aloud in their archaic language. This was a problem.

I hoped my experience would be different. Certain texts in the Congress library provided pronunciation keys. With any luck, the answers I searched for would be in a book with such a guide.

This assumed I would find the right book to help me translate the spells into a recognizable language. I allowed this worry to overwhelm the sadness permeating my energy after seeing Rabbit. The vodka only obliterated the new memories for a while. To cope, I opened a box inside the back of my brain and crammed them all inside. Then I put the box on a shelf. I could only handle one problem at a time, and right now, it was understanding the words in Templeton's book.

Just focus on one damn thing at a time, I thought as I stared out the window while the cab zipped up the last street, reaching the block where the formidable Congress of Empire Witches building sat.

∞∞∞

The Congress was located in the northeastern part of Matar. The witch community favored this section of the city. Here you would find a concentration of witch-owned businesses, organizations supporting witch interests, and even a limited number of residential areas that urban-preferring traditional witches called home. Not every city-dwelling witch lived there, of course. I was quite content in the relatively diverse Clover District.

As the cab pulled up in front of the impressive granite and marble building, I marveled at its massiveness. I'd been in the building many times, but it never failed to impress me. It covered an entire city block, housing a multitude of offices and chambers, a grand ballroom, large and small rooms for rituals and magic, a dining area, a legal wing that included the Elders Panel, and of course, the two-story library. Below ground, the CEW contained a maze of corridors leading to demonstration rooms where witches sat on the other side of reinforced glass and watched rituals and magical acts. I'd suffered under my former teacher's brutality in one of those chambers only months ago. Guillaume had abused his position to abuse my body.

It gave him pleasure.

But Templeton was one of the Congress members watching from behind the glass that day. When Guillaume conjured Sebastian as a demon to 'play' with me – Templeton lost it. He broke into the demonstration room, and after conjuring an indoor tornado, door traveled out of the Congress with me in tow.

For his part, Sebastian didn't intend to do Guillaume's bidding. But that's another story.

Even though Templeton acted to save me from harm, the Congress easily terminated his membership on technicalities: using magic without authorization, 'interrupting' an official demonstration for Congress elders, and spiriting me away before I'd been permitted to leave. But Templeton, a non-witch, was not well-liked by most in Congress. Yes, his personality was an acquired taste, but if the real truth were to be told, most witches were jealous of his magical abilities.

I paid the driver several bills, and he pulled away, leaving me to stand in front of the elaborate security gate which kept non-witches – *and unwelcome witches* – at bay.

Since I was a witch, terminating my membership was more difficult. I'd be afforded a review after a three-month investigation. I honestly couldn't care less if the Congress reinstated my membership – but it was the library that would cause me to grovel for mercy. This library held a wealth of information. I could spend a lifetime studying in it and still only learn half of its secrets.

However, I'd come to realize that I would be reinstated as a full member. The elders were quite keen to keep their fingers on the independent witch who managed to learn how to strengthen her thinning witchline. This gave me some power but also put me at risk. More than once, Loren had intimated certain families might want me to bring my witchline into their family trees. The thought of the Congress compelling me to marry or mate with a member of an influential family was laughable – but it also put a fear into my belly I wasn't ready to entertain.

Again, I could only deal with one problem at a time.

Once the bored security guard allowed me through the gates, I strolled up the walkway to the CEW's entrance. Green sprouts were beginning to line the cement path – maybe daffodils or tulips. The color would be a welcome arrival. The last time I'd made this journey, winter was still clinging to Matar, and I was entering the building knowing I was about to be subjected to intense physical and emotional pain. I gave my head a firm shake. I needed to let that go today. I needed to focus on the task at hand.

As I passed through the double doors into the building, I felt the protective wards judder once as I passed through. The next test would take place with the blind being sitting to the side at the set of doors leading into the actual Congress lobby. The ritual of recognition was conducted by a non-witch, a woman whose origins I couldn't determine. She wasn't human. I'd had one or two odd experiences with her when all the craziness was unfolding earlier in the year. I'd realized she'd seen the demon who broke into the Congress the night of the Witches Gala. I'd learned later the demon was, in fact, Sebastian. I still didn't know why he broke in – or how he managed to get into the CEW. It was all too strange.

As I approached the blind being, her cloudy eyes zeroed in on my face. While I knew she could not see me, I was convinced she recognized me long before I bared my wrist to her for inspection.

"Hello," I said. I'd engaged with her briefly before, but I was wary.

"The light is back at the Congress," she chortled before sliding into a fit of wet coughs. She grasped my hand and pulled me closer as her bent fingers stroked the skin of my wrist. "Who will want and who will win? Who will shine on those who sin?"

My gaze rose from the black tattoo she pulled to the surface of my skin. Rhyming was new. "What do you mean? I don't understand what you're trying to tell me."

"Be aware, witch. He needs you." She blinked, the film covering her protruding eyes appearing shiny, slippery. Her toothless mouth contorted, revealing sickly gums. A whitish tongue ran back and forth over them, the tip dipping into the indentations left behind by missing teeth.

"Who needs me?" I could feel the tremor running through my shoulders and zipping up and down my spine.

"Will you shine your light on he who needs it the most and deserves it the least?" She suddenly growled, clutching harder at my arm and causing me to stumble forward. Her hand wrapped around my wrist, and her voice dropped so low I could barely make out her next words. "You must go through the dark to bring the light, light, light!"

The being's agitation was winding her up. She gasped, clinging to my arm with both hands. I remained rooted where I stood. Although unsettled by her behavior, I waited until her labored breathing calmed. She still held my hand, and her fingers returned to caressing my sensitive skin. The black tattoo began to rise and fall again.

"You may enter, witch," she wheezed.

Unnerved, I nodded, pulling my hand away. "Thank you."

The ritual of recognition ended, and I stepped past the being as she hunched over to rest. I cast a wondering look back before I crossed through the doors to meet the official escort who would take me to the library to search for the answers I needed.

∞∞∞

Several witches were in the lobby, and none appeared to be waiting for me. Between the security guard and the wards, those who wanted to know when I arrived were certainly aware I was there. I would need to be patient.

I adjusted my blazer and shirt sleeve, touching my wrist where the blind being had called up the black tattoo living underneath my skin. Soon after birth, natural witches are often baptized with such a mark. It's a fairly conservative practice, but one many in the Empire still follow. The Congress also requires this mark for its member witches. A handful of non-witches are granted membership at the CEW, but it's extremely rare and the circumstances must be extra special. Templeton had been – *reluctantly* – granted membership but only because of the legacy of a late respected witch, Theodosius. The Congress elders understood Templeton was an approved member, but they did not know why.

But I knew the reason. Templeton's paternal grandfather was a Sorcerer, a fact Templeton has shared with precious few. Theodosius was also privy to this fact, and I can only extrapolate that he smartly attempted to bring a potential future Sorcerer into the witch community's fold. I wondered if Theodosius had any inkling as to how unmanageable Templeton would be inside the witch community. Oh, he 'followed' the rules while in the Congress building, but he was no fan of the CEW. He'd made it clear more than once. His great attraction to the Congress was similar to mine: the library.

Templeton consumes knowledge. Publicly, he's known as a Salesman with magical abilities, but privately he told me he was also a Magician. He revealed his secret to me right before I lost him.

My melancholy thoughts were interrupted when my official escort appeared at my side. "Lucie Bellerose." It wasn't a question.

"Yes." I offered a polite smile.

The man returned one of his own and gestured across the lobby. "You know the way."

I nodded, and we headed for the hall that would deliver us to the library. My feet hurried along, eager to get to work.

"There's no rush," the man said. "The library will be there when we arrive."

"I'm not sure how much time I've been permitted," I explained, glancing up at my escort. He had a pleasant face, but he probably wouldn't turn many heads. He was mostly ordinary. His light brown hair was short, his plain blue eyes friendly enough. I guessed his age to be between 45 and 50. Under his navy-colored suit, he appeared to be fit. His clothing reminded me of Templeton – these garments didn't come off the rack. The suit was custom-made. I noted the gold cufflinks when he opened another set of doors leading farther into the CEW. My official escort was scented with wealth. I frowned; this wasn't a library employee.

"I'm sure the staff in the library will endeavor to bring you what you need today," he replied.

"I'm sorry, I didn't catch your name in the lobby?" I asked casually.

"I didn't give it to you," he answered before greeting another witch as he passed.

"And you are?" I prompted.

"Taking you to the library. And here we are." The doors were open, and we passed through the wide opening into the one space in the CEW where I found comfort.

Immediately I was caught up in centuries of worn books, furniture polish, low lighting, and deep magic. I basked in the familiar scents and soft sounds of pages being turned. Yes, it was like coming home. My memories wandered beyond the front desk to the spiral staircase leading up to the second floor. Templeton had kissed me halfway up those stairs one extraordinary night. It was a bittersweet memory, but for a moment, I remembered how he'd shared a couple of personal details, letting me crack him open a sliver before he leaned in and –

"Lucie?" My escort had asked me a question.

I blinked away the shadows hovering precariously on the staircase. "I'm sorry. What did you say?"

The man raised an eyebrow. "I asked if you had a preference as to where you would like to conduct your research."

"I do, actually." I gestured to the right. "Historical Meaning."

"She'll be working in that section," he told the library assistant who had joined us. "Please check in periodically to see if she needs anything."

"Of course, Mr. Richardson," the woman replied.

Mr. Richardson – *why was the name familiar?* – beckoned, and we veered off to the right, walking quietly single file down the long hall toward the back of the old library before weaving through more towering stacks. As we entered a window-lit space grouping half a dozen tables together, I imagined Templeton sitting there, his head bent over an old text while he waited for me in the space where we'd conducted research together in the past.

But only the memory of the Salesman was there to greet me.

"Any special table?" Mr. Richardson waved a hand, once more breaking into my sad reminiscences.

"The back," I answered automatically, crossing the aisle separating the tables. I set my purse down and hesitated before digging for my notebook. "Thank you, *Mr. Richardson*. I appreciate you escorting me today." I waited for him to say goodbye and leave me to my task.

Instead, he joined me at the table, pulling out a chair and sitting. "Have a seat, Lucie."

It took everything I had not to groan out loud. In my brain, I repeated his name: *Richardson. Richardson.* Was he someone I should know? Did

Loren ever mention a Richardson?

Acquiescing, I took the seat across from him, folding my hands and setting them on the table. I waited.

"Templeton spoke very highly of you," he said, that polite curve of his lips returning. "And you know as well as I do, Templeton rarely speaks well of anyone – except himself."

"Mr. Richardson," I began. "I'm at yet another disadvantage here in the Congress today. You clearly know who I am, but I have no idea as to who you are."

He held out his hand across the table. "Timothy Richardson. Please call me Timothy."

My hand was enveloped in his, and I drew it away after one customary pump. "I'm sorry, but I'm still not sure who you are."

"A friend, perhaps." He sat back in his chair, his hands disappearing into his lap. His unremarkable eyes grew shrewd. "Loren mentioned in passing that Templeton's been missing for almost three months now."

I dropped my attention to the tabletop. *Damn, Loren!* I was sure Templeton would not want that to be common knowledge.

Timothy read my expression accurately. "Oh,

don't be too hard on Loren. I'd realized something was amiss when Templeton missed several poker games."

My head lifted. Poker? Seriously? No.

Timothy's eyebrows raised. "You're surprised? Templeton's quite the card master. He brings a nice challenge to our game."

"I was unaware Templeton was interested in playing cards with witches," I said. "He's not a social creature."

"That he is not," Timothy agreed. "But I'm the only witch sitting in with the others. It's a routine 'off the record' game played in a private room at one of Matar's jazz clubs. It used to be one of Templeton's occasional haunts."

I knew Templeton favored jazz. Timothy's revelations weren't impossible to believe but unexpected. "I see. And that's how you know him?"

"Mostly." A sly expression crossed his face. "On Saturdays, Templeton's favorite jazz singer takes the stage. That's where I first noticed his absence." Timothy's gaze swept over my face and briefly bounced down to the front of my shirt before lifting. "Apparently, Templeton likes redheads with..." Again, he looked down and back up. "Blue eyes."

I didn't care for the leer or his story. "Mr. Richardson –"

"Timothy."

"What Templeton prefers or doesn't prefer is not my business." Slight lie. On the spot, I developed a hatred for every busty, redheaded jazz singer in Matar. "And my purpose here today is to do research, which I should get to. If you have nothing more for me –"

"Loren also indicated Templeton might be in trouble – that his return is being prevented by some force. One you've dealt with in the past."

Thanks again, Loren. I was between a big rock and a hard place. This Timothy had way more information than he should. I played it cool. "I'm not sure what's delaying Templeton's return."

"Perhaps if you told me the whole story, I could help you." Timothy slanted forward, resting his elbows on the table. He pressed the fingertips of his soft hands together. "But you need to take me into your confidence. You need to tell me everything."

I shook my head. "I'm appreciative to the Congress for letting me come here today while

I'm suspended, but –"

"You're welcome," Timothy interrupted yet again.

I faked a patient smile. Great, Mr. Important was giving me a blessing on behalf of the Congress. "Yes, please pass along my thanks. I –"

"To whom?" His condescending tone was getting old.

"To the elder Loren spoke with on my behalf. The elder who helped me gain access here to –"

"To the elder who called in enough favors to grant Templeton permission to join the group who witnessed your brutal demonstration with Guillaume?" Timothy's voice grew icy, his countenance no longer holding any friendliness.

My mouth formed a small 'O.' I'd realized who Timothy Richardson really was. "Yes," I said quietly.

"You're welcome, Lucie Bellerose."

Chapter 6

This was *the* elder – the one who Templeton went to before the demonstration with Guillaume. This was *the* elder Loren went to on my behalf following my birthday lunch to ask for permission to be here today.

The elder. And Templeton's poker buddy? No. I didn't believe it. They might play poker – strange, yet I decided it was possible – but Templeton did not have buddies. Or friends.

I recovered from Timothy's reveal. "I see. Well, thank you for all your help." I paused. "I made the assumption Loren spoke to an older man. You're somewhat younger than most of the elders I've met."

Timothy's expression remained unchanged. "It's less about age in the Congress – it's about power and influence. Or tradition where some witches are concerned. Like Loren."

I wasn't sure if his flippant comment with respect to Loren's clout within these walls was accidental, but I didn't care for it. "Yes, I owe a lot to Loren for his advocacy. Without him, I never would've received support from the Congress to experiment with Guillaume. The strong connections Loren's built over the years were an asset. And he's a good man. What he brings to the table, other witches respect."

"Yes, of course." His elbows remained on the table, but he lowered his folded hands, mirroring my position. "And it's clear you care for each other."

"We do."

"I was fascinated by the work you accomplished with Guillaume." He switched the subject.

I didn't want to discuss my experience with my former teacher. I wanted to begin my search for the resource that would help me translate passages from Templeton's book. "Yes, it was successful. I don't want to be rude, but –"

"You're the only witch who's been able to strengthen her witchline, Lucie. This is extremely important to our community," Timothy said.

"As a member of the community, I am well aware." Where was he going with this? "It's my understanding another witch is in France with Guillaume now, learning to reinforce his witchline. What I accomplished with Guillaume can be taught to –"

"He's dead."

"The...The young man sent a few months ago?" I stammered.

"Yes. Last week. Turns out he had a heart condition – which remained hidden until a particularly intense session with Guillaume." Timothy's face and voice were devoid of any emotion.

"That bastard." I felt sick. "Why do you allow him to continue to teach? Why does he have the Congress' blessing?"

"Because he achieves the goals set for him. You know what a master teacher he is." Timothy scowled. "Lucie, you recognized what could be accomplished under him. That is why you begged the Congress for support."

I sat back. "I did not beg. I petitioned." Angry, I lifted a hand when he moved to speak. "Don't interrupt me again, Mr. Richardson. Do not confuse my politeness for weakness. As a member of Congress – *as an unfairly suspended member* – I'm affording you the respect I would pay to any elder. But I will not be talked down to by you or anyone else here. My strengthened witchline is something I deserve – and trust me, I earned it over and over under Guillaume's hands." The last bit I spat out.

Timothy nodded, his head tilting slightly as he studied me. "Yes. I witnessed a slice of what you endured. I realize it was only a demonstration, but I could see Guillaume did not restrain himself."

That was an understatement. "He did not."

"The fact you could tolerate what he inflicted upon you and use it to feed your witchline makes you incredibly special." Timothy sighed. "You are very valuable."

I hated being labeled as such. I was a person, not an object. "I'd like to get to my research now. It's why I'm here, and I don't want to squander away the time I've been given."

He pursed his lips. "This conversation can continue at another time. But tell me, exactly what are you hoping to do today? Since you are unwilling to tell me about Templeton's disappearance, maybe you would be open to explaining how using the library will help?"

The man just won't stop, I grumbled silently. Frustrated, I motioned to the bookshelves around me. "I need to translate some text. It's written in a language I don't recognize, but I'm confident one of these books will help me develop a key."

"Would you like to show me what you hope to decipher? I'm adept with translation."

"No, thank you." Not on your life.

"Very well." Timothy accepted my rejection, pushing his chair back and standing. Although he wasn't particularly tall, the elevated position underlined his authority. "Then again, I'd assume if this passage was as important as you imply – maybe even something you hoped to use to facilitate Templeton's return – you'd want all the help you could get."

"The passage is private," I replied, shrugging.

"Hmm." He pinned me down with an impassive stare. "Lucie, I do want to be your friend. I want you to be able to come to me for help when you need it. In fact, I want you to bring all your concerns to the Congress so we can work together for our common interests. Think of the wealth of magical resources filling these halls. Think of what you've been presented with by your own kind." His words puzzled me, but he continued. "This translation you need to do – I'm rather amazed you haven't thought of it yourself, but maybe you've already used it for something else." He lifted a shoulder, letting his confusing words fall around me.

"What are you saying?" As much as I wanted him to leave, he'd made me curious.

"The elders are aware you were given a blank page from Guillaume's personal book of magic upon completing your year with him. This act alone proved your worth to the Congress." He raised a hand and stopped me before I could speak. "Like it or not, it's true. I suggest you use the page to see if it will translate the text you believe will help you. Spell it and copy the letters. At a minimum, you might be able to create a legend."

Oh, no.

"Unless you've already used the page for something else and that's why you're here?" Timothy prompted.

"Um, yes." I faltered. "It was used in a different ritual." Yeah, a *ritual barter*. Damn it!

I feared Timothy saw through the lie, but he

let it be. "Well then, I guess I should leave you to your task. The library staff has been informed that you're welcome to conduct your research until the library closes. If you should need anything, they'll assist you."

"Thank you." Clearing my throat, I told another lie. "It was nice meeting you."

"The pleasure was all mine," he replied smoothly. And that *was* the truth.

He lingered. "I'll call upon you in the next day or two to learn if you were successful, but I'm sure you will be." Sharp eyes regarded me one last time. "I can see why Templeton is drawn to you. Like him, you have a great deal of determination inside. Make sure it doesn't deal you the same fate he met, whatever it was."

Before I could answer, Timothy spun on his heel and strolled out of view, blending into the shadows nestled between the stacks.

∞∞∞

The page from Guillaume's book of magic. I knew this would come back to bite me in the ass.

Timothy made a brilliant suggestion. I hadn't

even considered it because the page was no longer in my possession.

Last October, I'd traded the page to Nisha, a powerful supernatural priestess with desperate devotees. She'd siphoned off a year of Templeton's door travel energy as payment for her help in another matter. It rendered him useless when we needed him the most. We were fighting the Fringe and it was crucial for him to be at full power. I gave Nisha the unique piece of witch magic to repay his debt so he could door travel again.

Nisha's origins were unknown to me, but I knew she practiced a sinister magic. Templeton seemed to know her well, and for some reason, Rabbit was familiar with her, too. Emily crossed paths with her more than once, and we both agreed: Nisha was dangerous and should be avoided whenever possible.

Templeton was furious when he learned what I'd done. He knew if my trade was discovered by the Congress, I'd be in a world of trouble. They would punish me. And if Guillaume found out I'd traded his gift to help Templeton...I shuddered. He'd make any action the Congress took against me look like a day playing in the sunshine.

If I could get the page back from Nisha, Timothy was right – I could spell it. There was a good chance the inherent power in the page would work in the way I needed it. I chewed on a thumbnail while I contemplated my options. It was likely Nisha had used it for her own purposes already. But if she hadn't...The packed shelves forming walls around me suddenly seemed overwhelming. It would save me a lot of time. Despite what I'd said to Timothy, there was no guarantee I'd find what I needed here in the library.

I made my decision. Since I was given access, I'd conduct my research as planned. It was possible Nisha would deny me the chance to barter for the page even if she still had it, so I needed to continue what I'd started. I pulled my notebook out of my purse and silently read a line I'd copied.

Okay. Time to get to it.

∞∞∞

The library closed at 5 o'clock. I wouldn't call my day particularly successful, but I'd ruled out several ancient languages no longer used in the Empire. That had to count for something, right?

However, I stumbled across an interesting spell one could use to compel another to tell the truth. As handy as it might be, forcing another to do my bidding troubled me. Still, I copied the phrases and instructions into my notebook. I could adapt it into something I was more comfortable using. I wasn't about dismissing something entirely simply because it didn't follow my practices. I added my thoughts underneath the lines of the spell – perhaps I could imbue it with an intention to test if something was true.

This is how I built my book of spells over time. I learned from more experienced witches and other practitioners of magic. Everyone had something to teach. Then, I adapted what I learned and added my own unique abilities into the mix. I studied and practiced. Spellcasting, like reading Tarot, was an art form using natural elements, personal power, and the mind. Intention influenced the outcome tremendously.

At 4 o'clock, I decided I'd gone as far as I could. I was brain-fried. Admittedly, I was distracted by

Timothy's suggestion to use the page Guillaume had given to me. But it had to be a moot point. Surely Nisha had used it or maybe even traded it away – although she was keen to acquire the valuable magical object. I couldn't see her casually letting it go.

I tapped my pencil on the open notepad in front of me. *Chances are she's used it,* I argued again inside my head. *Shit.* I stuffed my notes into my purse before carrying the books I'd gathered during my day of research over to the returns cart. Another hour in the library was unlikely to make much of a difference. The library sometimes yielded the answer, but other times it did not. I was frustrated. At the end of the day, I was no closer to creating a letter key or translating the words in Templeton's spell book than when I began.

Plus, after six hours, I was hungry and tired. The hangover I'd chased away in the morning had remuddled my mind two hours ago. It was time to leave. I slung my purse over my shoulder and wound my way through the lonely stacks back to the front of the library. At the circulation desk, I thanked the assistant who'd checked in with me – and who was also probably checking up on me – while I pored over the books I'd collected.

Since no one told me I needed an escort when I was ready to leave, I walked alone to the front of the building, passing through mostly empty halls leading to the lobby where I'd met Timothy earlier. The Congress was oddly quiet for a weekday, and the soles of my heeled loafers added no noise to the oppressive silence. Outside the lobby doors, the blind being performed the ritual of recognition with two waiting witches. As I passed, she paused, her gnarled, arthritic fingers stroking the wrist of an older woman while her unseeing eyes tracked me to the building's entrance. I looked over my shoulder as I passed outside into the late afternoon light and realized her face was still pointed in my direction. A shiver ran through my shoulders, and I hurried away. At the security gate, a guard whistled for a cab and held the door as I climbed into the vehicle.

Usually, the guards were less than friendly, and this was a pleasant change. He was younger than the others I'd encountered at this first line of defense in front of the CEW. Perhaps a nicer way of being was the new order. After giving the driver my address, I was whisked off back to the Clover District and home.

∞∞∞

Flame met me outside the front door in his cat form, meowing furiously for me to hurry with the lock.

"You can get in through the back," I reminded him.

He thwapped my calf with his furry tail.

"Don't give me that," I said, unlocking my door after testing the wards and noting nothing out of the ordinary. Flame swept by my feet. As I shut the door behind us, he spun around in a tight circle. I was sure it was part of his performance rather than a necessity. Mesmerized, I watched as his form grew, the front half of his body lifting and twisting as he rose. His tail drew in snugly to his body, and his head rolled on his neck while his shoulders shuddered rapidly as if he were shaking off his coat. Instead, the orange and white fur retracted and folded against his tan skin. The soft feline fluff morphed into blond fuzz, peppering the tops of his forearms and slim but athletic legs.

A smattering of light hair spread across his stomach and trailed down into a thicker patch between his legs.

I tried not to look, but frankly, it was fascinating.

The transformation, that is, not the half-erection he *always* sported when he shifted into his human form. I shook my head. Good god.

As the planes of his face reformed into the young man who'd taken over my spare bedroom, the pointed teeth inside his mouth drew back, leaving him with his trademark grin. He pushed an errant strawberry blond lock off his forehead.

"I see you checking it out," he teased.

"Seriously, Flame," I sighed. "It's hard not to notice it when it's flapping around like that. I can tell you're flexing it. Now go put some clothes on." I stalked by him toward the kitchen, ignoring his chuckle.

"What's for dinner?" He called after me. "Oh, and I need hair gel."

I paused in the kitchen doorway. "You know, Flame. You're a grown man. Perfectly capable of making your own dinner and picking up hair products at the store."

He brandished a broad grin. "Cash flow is somewhat of an issue these days."

"Yeah," I said, turning into the kitchen.

"I still have your card," he called after me. "I'll use it."

"Freakin' hell," I muttered, tossing my purse on the counter.

"I'll get dressed now and run to the grocer," he continued. "Want me to buy us dinner?"

The clock on the stove indicated it was almost 5 o'clock. "Fine!"

The sound of Flame's bare feet slapping up the stairs carried into the kitchen. What was I going to do with him? I shook my head. Later I'd have him show me the clothes he'd purchased from *Second Act*. Job hunting started tomorrow.

"Never in my life did I think I'd have a big-assed kid living with me," I groused as I set the kettle for tea. Then I smiled.

Flame returned in yet another pair of basketball shorts – apparently, they were more comfortable because he skipped wearing underwear – and a bright red tee shirt. He'd pulled on a pair of canvas tennis shoes with missing shoelaces. He waved my card at me and asked how I felt about barbeque chicken wing pizza. I told him my feelings for such a thing were unremarkable and waved him off.

We'd have to talk about him going commando underneath the shorts, however. I wasn't convinced the no underwear choice was a good one.

He was almost to the front door when it hit me. I abandoned the raspberry tea I'd made and called after him to wait.

"Yes?" Flame paused with one hand on the doorknob.

"Why are you so hot for an early dinner?" My arms folded, I leaned against the door jamb separating the kitchen and the hallway.

"Well," he began, slowly picking his next words. I could tell this wasn't going to fill me with joy. "Thursday evenings, David usually goes out to a particular bar downtown with his colleagues. Now that I have some new threads – *and thank you, Luscious* – I thought I'd meet up with a new friend, too."

I ignored his well-timed gratitude and the nickname. "Uh-huh. And you are meeting this new friend at the same bar David is going to?"

"Weird coincidence, isn't it?" Flame's not-so-innocent eyes widened as he lifted his palms toward the ceiling.

"Flame," I shook my head.

"I only want to show David there are no hard feelings. I have moved on." He put a hand to his chest. "And I have clothes again."

"You're not going to make a scene, are you?" I winced, imagining the call coming through the service line from the closest Empire guard station.

"Absolutely not! I'm only having a drink with a special friend," Flame protested. His hand returned to the doorknob, and he drummed his fingertips on it. I swore it sounded like someone tapping pointy nails on a metal surface, the scratchy swiping sound giving me chills. "It's a convenient spot to meet downtown."

"This new friend," I said, stepping into the hall. "What's the hotness factor?"

He waggled his blond brows. "Smokin'."

"No surprise there." I wiped a hand over my forehead. "Please stay out of trouble."

"Relax! Now listen, I'm going to get us pizza. I'll need to hurry so I can shower before going out tonight." Flame stepped outside. "I'll get hair gel, too. You need anything?"

I waved him off. "No. Go."

He started to shut the door behind him but quickly reopened it and popped his head back inside. "While I'm gone, could you order a cab through the Empire service? Ask them to be here at 7 o'clock? Thanks, Luscious!"

"Fine," I answered. My headache was returning.

Flame disappeared back out the door, leaving me behind to wonder how he was going to pay for a cab downtown. I caught my bewildered reflection in the hall mirror. *Oh.*

Whatever. I had somewhere to go tonight as well, and it would be easier if Flame was out. I didn't want to explain my plans.

I was also heading downtown to a luxury high-rise building where I'd find a priestess living in a penthouse on the top floor. I'd mulled over what I could possibly trade for the page I'd given her last fall. The cab ride home from the CEW gave me time to run through a short list of what I possessed that Nisha might find valuable.

I doubted she would have too much of an interest in the spells I'd developed over the years. Even if she did, they were not equal in value to the page from Guillaume's personal book of magic. Templeton's book of magic, on the other hand, would be of interest – and I'd never, ever part with it. The Crimson Stone also held great value, but again, it wasn't an option.

The answer came to me during the trip home. I'd been staring out the cab window when I saw a billboard promoting a new medicine for springtime allergy sufferers. The woman appearing in the advertisement was featured mid-sneeze, a hand holding a crumpled tissue near her nose.

Realization washed over me. There was something I possessed that Nisha might want to add to her magical tool chest.

A tissue covered with dried demon blood.

After I'd bloodied his nose, Sebastian made a costly mistake by leaving those tissues in my trash. And yes, I was going to try to profit from his poor judgment. I'd do whatever I needed to do to get that damn fifth door open.

Plus, I'd hidden away several tissues. I was willing to give up one – it would be enough. I'd hold onto the remaining few. I might need his blood for something in the future.

After Flame left for the evening, and hopefully for a drama-free night out on the town, I'd box up a bloody tissue and take a cab downtown. There'd be no need to send a message in advance, and I didn't want Nisha to know I was coming. I'd need every extra edge I could squeeze out of the situation.

I did not look forward to doing business with the dreadful priestess.

I opened the cupboard, lifting the handset from the Empire phone. I bopped its cradle up and down once. Ticking indicated I was being transferred to an operator.

"Hello, this is Lucie Bellerose of 1106 Autumn Avenue. I need to request two cabs for pick-up. I'll need the first one at 7 o'clock and the second one can arrive 30 minutes later. There will be one passenger for each car."

Chapter 7

Dinner with Flame was quick – he was eager to shower and primp afterward. The final result was a sexy young man in a pair of gray plaid chinos with the bottoms turned up, an Aegean blue button-down, and a pair of gray-to-beige dress sneakers without socks. His hair was brushed up and swept in soft spikes to the left. I sniffed. Strawberries. He was still using my shampoo, dammit!

"*Second Act* came through," I noted. He looked fantastic.

"Hmm," he purred. "Yes, lucky day. By the way, when does your credit card statement arrive?"

Wait, what? "Flame?"

"Just asking – nothing to worry about," he assured me. "I'm going to check and see if the cab's arrived."

I had no one to blame but myself. I'd given him

the credit card. I finished my pizza crust while I wondered about the amount I'd find on my bank statement. Sighing, I washed the plate in the sink.

"Hey, it's here," Flame announced as he hurried back into the kitchen. He pulled a new leather wallet from his pants pocket and waved it at me. "Nice, huh? Soon to be loaded with paycheck money all because Luscious bought me a new wardrobe."

Wardrobe?

"In the meantime, um, does the cab driver take cards?"

"Yes," I answered slowly.

"Can I hold onto yours?" He flashed what my friend Emily would call a 'winning smile.'

"Alright, listen. One night with the card. You're allowed to use it for a cab ride downtown and back home. And for one drink. One." I eyeballed him as he made sure the card was tucked safely inside his wallet. "And only if you promise on your nine lives that you will absolutely not get into any drama tonight. None. No drama. And you are to return home with the clothes you are wearing still on your back. If you can promise me to –"

"Will do, Luscious," he interrupted before smacking a loud kiss in the middle of my forehead.

"I mean it, Flame," I tried again. "If you can swear on your nine lives –"

"Oh, we really don't have more than one life," he laughed. "I gotta run. Don't wait up for me!" He whipped around and out of the kitchen so fast I would've thought he was in his cat form. The front door opened and slammed shut.

Great. He was something else – but then again, he always seemed to land on his feet. Had to be a cat thing.

I checked the clock. In 25 minutes, my cab would arrive. Pulling a face, I contemplated changing into a pair of sneakers in case I needed to make a run for it after dealing with Nisha. Then again, the heeled loafers added 2 inches to my height. Barefoot, Nisha was 6 feet tall. I wasn't short, but I'd have to be on stilts if I wanted to tower over her.

Upstairs, I retrieved one bloodstained tissue from my jewelry armoire. It was already folded, and I gently eased it into one of the plain wooden boxes I kept for storing and transporting magical items. This one was small, and I nestled the tissue inside carefully. In magic, many things were possible. If Sebastian still lived, the blood I'd saved could be even more potent in certain spells. Would he be affected by how she might use it?

Pressing my lips together, I closed the lid and secured it. I couldn't let any troubling thoughts stop me now. I'd made my decision.

∞∞∞

The cab was on time, and the ride downtown ferrying me to the foot of Nisha's high-rise seemed too short. I handed over several bills to the driver before stepping out onto the curb. The sun was no longer visible, and the last light was fading. Perfect timing for damnable dealings, I supposed, with no little amount of unease.

The doorman welcomed me inside the luxury building, directing me to a reception desk where I recognized a staff member from my previous visit. The concierge spoke in hushed tones on the phone. She acknowledged me with a nod, and I waited until she finished her conversation.

"How may I assist you?" The woman's curious

gray eyes swept over what she could see of me from the other side of her counter.

"I'd like to meet with Nisha." This was the same process I'd experienced before. Rabbit had coached me on what to say when he grudgingly led me to Nisha's residence in the past. He also warned me against asking her too many questions. I could find myself in a world of trouble if Nisha believed I owed her even more for the answers she gave. It would be wise to avoid asking questions – or at least limit them to the basic ones necessary for our dealings.

"I'm sorry, there is no resident here by that name. Perhaps you have the wrong address," she replied, the same response I received months ago passing smoothly through her lips.

I stuck to the script I'd used before. "My name is Lucie Bellerose. I'm here on behalf of John Templeton." I paused, then added. "I've met with Nisha in her penthouse before. She's not expecting me, but I have something of value with me tonight. She benefitted from my prior visit. Would you check to see if she is available?"

The concierge weighed my request, her mouth pulling to the side. "You do look somewhat familiar. Wait here."

She disappeared through a door behind the wide desk, and I assumed she was ringing Nisha's penthouse in private. Minutes later, she returned and waved for me to follow her to the elevator. As before, we both stepped inside when the doors slid open. She would escort me to Nisha's floor at the top of the building. After she punched in a secure code, the doors slid shut.

The elevator ascended quickly. When it stopped and the doors reopened, the concierge motioned for me to step into the wide hallway where visitors waited to be granted entrance into Nisha's lair.

"She's expecting you," the concierge said as she tapped a button on the elevator wall. "Go ahead and knock."

I offered my thanks to the sliding doors before crossing to the entrance leading into Nisha's penthouse. This heavy door was unlike any other I'd seen in the building. It was made from reddish-brown mahogany wood, and a pattern of carvings covered its surface. A couple resembled symbols I might use in a protection spell. Several prominent designs appeared to be warnings – figures on their knees, their arms wrapping around their heads as if to protect themselves while they groveled. Beneath those, figures with snapped necks fell through the air.

Were these symbols presented to keep out magical nasties or to remind visitors to be cautious? Probably both. I tapped on the door and waited. Almost immediately, one of her staff members opened it and directed me to come inside.

The penthouse was large, and I'd only ever seen the first room where Nisha gave an audience to her visitors. The room was lush, filled with plush couches and chairs in rich shades. A scarlet-colored carpet muted my steps as I followed the man who encouraged me to take a seat. As with my first visit, as soon as the man's figure faded down a shadowy hall, I couldn't recall what he looked like. This level of spellcasting put me on edge.

I remained standing and did not wander. White candles in various lengths and widths decorated surfaces throughout the room. The heady scent of perfumed incense drifted seductively under my nose, the unseen smoke rising in a different room. A wall of windows faced Matar's dusky cityscape, the light disappearing while the sound of water trickling from deep inside the penthouse tickled into my ears. The temperature was pleasant, almost cool, yet not cold. The atmosphere left me feeling safe and relaxed.

This place was dangerous.

While I waited, I noted nothing personal in the way of décor – no artwork or knick-knacks, no shelves lined with favorite books or photos. The space was designed to encourage visitors to let down their guard while revealing nothing about their hostess.

I was searching the darkening Matar skyline for landmarks through a wall of windows when the priestess glided into the room.

"The Bellerose Witch returns," Nisha cooed, startling me.

I turned, nodding once. "Nisha."

"You are here on behalf of Templeton again?" The woman's full, wide mouth opened in a dreadful smile. Over her generous curves, she wore an ankle-length ivory-colored dress that clung to her round hips before revealing two long slits on each side beginning mid-thigh. The dress was sleeveless, with a deep neckline. When she turned to adjust a flickering candle, I saw it was backless, revealing her flawless ebony skin.

Rows of silver bangles rose up each arm, and around her ankles, more bracelets appeared. On both hands, she wore several rings – gold and silver bands sporting various gemstones. Her sleek black-as-the-night hair was worn down and loose, spilling over her shoulders. The light color of her dress and the shining silver of the jewelry she'd adorned herself with were in sharp contrast to her skin. She was barefoot.

"Somewhat." I raised a shoulder.

A winged eyebrow lifted. The candle repositioned, she stepped toward me, the waving light reflected in her large sable eyes. "What is your purpose here today?"

"I'm here to inquire about the magical item I brought to you last fall." I waited to see how she'd react. "It's the page I traded to erase Templeton's debt to you."

"Yes," she exhaled. "The blank page from another witch's book. Oh, Templeton was livid. He was so angry with you. I could…barely console him that night."

You wish, I thought. Templeton wouldn't be interested in any soothing Nisha offered. I wouldn't take the bait. "Is the page available for a new trade?"

"You would like to regain this piece of witch magic?" She breezed past to stand in front of the windows, her back to me. The smell of cold, wet earth followed in her wake.

"Yes."

"Are you being directed by your Congress to do so?" Nisha spat out the word 'Congress.'

"I am not."

"It is something you need from me for personal use?" She faced me again, her chin lifting. Even though we did not stand close, I could see her nostrils flare as she sniffed the air.

"Yes, I would like to trade for it – if it is unused."

Nisha's lips parted, and I imagined a forked tongue darting out. "It is in the condition in which it came to me."

I'd have to trust it was unused. From what I understood, Nisha didn't lie, but she would mislead. "I would like to make a trade for it then."

"What is your planned use?"

"Translating a passage." Simple answers, nothing more.

"Hmm," she hummed. "Magical text?"

"I assume."

"You do not know the language?"

Clearly not, I thought. "No."

"One of the Empire's archaic languages?"

"I'm not entirely sure, but yes, I believe so."

"You implied you came here 'somewhat' on behalf of Templeton. I have taught him many of the ancient languages. Will he not help you with your translation?" Nisha stood in front of me. I resisted the urge to give any ground by stepping back. Unfortunately, this also meant I had to look up.

"Templeton is not available at this time." My lips pressed into a thin line.

For a long moment, Nisha searched my face for information I was unwilling to give. "I have not seen Templeton in many months. I sense you have not either. He is no longer in the Empire?"

I waved a hand. "I cannot say exactly where he is, Nisha."

"This translation you need to make – is it to assist Templeton?" She watched for my reaction. "Do not lie to me, witch."

"The translation will assist *me*."

She laughed. "What you say is, indeed, a truth.

Very well. You will not tell me where Templeton has gone. I will accept your answer. But if you should desire to share Templeton's whereabouts in the future..." Nisha tilted her head back, her eyes sliding upward as her irises and pupils disappeared under her lids. Cloudiness appeared in the milky orbs, and I sensed the magic swirling around her. The language she whispered was unknown to me, and she conversed with an unseen force. Her eyes lost their murkiness when she lowered her head and refocused on me.

Nisha continued. "Bring me the passage you need to translate. I will decipher it for you. In return for my help, I will keep the original document on which it was written. That is all the payment I require."

"That's not something I'm willing to do."

"And yet you think you can offer me something equal in trade to the value of the page from Guillaume's book of magic?" Nisha sneered.

I blanched. When I gave it to her, I hadn't revealed the page's origins. I wouldn't ask how she knew – it could cost me. I continued with my original request and made my offer. "I would like to trade for the page. In return, I can give you demon blood."

"Demon blood?" Nisha mocked. "A demon can be summoned and compelled to spill his black blood should I have a need. I rather enjoy harvesting it from their dead hearts. Try again, witch."

I pulled out my ace in the hole. "This blood is not what you expect. I don't know how this is the case, but this demon is *not* dead. What I'm trying to say, Nisha, is he never died before becoming a demon. He's alive with a beating heart. Living blood still pumps through his body."

She did a good job of hiding her surprise, but I knew she was intrigued. "Tell me more," she hummed, stepping away and pressing a tile. Within seconds, the man who'd let me into the penthouse appeared. She spoke low into his ear. He nodded and left the room.

"I don't know the details surrounding his transformation into a demon," I said. "At first, I thought it happened after his death and might've continued to think that was the case if it weren't for another witch familiar with the art of necromancy. He observed that the demon retains his human life force – his signature energy."

"Where is this demon now?" Nisha asked.

"I'm not sure where he is." That *was* the truth. I presumed Sebastian remained in the Below.

"How did you come to possess the blood?"

I lifted a shoulder. "Someone gave him a bloody nose. The details don't matter."

She didn't press me. "Let me see it."

"Do we have a deal? Will you accept the demon blood in trade for the page?"

"I am considering it. I want to see this demon first." Nisha beckoned to me as her staff member reappeared with a tray and placed it on one of the taller tables. In the center sat a black glass circle. It rested flat against the surface of the tray. The man was gone before I looked up.

"I'm not on board for conjuring a demon," I replied.

She waved a graceful hand. "No conjuring, but his blood will reveal his likeness to me. I need a droplet."

"The blood is dried on a soaked tissue."

"It does not matter to me. I will use a speck torn from it." She floated her hand over the smooth surface, her palm facing up. "Place a piece on my hand."

I pulled the wooden box from my purse. Nisha watched as I opened it and tore off the tiniest scrap possible from a bloody corner of the tissue. "Enough?"

"My magic rarely requires outside assistance," she said. "But this is necessary to open a connection."

I hovered my fingers over her palm and gently released the stained fleck of tissue.

After it landed, she balled her hand into a fist, her eyes rolling back a second time. It fascinated me as much as it repulsed me. The words passing through her fast-moving lips were unintelligible. A sharp gust of wind blew through the room – *impossible!* – extinguishing all the candles. The room grew dim, then immediately, the flames returned, each one swaying and casting shadows along the wall. They undulated in opposite directions, a trick of the eye or some sort of mystical beings assisting in Nisha's spell? I didn't like this.

Turning her hand over, she allowed the piece of tissue to fall onto the black glass. As it fluttered against the hard surface, it disintegrated and ripples appeared. The circle then filled with smoke and swirled. Nisha's eyes reopened, and we both bent over the tray.

A pinprick of light appeared in the middle of the glass. As it grew, the brightness morphed and an image formed. Sebastian's shaggy head turned and lifted. His reflection peered out from the surface of the glass, his face contorted in confusion. He looked from side to side, wary. His eyes roamed the gloomy space around him. His lips moved, and I read the question on them:

Who's there?

"Does he know we can see him?" I asked without thinking. I examined the man whose blood I would trade.

"Oh, he is a pretty demon," Nisha purred, ignoring my question. "I might conjure him and keep him bound to me. What is his name?" Before I could answer, she hovered her hands over the image inside the glass. "He is in Abaddon."

Abaddon? My brain took off on an automatic search for the term. Abaddon...*Hell?* "I know this place as the Below."

I didn't miss the flutter of recognition skimming across her face. "It came to be known as the Below by those who could not read the ancient texts. They believed the life force, when it escaped the corporeal form, would be directed to the light or the dark. Those judged to live in the darkness were sent to the Below, where they would spend eternity seeking the light. Those judged to live in the light were directed to the Above."

Nisha didn't surprise me with what she knew of the Above and the Below. I wondered if Templeton had discussed any of this with her. Before I could reply, she spoke again.

"These ignorant beliefs are, of course, untrue. There is no external judgment. The life force, upon leaving the body, chooses where to go. However, neither place is hospitable. In the Below, they cry for the light. In the Above, they receive the light and cease to be." Nisha's dangerous smile returned. "And how did you come to know this demon who lives in the Below, Bellerose Witch?"

When I didn't answer, her hand shot out like a striking snake. Nisha's fingers wrapped around my upper arm, and she dug her fingernails into my clothing – yet I felt her claws sinking into my skin as if my arm was bare. Was it my imagination, or was she employing a form of menacing magic? Immediately I raised the fire living under my skin to a blistering level. She released me, abruptly pulling her hand away and hissing.

"You do not have permission to touch me," I warned. My voice had also dropped, the low tone resonating in my upper chest. I did not trust Nisha, but I realized despite all I'd witnessed and learned, I wasn't afraid of her either.

Nisha's upper lip curled, and she sniffed her fingertips. "I can smell his memory on your skin. Tell me, was he a pleasing lover? Did you let him touch you in his demon form?"

This was not a time for girl chat, and we were not from the same sisterhood. "Do we have a deal? His blood for the page?" I held up the rest of the bloodstained tissue. If she reached for it without agreeing to return the page from Guillaume to me, I'd set the dry tissue on fire in front of her.

The wicked priestess lowered her hand back to the surface of the glass. She stroked Sebastian's face, and the demon jerked his head back. Again, I read his lips:

What the fuck?

A pang of remorse flitted through my chest.

Nisha continued to stroke Sebastian's likeness until he swatted the empty air around him and let out a yelp I could see but not hear. "We do."

"I'll take it now, then."

She snapped her fingers, and the page from Guillaume's book appeared. She held it between her sharp fingernails outside my reach. "Tell me, this demon, does he know where Templeton has gone?"

I glared at the bitch. I was so done with this miserable transaction. "Yes."

"And has this demon also traveled to this place, this *special* plane Templeton is now... *visiting*?" Her voice melted in the air around me.

A dull buzz rose inside my ears. "Y-yes."

Why was she asking these questions? *Why was I answering them?*

Nisha rolled her hips in a figure eight, her body responding to a rhythm pulsing in the air surrounding us. "I am feeling generous, witch. I will give you a present."

"I want nothing more from you," I answered, my eyes darting to the page she held. I felt lightheaded. The incense was heavier and flooding the air. It stuck in the back of my throat. "A simple trade. One tissue with demon blood for the page. Done. Nothing more expected on either end."

She straightened, ignoring me. "My present is this advice: Conjure this demon and learn how he traveled into the plane where our precious Templeton is delayed. Then send him back to the place you call the Below." Nisha leered at Sebastian gritting his teeth on the other side of the glass. "But do it before the next full moon. I will want my new pet at my side by then. He can pledge himself to me during my ritual."

My thoughts reconnected in my brain, and I snapped out of whatever haze Nisha had floated into it. *What?*

I pulled my attention away from the image of Sebastian. A satisfied expression filled Nisha's face as she passed the unused page from Guillaume's book of magic back to me. In trade, I gave her the tissue saturated with Sebastian's blood.

"What is the name of my new demon?" Nisha licked her lips.

"Sebastian. Sebastian St. Michel." A pang of sadness bounced around the inside of my rib cage.

What was done was done.
But I certainly did not wish Nisha upon him.

Chapter 8

The doorman stood outside in front of the building, the sound of firetrucks and stalled traffic drawing his curiosity. I pushed through the set of doors, exiting the building.

"What's going on?" I peered down the street.

"The next block down houses a number of restaurants and bars. There's a fire. Probably started in a kitchen," he explained. "I can hail you a cab, but you might be better off walking to the corner and turning toward Harrington Avenue. It's a one-way street, and you should be able to catch a cab there."

I hooked my thumb and motioned over my shoulder. "This way?"

"I'd head toward the mess." He pointed in the opposite direction. "The fire is farther down, and you should be fine. The walk to this corner is shorter."

"Got it." I pulled my purse up over my shoulder and tucked it securely under my arm. The page from Guillaume's book of magic was safely stored in the envelope I'd brought and slid inside one of the purse's large pockets.

Foot traffic flowed against me in fits and starts, but it wasn't bad. I supposed a fire on a weekday evening was better than a weekend night blaze. Right before I reached the corner where I'd turn, an orange flash darting across the street in front of me snagged my attention. A very pretty mackerel tabby landed on the curb and trotted in my direction.

Son of a bitch!

"Flame," I hissed as he drew near. A bad feeling about the fire crept up my spine. "Flame!"

The cat slowed, his progress coming to a halt when he turned his wide eyes on me. He spun around and dashed off back down the block. At the corner, he turned where I'd planned to do the same, disappearing from sight. My heeled loafers weren't made for running, and I quickly bent and pulled them off. They dangled from my fingers as I raced after him. By the time I'd rounded the end of the block, he was gone.

I wasn't sure what he did, but he was in a world

of trouble.

∞∞∞

It took me an hour to find an empty cab and return home. During the ride, my thoughts alternated between plans to kill Flame – because I *knew* he had something to do with the fire – and the transaction I'd completed with Nisha. I was thankful I could get the page back unused, but guilt over what nastiness I might've inflicted on Sebastian surfaced. I attempted to console myself with plans to use the page to translate the text from Templeton's book of magic.

I was getting closer to finding and deciphering the spell that would reunite the three pieces of the Crimson Stone. Then I could open the fifth door to the Above.

Yes, this was what I'd focus on. Sebastian becoming a casualty of what I'd done – *what I had to do* – would not be my problem. He would've done the same thing and had no regrets. This was another consequence of the man he chose to be.

I chewed on my thumbnail as I stared

unfocused at the world rushing by on the other side of the cab's window.

∞∞∞

That night, my guilt wouldn't let me sleep. Visions of Sebastian's likeness in the black glass, swatting at invisible touches delivered by terrifying magic, created gruesome shapes on the insides of my eyelids. His confusion and fear made my stomach hurt.

I buried my face into the pillow and tried to redirect my thoughts to my troublesome shapeshifter. Flame hadn't returned home – not a shock. I left a note on the kitchen counter telling him we were going to talk in the morning or he'd have to find another place to stay. I put the same note on his bedroom pillow – no, the *spare* bedroom's pillow. It was an empty threat, but hopefully it would keep him from sneaking out early in the morning. If he even came home.

Sleep eventually came to rescue me, but my dreams were visited by three vastly different men: my lost knight, my angry Rabbit, and my desperate demon. Sebastian was the last one to make an appearance.

He begged me to glow for him. Dream Lucie felt as guilty as the real one, and she told him she would. I woke before I could figure out what she planned to do.

∞∞∞

The next morning, before going downstairs, I checked to see if my roving shapeshifter ever made it home. The covers were pulled down and balled up at the bottom of the mattress. Two pillows were stacked one on top of the other in front of the headboard. He'd slept in the bed, but he wasn't an early riser. I worried Flame might've escaped before I woke.

I found him in the kitchen, eating a bowl of cereal with more milk than grains and reading a magazine I'd left on the counter. He cupped the bottom of the bowl in the palm of his left hand while he spooned in mouthfuls of cereal with his right. When I opened my mouth to announce that we needed to talk about what went down last night, a page of the magazine rose and gently fluttered to the left. Well, *that* was unexpected. We'd need to discuss these magical inclinations at some point. But first, there were more pressing items.

Such as his role in a building fire.

Flame crunched his cereal. "Morning, Lucie," he sheepishly greeted me around a mouthful.

"Good morning, Flame." He'd made coffee, and I poured myself a cup. The whole milk waited on the counter, and I added a dollop. I watched him squirm out of the corner of my eye.

He coughed. "Did you sleep well?"

Turning, I took a sip of coffee before answering. "Not really, but I'll live. And how did you sleep?"

Flame scrunched up his nose, which lifted his upper lip and bared his bright, white teeth. "Horrible. I know you're mad."

"Do I need to report my credit card as lost?"

"Probably a good idea. My wallet was torched in the fire." He took another bite of cereal and mumbled 'sorry, Lucie' into his bowl.

"Tell me what happened."

Flame took his time chewing. I figured he was choosing his words carefully. "There was a misunderstanding, and somehow a waiter carrying a tray full of flaming shots got knocked over. The alcohol went everywhere – and so did the fire."

I stood on the other side of the counter and faced him. "Was anyone hurt?"

"I don't think so, but it was chaos." Flame slid his spoon into the bowl and set it down on the countertop. "For the record, it wasn't me, Lucie. I didn't cause the fire." His cat eyes didn't blink.

"Why don't you walk me through what happened? I'm guessing you met your 'new friend' and that David was there, too."

"David was already there when I arrived – with people from his office. I think I saw him first because he was surprised when he looked my way," Flame said.

"I'll bet." I took another drink from my cup.

"Yeah." Flame's tongue poked at the corner of his mouth. "I could see he wasn't happy, but he wasn't about to make a scene in front of his co-workers."

"And you? Did you make a scene?" Visions of Flame hovering over David's table with his date floated through my mind.

"Absolutely not," he replied. "I don't need to make a scene to make a point."

"And your point?"

"That I don't need him. There are plenty of

others who enjoy my company." Flame folded his arms across his chest.

I was somewhat relieved, but I knew there was more to the story. I wasn't ready to absolve him yet. "Go on, tell me what happened next."

"Well, here's where it gets interesting." Flame squirmed. "Madison's ex-boyfriend is a server at the bar."

"Who's Madison?"

"My new friend," Flame answered. He continued without missing a beat, but the tips of his ears grew red. "Turns out this ex-boyfriend wasn't too keen on seeing me kiss her."

I set my coffee cup down. "Wait, Madison is a girl?"

He cocked his head to the side. "Didn't I mention that?"

"You might have skipped that piece of information when you said you were meeting a friend."

"Does it matter?" Flame's blond brows knitted together. "I told you, I like all people equally – guys, girls, or whatever people see themselves as being. It's the person, not the private parts."

"Of course it doesn't matter, as long as you're

dating good people," I answered. "I assumed you were meeting a guy to make David jealous."

"I wasn't trying to make David jealous," Flame argued.

"Whatever." I waved off his denial. "This ex-boyfriend, did he hurt you?"

Flame laughed. "No, but after coming up to us and shouting at Madison, he took a swing at me when I told him he needed to step away."

"He hit you then?"

"Nope. Cat-like reflexes, remember?" Flame's normally sweet face developed an edge I hadn't seen before. "But Madison was scared, so I gave him a push. That's when David punched him."

"Oh, that's not good." I shook my head. "But how does the fire-carrying server come into play?"

"David hit the ex-boyfriend hard." Flame grinned. "He works out. He's got incredible arms."

I didn't want to dive into a discussion of David's body. "And?"

"And the ex slammed into the server with the flaming shots. *Bam!* Lit alcohol all over the place. It was one of those freak things – people were trying to slap the flames out, but it spread across several tables, and people panicked. I turned around to grab Madison, but she'd already fled the bar."

"What about David?"

Flame shrugged. "I'm not too sure. A bouncer grabbed me. He made your Big Rabbit look tiny."

I motioned for him to continue. "Keep going."

He sighed. "Well, I shifted."

I gaped at him. "In front of everyone?"

"Sometimes I can do it super fast if I'm... *motivated*. It hurts a lot, but sometimes you've got to move." His shoulders hopped up and down. "I took off in the opposite direction of the entrance so I wouldn't get trampled. I left through the kitchen – the door to the alley was wide open."

"And David?"

"Hopefully the bouncer didn't get him." Flame abandoned his barstool and carried his bowl to the sink.

"He could be in a lot of trouble," I said.

Flame rinsed out the bowl. "He's a lawyer. He'll be fine. Besides, he was trying to break up a fight. An innocent patron was attacked, and David intervened." He lifted his head and looked out the window into the backyard. A dreamy smile flirted with his lips.

Oh, brother. I shook my head. What a mess. Well, hopefully, Flame would survive this one, too. "Wait, didn't you say at the beginning of this story that it was all due to a misunderstanding?"

"I did. It was." Flame twisted his mouth to the side.

"I'm not following," I frowned.

"David didn't think I could take care of myself and got involved. If he just would've let it be, none of this would've happened."

I passed a hand over my forehead. "Well, if there was no real damage to the –"

"Oh, it went up in flames," he interrupted.

"Great," I groaned. Before I could add anything else, someone firmly tapped the brass knocker several times against the metal plate on my front door. Flame and I both froze. I pointed at him. "No shifting and no going anywhere."

I grudgingly traipsed to the front of my house, stopping to peek through the side window before opening the door. Outside, David Mattison stood on my front stoop. Wow...And here I believed it couldn't get any crazier.

I opened the door. "Hi, David."

"Is Marcus here? Is he okay? I couldn't find him outside the bar last night." David had the presence of mind not to push past me into my home, but he bounced back and forth as he tried to see behind me.

I held up a hand. "He's here. He's perfectly fine."

"Thank god." David ran a hand through his wavy hair. "I was at the Empire guard station for most of the night, and I've been worried sick."

"David?" Flame appeared behind me. "What are you doing here?"

"You're okay?" The other man leaned into the doorway, and I had to step back. I bumped into Flame.

"I'm fine," Flame answered, placing his hands on my shoulders and guiding me to the side.

"Wait a minute," I stepped back between the two men. "Flame isn't in trouble, is he?"

David shook his head. "Absolutely not. Flame was an innocent bystander in last night's mess." His concerned blue eyes swung to the shapeshifter. "I told the guards I saw one of the servers hassling a couple at the bar. When I intervened, the altercation ended up knocking a tray of fire shots over." Here David paused, and an expression I could only describe as crafty slid into place. "Did you know flaming alcoholic drinks are illegal in Matar?"

"I was not aware," I answered.

"And the bar let their insurance lapse – which isn't only a shame for them, it's also illegal to operate willfully without the proper coverage." David's tone was reassuring. "I was thanked for my time and released. I don't expect to hear from them again. Flame isn't even on anyone's radar."

I looked up at my young boarder. He hadn't done anything wrong, I supposed. But what drama!

"Marcus? Can we talk?" David's face grew serious. "Maybe go for a walk? Coffee?"

A wide smile lit up Flame's whole face. "There's a cool place a block over called *Coffee Cove*."

∞∞∞

With Flame gone and the events of the night before explained, I put my worries to rest. I still needed to contact the bank to cancel the credit card and get a new one, but since it likely burnt to a crisp in the fire, it wasn't my top priority.

Translating the text from Templeton's book was the most important task at hand. With the page from Guillaume, I was hopeful I'd begin to get answers immediately.

As eager as I was, I forced myself to eat a piece of toast, followed by showering and dressing. I pulled on a stretchy tee shirt and a pair of jeans. Flame was still out with David. I could work uninterrupted.

I cleared the counter by the barstools, wiping the surface clean before setting Templeton's private spell book beside the page from Guillaume's personal book of magic. Seeing them side by side drove a shiver down my spine. Two men who influenced me with their magical mastery. One man I loathed, the other I...My fingertips automatically touched my chest and remained. I missed Templeton horribly. It hurt my heart to think about him sometimes. What if I was too late? My gaze strayed to *Empire Tales for Children* sitting to the side. What if he 'ceased to be' as described in *The Ending*? What if he'd already disappeared into the bright light of the Above?

I swallowed the rock-hard lump forming in my throat. No, I wouldn't do this to myself.

I pulled out the notes I'd made while using the CEW's library. After spelling the page from Guillaume, I'd simply copy the lines and letters I'd attempted to research onto the enchanted paper. Then I'd cast a spell to translate them, using the page as a foundation to support my work.

My fingertips stroked the surface of the paper. *"Paras."*

Vibrations from inside the paper formed and resonated up my fingers. I met them with my own energy, holding back the fire coasting under my skin. I concentrated on connecting with the magic inherent in the blank page. It was strong, powerful, domineering. *Familiar.*

I lifted my hand, studying the page before cutting my eyes to Templeton's book of magic. Second thoughts crept in. What would I set in motion by writing Templeton's words on Guillaume's page?

"Dammit!" I slapped my hands down on the counter. No, I couldn't overthink this. I had a plan, and these doubts would only delay me. My hands balled into fists. I turned on the barstool and angrily hopped off, stalking across the kitchen. I glanced back at the magical items waiting for my direction, the translation waiting to come to light.

But I knew I couldn't trust Guillaume. *Ever.* Even when I was his willing pupil, the dutiful student who knelt at his feet and did what I was told, I didn't fool myself into believing he would someday grant me full freedom from his reach. I wiped my hand over my mouth, my heart fluttering in my chest as if it housed a hummingbird. I never imagined the page he presented to me – this 'gift' – might be yet another way for Guillaume to keep me tied to him, to know my magic long after I left France.

"Think, Lucie," I said aloud. I needed to run this by someone. Or *something.*

I opened the door leading into my rarely used dining room. After I'd left my reading room at *Coffee Cove* behind, I'd stacked the boxes I'd brought home against the wall by the buffet table. I pulled a knife from the buffet's drawer and slit open the top box. A blend of various incense smells wafted up as I pulled the cardboard flap aside.

Inside there were at least a dozen wooden boxes holding different Tarot decks, the artwork on each unique and representing its overall theme: health, creativity, relationships, and so on. I rummaged through the cardboard box until I found what I was searching for – a relatively plain deck with limited artwork displayed. I needed simplicity.

I hadn't consulted the cards in a long time. I kept a special deck for personal readings, but I couldn't bring myself to use it. Months ago, it showed me the dangerous path I'd traveled. I wasn't able to change the outcome, and in a moment of anger, I set fire to one of the Trump cards.

The deck I pulled out now held no special significance for me. In the kitchen, I rested it on a bed of salt, passed it through the smoke from the sandalwood incense I'd lit, gripped it between both hands while I raised my fire around it, and then stroked the top card with a damp fingertip.

"*Purgo*," I whispered over the deck with each step. It was a fast-track method of removing any leftover energies from the card but efficient. Not all spellwork needed to be grandiose. Simple was sometimes better.

Before returning to the counter where the page from Guillaume waited, I gathered a white candle and a vial of rosemary oil. The scent was particularly effective for clearing the mind before a reading. I popped the cap open and took a sniff.

I climbed back onto the barstool, the lit candle off to the right and the sandalwood smoking to my left. I'd placed Templeton's book of spells to the side with the book of fairy tales. Before me sat the blank page from Guillaume's personal book of magic. I mulled over how I wanted to make the cards work for me, considering the paper as I shuffled them between my two hands. I pictured Guillaume, and the moment he'd revealed what he was giving to me. I'd been floored, flattered even. Another blessing from the master teacher. Another sign of my worth.

My worth. My upper lip curled, and I shook my head with a measure of disgust.

The deck properly shuffled, I skipped pulling a querent card. Instead, I placed the deck in the center of the paper, covering it with my hand. Closing my eyes and taking a full cleansing breath, I pressed my energy down through the cards to the page below. I sensed it flowing across the paper and spreading to the edges. As the connection to the page was forming, I allowed my eyes to open. A whitish glow surrounded my work. I waited until I felt the distinct signature of Guillaume's magic threading through the page. *There!* Not unexpected, not necessarily a menacing force, but I would use this leftover energy to test the page.

I would pull it through the Tarot deck resting on top of it.

The energy I'd pushed from my palm and through the cards sought the traces of energy left behind by Guillaume. It struck like a snake, biting into the vibrations flowing over the surface of the page. It held on, refusing to let go.

I kept the power flowing from my palm – actively pushing energy out. In a blink, I snatched my energy back, pulling it through the Tarot deck and into my hand. Guillaume's leftover energy was ripped along with it, tearing through the cards and blasting against my hand. My timing was a fraction off – a snippet of his power slipped along with the personal energy I drew inside. I coughed, my hand darting up to my neck as a puff of ashes parted my lips. I gagged, almost falling off the barstool as I stumbled to the kitchen sink and spat. Another mouthful of ash erupted from my throat. I bent forward, hacking up the gray sludge as it coated my tongue. My left hand grabbed wildly for the coffee cup I used earlier. I filled it with tap water and gulped it down.

Still hanging onto the sink, I coughed until I caught my breath. *Son of a bitch!* If that wasn't a sign...Turning my head, I scowled at the innocent-looking blank page.

After sipping more water, I wiped my face with a dish towel and returned to my work. Perching on the barstool, I once more rested my palm on the deck. This time I simply let my energy touch the cards. The connection opened, and I silently formed my question to test the reliability of the deck.

To whom does the paper belong?

I lifted my hand and snapped my fingers above the deck. The cards vibrated, then jumped. I drew the top card and flipped it over. A court card, the *King of Swords.* I nodded as it often represented Guillaume in spreads when I've read for myself. However, I'd expected the deck to indicate the blank page belonged to *me.*

Another sign, perhaps?

I repeated the process. This time my question

asked: *Will this paper keep my magic private?*

A finger snap, another hop, the top card pulled revealing a Trump card.

The Moon.

Often this card pointed toward deceit and liars – but even in its most positive aspect, it suggested uncertainty. That was good enough for me.

"Third time's a charm," I said aloud. Once more, I let my hand cover the deck. "Would Templeton approve of my plans to write his words on this paper?"

I snapped my fingers, and before I could pull the top card, it flipped over and landed by the deck.

The *Ten of Swords.*

I felt the skin tighten across my forehead, and for a brief moment, I was torn.

When I read for others, this card often represented a lost battle or being defeated in some way. It's the end of the line for a situation and one without a happy ending. The appearance of this card seemed obvious: Templeton would not approve. Don't use the page from Guillaume.

And yet, in the handcrafted deck of Tarot

cards a friend created for me in college, the *Ten of Swords* revealed a Lucie in control – a Lucie destroying the swords lifted against her. Defeat might have sat at the end of the journey, but the Lucie represented in those cards would not remain beaten. She'd rise up again.

Regardless of the deck used, the *Ten of Swords* suggested a 'no' to my question. Combined with the first two cards I'd pulled, the answer was clear.

I could not use the page from Guillaume to translate text from Templeton's book. It was too risky.

"Fucking hell." I pressed my palms together and brought my hands to my lips. Frustrated, I consoled myself with the fact I'd retrieved the page from Nisha before she used it. Had she done so, Guillaume might've detected it had left my possession. He would've been livid, and he would've found a way to punish me for such a 'transgression' against his 'generosity.' I dropped my hands, squinting. Had Nisha detected a similar risk? She wouldn't be foolish enough to share her magic unknowingly, nor would she trust whatever power Guillaume might've instilled into the page to play well with her intentions.

Defeated, I blew out the candle. No wonder she was willing to make the trade. The page was useless. The stick incense I'd used wasn't quite at its end, and I turned the tip into the sand at the base of the ceramic holder, snuffing it out. I picked up the Tarot deck, giving the cards a shuffle as I silently brought the reading to a close. I reached for the wooden box where they'd been stored. My thumb pressed up against the side of the deck, and a card popped out, faceup.

The *Eight of Swords*. Feeling trapped, reluctant to move forward. Recommendation: Whip off those self-imposed limitations. Seek counsel, if necessary, but step beyond the fear.

Returning the *Eight of Swords* to the deck, I knew I'd already been advised. Nisha recommended conjuring a particular demon to learn how to get to the plane where Templeton was trapped.

I knew what I had to do. I would conjure Sebastian.

Chapter 9

It was late morning when I finished carrying the supplies I'd need into the basement where I'd do this...*dirty work*. I brought one of the remaining bloody tissues along with the consecrated salt, incense, and candles I planned to use. I was on edge, my stomach in fits. The thought of actively calling Sebastian to me, of bringing him into my home...My skin felt clammy.

I'd never conjured a demon before – *because I wasn't insane* – but I still had textbooks from college with passages from which I could draw. I'd scribbled notes in the margins referencing various arcane wording that might be useful.

One thing I knew for sure: The conjuring Guillaume performed months ago when he brought Sebastian into our demonstration was flawed. Sebastian wasn't dead. Demons were formed *after* death. I'd amend the wording to fit.

As I prepared, my confidence grew. I was adept, and I'd craft my magic precisely. As his conjurer, I'd have control. I'd keep him in his salt circle so he couldn't escape. I'd bind him to me. He wouldn't be able to act in opposition to my desires.

I'd also need to amend the wards placed around my home. Templeton had cast his spells alongside mine, and I felt a sadness press over me as I cut through some of his protection. It hadn't lessened in the time he'd been gone.

Ingredients gathered, supplies shuttled to the basement, and my determination firm, I raised a hand. There was one more step before I'd be ready to begin. I needed to attach a permission I never imagined I'd add to the wards still standing.

"*Permitto*, Sebastian St. Michel."

∞∞∞

Before I could slink down into the basement, Flame returned from his coffee with David. He was cheerful, and even though I wasn't thrilled with the havoc he seemed to draw into his world

– and therefore, mine – I was glad he seemed to be happy.

He was feeling so good, in fact, that after his shower, he dressed in one of his new 'job hunting' outfits and disappeared out the front door. He told me he'd be back in the evening to get ready for a date.

With David.

Convinced I'd have the house to myself for a while, I stood in front of my basement workbench along the northern wall. Two of my textbooks were opened to passages on conjuring a demon. To be clear, conjurings of this sort were not sanctioned by my professors. Only basic history and facts were referenced, as well as notable conjurings recorded by everyone from practitioners of dark magic to religious monks. The monks were more intent on banishment, but they included their set of invocations. I noted Guillaume had drawn inspiration from one of them.

I skimmed the wording. I'd put my own stamp on it. Plus, I needed to weave through the text that Sebastian was alive and adapt the lines accordingly. Loren believed the conjuring and subsequent binding Guillaume used were more appropriate for a demon created upon death – which makes sense.

Because demons, ultimately, were dead.

And Sebastian was not.

I inspected the invocation, but the words blurred as I went inside my head. If Sebastian was still alive and a demon, were there others like him, or was he the only one? Why was there no record of such a thing? Or maybe there was, but it was not available to me. This was something I would've liked to discuss with Templeton. Our debates and discussions about working magic were some of the most enjoyable times I'd had with him. Even if we didn't fully agree with one another's approach or opinion, we were respectful of one another. And frankly, although I dared to believe my level of power was equal to his, Templeton's experience and magical abilities were superior to mine. While he was frequently a difficult man to be with, he was generous with his knowledge when we crafted spells together or blended our strengths – my fire with his intense energy.

I straightened my shoulders. My mind had wandered, and I couldn't afford to lose more time.

Sebastian. Right.

"Okay." The sound of my voice bounced off the chilly walls in the empty basement. "Let's see." My fingertip traced over another paragraph. The academic text quoted early monastic literature in which observers described witches who consumed small amounts of a demon's sticky black blood to bind the demon to them. I grimaced, my gaze sliding to the tissue stained with Sebastian's dried blood.

Lovely.

I'd been unable to determine the perfect incense for the conjuring. Guillaume had used yew, but it was for raising the dead. So was wormwood. I skipped through those sections highlighting ingredients often used for such manifestations. Many of the herbs and incense used in protection spells were risky because they often contained elements that supported magic geared toward exorcisms and banishment. They would ultimately work against me. I settled on cinnamon. Protective, but not restrictive.

"It'll be a festive demon conjuring," I mumbled as I set the ceramic incense burner near the spot where I'd create the salt circle containing

Sebastian.

I also included thin strands of hellweed in my supplies. Useful in knot magic, I would form three miniature knots in the binding portion of my spell. This I would secure in the circular wooden box in which I'd store the tissue with Sebastian's blood.

Once my supplies were set out in the order in which I'd need them, I began to write the conjuring on a piece of paper I'd cut from my personal book of spells. I'd made the decision not to leave such a working in the book. My book housed spells of healing and protection; it was not a place for deviant magic.

I started with a standard invocation and made my adjustments. As I wrote, I debated with myself about the power inherent in the tissue of dried blood. One of my biggest fears was that I wouldn't be able to successfully bind Sebastian to me to do my bidding. I had nothing diabolical planned, of course. But I needed to be able to compel him.

I set my pen down and picked up the tissue. "How much of this disgusting thing do I have to eat?"

∞∞∞

The circle of consecrated salt had been drawn: 9 feet in diameter as the text described. Cinnamon incense burned, ironically creating a pleasing environment despite the unholy work I'd perform. I'd chosen white candles and placed four around the circle of salt to represent north, east, south, and west. Candles also sat along my bench, adding additional light. When the time came, I'd shut off the brighter basement lights.

I'd dressed simply, removing all jewelry. The Crimson Stone remained upstairs, locked away behind a protection spell in my jewelry armoire. My hair was down. There was no need to change my clothes. Jeans and a tee shirt would suffice – I was conjuring a demon, not going on a fancy date.

I did, however, take off my shoes and socks. I wanted to stay grounded to the earth. I stood at the circle's edge, the box with the tissue sitting on a low table at my feet.

After lighting the candles and turning off the overhead lights, I rolled my shoulders and gave my hands a shake to loosen up. I lifted each leg, bending each knee and wiggling my toes. There was fear inside me, but a logical part of my brain pointed out how during the last time I'd faced Sebastian, he was actually protective of me. I remembered his behavior at the Fringe's old compound. He'd warned me about the Beams of Light from Above. He'd put himself between me and one of those terrifying creatures, placing himself in danger. When he was compelled to return to the Below, he begged me to go with him, but he didn't try to drag me through the horrifying gash in the ground.

I pressed my palms together. Breathe in. Hold. Breathe out. Repeat.

When I felt centered, I retrieved the paper with the invocation I'd crafted. My mouth felt dry, but I licked my lips anyway.

"I do invocate and conjure thee, Sebastian St. Michel, demon; and being with power armed from the Spring of Dwelling, I do strongly command thee, in the vein of the Witch of Endor." These were the same words Guillaume used.

"I command you to enter this circle before me, rising from the depths of the Below, *alive* and in your demon form." I set the paper on the table and pulled the tissue from the box.

"With your blood, I bind you to me, Sebastian St. Michel. I consume your free will." Before I could talk myself out of what I was doing, I ripped off a sizable piece of the stained tissue and pushed it past my lips. It tasted like nothing, but the thought of what I'd put in my mouth threatened to make me gag.

Don't chew it. Swallow it. Swallow, swallow, swallow, I chanted silently. I forced the wad of tissue, wet with my saliva, down my throat. My tongue pressed against the roof of my mouth, and the muscles in my neck worked to drive the mass down.

I paused, allowing myself a moment to regain my focus and placing the remainder of the tissue back into the box. I shuddered. That was gross, but I wasn't done.

"Your freedom is surrendered to me. Your actions will be according to my direction. I compel you to obey me." I resumed the conjuring, picking up a strand of hellweed. I meticulously tied three knots in its length. "*Oboedite mihi, oboedite mihi, oboedite mihi.*"

The air around me charged with static electricity as I set the knotted herb on the rest of the bloody tissue. I fastened the lid.

"I command you, demon, to come to this circle fully formed and bound to me and my orders. I command you, Sebastian St. Michel, as named in this invocation, to appear before me now and remain contained and at my service until I release you," I ordered. "So be it!"

As I finished my invocation, my eyes darted to the circle where a thin line of charcoal-colored smoke spewed from the basement floor. The curls twisted upward, the smell emanating from the churning air not the putrid stench I expected. This did not call to mind the rotten odor leaking up from the sixth door when the frozen ground was split open inside the compound. No, this was an altogether different scent. Bergamot. I recognized it.

It was reminiscent of Sebastian's cologne. I pressed my lips into a hard line and forced a breath out my nose. Was this truly the case, or was it a bizarre olfactory hallucination?

The smoke billowed and filled the circle before the hue of the dense clouds lightened. Inside the circle, I could make out the silhouette of a man. I concentrated on the standing figure as the smoke peeled away.

When Guillaume conjured Sebastian months ago in the Congress of Empire Witches, Sebastian made his appearance in a crouch, rocking back and forth on the balls of his feet. The sound coming from him then was a keening laced with growls. His eyes were wild, skittering around the room like a spooked animal.

The man – *the demon* – standing in my circle now shared no such similarities. The only thing Sebastian had in common with his former conjured self was nudity.

As the smoke dissipated, a silent Sebastian came fully into view. At 6'2", he towered over me. His body was lean and sinewy – I sensed rather than saw the tensing of hard muscles under his skin as he dropped his attention to the floor and registered the salt line. His eyes snapped back to mine, his upper lip curling. I held my ground at the circle's edge.

There was more red than brown in his irises since I'd last seen him. His skin retained its olive tone, and his hair was still shaggy and dark – although it was noticeably longer. I'd never seen him without facial hair, and this time was no different. Black hair trailed in a thin line over his upper lip and was paired with a narrow path of the same running from under his lower lip and into a small patch on his chin. Stubble dotted his stubborn jaw as if he hadn't shaved in days, creating more than a 5 o'clock shadow. His nostrils expanded marginally at the bottom of a straight nose as he pulled in an angry breath. He was uncharacteristically still.

"Sebastian." Grounding myself by pushing the excess energy out of my body through the soles of my feet, I waited. He said nothing. His sneer slid slowly from his face, but he did not acknowledge me. I blinked. Maybe I needed to give him the go-ahead on speaking since I'd specified in the invocation that I controlled his actions. "Sebastian, you're allowed to talk. I want to ask you some questions."

He snorted, letting his head fall back as he stretched his long arms upward, his fingers hovering under the surface of the basement ceiling. A thin scar stretched horizontally across his neck where a vicious Beam of Light had wrapped one of its fiery tendrils around him, lifting his body and strangling him. His eyes fluttered closed as he let his arms sink back to his sides. When he reopened them, they were a shade less red – *maybe*. "I don't need your permission to speak."

I was not going to be intimidated by him. "Good. Then let's begin. I need information. You told me last fall you went through the fifth door into the Above. I need to know how you opened the door without the Crimson Stone."

Sebastian abruptly stepped to the edge of the salt circle, narrowing the distance between us. I flinched but held my ground. He couldn't touch me. "Let me out of this circle, and I'll answer your questions."

"No way," I replied.

"Then you don't get any answers." He looked down his nose.

I frowned. "You're compelled to obey me by the binding."

He shook his head, his feathery black eyebrows lifting. "You've claimed compulsion over my actions, not my speech."

Shit. I worked through the invocation in my head. The bastard was splitting hairs. "I've demanded your obedience. Speaking *is* an action. You must answer my questions."

"Sorry, witch. I'm not telling you anything until you open this circle." He rolled his shoulders, then his head back and forth on his neck. I heard a crack as his chin lifted.

"Let's see if you're still singing the same tune after standing in that circle for a week." Angry, I turned away, making for the stairs. This was bullshit. I wasn't playing games with him.

"You don't have the stomach for it, Lucie," he insisted as my foot touched the bottom stair. "You won't leave me down here. It would be cruel, and I know better. You're too softhearted."

I paused and looked over my shoulder. "You'd be amazed. A lot's changed since we last saw each other."

He studied me, his brow lowering as he ran the point of his tongue along the bottom of his top front teeth. I watched the pink tip glide back and forth. "Why do you want to open the fifth door? It didn't go so well the last time." A mean smile took over his lips.

"Can you tell me how to open the door or not?" I turned around, stepping down onto the basement floor.

He cocked his head to the side. "It's Templeton, isn't it? He never came back from the Above. Am I right? Mr. Almighty Magic met his match in the light?" Sebastian nodded, answering his own questions. "What a shame."

I was not going to rise to the bait. "If you're of no use to me, there's no point in keeping you here."

"What month is it?" Sebastian asked suddenly.

"April," I answered, irritated. "Are you going to explain how you opened the fifth door or not?"

"Is it day or night right now?"

"Quit stalling." I crossed over to the workbench where I'd left the textbooks I'd used to form my version of the demon invocation. I turned on a lamp before skimming the language I'd drawn from to conjure him. I'd bound him to me, but how could I tell? Was I supposed to feel something between us? A metaphysical connection?

For the love of the Empire, I'd eaten a bloody tissue!

"What time of day is it?" He pressed again.

I ignored his question, choosing instead to return to the circle's edge. I picked up the paper with the invocation I'd written. "I've bound you to me, Sebastian. I compel you to answer my question. You're not getting out of this on some perceived technicality. How did you open the fifth door? Answer me."

But Sebastian was preoccupied with the stairs leading out of the basement. His eyes cut to mine. "Is the sun out? Let me go outside. Let me out of this circle, and I'll tell you everything I know about the fifth door."

"Not going to happen." Disappointed, I picked up the round wooden box from the table and returned to the workbench, scooping up the books into my arms. I'd known it wasn't going to be easy. I returned to the stairs a second time.

"I haven't seen the sun in what, three months? You have no idea what it's like, what it does to you when you're without light for so long." Sebastian's voice sliced into the anxious air between us.

Once again, I stood with my foot on the bottom stair. I didn't turn around. "You can't go outside naked," I stalled.

"Then get me some clothes," Sebastian pushed. "I need to feel the sun on my face. You can't conjure me and torture me like this."

I kept my back to him. "Actually, I can."

"But you won't. I know you won't. Please, Lucie."

Shit.

I pictured Flame's clothes in the spare bedroom's closet. The shapeshifter was tall, but he was a couple of inches shorter than Sebastian. The younger man was a touch skinnier, too. With two more decades than Flame under his belt, Sebastian had a certain solidness that came with time. Still, I might be able to find a pair of loose shorts and a tee shirt for him to wear. I sighed, shaking my head. "Fine. Fine! I'll get you something to wear."

"But nothing stupid," he called after me.

I hesitated mid-stairs. Why couldn't he ever keep his mouth shut? Pressing my lips together in an impatient line, I resumed my climb. I hoped to find something ugly in Flame's closet.

Ugh! My closet – my spare bedroom closet.

I left the basement, stopping in the kitchen to slip on a pair of canvas shoes. I set the books and the box with the tissue on the counter before grabbing a glass of water. I stood at the kitchen sink, peering out at my backyard. Having a loose Sebastian bound to me was going to be difficult. I'd have to set boundaries. How does one control a demon after it's been let out? I took another sip from my glass. I'd set clear parameters and make him repeat them. Oh, sure.

This was going to be so much work.

Groaning, I took the wooden box and the paper with the conjuring upstairs and stored both inside my armoire. I lifted my right hand and whispered a short spell to conceal both. As I left my bedroom, I paused in front of the cheval mirror. I brushed several stray hairs out of my face and wiped a smudge of mascara off my eyelid, stilling when I realized what I was doing. I backed away from the mirror. I didn't need to primp for the demon in my basement.

Because that's what Sebastian is, I reminded myself. *A demon.*

In the spare bedroom, I stood with hands on my hips, appraising the unmade bed and the clothes scattered across the floor. Seriously?

"One disaster at a time," I grumbled, opening the door to Flame's – *no, my!* – closet and skipping past several tee shirts. I hesitated, remembering how Sebastian favored shirts in stark white or pitch-black. I snatched a blaze orange tee shirt bearing a local club's goofy logo from a hanger.

Spinning, I spotted a pair of shiny, gray basketball shorts on the floor. Perfect. I picked them up as I left Flame's room. *My room.*

Downstairs my footsteps slowed. Letting Sebastian out was a huge risk. It wasn't going to be that simple. And who was I kidding? I didn't trust him. He had to give me something first. If it was good enough, I'd let him have his 'moment in the sun.'

Back in the basement, I saw he hadn't moved an inch. Certainly, he was limited to the circle, but he either stepped into the same position when I descended the stairs, or he waited in the exact spot. He reminded me of a caged animal brimming with a coiled energy, waiting to leap out at the first chance of escape.

"Here's the deal," I said, waving the ball of clothing I held in my hand. "I'm going to let you out of this circle so you can spend an hour in the sun in my backyard. That's as far as you're allowed to go. But I'm only letting you out if you tell me what you used to open the fifth door. You tell me, I'll let you have the hour outside. You don't, I'm sending you back to the Below right now."

At my final words, Sebastian shifted his weight from one foot to the other. "I'm of more use to you here, not in the Below."

"Maybe," I replied. "Start by proving it. What

did you use to open the fifth door, Sebastian?"

He sucked his lower lip into his mouth and inhaled through his nose, glowering at me. Eventually, he answered. "Nothing."

I cast my eyes upward. He was going to act like a petulant child. "Nothing," I repeated.

He smirked. "It was already open."

Okay, that was possible. *Empire Tales for Children* even included a fairy tale in which the girl searched the Empire for open doors and closed them with her 'pretty stone' when she found them. "Who discovered it? You or someone else?"

He looked down at his hands and flexed his fingers. "One of Ivanov's men."

Ivanov Transport had owned the compound where the fifth and sixth doors were located. "Do you think he opened it?"

"Oh, sure." Sebastian lifted his head, raising an eyebrow. "Some grunt loading trucks? Yeah, he researches how to find and open portals to other worlds in his spare time."

I squeezed the clothes I held in my fist. Maybe I *should* leave him in the basement. "Do you know if this guy did something to trigger its opening? Maybe all the activity set something in motion?"

Sebastian hesitated, then shook his head. "No. I don't think any of the men there could've caused it to open like that. It was a coincidence."

At those words, I thought of Templeton. He didn't believe in coincidence. I questioned it, too. "After it was found, how did you learn about it?"

"They told me."

"Because...you're a trusted advisor to the trucking industry?" I mocked.

"Because I have a vested interest in Ivanov Transport's business." He paused. "Had a vested interest."

The transportation company had been deep between the sheets with the Fringe – and Sebastian sat at the top of this rogue group. He didn't only rub elbows with terrorists in the Empire, he'd led them.

"Alright," I continued. "So, someone at Ivanov gets ahold of you and tells you about the door opening – did you know it was the fifth door?"

"Hey warden, at what point do I get let out of this circle so I can go outside?" Sebastian argued.

"When I'm ready," I shot back. "I asked you a

question. Did you realize right off it was the fifth door? What happened?"

"No. I'm done answering your questions until you release me." He rubbed a finger over his chin, a speck of mischief sparking in his eyes and catching me off guard. "Unless you're stalling because you like keeping me naked. Getting an eyeful?"

"I've seen it all before," I huffed. I needed to assert my control over him – I was allowing too much latitude.

"I remember you liking it." His hand dropped to his penis.

I whipped my head to the side and threw up a hand. "For fuck's sake, Sebastian. Knock it off."

"I've decided if I'm forced to stay in this circle while answering your questions, I'm going to try to enjoy myself."

Out of the corner of my eye, I saw his fist slide back and forth. "God, just stop. *Stop.* Fine – I'll let you out now. But I'm not kidding. You make one move to leave or do anything stupid, I'm shipping your ass back into the Below like that." I snapped my fingers. A stray spark flew through the air.

"Am I making you hot?" Sebastian needled me.

"I'm warning you," I told him. "Now stop it."

He grinned, releasing his rising erection. It bobbed up and down. "I think he's missed you."

"I hate this," I muttered, eyeballing the circle containing him. I waved my hand over a narrow section in the line of salt. *"Patefacio."*

I retreated as grains of salt individually tumbled to the right and left, effectively creating a gap in the circle's edge. It took a minute, maybe longer, for the door to fully open. I glanced up and realized Sebastian was staring intently at me, a familiar wild look rising in his eyes, his lips parting.

Oh, no.

As soon as the opening was wide enough, he was outside the salt prison in a blink. Only inches apart, I could feel the heat of his skin. My body, remembering our past, tipped toward him automatically. I jolted, swaying backward when a hardening part of him bumped into my midsection. No! No, he was my demon to control now, and I wouldn't put up with this. He lowered his head.

"No." I stepped away before he could kiss me, my heart ramming against the inside of my chest. "That will never, ever be a part of this arrangement, Sebastian. Now put on the damn clothes." I dropped the shorts and brightly colored tee shirt at his feet.

His laugh was characteristically loud, the sound echoing off my bare basement walls. "You don't fool me, Lucie. Maybe you should stop trying to convince yourself that you're not attracted to me anymore."

My shoulders stiffened at his words, and I glared at him. "Get dressed. I'll be in the kitchen waiting." I turned and fled, stomping up the basement stairs and away from the naked ex-lover in my basement.

Chapter 10

Sebastian appeared in my kitchen wearing the obnoxious orange shirt and the loose-fitting shorts. I gave him the once over. He seemed comfortable in the outfit. I'd never been so annoyed.

He surveyed the kitchen before peeking down the hall toward the front of the townhouse. He nodded. "It looks like you."

Sebastian and I might've been involved, but I'd never invited him into my home. It was a barrier I instinctively kept while the other side of me dove deeper into a relationship with him. Yes, it was weird, but it was intoxicating, too. The nights we spent together were either in a luxury penthouse in downtown Matar or at a massive cabin to the west of the city. He told me the cabin belonged to a friend. I found out later it was, in fact, his. The penthouse, he'd claimed, was used for 'corporate functions.' He never discussed the details of what he did for a living beyond saying he was 'in finance' – a half-truth. His family owned the largest private bank in the Empire. I also learned later the penthouse belonged to his family. Both residences were devoid of personal items, like photos or family mementos. Sebastian was meticulous in his deception.

I wasn't without blame. I overlooked a lot of questionable explanations. Even now, my ears burned when I thought about my wanton ignorance.

And yet, he never pushed to come into my townhouse, either. I now suspected it was because he didn't want to be recognized if Emily, Templeton, or Rabbit showed up unannounced. He didn't ask to come in, I didn't invite him, and we both ignored the weird raging pachyderm in the center of the metaphorical room.

"Do you want water?" I gestured to the dispenser on the refrigerator. I was starting to feel uncomfortable. Strike that – *more uncomfortable.*

Sebastian, on the other hand, made himself at home. "I don't suppose you have any strawberry

Toro?" He opened the fridge, bending and tapping his fingers on the edge of the metal door while he browsed.

"You still drink those horrible chemicals?" My nose wrinkled. "It's disgusting."

"Yeah, they keep a stocked fridge of your favorite drinks in the Below," he snarked. He rummaged around the shelves. "What's up with the full-fat milk? You should switch to 2%. Healthier."

I sighed. I did not sign on for this. "Get a glass of water and go have your moment in the sun. But don't even think of leaving."

"Compelling me to stay here with you?" He lifted his head, tossing a mildly challenging look my way.

"Yes." I crossed my arms and waited.

"Well, you're the boss." He'd skipped the water in favor of a rogue bottle of *Rooster Broo* he found hiding behind the ketchup. He twisted off the cap and took a sip.

We considered each other. I wondered what he was thinking. A few moments of quiet passed.

Eventually, I pointed toward the pantry door with my chin. "Through there. Past the shelves, you'll find the door into the backyard."

"Want to come sunbathe with me?" He took another sip of beer.

"This isn't a vacation." I gave him a steady look. "We're not friends – we're not anything anymore. The only thing I wanted from you was information about the fifth door. Now I'm not convinced conjuring you was worthwhile. You didn't open the fifth door. You can't give me anything I can use."

"But I do know about a second door leading directly into the Above. And I know where this door is and how to get to it."

"Where?" Believing a pathological liar took a lot of effort.

"Tell you what, Lucie," he began as he gestured to the pantry door. "I'm going outside. You gave me an hour in the sunshine, and I'm taking it. You want answers? Come see me then." He flashed a toothy smile before leaving the kitchen, crossing through the pantry, and strolling out the back door.

I turned and watched through the window. Barefoot, Sebastian stood in the grass and rolled his shoulders yet again, arching his back and turning his head from side to side. He spied the garden table I'd nestled into a corner. Dragging it along with a chair into the sunnier part of the yard, he rearranged the outdoor furniture. He set the beer bottle on the round table and pulled Flame's bright orange tee shirt off over his head, tossing it across the chair. Tight muscle rippled across his back.

After retrieving the bottle, he settled himself into the chair, stretching out his long legs and propping his feet up on the matching table. His head swiveled to the side and his gaze lifted expectantly to my kitchen window. Sebastian already knew I was watching him. Grinning, he raised his beer in a toast before taking another swig. Balancing his elbows on the armrests and the bottle on the low-slung waistband of the basketball shorts, he made himself comfortable. His eyes drifted shut, and his face tilted up toward the sun. He looked...*happy*.

Shit.

My head dropped. My hands raised, and I pressed my fingertips into my forehead above both eyebrows. This was not good. This was very much the opposite of good. This was bad. So very bad.

I let my hands fall away and studied him through the window. Sebastian was in the same pose, his body relaxed. This was not the crazed demon who'd invaded my home months ago. This was not the angry demon conjured by Guillaume during our demonstration at the Congress of Empire Witches. This was not the fearful demon who'd resignedly returned to the Below after I'd lost Templeton to the Above.

The man soaking in the sun in my backyard was more *Basha* than Sebastian and more *human* than demon.

"No. No, it's okay. I can do this," I said aloud to reassure myself. "He *is* a demon, and I can control him. He's got one hour."

I reached over and fiddled with one of the knobs on my stove, setting the timer.

∞∞∞

After I made sure the lit candles I'd left in the basement were safely extinguished and the door leading to the space where I'd conjured Sebastian was securely locked, I spent the rest of the 60 minutes thinking about what other door Sebastian referred to and how we would open it. I assumed I'd still need the Crimson Stone in its united form, which meant that hurdle remained. I flipped through *Empire Tales for Children* but saw no reference to yet another door leading directly into the Above. Although, in the final fairy tale, *The Ending*, a passage mentioned a row of doors sitting on top of the Between:

...She noted a row of doors, hundreds of miles long, sitting atop the Between. "There are so many!"

"Each door leads to its own imagined place or reality. One door opens into your land in the Between. These doors blend into the Above. The Beams of Light from Above live there. It is a hard space for other creatures to endure. Most do not stay. Some get trapped," the bird finished...

My hand trembled as I skimmed my fingertip over the last lines uttered by the bird.

Trapped.

Don't let worry get the best of you, I thought. One step at a time. Get the information from Sebastian, then decide what problem to tackle next.

I checked the time. His hour was almost up. I'd forced myself to stay away from the kitchen window. It was a test of sorts. I would 'trust' him not to leave, and he would obey my command. Or my command would compel him to stay.

Or he'd sneak away, and I'd have to figure out how to get him back.

On top of all the information I needed from him about this other door and what I should expect to find on the other side, I was growing increasingly curious about his changed personality.

Why did he seem much calmer when compared to the last time I'd seen him? What had happened between the moment he held his hand out to me, begging me to go into the Below with him three months ago, and now? This mattered. I needed to understand what I was dealing with – especially since my original plan was to conjure Sebastian for the information I needed and then send him right back. Letting him out of the salt circle was definitely a detour on my way to getting the answers I needed.

I wasn't looking forward to adding another layer of complexity to the situation, but the less I knew, the greater the chance of failing to get into the Above.

The beeping from my stove told me his hour outside was up.

I didn't expect him to come wandering in on his own. Sighing, I pulled a glass from my cupboard and filled it with ice water. I topped off my own glass, carrying both outside.

Sebastian heard the door shut behind me. He opened one squinty eye before pulling his big feet off the table as I marched over and set both glasses down. He sat up, straightening when I retrieved the other chair, an eager expression forming. His forearms rested on the tabletop when I sat down across from him. Again, we allowed a long stillness to stretch between us.

"Feels familiar, doesn't it?" He finally spoke, his pouty lips stretching in an easy smile. "Remember that hot night last September when we went skinny dipping in the lake up at the cabin? The moonlight lit up everything, and the air was still. The water was like glass."

Baffled, I could only gape at him. How could he be this clueless? "You know what, Sebastian? Please don't bring up things like that. It hurts to think about how you lied to me, how you misled me. Those memories of us..." My voice trailed off. "They don't bring me happiness. They make me feel foolish and used."

Sebastian fixed his attention on the glass in front of him. He shook his head. "Not everything was a lie."

"I don't believe you, but I don't want to talk about it either. It's done. It's gone. I conjured you to find out how I can get into the Above. That's it. That's all I want from you. Then you're going right back into the Below."

"You really make me want to help you out," Sebastian scoffed.

"You have the opportunity to do something good for me. How about breaking the mold and being selfless for once in your damned life?" I let go of my glass and placed my palms on the metal tabletop. The surface was warm from the sunshine.

The empty bottle of *Rooster Broo* sat on the table by his water glass. Sebastian picked at the label, peeling it away as he spun the bottle. When he spoke again, his voice was unusually soft. "The Below...You can't imagine the things I've seen and done down there. It gets bad, Lucie. The screaming is so loud, and you can't tell the difference between cries for help and cries of pleasure made by the monsters inflicting the pain. It's brutal. Then it turns silent – that's when I get scared. The only fucking thing I can hear is my heartbeat. And if I can hear it, I know other things can, too. A heartbeat fucking stands out in the Below." He wadded a piece of the label into a paper ball between his thumb and index finger.

"Because you're not dead," I stated quietly.

He nodded, still focused on his fidgeting fingers. "Alive and unwell."

"Tell me what happened last fall, after I opened the sixth door and you door traveled into the Below for the first time." My throat grew tight when I pictured those final moments. I wanted to rewind time and do something differently. The role I played that night continued to haunt me no matter the terrible things he'd done.

"Door traveled?" Sebastian's tone developed an edge. "We have conflicting memories."

I nodded, dropping my eyes. My heart followed my throat's lead and constricted, too. "Okay, then you tell me your version."

"Look at me," he demanded.

I gave in, watching the red haze swirling madly in his eyes. "I'm looking."

He clenched his teeth, then continued. "After Emily pushed me through the sixth door, I did door travel, but it wasn't normal. There was no door on the other side to cross through. It was a free fall into the Below. My body smashed into the ground, and I was knocked out. When I came to, the pain was excruciating. I'd broken bones, suffered a concussion, and was bleeding internally. I was going to die – but I had entered the Below alive. Let's just say that's not typical. I drew attention."

"Who found you?" I watched him carefully. Was he telling me the truth?

"There are these things...They're hard to describe. They're mostly made of shadow, but you can see them *in* the shadows if you know where to look. They talk to you inside your head. I hate it. They follow you around. They can't touch you, but you can't get away from them either – and they spy on you. They're spies for him." Sebastian shuddered. He abandoned his label peeling and crossed his arms, his shoulders rounding as he curled in on himself.

"Spies for whom?" I asked gently.

"The Darkness." Sebastian winced.

"It's okay." I automatically made to comfort

him, gritting my teeth at my inclination. I tried again. "You're not in the Below right now... What did this shadowy being do?"

His eyes met mine again. "It brought the Darkness to me."

"Then what happened?" I prompted. "What did the Darkness do to you?"

"We made a deal. He'd let me live, and he'd let me go – but only if I brought him something from the Between, something he believed I could get for him. But he knew he couldn't send me back without holding something over me. He would slowly turn me into a demon until I brought him what he wanted. That's the catch. I'm alive, but I'm becoming a demon, one who didn't have to die to become...*this*." He directed his hand toward his chest. The emotions flickering across his face ranged from anger to despair.

I was horrified. Sebastian was not a good man – okay, he was a terrible man – but this was cruel torture. "What does the Darkness want you to bring to him?"

"He wants what he sensed at the mouth of the sixth door. He wants the Light. He wants *you*, Lucie. That's why the sixth door opened that night in the Walled Zone. You didn't open it. *He did.* He knew you were there. You might've had the Crimson Stone in your hand, waving around a bunch of energy, but guess what? The Crimson Stone doesn't open the doors. It only closes them." Sebastian shrugged. "Surprise, surprise."

The Crimson Stone doesn't open the doors... His words slammed into my chest. The Stone doesn't open the doors? No! He had to be lying. The Stone *had* to open them – how else would I get into the Above if I couldn't open the door leading into it? How would I get to Templeton?

My mouth had popped open during his great reveal. I snapped it shut as I stood, carelessly banging into the table and causing the empty beer bottle to tip. Slapping my hands together, I raised the heat living under my skin to a blistering level. The explosive energy built rapidly, and I pulled my palms apart, allowing it to gush forward as I pushed all I'd called up against him. An enormous wave rose between us and crashed over his unsuspecting body. *"Dicere veritatem!"*

He jerked as if zapped sharply, the muscles under his skin seizing violently and pulsing in an angry tattoo before releasing. His mouth hung open while the pain reverberated through his bones. Gasping, his hands gripped the arms of the chair as he sucked in several gulps of air in quick succession. The arrogance in his haze-filled eyes slipped away, and he became guarded. His jaw tensed angrily as he recovered.

Around him, a white light shimmered in the air.

My demon had told the truth.

∞∞∞

After laying my spell down on Sebastian, I whipped around and bolted back into my home. His revelation crushed me. Even if I could reunite the three pieces of the Crimson Stone into one – what was the point? It wouldn't open the doors!

I was furious – at myself, at Sebastian, at the whole situation. The page from Guillaume was worthless since I didn't dare use it, and now I learned the Crimson Stone didn't do what I thought it did. *Empire Tales for Children* sat on the counter where I'd left it earlier. Furious, I flipped through the pages, wondering if there was an answer I'd missed.

As I read, I heard Sebastian come into the house behind me. He appeared at my side, his arm brushing mine. My fire crackled under my skin where we touched. "I don't know why I deserved that."

"You deserve everything you get," I muttered, shifting my weight to the opposite foot while I skimmed the fairy tale called *Six Doors*. The little girl featured in the book's nine tales used a 'pretty stone' to close each door she found in the Empire to keep out 'Beasties from Below.' There was no reference to using the stone she carried to open any door – *ever*.

Sebastian ignored my reply, instead nodding toward the book in my hands. "This is where it ended up."

"Yup."

"It was stolen from me," he continued.

"You stole it from someone else." I looked up. "And now it's mine. You are not to touch it."

He pointed at the book with his chin. "Trust me, I know this book better than anyone. I've met the *delightful* cast of characters living in the Below – not to mention the vicious Beams of Light from Above. I'm waiting for the stupid bird to show up."

I closed the book. I was so far behind I wasn't even at square one anymore. Shaking my head in frustration, I turned to Sebastian. "This second door you mentioned – the one leading directly into the Above. Can it be opened upon command?"

The left corner of his mouth quirked up. "It can."

"Do you know how?"

"Mostly."

"Mostly? That's reassuring. Are you going to tell me what you do know, or do I have to compel you to answer me?"

"You can't compel my speech, only my actions."

"Bullshit," I spat.

"Let's make a deal," Sebastian countered.

"No deals," I said.

"You sure you're not interested? I'm offering to take you to a door leading straight into the Above. I'll even tell you where you can find out how to open it."

I tapped my fingers on the cover of the book of fairy tales. "Finding out how it's opened is one thing. Me being able to open it is another."

"You'll be able to open it." He leaned near,

looking me squarely in the face. The sly curve of his upper lip was back. "You're the Light, after all."

I froze. There was no way Sebastian could know about the prophecy. "What do you mean?"

"The Darkness calls you the Light. The Light is what opens the door. I take you to it. You open it." Sebastian sniffed, his eyelids dipping. "You smell good."

I stepped back to put some distance between us. He hadn't been referring to the prophecy after all, and for that, I was grateful. I didn't need to be blindsided by any more of his bombshells. "You're saying I simply show up at the door, and it automatically opens? Why don't I believe it? Oh, I know – because the words came out of your mouth."

He straightened. "There's a book that explains how to do it. You get the book first, learn the trick, I take you to the door, and you're golden."

"That sounds like a majorly oversimplified version of the process." My right hand balled into a loose fist, and I bounced it on the countertop. "Where's this book?"

"In the library at the Congress of Empire Witches."

"You're kidding me?" Figures.

"Nope."

I thought about the Witches Gala I'd attended several months ago. The Congress admitted a demon had made it past their wards during the event. Eventually, I realized it was Sebastian. "That's why you were there in the library."

"That and I hoped to catch a dance with my favorite wayward witch," he taunted before his expression slipped from playful to ugly. "Watching the make out session between you and pencil dick was dis–"

"Enough, Sebastian, before I compel you to wrap duct tape around your head and over your mouth." A headache was forming behind my eyes. I pinched the bridge of my nose. "You didn't find the book?"

He reached across the counter, pulling a pencil and my notebook toward him. Turning to an empty page, he sketched a shape. "I couldn't find the book, but it has this symbol on the cover." He drew a square with a horizontal line through the center from one side to the other. He proceeded to shade the lower half of the square with the side of the pencil point. "The top of the square represents the Light, the lower half the

Darkness. The same symbol is on the door."

"How do you know about the door and this book? Why should I believe any of this?" I dropped my hand.

"I know about the door because I've seen it. I know about the book because some demons like to talk." He pursed his lips. "Some never shut up."

"Gee, I wonder what that's like?" My eyes narrowed. "Assuming I believe any of this crap, you're telling me a demon went out of its way to tell you about this book? Around-the-watercooler morning chitchat?"

"I overheard a conversation."

I was wary. "What's the catch? Where is this door?"

A wicked grin spread wide across his face. "It's in the Below, Lucie. If you want to get into the Above, you've got to come with me into the Below."

Chapter 11

"No way," I told him. "I'm not falling for your shit, Sebastian. And I'm not going into the Below with you – *ever*."

"It's the truth. The door is in the Below." He didn't blink, he didn't flinch. "Find the book in the library. It'll prove it."

I contemplated his words. He had plenty of reasons to lie to me, but if there was a book in the Congress' library, and if I could use it to determine the door he described truly existed...I turned away, picking up a dish towel and wiping a counter. I snuck a look over my shoulder. He watched me – curious but relaxed. This was drastically different from what I expected when I was preparing to call him to me.

"Why are you so calm, Sebastian?"

He made a face. "What do you mean?"

"When you were in the Empire a few months ago, you were beyond agitated. You were practically pinging off the walls." I hung the towel over a drawer handle.

Sebastian opened his mouth to speak.

I cut him off. "And you attacked me. You kept me in a chokehold until I passed out. You imprisoned me in a circle of demon ash."

His mouth shut, his lips pressing so firmly together I could see tiny lines forming. He nodded.

"What's different this time around? Besides the obvious – I conjured you instead of you breaking in while I slept." I crossed my arms.

He rubbed the tip of his tongue over one of his pointed canines, considering his answer. "Time has a way of changing things."

"Yeah, I need more than that."

Sebastian moved around the end of the counter and sat on one of the barstools, his long legs allowing his bare feet to remain on the floor. This simple act jarred me – there was Sebastian sitting in my kitchen, the two of us having a conversation.

Templeton was lost in the Above. Rabbit had pushed me out of his life. The man they both hated was my conjured guest. My world had turned upside down.

"You have two choices in the Below, Lucie. You can either join in and go crazier, or you can go numb. At least, that's the way it's been for me. Maybe because the other demons are different. *Dead*. Full demons." He folded his arms and rested his elbows on the counter. His face blanked. "For the first, what? Four months? My brain was wrecked. My thoughts were scrambled – all the time. It's hard not to give in to the crazy. And when it happens in the Below, you give in to the things they make you do. Really bad things. Things that would make you sick."

"I don't want to know what those things are," I said.

"I'm not going to tell you." His eyes focused on me for the briefest moment, then the vacancy returned with his memories. "When I came back the first time, it was like everything here in the Empire was whirling around me. I felt out of control. My sense of time was off. I'd hear voices inside my head – and they were real. They were from the Below. Fucking drove me insane."

He continued, his face contorting. "After we

were on the quad together and I went back into the Below, the Darkness punished me. He said I failed because I couldn't get you to come with me. He wouldn't let me come back to try again, no matter what I said. He told me I deserved to suffer. The nightmare started all over again. This time, I went numb. No matter what the other demons did to me – no matter what they made me do...over and over." Sebastian shuddered. "I wouldn't give in. I shut down. I just...*existed*. Nothing mattered anyway. Until you conjured me. He couldn't keep me in the Below when you called for me."

My conjuring outranked the Darkness? I wasn't sure Sebastian was right about that, but I tucked the thought away. "And what? A different attitude in the Below, and you're not 'crazy' now?"

A ghost of a smile coasted over his lips. "No more than usual."

"Don't confuse committing violent crimes with chasing some sort of wild mischief," I barked, smacking him down. "You cultivated a reputation for being unhinged because it's a sick kind of fun for you, but in reality, you simply enjoy hurting people."

"It's not about enjoying –"

"You put a gun to my head." My eyes grew hot. I wanted to feel anger, but instead, I felt...*broken*. Damn, him.

He looked down at the counter, his cheek twitching. "I'm sorry, Lucie."

I waited for an excuse – a weak *'I wasn't thinking,'* or *'things got out of control,'* or even an accusatory, *'I was provoked.'* None came. The house sat deathly still around us. When a foolish tear broke free, I hurriedly wiped at it with my fingertips. Sebastian raised his eyes at the right moment and caught me. I turned my head away. This hurt too much.

"After getting thrown in the Below the first time, you were all I could think about," he said softly. "There are no days there, Lucie. There is nothing to mark the time as it passes. Sometimes it seems like only minutes have gone by because I can remember things like they just happened, but mostly it feels like unending night. There is nothing good there. You were the only good I had – even if it was only in my head."

"Don't." I lifted a hand, my fingers splayed.

"It's true. I know you don't believe me, and I understand why, but it's true." He wet his lips with his tongue. "And now, when it gets so bad and hopeless, and all the...I've done things. But I hold onto a picture of you. Here." He pressed a finger against his temple. "I picture you. Us."

"There is no us," I rasped.

He ignored me. "I remember how you glowed for me – how I felt that last night at the cabin." The hand drifted away from his face, and he pressed the same finger against the center of his chest. "Here."

"What do you expect me to say? You lied to me. You hurt my friends. You're a criminal, Sebastian. You broke..." I bit my lower lip. I couldn't finish. It didn't matter. The look in his eye told me he wasn't listening.

"Focusing on you is the only thing that's kept me going in the Below. It's the only thing that's kept me from losing it completely." His hand roamed back up to his face. He stared at an invisible spot above my head and rubbed at the smattering of hair growing around his lips. "Last fall, when you left the Empire, the Darkness realized you weren't in the Between anymore. He wouldn't let me out. I lost all hope. I don't remember everything after that. Everything was so loud in my brain. I couldn't put my thoughts together." His gaze returned to me. "But you came back to Matar, and he let me out. He let me leave the Below so I could come get you."

Turning away, I pulled a new glass from my cupboard and filled it with tap water, the mundane activity grounding me. In February, the Rabbit network reported the static and pulsing they detected in the Walled Zone – and pinpointed it to the compound where the fifth and sixth doors appeared. The unusual noise coincided with my return to the Empire. Was that when the Darkness sensed my return? Was that when he freed Sebastian to come after me? I sipped the water.

Sebastian was quiet, his attention back on the counter, his brow pulled down. A finger poked absently at the notebook page where he'd drawn the symbol for the door he claimed was in the Below. I sensed he was caught up somewhere in his black thoughts. For a moment, he reminded me of a damaged child lost in his own world.

"Okay." I cleared my throat. "I need to think about some things. Even if I agree to...I can't believe I'm saying this. Even if I agree to go into the Below with you, we've got a problem. My membership with the CEW is suspended. I can't waltz into the library and borrow a book."

"Suspended?" The haunted expression he wore slipped away in an instant as he returned to the conversation. The annoying smirk he always seemed to easily find resurfaced. "What did you do?"

"It doesn't matter," I told him. "The problem is I'm not welcome there. I don't have permission to enter the building." I eyeballed him. "How did you get in?"

He winked, the melancholy he'd dipped into only minutes ago now forgotten. "Demon door."

"You door traveled into the Congress?"

"No, not like a Salesman. Let me show you." He slid from the barstool and spun around, inspecting my kitchen. "I can't in here. I need a bigger surface." Before I could stop him, he turned into my hall.

"Wait, Sebastian, I don't want you wandering through my house." Exasperated, I followed behind him.

"Relax. The wall in the hallway is fine." He paused, examining the narrow corridor. "I need to move this." He pushed the hall table to the left and in the process, revealed a burnt handprint pressed into the wall. He hesitated, reaching out to trace it with a finger. "What's this about? You lose control or something?"

I studied the reminder of the steamy encounter I'd experienced with Templeton before everything went to hell. "You could say that."

He shot me a quizzical look but let it go. Instead, he straightened and hovered his palms in front of an unblemished portion of the wall. "Throughout the Empire, there are portals into certain places housing magic. I only know where a handful of them are located, but one happens to be inside the Congress of Empire Witches. All I need to know is where it is, find a wall big enough to open a conduit, and..."

I sensed the energy he directed against the surface. Fascinated, I watched as a circular rippling peeled back the wall onto itself, forming a round hole. As it grew bigger, a light blinked through the middle of the opening before dimming and revealing the other side of the demon door. The hole was large enough for a person to duck through. I realized I was staring into the space where the blind being sat beside the entrance leading into the Congress' main lobby. From my vantage point, I guessed the opening was located near the front doors of the building itself.

The creature who performed the ritual of recognition for the Congress lifted her head. Her unseeing eyes turned toward us, her toothless mouth opening in a wide grin.

"She knows we're here," I murmured. "She knows we've opened this portal."

"Yeah." Sebastian didn't elaborate but instead raised his palms a second time, swiping them over the wall. The opening shrank, my wall reappearing without damage. Seconds later, you couldn't tell anything had been there. Sebastian glanced down at me. "Demon door."

"That night, you searched the library but couldn't find the book?" I touched the wall to see if I could sense any leftover energy. There was none. I was glad but also concerned. Sebastian wasn't exactly performing magic, but he had strange powers connected to this demon he was becoming. I'd witnessed the strength and speed months ago – what else could he do? Did he even know? His nonchalance – this casual *'look what I can do'* behavior – was dangerous. He was too unpredictable to have these abilities at his disposal.

"Several areas were spelled, and I couldn't get into them. I think the book is in one of the Symbolism aisles. I was blocked from pulling certain books from the shelves and couldn't search the whole section. It's huge, and I didn't have a lot of time. But I think that's where you might find it."

"Maybe." I went back into the kitchen and checked the time. The library would be open until 5 o'clock. The challenge was getting inside and finding the book fast. I couldn't risk taking the time to look through it there, though. Inwardly, I groaned. I'd have to sneak it out of the library – assuming it wasn't spelled to prevent it from leaving the building, which was a distinct possibility.

Sebastian followed me. "You know, just because I'm a demon doesn't mean I'm not hungry."

I waved a hand at my refrigerator. "Help yourself. Listen. I'm...I'm going to go to the CEW and see if I can get past the gate. I'm worried about triggering some sort of silent alarm announcing my presence, but there's no way I'm going to get permission to browse the library." *Again*, I thought. And on such short notice.

Sebastian hooked his thumb and gestured toward the hallway. "You want to try using the demon door?"

"No," I answered. "I'm not risking it."

"It's even more accurate than door traveling as a Salesman." He looked inside my refrigerator as he spoke. "It only has one destination. No wrong turns."

"Again, no."

He pulled out a box holding the leftover pizza, lifting the lid. He scowled. "What the fuck is on this?"

"If you're hungry, you'll eat it. But you're taking it with you. You're not staying here." Sebastian was *not* hanging out in my house while I was gone.

He grabbed a cold slice and tossed the box back into the fridge. "Works for me. I'll meet you back here later."

"No," I told him. "You are not taking off and doing god knows what. I'm only giving you permission to go to your cabin. Nowhere else. You can door travel from my home to your cabin and vice versa. No wrong turns, no detours, no excuses. Here, there, here. You understand me?"

He grinned as he chewed a mouthful of pizza. "I love how commanding you've become. It suits you. It kind of turns me on."

My hands clenched. I needed to find a spell to reduce his speech to 'yes' and 'no.' "Sebastian, you're only allowed to door travel to your cabin. That is it. Then you'll come back here. That is it. I'm compelling you to adhere to the limitations I'm setting for you. Do you understand me?"

"Yes, warden."

"Don't call me that." I watched as he reached back into the refrigerator, snagging another piece of pizza. He'd consumed the first slice like a starved man.

"I don't suppose I can have visitors? Conjugal visits?" He ripped a paper towel from the roll on the counter and wrapped it around the pizza.

"No visitors, but you can go fuck yourself." I smiled. That felt good.

"Ouch," he rolled his eyes. "Alright, warden, I'll be waiting by my lonesome at your beck and call. Do your *'summon the demon'* thing when you're back."

"Wait." I dropped my chin to my chest and gave my head a shake. This was probably a bad idea, but his mention of visitors made me think of his family. I sighed. "Listen. Do you want to go see your parents? I don't know where they are, the Salesman Court confiscated your family home, but they still must be in the Empire. I'll give you permission to –"

"I don't want to see them." Sebastian's expression turned to stone.

I stopped. "Oh, okay. Maybe another family member, then, like –"

"The only family member I'd care to see died right after I got pushed into the Below. My grandmother didn't survive her heart attack when the Empire guards came and arrested her entire family." His posture grew rigid, and his voice flattened. "Can I go now?"

"Yes." I resisted the urge to say I was sorry for what he'd lost. I *was* sorry the poor woman passed away before he got to see her again, but I didn't want to continue the conversation.

Sebastian said nothing more, turning away from me and door traveling through my pantry door to the massive cabin he owned at the edge of the Walled Zone.

Hopefully.

∞∞∞

Only a couple of hours passed since I'd conjured Sebastian in my basement. It felt like days. With him gone, I examined the image he'd drawn in my notebook. There were hundreds of books on symbolism in the Congress library. Even if I made it in under the radar, there was no way I could show the drawing and ask for help at the circulation desk.

I worried the side of my thumbnail with my teeth as I evaluated my options. Working magic in the Congress building was strictly forbidden without prior approval. Any spell I used would alert the Oversight Office. They'd know it was me.

My brain mulled over my options. I might be able to do a workaround. If I spelled a copy of the symbol beforehand – right before I went into the building – and used it to seek, I might be able to fly under the radar. I'd have to limit myself to the natural energy coursing under my skin. No other magic. What's the worst that could happen? It wouldn't work? I'd be caught? Banned from the Congress forever?

Punished?

I wasn't sure how they would enforce any particular punishment, but if my experience had taught me anything, the Congress was comfortable exercising rights it *perceived* it had.

In magic, there is the concept of like attracting like. I'd use the symbol to seek that which it most resembled. Sebastian said the cover displayed the square with half of it in the Light and the other half showing the Darkness.

I ran through a timeline and a plan. I'd take my vehicle instead of a cab, so I could spell the symbol right before going into the building. Getting past the security gate was the first hurdle. I'd rely on charm over magic – and a teensy white lie about leaving something important behind in the library. Next, I'd pass through the wards guarding the building, but I didn't expect a problem. True, I was a suspended member, but the Congress was like any other bureaucracy. It would be too much of an effort to constantly amend wards to let individual witches in and out. No, wards were put into place to prevent real threats and other unwanted elements from getting inside.

I huffed. The Congress clearly had no idea

Sebastian's demon door bypassed the wards and rendered those layers of protection useless.

The ritual of recognition was a slight concern. But the blind being...My gut instinct told me she would let me pass. Something was going on there. She'd seen – well, sensed – Sebastian entering the Congress through the demon door the night of the Witches Gala and told no one but me. She called him a *'brother to her kind.'* Eventually, I needed to determine her connection to all this chaos.

There would be a chance of bumping into a witch who might recognize me. That's a risk I'd have to take, but the day was in my favor. Late afternoon on a Friday wouldn't see a lot of busy halls in the Congress. The second part of the challenge was entering the library without being noticed. Again, I'd count on light staffing on a Friday – but it was not a given. If questioned, I'd go with the same excuse I was giving at the security gate: I left something of value behind and hoped to recover it. In fact, I'd 'admit' it was a spell I feared would be kept if found instead of being turned in. That might preempt any 'lost and found' conversations.

The most dangerous part of the plan was

getting the book out. Some books are spelled in such a way that they literally cannot be removed from the library. If this was the case, I was in a pickle. I'd have to skim through the information as quickly as possible and hope for an answer. Not ideal.

If everything went perfectly, however, I would simply take the book. I wouldn't keep it, of course. The review of my suspension was coming up, and I'd sneakily return the book then. I'd leave it on a returns cart, and eventually, staff would reshelve it to where it belonged.

This was the plan. What could possibly go wrong?

Everything.

∞∞∞

Before leaving, I'd changed into something more presentable, choosing a respectable yet casual outfit so I wouldn't stand out. I paired a long black broomstick skirt with a tan leather belt and a short sleeved white top. A gold scarf wrapped around my neck and dressed up the ensemble. A pair of flat brown sandals graced my feet. I slid several gold bangles over each wrist and hung dangling leaf-shaped gold earrings from my earlobes. To keep everything informal, I added a cropped blue denim jacket.

The pièce de résistance, however, was an oversized brown leather purse with a short curved strap. It was perfect for pulling over my shoulder and tucking under my arm.

It was perfect for smuggling a book out of the Congress library.

I brushed my hair and pulled it into a low twist at the nape of my neck. Black mascara and toffee-colored lipstick completed the look. I stuffed a black pen into my purse and grabbed my keys.

It took 30 minutes to drive to the northeastern part of Matar where the Congress was located. I spent another anxious 10 minutes looking for parking.

I'd left the radio off during the drive, instead leading myself through deep breathing exercises as I drove. Some witches ignored the role their breath played in spellwork. I found it not only helped provide a solid foundation for my magic, it also helped me control the ebb and flow of the energy I used. When I pulled into the parking space – a half-block away from the security gate – I took another several minutes to ground and center.

When I felt as though I was ready, I retrieved the black pen from my purse, clicking it. The ballpoint pressed out of the end, ready for use.

I had two choices. I could draw the symbol on my left palm and attract the corresponding symbol to me. Or I could sketch it on my right palm, my projective hand, and use it to seek out the symbol appearing on the book I needed to find.

I opted for the latter, outlining a square on my right hand. Next, I drew a horizontal line through the middle. Wielding my energy down my fingers and through the pen, I colored in the lower half of the square. It wasn't fine art, but it was clear enough for my purposes.

I pressed my palms gently together and raised my hands to my lips, brushing them over my fingertips and murmuring, "*Quaerite.*"

Seek.

A tingling danced in my hand. The sensation matched the light fire smoldering below my skin. I waited until it lessened, then grabbed my purse.

Showtime.

∞∞∞

The young guard who'd hailed a cab for me the day before was stationed at the gate again. He offered a welcoming nod before scanning the paper on his clipboard. "Your name, Miss?"

"You won't find me listed on today's visitor roster," I told him, wincing and putting my left hand to my forehead. My right hand stayed wrapped around the short strap of my purse. I intended to keep my palm – and therefore the symbol – out of sight. "Remember me? I was here yesterday."

"Oh, right," he nodded. "How can I help?"

"I'm terribly embarrassed to admit this, but when I was in the library, I...Um..." I stammered intentionally, the fingers of my left hand now playing nervously with the scarf at my neck. "When I was studying in the library yesterday, I left a piece of paper with a spell I'd developed based on the information my mentor gave me. It's for an important test."

I was improvising.

"It's bad enough I left behind something so

special with my handwriting on it," I continued, dropping my voice and forcing him to lean in to hear me. "But he shared several words of power he uses personally. And I wrote them on that paper."

Another dramatic cringe made by me.

"If another witch finds this paper, I'll be... *disciplined*." I forced a shiver, then looked at him hopefully. "I'm sure I left it on a shelf. I can picture holding it in my hand. I remember setting it down. I need to get it before my carelessness is found out."

I bit the inside of my lower lip and widened my eyes. "Can you help me? Can you let me in so I can hurry and get it back? I'm worried someone else will find it first."

Now here's the thing. Witches recognize each other. I don't have to know you, I might never have met you before, but if I pass you on the street, I'll know you're a natural witch if you are one. You'll know I'm one, too. And I knew this security guard was *not* a witch. I also banked on the belief that, like many non-witches in the Empire, he thought witches didn't trust each other. I wanted him to think I was desperate to find the paper I'd 'lost' before another witch discovered it and used it against me.

He balked. "I might need to call someone."

"Oh, I understand," I said, my left hand gripping a bar on the gate. I pressed my cheek against the metal and blinked rapidly. "Do you, um, well, do you think I can trust the library staff to be honest and tell the truth if it's there?"

A troubled look crossed his face. "Well, probably." He glanced over his shoulder at the Congress building. "Then again, I get your point."

"I'll go in and out," I promised. "Like I said, I'm pretty sure I know where I left it." I held up my left hand with my fingers crossed.

He unlocked the gate. "I probably shouldn't do this, but I know you were here yesterday. And you're just going in and out? You'll be quick?"

"Absolutely," I answered. I passed through the gate, turning to face him and walking backward for several steps. "Thank you so much. Give me a few extra minutes in case the library staff delays me." I gave him a thumbs up.

He was nervous, but his hand lifted in a tiny wave. I turned right as I passed through the wards guarding the Congress. I felt the normal shudder as I crossed. Nothing unusual there. I'd called it.

Two hurdles down. Next, the ritual of recognition.

∞∞∞

Inside the outer doors, I stopped and sized up the place where I believed Sebastian's demon door had opened. In the wall, there was a rectangular door bearing the words *No Entry*. The doorknob was missing. In the past, I'd assumed it was an emergency exit that was opened from the other side. I wondered if it was a coincidence his demon door formed in the same space.

The room where the ritual of recognition was conducted was empty except for the creature who sat by the doors leading into the main lobby. I padded over to her, but I didn't pull up the sleeve on my denim jacket in preparation like I'd normally do. Instead, I stopped a step away and waited, remembering the last time when she'd grabbed my arm and told me 'he' needed me – that I'd need to go through the dark to get to the light.

"Do you see things the others don't?" I asked.

"Is that how you know things?"

Her cloudy eyes lifted to mine, her face so gaunt the orbs appeared to pop out of their sockets. "I see the Light and the Darkness."

There were many things I wanted to ask, and I was tempted, but I had limited time. Instead, I replied, "I need to go to the library, but no one can know I'm here."

Her gnarled hands cupped the sides of her face, and she pressed dirty jagged fingernails into her sunken cheeks. She tilted her head to the side as she peered up into my face. "I can hear them. They call for the light, light, light."

"You can see me, can't you?" I realized. "You really can."

"I can see the Light." Her scrawny arms trembled. "The Light must go to the Darkness, but the Light always has free will. The Light can stay, the Light can go. The Light must shine on him and cast the shadow out."

"On him? On the Darkness?" These muddled words only confused me more.

The being's head snapped to the left and her lips pressed together as her toothless mouth worked, her bottom jaw almost disappearing into her head. She froze for a beat before her murky eyes cut to mine. "Someone comes! You may enter, witch."

I didn't hesitate. The ritual of recognition skipped, I passed through the doors and into the main lobby.

Chapter 12

I saw one lone witch as I made a beeline toward the hallway leading to the library. He barely noticed me as we passed, the acknowledgment brief as his eyes tore from the document he carried to the vicinity of my chin and back to his hand. The coat check counter was unstaffed, a sign directing visitors to ring the bell for assistance. I rushed by it.

Occasionally, I'd hear a door shut or heels clicking across a hard floor in another hall, but I scurried to the library in record time without passing another. Despite the unusual experience with the blind being, my mission was staying as far under the radar as it could. The first room in the library was the next test.

"Please don't let anyone be at the circulation desk," I prayed. The double doors were propped open, and I cautiously stepped on through. Two younger witches sat poring over a book at one of the tables to the side. Their heads stayed bowed. The assistant at the circulation desk stood with her back to the door, and I trekked as stealthily as I could to the right. I forced myself to keep a relaxed pace in case anyone turned a curious eye my way.

The section on symbolism was housed at the back of the library. Once I entered the stone hallway on the right, I made my way to the end and hooked a left. I doubled back through the stacks and entered the rows at the opposite end of the library. For the moment, I was alone. I put my right hand over my heart as I calmed myself.

Instead of traipsing up and down every row, I first targeted some obvious stacks – specifically those beginning with A, B, D, and L: Above, Below, Darkness, Light. I didn't intend to push out any of my magic or cast any additional spells. I would simply hold my right palm facing the shelves as I went along. I was hoping to feel a tingle or a tug as I got closer to the book Sebastian claimed would prove the existence of a door in the Below leading into the Above.

The stacks were much taller than my reach. I started with the lowest shelves hoping the book would be amongst those. I found the section beginning with Ab…Abo…Abov…Above.

Nothing.

Next, I skimmed through the books with titles beginning with Below. This time I had to climb a sliding ladder and stretch my arm out to the right to pass my hand along the spines.

Nothing. Strike two.

I repeated the process with titles beginning with Dark, Darkness, and Light – again spending time on the ladder moving along the shelves.

No luck.

I didn't have a lot of time. I'd already been inside the building longer than I believed I should be. Anxious, I made my way back to the 'A' section. I'd skip the topmost shelves for now. I could move more swiftly if I focused on the ones I could reach.

"Please, please, please," I chanted as I waved my hand along another line of books. My heart rate had sped up, and I worked to pull it back. I did not want to lose control of the natural energy powering the silent symbol on my right palm.

Passing my hand over the beginning of the 'B'

shelf delivered a hit. A cool tingle tickled in the middle of my palm. It was so slight I thought I'd imagined it. A second pass assured me I had not. I narrowed it down to a row holding a dozen books beginning with 'Ba.' However, a couple were missing titles on their spines.

I pulled out the first one, but it was not the book I sought. The second wasn't either. I glided my fingertips along the spines of the remaining tomes. The seventh – one with a naked spine – delivered the biggest vibration. I pulled it from its dusty spot. The black cloth cover was faded, and a gold embossed square appeared on the front. It was divided horizontally, with a gold band filling the upper half of the square. In contrast, the bottom half was free of embellishment, showing only the plain black cover.

Light above, Darkness below.

Above and Below.

I hugged it to my chest. I was back on track. In my hands, I held a way to get into the Above. To get to Templeton. My heart felt a little lighter.

"Okay," I muttered as I shoved the book into my bag. I zipped it shut. "Time to get out of here."

Peeking around the end of the aisle, I determined the coast was clear. I'd head back the same way I came. If I could get past the library assistant without being noticed, even though I was still not all the way out of the Congress building, I felt like I'd be home free.

I kept my head down as I hurried, slowing only when I heard a woman's voice complain in a shrill whisper about the library staff not reshelving books fast enough. I dove into the closest row of stacks and dropped my head back.

Roberta – *gah!*

The older witch was a longtime Tarot client and a huge pain in the neck. I'd managed to avoid her since I'd returned to Matar in February. She was a busybody and a card reader's nightmare. When I was actively consulting Tarot for clients, I had to limit Roberta to once per week. Whenever she faced a question or a choice, she wanted to run it by the cards – no matter how inconsequential. Even more infuriating, she was also a diviner. Roberta's forte was runic divination, although she also read Tarot. She liked to use me to confirm her interpretations since I was 'the best.'

Her words, not mine.

If she saw me now, not only would I be trapped – Roberta was quite talkative – she would tell everyone she ran into me at the Congress. Dammit! This was bad. I spun around and hurried in the opposite direction. Her complaining about the library's negligence followed me.

As I weaved my way through the towering stacks, I cast another look over my shoulder. I seemed to be safe – she didn't realize I was near. I rounded another row's end and came face-to-face with one of the last people I wanted to see in the library.

Timothy Richardson.

I stopped short. "Oh, just...*fuck*."

He raised an eyebrow, an amused smile playing at the corners of his mouth. "And good afternoon to you, too, Miss Bellerose."

I could feel the heat rising in my cheeks. "I'm sorry. You startled me."

"I bet I did," he replied. "But I'd say it's more of a surprise to find you here."

When I was forming my plan, I decided if I did get caught inside the library, I'd stick with the same story I'd offered at the security gate. I saw no reason to do a changeup, but I amended it somewhat for Timothy. "I lost something important of mine here yesterday, and frankly, I didn't trust anyone in the Congress to try and find it for me."

His gaze roamed over my face. "Is that so?"

"Yes. Unfortunately, my recent experience with the Congress has colored any confidence I'd had with it in the past. I was running errands and thought I'd stop and look for it myself." I sniffed, taking a moment to adjust the hem of my cropped jacket. I kept my right hand wrapped around the purse strap at my shoulder.

"Care to try again?" Timothy chuckled. "See if you can come up with something better this time."

"I'm not sure what you mean," I answered, raising my eyes to his. I kept my voice low. Thoughts of the stolen book buried inside my oversized purse made the skin between my shoulder blades feel clammy. My heart skittered like it was skipping beats, but I hid any overt uneasiness by listing to the side and looking past the Congress elder. "I thought I heard a friend a minute ago. Do you know Roberta?"

"Lucie, here's a piece of advice: Never play

poker." Timothy reached for my right elbow, ushering me off to the side and into a shaded corner where we'd find more privacy. When I pulled away to face him, I realized his position effectively blocked my path.

"Mr. Richardson, I'm not comfortable with this." I kept my hand loosely folded around the purse strap. I did not want him to see the symbol on my palm.

"I'm not exactly sure what you're doing here, but you're not supposed to be in the Congress building," he admonished. "The courtesy of doing research in the library was only for yesterday."

"I'm aware, and I apologize for returning without permission. Like I said, I'd lost something and thought I could take a second to pick it up." To leave the conversation, I'd have to push past him. I didn't want to have to do that.

"Did you find it?"

"I, um. No. Unfortunately, I did not. Perhaps I'm wrong, and I didn't leave it here after all." I shrugged. "I'll check again at home."

"Or maybe someone took it?" He shook his head, forcefully sighing. "I mean, you pointed out members of the Congress couldn't be trusted."

"Right." I pressed my lips together to signal I had nothing more to say.

He kept studying my face. Eventually, his gaze wandered to the hand holding my purse strap, then to the purse itself. I didn't know Timothy's magic, what he used or what his abilities included, but I didn't feel any pokes of energy coming from him. With his powerful status as an elder, he might be allowed to use a limited amount of magic in the building. However, my sense was Timothy didn't need to dip into his magical tool chest to know I was lying. His astuteness was mundane but well-honed

"What's in your purse?" His voice was soft.

"Personal items," I replied.

"Nothing belonging to the Congress? Or specifically, to the library?"

"No." I pulled my jacket closed with my free hand. I drew in a short breath through my nose.

He nodded, a patronizing smile holding me captive. "Okay, Lucie."

We stood there a moment longer. I knew he was waiting to see if I'd bend and admit any wrongdoing. I remained silent.

"Alright, let me escort you out – that way,

your presence, if anyone else notices, will not be questioned." He stepped to the side and motioned for me to go ahead.

I certainly wasn't home free, but I still had the book. *Almost there,* I thought.

"Did you have any luck translating the text you needed?" Timothy's pace kept us moving more slowly than I preferred. It was intentional.

"I did not," I answered. I attempted to put a button on it. "But it's fine."

"Is it?" We strolled to the front of the library. He stopped at the circulation desk and spoke in a low tone to the assistant. Her eyes bounced to me once before returning to Timothy. She nodded. He pointed forward, and we walked side by side once more. Outside in the hall leading away from the library, Timothy immediately resumed our conversation. "It's fine? I was unaware Templeton had returned home."

"He hasn't." The stress of the day was getting to me. I called up an image of Templeton in my mind. I tried to picture his face in my home – door traveling through the pantry door, sitting beside me on a barstool at my kitchen counter, showing me his secrets...Kissing me in my hallway while my fire raced through my body and burnt my handprints into the wall. Instead, I saw his limp body dangling in the air, light ravishing it and bleeding him of his energy. I saw the Beam of Light cross through the fifth door, carrying him away, trapping him in the Above.

"Stop." Timothy again put his hand on my elbow. We were alone in the hall, and he turned me to face him. "I'm going to do you a favor, Lucie. Whatever is in your bag, I'm letting you leave with it. I expect you to return it in due time."

I focused on the buttons of his pin-striped dress shirt. "I don't have anything." I couldn't have sounded less convincing if I tried.

"Whatever it is, I'm guessing it's something you think will help you bring Templeton back." He paused. "Therefore, I'm looking the other way. I want you to remember this. I've been willing to help you several times now. I want to be your friend, Lucie. And friends do favors for each other. Do you understand what I'm saying?"

I did. And this was downright dangerous. "I do. Thank you."

Timothy squeezed my arm gently. "Good. I'm glad. And I hope you'll let me know how this goes – whatever you have planned. I'm sure Templeton's counting on you. Remember, you can come to me for help. You should come to me. Not only am I a fellow witch, I'm also an elder. I have resources I can access on your behalf."

And put me in more debt to you, I thought as we continued toward the lobby. I couldn't wait to leave. "I'll let you know."

"That's what I want to hear." A handful of witches were leaving ahead of me. Timothy waited until they were gone. "Your review is coming up. Hopefully, your membership will be reinstated, and these violations won't be repeated."

"I look forward to it," I lied, stepping away and motioning to the next set of doors. "I should go. Thank you again."

"You're welcome. I'm sure we'll see each other soon."

I didn't reply but left the lobby, entering the space where the blind being sat. I paused, desperate to learn more from her but fearful Timothy would find out she told me strange things – if he didn't know already.

When she raised her face in my direction, I simply waved before turning and leaving the building.

∞∞∞

A different guard was at the security gate, and I hurried past. The sky had grown overcast, and fat raindrops fell as I climbed into my RAV4. Through the car window, I caught a glimpse of a dark-haired man in black skinny jeans and work boots pulling up the hood on his sweatshirt, his curls disappearing under the gray material. He fished out a small phone from his pocket and stepped backward into a doorway to avoid the spring shower.

I shook my head. Another Rabbit.

I started my car. I couldn't wait to get home.

∞∞∞

By the time I returned to the Clover District, the rain had stopped. I parked in the garage and walked the block home, my flat sandals slapping against the wet ground. I was impatient to go through the book I 'borrowed' from the library. My stomach growled. I was also starving. I'd make a sandwich – or maybe there was still leftover pizza.

When I reached my front stoop, I sensed something was off in the wards. Nothing appeared to be torn, but there was an element I couldn't place my finger on. I unlocked the door as quietly as I could and pushed it open slowly while I listened for unusual noises.

I didn't hear anything strange, but I could smell something as I stepped inside.

It was like strawberries on steroids. My head dropped back, and I raged silently at my ceiling. Seriously?

I shut the door behind me. I could already see Sebastian sitting at the kitchen counter. He was drinking a strawberry *Toro* and reading the paper. I stood in the doorway leading into the kitchen, my mouth hanging open.

He looked up, then frowned. "What?"

I crossed to the other side of the kitchen and set my purse on the counter. Turning, I lifted a hand, then let it drop. "What are you doing here?"

"I was hungry." He pulled a face and went back to reading the paper.

I stuttered through my words. "But, no. You have food. No. Wait."

Sebastian raised his head a second time. "Come again?"

"You have food at the cabin," I argued.

"No, I don't." His head cocked to the side. "I haven't been at the cabin in months."

"Don't give me that shit, Sebastian," I fumed. "I'm sure you have enough nonperishables to get you through the night."

"What I don't have –" he began, a wicked smile putting a glint in his eye, "– is sushi. I called for takeout." He held up a hand and listed off the rolls he'd ordered on his fingers. "California, Spicy Salmon, Ocean Wave, and Dragon. I know you like the Unagi Rolls, and I ordered you one of those, too."

I didn't know whether to laugh at the absurdity of the whole fucking nightmare playing out in my life or to simply break down and cry.

"As for 'nonperishables,' I brought wine. There's a nice Riesling chilling in the fridge. I added your favorite Pinot Noir to your wine rack." He slid the barstool back and stood.

He'd showered and changed clothing at the cabin – of course. Gone were the stupid blaze orange tee shirt and the basketball shorts. The new outfit was trademark Sebastian: a long sleeved white tee shirt and a pair of low-rise bootcut jeans. He'd run product through his wild shaggy cut and trimmed up the facial hair around his lips so meticulously it looked like an artist's rendering. He sauntered around the end of the counter and opened the refrigerator. Sebastian was taller, too. My gaze lowered to his feet. He'd slipped on a pair of boots.

"This is so bad," I exhaled, noting the two wine glasses waiting on the counter, a bottle opener beside them. I pulled off my jean jacket and laid it over my purse.

"We probably have 10 minutes before the sushi gets here." Sebastian didn't miss a beat. He pulled the white wine from the refrigerator. "Shit, you like that calamari salad, don't you? I didn't order any."

"You've got to stop this." Oh, my god. He *was* still crazy. I was wrong earlier. Just because Sebastian wasn't acting insane didn't mean he wasn't.

"What I've got to do – and you do, too – is eat." His eyelids dipped as he worked the cork out of the wine bottle. "You look nice. I see you went with light on top and dark on the bottom. The Above and Below? Some sort of witch thing?"

I looked down at my outfit. I hadn't realized the coincidence. "Um, no."

He poured two glasses of wine, eyeballing my chest. "The shirt is a perfect fit."

I picked up my jacket and pulled it back on. Wait, had Flame come home? When did he say he was coming back to get ready for his date with David? My eyes flicked to the pantry door. A bigger fear wound through me. What if Emily Swift door traveled into my home right now? How would I explain this? Would she understand?

Sebastian set a glass of wine next to my purse. I caught a hint of his cologne and automatically leaned in his direction to sneak a whiff. He noticed my reaction and stepped closer.

"No," I held up a hand, getting a grip on myself. "You need to leave."

"I'm not leaving, Lucie," he shook his head, fixating on my hand. He nodded at the inked symbol. "What's this about?"

I needed to put some space between us. I snagged my purse and carried it to the counter where he'd been reading the paper. "It's from earlier today."

He turned, tracking my movements when I stepped around him. "And? Did you get the book?"

"I did," I said, setting my purse on the barstool.

He waved his wine glass at me. "Where is it? Let me see. Are you sure you got the right one? What does it say?"

"Slow down," I told him. "I haven't gone through it yet. I didn't want to waste time at the Congress. I planned on reading it when I got home."

"So, let's read it," he said, gesturing toward my purse.

"You are not allowed in my purse. I compel you to not open my purse." The wording was awkward, but the point was made.

He sneered. "I changed my mind. I don't like this new side of you."

"Deal with it." Absently, I reached up and pulled the pins from my hair. I was tired – I wasn't even sure I was hungry anymore. "I'm going to read it tonight and see what it says about the door you claim exists in the Below. Assuming it does, I want to learn how it's opened. I'm still not convinced any of this will make a difference, but it's all I've got right now. It's my only hope."

Sebastian watched as I set the pins on the counter. "You really think he's still alive, don't you?"

My head jerked up. "Yes, of course. Look, even you made it back, right? You've been to the Above."

"Yup." He took a gulp of his wine. I wondered then if I should've compelled him to only drink water. An intoxicated demon I did not want.

"No offense, but if you can make it back..." I let the implication fall between us.

"Precisely." Again, another swig of wine.

A rapping on the front door announced the sushi delivery. Sebastian set his glass on the counter and pulled a wallet from his back pocket. He dug out a wad of bills. I assumed he kept a stash of money at his cabin. "I've got this."

Mystified, I watched as he stalked past to answer the door. Why did everyone make my home theirs?

Sebastian returned with the order, unloading boxes onto the counter and retrieving plates from my cupboard. He set a pair of chopsticks on a plate. "Yours." He proceeded to load up his dish, snagging a piece from a roll and popping it into his mouth while he nosed through the containers. I watched his jaw work as he chewed.

"What did you mean by 'precisely'?" I asked.

He swallowed as he sprinkled soy sauce on several lumps of rice. "Precisely what?"

"I said if *you* could make it out of the Above..." I twirled my wrist, waving my hand at him. "Meaning if you could make it out, surely Templeton could make it out, and you said, 'precisely.'"

Sebastian plopped a wad of wasabi onto his plate. "Are you going to get your sushi or what?"

"Answer me."

"I told you, you can't compel my –"

"Answer me, dammit!" The fire under my skin surged to the surface. I gripped the edge of the counter, forcing it back down.

Sebastian ignored my outburst. "Precisely, Lucie, as in, if I could make it out, so could pencil dick. If he didn't, he's either dead or he doesn't want to come back." Sebastian used his chopsticks to pick up a piece of the salmon roll.

"He's not dead. He's trapped." I watched as the sushi disappeared into his mouth. "And I'm not putting up with this 'pencil dick' crap anymore, Sebastian."

"Oh, massive, is it?" Sebastian raised an eyebrow. "Satisfied you in every way, huh?"

Without thinking, I looked toward the hall and thought about the handprints burnt into the wall.

"Tell me what you want, Lucie," the ghost of Templeton whispered.

Why didn't I answer him that night? Why couldn't I tell him? Why couldn't I say: *I want to be with you, Templeton, in every way. Please stay with me tonight. I want you.*

The silence stretched awkwardly, my eyes still seeing the two stubborn shadows kissing in the hallway.

"Wait a minute." Sebastian's voice cut into my memory. I tore my thoughts away from the hall in time to see his eyes light up. "You haven't slept with him, have you?"

"We're not discussing this," I replied. My face felt hot.

"You didn't!" Sebastian was euphoric. "You didn't sleep with Templeton!"

"Enough," I hissed.

"Wait, were you playing hard to get with him?" Sebastian tsked. "Although, I admit it's fun to imagine you as a cock tease."

"Stop it, Sebastian," I warned, my fingertips burning again.

"But what about the other one?" His lip curled back. "Were you fucking that animal instead? Is that why the filthy Rabbit was sniffing around you, too? The one the dog chewed up on the quad?"

"Shut up!" I shouted, taking a step toward him. How dare he? He wasn't half the man Rabbit was. "Get out. I don't care where you go – we're done. Done! No deal. No...*nothing*. I want nothing from you, Sebastian. *Ever*. I'll find another way into the Above. Get the fuck out of my house."

"I bet Templeton was beside himself," Sebastian laughed. He'd found a wound and couldn't resist sinking a finger into it. "You, fucking a Rabbit instead of him!"

The anger erupting from my skin did little to affect Sebastian in his demon form as it poured over him. Still, I singed the front of his shirt – and set the dish towel hanging from the oven door on fire.

"Shit, Lucie!" he swore, grabbing the flaming towel and throwing it into the sink. He turned on the faucet, submerging it in water. He cast an indignant look in my direction as he passed damp hands down the front of his shirt. "Get some fucking control."

"I have control," I snarled. "You're lucky I didn't blast you through a wall. Don't you dare speak of Rabbit ever again. *Ever*."

"Fine, you want to fuck your way through Matar, have at it," he needled, dropping the destroyed towel back into the sink.

"I wasn't fucking anyone," I gritted out. "Rabbit was my friend – *is* my friend." My voice shook with anger. I balled my hands into fists, jamming my fingernails into my palms. "It's none of your business what I do or don't do."

Sebastian took in my words. He quieted, then it hit him, his face shifting into surprise. His lips formed a soft 'O.' "You haven't slept with anyone since we were together."

"Leave it," I warned, my face still burning.

"You haven't been with anyone since me, have

you?" Sebastian's voice dropped to a quieter tone. He stepped closer, his eager eyes searching my face.

"No!" I pointed at him. "Don't get the wrong idea. What was between us is over. So over."

"Is it?" He snorted. "I don't believe you. Think of me what you will, but I know people. I can read a person fast, and you were never hard for me to see, Lucie. You were wide open from the beginning. I saw it earlier, and I can see it now. It's written all over your face. You still care about me. Lie to yourself if it makes you feel loyal to 'him,' but don't think I don't know the truth."

"The truth," I snapped. "That's rich. You wouldn't recognize the truth if your face was shoved into a pile of it."

"Yeah, because I'm evil. I get it. Sebastian's rotten to the core, a threat to all that's good and holy. Treated Lucie like shit."

"You lied to me! You are responsible for so many deaths." I ran both hands through my hair, yanking on fistfuls. I froze when I realized I'd mirrored one of Sebastian's crazed habits. I lowered my arms. "You attacked Emily when she went after you for strangling the Warden of the North Door."

Sebastian scoffed. "What are you talking about?"

"Rene Blackstone – the Record Keeper. You killed him."

Sebastian swayed from foot to foot, confused. "No. No, I didn't."

"You did! After all your lackeys were rounded up, they told the Empire guards what they saw you do. You were there. You killed him," I challenged.

"I didn't." He shook his head slowly, his eyebrows lifting. "I was there but left when I got what I wanted. He was still alive."

"Even if that's true, are you suddenly claiming to be a choir boy? Because that's a joke. Your hands are covered in blood, Sebastian."

He turned his head, looking out the dusky window over my kitchen sink. "I didn't say that."

"You're a killer."

He pursed his lips, still staring outside. I watched as they parted, and I could see his tongue moving under his cheek. Sebastian blinked once before facing me again. "I am. I was."

"Wow, the truth," I mocked.

"You think that Rabbit of yours has never killed anyone? With his own hands, I might add?" The mean look reappeared.

I faltered. "Rabbit's situation is different from yours. He's not a greedy psychopath merrily leading a terrorist group."

"Funny you should say that," he shot back. "You know the Empire basically sees the Rabbits as a threat to their government, right?"

"I don't think that's quite –" I began.

"No?" Sebastian interrupted. "The Rabbits built their little world inside the Empire – you think the Salesman Court likes that? They want Rabbit technology so bad they'd love to label them as terrorists and go after them full-on. And you know, they wouldn't have a tough time pushing the initiative through with the right people on the bench. Rabbits are already known as vigilantes. No one can deny that. Not even you."

I swallowed. How did we get here? "We're not talking about –"

"And your precious Templeton," Sebastian spat. "Tell you what. If he's not dead, the next time you see him, you ask him. Ask him. Has he ever been 'a party' to anyone's unfortunate demise? See how he answers you. If he even answers you."

I held up my hands in surrender, trying to reel in all the miserable feelings Sebastian stirred up inside me. I couldn't do it anymore. "Please stop. Let's stop this."

Sebastian's long fingers rubbed at his shirt's neckline. His gaze didn't waver. "Seems like the good guys might have more in common with me than you'd care to admit."

I let his words hang in the air. He waited, but I didn't respond.

Briiing! The interruption made by the Empire service phone sliced into the tension filling the kitchen. I jumped at the noise but automatically crossed to the cupboard and answered the call.

"Yes?" I spoke into the handset, eyeing Sebastian warily.

"This is the award-winning Empire messaging service line," the operator's clipped tone assaulted my ear. "I have a message for Ms. Lucie Bellerose from Ms. Anne Lace. Am I speaking to Ms. Bellerose?"

"You are," I sighed, watching as Sebastian put several pieces of sushi onto a plate and set it on the counter by my purse, along with the wine he'd poured earlier. He placed a pair of chopsticks across the plate. I looked down at my feet.

"Ms. Bellerose, the message from Ms. Lace is as follows: 'Gavina has met with the family lawyer to begin the process of having Templeton declared dead. There will be a reading of his will, and the distribution of his assets will be determined.'"

Gavina was Templeton's mother.

"Ms. Lace also included the following: 'Mr. Archie reported he knows Templeton amended his will to include you. I'll let you know when I hear more. I'm sorry, Lucie.' Ms. Bellerose, that is the end of the message," the operator concluded.

"Thank you," I mumbled, returning the handset to its cradle and shutting the cupboard door.

It was the final blow.

Outside, the sky opened up, and a punishing rain swept through my backyard. The sound of heavy drops pelting the lawn furniture carried in through the window, the noise climbing as the spring storm surrounded my home.

Lightning split the air with a nerve-rattling crack. The rumbling of angry thunder replied immediately.

It's right on top of us, I thought.

Defeated, I looked at the feast Sebastian laid out on the counter for me. I lifted my eyes to him, rubbing my hand across the back of my neck. "Alright, let's...Let's move beyond all this tonight. Why don't you tell me what happens when we get into the Below?"

Chapter 13

Sebastian didn't give me much. Basically, his plan consisted of door traveling with me in tow through the sixth door, then leading me to a metal door connecting the Below to the Above. There I would – as he put it – 'do the witch thing' and open the door. I left the book I'd taken from the library in my purse. This was witch property. No demon perusal allowed.

I nibbled on pieces of sushi while I listened. "And what about the Darkness? He'll know I'm there."

Sebastian refilled his wine glass. "Yeah, he'll know you're coming as soon as we step onto the quad in the compound. He'll open the sixth door."

"Wait a minute." I made a wry face. "You said there's no door on the other side – it's a free fall."

"It is." He lifted the bottle in his hand. "More?"

"No." I'd taken only several sips from my glass. "About this free fall, that's not going to work for me."

"Relax," he dismissed me. "Becoming a demon has its advantages. I've done it before. I'll land on my feet – like a cat."

"Again, the free fall is not for me. There must be another way in," I pressed.

"Nope." Sebastian folded the lids on the sushi containers. "I'll hold onto you. You'll be fine."

"Sebastian –"

"You think the Darkness wants you to fall to your death?"

I lifted my hand. "Maybe?"

"He doesn't. He wants you to come to the Below of your own free will," Sebastian replied.

"If he knows I'm coming, won't he try to keep me there?" Oh, this was such a bad idea.

"He can't." Sebastian pointed to the book of fairy tales. "There's a story in there – the Light leaves the Darkness behind. You can leave."

"The Light ran away from the Darkness," I clarified.

"Because she was afraid of it." Sebastian stood on the other side of the counter across from where I sat. "Are you still afraid of dark things,

Lucie?"

I nodded as I stabbed a chopstick through a blob of wasabi. "Yes, I am. Because dark things never truly go away. They hide in places where you can't see them."

∞∞∞

There wasn't much more to discuss. Sebastian might've been nonchalant about the whole plan – the pathetic excuse for a plan – but I knew better. I'd have to face the Darkness. I had no idea what it would entail, but there'd be no avoiding it. And while Sebastian held up the book of fairy tales as proof the Light could leave the Darkness behind, I found myself taking more comfort in the blind being's words from earlier: *'The Light has free will.'*

I told Sebastian to leave and that we'd regroup in the morning. For now, I wanted to look at the book and learn more about the symbol. Maybe it would give me the confidence I needed. However, with or without the book's reassurance, I was still going into the Below.

I'd do anything to bring Templeton back. The fact his mother was preparing to have him declared dead so quickly shook me to my core.

He was *not* dead. I'd know it if he didn't survive. *I'd know it.*

Sebastian didn't argue when I directed him to return to his cabin for the night. I reminded him he had no permission to go anywhere else – and again, absolutely no visitors. He didn't seem to care and admitted to looking forward to a full night's sleep. I was somewhat suspicious of his easy acceptance, but I didn't push.

I watched as he passed through the pantry door, the remnants of his door travel energy leaving a footprint in my kitchen. I could only sense Sebastian's energy; I could not see it. Templeton's door travel energy was a magnificent royal blue, and it rose in tremendous waves around him. More than once he'd surrounded me with them – to lend power to my magic, to protect me, to connect more intimately with me. It made my heart ache to think about it.

I remembered the moment when Templeton sat on the barstool next to me and dipped his powerful energy inside my witchline. Goosebumps rose on my skin when I recalled the feeling. It was like nothing I'd ever experienced. The sensation was exquisite. In that moment, I wanted him inside *me*.

Giving myself a shake, I pulled the book I'd 'borrowed' from the library and touched the square symbol on the cover. It wasn't a particularly elaborate one, but I knew better than to judge any symbol by a first impression. Simplicity didn't mean it wasn't powerful. I opened the book for the first time.

Pages had been ripped out of several sections. Still others were damaged by water, and the ink had bled, rendering the content indecipherable. More than once, sketches had been scribbled out, and new ones were added beside the originals. I was disappointed to find the book contained no lines of text. Essentially, it was a picture book.

I turned through the delicate pages, seeking the symbol represented on the front cover. In the second half, I discovered a series of squares. In some, the upper portion was larger than the solid-colored lower half. These were followed by renditions with the dark overtaking the light in the upper half. I also found sketches of doors bearing the symbol. They were either filled in or left empty. The symbols featuring more light appeared on the doors without color. Those squares with a greater amount of dark were matched with sketches of doors that had been inked in.

I turned yet another page and was greeted with the symbol found on the front of the book – the same one Sebastian had drawn. The square was evenly divided between the light section without any color or shading and the bottom half with its solid black. Finally, the symbol I needed.

The next handful of pages had been ripped out of the book.

Of course.

I checked the remaining pages, but there didn't seem to be anything I could use. I wasn't even sure what to do with the pages that were intact. Closing the book, I examined the perfect square on its cover. The light and dark were balanced equally.

I raised my head, not seeing the kitchen before me but imagining the shelf where I'd found the book. I was in the 'B' section – 'Ba' to be precise.

"It's balance," I said aloud. "Balance. The Light and Dark need to be balanced."

Sebastian had drawn the symbol as balanced

when he first showed me. I'd need to question him about this.

"But for now –" I yawned as I glanced at the clock on the stove, "– I should go to bed."

And yet, as exhausted as I was, I pulled out the bottle of Pinot Noir Sebastian had added to my wine rack. It was my favorite. Damn. What was I going to do with him? I replaced the bottle and instead chose another, removing the cork and pouring myself a sizable glass. I grabbed a dish towel – one that hadn't been set on fire – and crossed through my pantry and into my backyard.

The rain left its memory on the table and chairs sitting in the center of my yard. I wiped off a seat and sat back, my eyes searching the night sky. It was still overcast, but you couldn't see the stars in the city anyway. You'd find the full moon when it hung low in the sky, but it would be two weeks before the celestial body achieved its completeness. I grimaced. Nisha wanted Sebastian unbound before the full moon. She planned to call him to her.

I shivered. This was something to think about later. I certainly wasn't telling Sebastian about the frightening priestess.

"Lucie?" Flame's voice carried from the doorway. "What are you doing out here?"

I lifted my glass. "Having a nightcap. Are you home to change for your date?"

"Sort of," he answered. "I've already been to David's – we had takeout. It looks like you did, too."

"Sort of," I also answered.

"There was more than one wine glass. Did you have someone over?" He gestured to the house as he came outside.

I took another sip of my wine and winced. "Yeah, there was another person here."

Flame dragged the chair from the other side of the table, wiped off the seat with the damp towel, and sat on the edge facing me. "Spill."

I shook my head.

I was unprepared when he took my hand. "Lucie, you know shapeshifters can tell when people are upset, right?"

"I did not know that," I said, stiffening. "Are you telling the truth?"

He played with my fingers with both hands, rubbing each digit. "Well, yes and no. I can sense something is off with you – more than your usual sadness."

I was taken aback by his words. "My 'usual sadness'?"

He nodded. "It's always there."

"Maybe," I replied, feeling vulnerable.

"Who was here tonight?" Flame asked gently.

I couldn't look at him. "A demon."

Flame's fingers halted. "A demon?"

"Yes." My shoulders hopped up and down once. "The abbreviated version of the story is this: There was a man who became a demon – well, not a full demon. He's in the process of turning into a demon. He's not dead."

"So, demon-lite?" Flame resumed the finger massage.

"Sure, demon-lite. Anyhow, we're kind of... connected to each other because of our past. Today I conjured him for help. He's going to take me to where he lives. There's a door there leading into a place called the Above." I hesitated, and Flame squeezed my fingers. "The Above is where Templeton is trapped. I'm going to go through the door and find him. I'm going to bring him home."

He released my hand and sat up straighter. "You're going someplace with a demon?"

"Yes." Because I'm going crazy. And getting

desperate.

"No," Flame said. "You can't go with a demon – anywhere. This is a bad, bad idea."

"It's my only hope."

"It can't be," he argued. "Maybe you can –"

"It's my only hope, Flame!" I sat up and set my glass down hard on the table. "I've made my decision. I've got to suck it up and do it. I'm running out of time. Templeton's running out of time."

Flame's sweet face was pinched. "When?"

"Maybe tomorrow. I don't know." My shoulders slumped.

"Will you let me know when you're leaving me before you go?" The distinct quiver in his voice caused me to raise my head. His amber cat eyes seemed to capture what little light there was in my backyard.

I nodded. "I will."

"I'm scared for you, Lucie," he whispered.

A door slammed somewhere in one of the townhouses attached to mine, and we both turned our heads toward the source as the sound carried out an open window. "I'm scared for myself, too."

∞∞∞

My dreams were filled with a light so bright, I struggled to see. The dream version of Lucie stumbled over uneven ground, her feet kicking rocks as she pitched forward. A persistent crying of 'light-light-light' filled my brain, and before I woke, the blind creature who performed the ritual of recognition at the Congress appeared before me, placing her thin-skinned hands on the sides of my face.

She leaned in close, her milky eyes unexpectedly clear and searching mine. "Will you shine your light on he who needs it the most and deserves it the least? Will you bring your light into the dark and cast out the shadow?"

Her question shook me awake, and I sat up, wringing my covers in my hands. The clock on my nightstand indicated it was after 8 o'clock. I groaned. I'd forgotten to set the alarm. Throwing back the covers, I climbed out of bed and wrapped a satin robe around me. I'd left the window open and was rewarded with a remarkably warm breeze. The wet world the rain left behind would create a humid day in the city.

After talking to Flame under the night sky, I'd gone straight to bed. My vagabond shapeshifter left the house on four feet. He told me not to wait up.

I checked his room, shaking my head when I realized my spare was going to stay his bedroom for longer than I'd expected. The bed was empty, however, and I paused to pick up clothes from the floor, draping the garments over the chairback. Then I made his bed.

Downstairs, I was relieved to find an empty kitchen. No Sebastian. I'd forgotten to clarify with him that he wasn't to come to me unless I called. I drummed my fingertips on the countertop. This I'd have to figure out. I wasn't going through a conjuring ritual every time I wanted him to come to me.

The kitchen looked much like it had when I went to bed, which made me believe Flame hadn't returned home. I set about making coffee and poured myself a bowl of cereal. Admittedly, it was better with whole milk. A point to Flame.

While the coffee maker worked its magic, I sat at the counter and searched again through the book I'd taken from the library. I was disappointed by the missing pages, but I didn't dwell on it. What I did piece together was the symbol wanted equal parts light and dark – this made sense. There needed to be balance.

I spooned another mouthful of cereal between my lips as Sebastian door traveled into my kitchen. Shaking my head, I stared at my bowl and chewed. I hated this.

"What?" He had the audacity to be annoyed.

I swallowed, shooting a withering look at him. "I told you I'd call for you when I was ready."

"No, you didn't," he replied, helping himself to a cup of coffee. He paused to survey my breakfast before pouring me a cup as well, retrieving the milk from the refrigerator and adding a dollop. Sebastian set the coffee by my cereal bowl.

"Yes, I did," I sighed, noting how easily he'd inserted himself into my morning. "Listen. I know this is fun for you, but I can't have you showing up whenever you feel like it."

"Really? Huh." He sipped at his brew.

"Sebastian," I groaned. It was too early for this.

"And how will I know you're calling me?" Mischievous eyes laughed at me through his thick lashes.

"Um," I faltered. "I'll need to do some research. In the meantime –"

"You need to want me to come to you. I'll feel it," he smirked, rubbing a hand over his chest. "You don't know how this works, do you?"

"Well, until you, my experience with demons was limited to a few chapters in textbooks," I retorted.

He raised a hand in surrender. "Alright, look. I'm bound to you. I don't know what you feel, but for me, it's sort of a...*tether*. It's always there, even when you're not. If we're apart and you want me to come to you, I'll feel it tighten. Luckily for you, I'm also a Salesman. I can door travel to you in an instant." He snapped his fingers.

"How do you know this?" It was hard not to believe he was making it up as he went along.

Sebastian shrugged. "I just do."

I considered him. "And you can't refuse me?"

"I could try, but the connection caused by the binding will keep increasing until it's impossible to do anything but come to you."

"If that's the case, then from now on, you don't come through that door unless I call you.

Understand?" I took a drink from my cup.

"You afraid I'll interrupt a date or something?"

"Yup. That's exactly it." I slid off the barstool and rinsed my cereal bowl in the sink.

Sebastian laughed but didn't continue to push me. Instead, he changed the topic, gesturing to my robe. "Is this what you're wearing to the Below? I mean, it's cute and all, but I'd recommend jeans."

I gave him a sour look. He was dressed much like the night before, swapping out the long sleeved white shirt for a black one. He was freshly showered. "I overslept."

"Well, go get ready," he motioned vaguely to the ceiling. "We'll leave as soon as you're dressed."

"Alright, this is how it's going to work." I faced him. "You're going back to the cabin, and you're going to wait until I call you. Then we'll talk about leaving for the Below."

"Don't get your panties in a bunch," he replied. "If you want to waste more time, fine. But I need to go somewhere else then."

"No. You can only go to the cabin."

"Hear me out. I want to try something. I need to go to my family's estate," he said.

"It's all boarded up," I told him.

"I know, but there's something I want to do."

"What?"

He started to shake his head, then stopped. "I want to see if I can make a case of water appear in the Below."

"What do you mean?" I searched his face. "Make it appear in the Below?"

Sebastian rolled his eyes. "You'll see when we get there. But I want to take a case of bottled water from the cabin and leave it at the estate."

I pulled on my lower lip, weighing his request. Dealing with him was exhausting. "Fine. You can go there. I don't know what you're up to, but it better not jeopardize anything."

"It won't. Trust me." He finished the last of his coffee and put the cup into the sink. In two strides, he was at the pantry. "Call me when you're ready, warden." He winked and pulled open the door, disappearing as it slammed shut behind him.

Trust him? Oh, sure. I slumped against the counter and finished the rest of my coffee, staring at the pantry door. My heart ached.

The wrong Salesman kept coming through it.

∞∞∞

After showering, I pulled on a pair of jeans and a plain tee shirt, topping it off with a black zip-up hoodie. I planned on wearing my old red sneakers, too. They certainly weren't Dorothy Gale's ruby slippers, but perhaps in a pinch, they'd help me get back home.

I debated for half a second about wearing the necklace with the three pieces of the Crimson Stone. It was obviously a bad idea, but I still thought about it. The fact I couldn't unite them was ultimately the reason I decided to leave the gemstones behind. Then I wondered if I should send the necklace to Templeton's Mr. Archie – in case I didn't return from the Below.

Because it was a real possibility.

I was afraid. There was every chance I'd make it safely to the Below and end up trapped there.

I made my decision, texting Big Rabbit.

It's Lucie. I'm sorry to bother you, but I need a favor, and there's no one else I can ask.

A moment later...

Never a bother! What do you need?
Are you in Matar?

About 15 minutes from your house.
Can you come over now?
Be there as soon as I can.

∞∞∞

True to his word, 15 minutes later, Big Rabbit was ducking inside my front door. He gave me a cheery smile. "I've been wanting to check in on you."

"You and your girlfriend should come by for dinner sometime," I told him. "With the weather getting nicer, we could dine al fresco. Big veggie and fruit salads. Grill up some veggie burgers?"

"We'd love it." He continued to beam at me. "Now, what's going on?"

There was no way I was telling Big Rabbit what I'd planned or where I was going. I picked up a wooden box and an envelope, carrying both over to him. "I need you to deliver this to Mr. Archie at Templeton's estate. Keep the box closed and make sure Mr. Archie reads the note first."

The happy face Big Rabbit wore melted away. "What's in the box?"

"The three pieces of the Crimson Stone," I answered. "They need to go back to Templeton's family."

The tender giant took the box and the envelope. He peered down at me, his brow knitting itself into a dismal line. "I don't know much about this, Lucie. But...wouldn't Templeton want you to keep it?"

I shook my head, my voice catching as I spoke. "His mother is having him declared legally dead. This needs to go back to his family."

"Oh." He looked down at the box.

"It's vital this letter and the Stone make it safely to Mr. Archie."

"I'll get it to him right away."

"Thank you." There wasn't much more to say.

"I'm sorry about Rabbit. I thought by taking you there..." His voice trailed off.

I placed my hand on his forearm. "I appreciate what you tried to do."

"He has his crew keeping watch over you, you know." Big Rabbit wouldn't meet my eyes.

"I suspected as much."

"He loves you." Big Rabbit's eyes shimmered. "But his head is messed up. He blames himself for everything that happened. He's full of anger.

And he was ashamed you saw him like he is now."

I sagged against the door jamb separating my entryway from my cozy living room. "I don't understand. Nothing was his fault – hell, half the shit that happened was my fault!"

"I know – I mean, I know it wasn't his fault, but it wasn't yours, either. It was...Sometimes bad things happen. That's all." Big Rabbit tucked the envelope into the back pocket of his jeans. The wooden box he held in his large paw. "Don't give up on him, though. He's come a long way. He couldn't walk at all a month ago."

My heart twisted. "Will he fully recover?"

Big Rabbit's head toggled from side to side. "I think so, but it's up to him – he needs to fight for it."

"What about," I hesitated. "What about his illness?"

"He's still sick," Big Rabbit nodded. "But he's a lot better."

"Are you ever going to tell me what's wrong with him?" I asked.

"Not my tale to tell." Big Rabbit's kind eyes glistened. "But maybe he'll be open to having you visit again."

"Was he pissed at you?"

A cheerless laugh passed through his lips. "Kicked me off his crew."

"What?" My mouth popped open.

"No worries," Big Rabbit replied. "He'll get over it. I'm letting him stew for a while."

"I'm sorry you got into trouble because of me." I scrunched up my nose.

"Oh, no. I got into trouble because of me." Big Rabbit gave me a hug. "And I'd do it all over again."

"Rabbits. What would I do without all of you?" I offered a halfhearted smile.

"Don't sweat it – we've adopted you," he answered. He held up the wooden box with the Crimson Stone. "I'll get this to Mr. Archie."

"I really appreciate it," I said. "He'll know what to do with it."

Big Rabbit nodded. "I'm off, then. I'll check in later, okay?"

"Perfect," I nodded, a place deep inside my chest aching as I let him believe I'd be here to receive his message.

He flashed a sweet smile and opened the door. I stepped forward and watched him hustle down the stairs leading up to the front of my townhouse before turning to the left. I searched out the spot where I believed the hidden camera was perched on the corner. I raised a hand and waved.

Just in case my Rabbit was watching.

∞∞∞

There was no reason to delay the inevitable. I stood in my kitchen, making faces at the pantry door. Resigned to what I was about to do, my fingers flexed as I considered how it worked. What did Sebastian say? I only needed to want him to come to me.

I snorted.

Straightening my shoulders, I concentrated on clearly forming the words inside my head: *Sebastian, I want you to come to me.*

Nothing happened.

"I know he's making this difficult." Glaring at the pantry door, I placed both of my hands over the center of my chest. "Come on, Sebastian. You can't resist me."

Nothing.

"Such an asshole." I glowered at the door. Even before becoming a demon, he was willful and delighted in being unpredictable. One minute he'd be moody; the next would find him trying to pull a smile from me. I winced. He was often playful – something I missed. And he could be thoughtful when it suited him. Unbidden, a memory resurfaced. On a hot late summer day, after finishing my last client reading at *Coffee Cove*, a hand holding a vanilla iced coffee appeared around the half-open door. The hand wiggled the plastic cup at me. I'd laughed, opening the door to find the Basha-version of Sebastian waiting. I reached for the cold drink, and he leaned in and kissed me instead. Then he let me have the coffee.

"And that's how it works," Sebastian announced as he stepped through my pantry door. "You wanted me to come to you, and here I am." A smugness settled across his lips. "This could cause some awkward situations in the future, though. Try to resist thinking about me when you're sleeping with someone else."

Chapter 14

The first step in the plan was to door travel from my house into the Fringe's old compound in the Walled Zone. I was dreading the entire journey, but I was most certainly not looking forward to standing on the quad where I'd lost Templeton and a mauled Rabbit had almost died in my arms.

"What if the devil dogs are there?" I asked matter-of-factly. I put up a brave front, but I was terrified. I'd had a working Crimson Stone in my hand when I faced off with the monsters before.

"They won't be. They were only there the last time because the Darkness sent them after me." Sebastian pulled a face. "But I get it. I don't like dealing with them either."

*Dealing with them...*I shook my head. He and I had different ways of putting it.

"And the sixth door will be open?" I pressed on.

"You're positive?"

"If it's not when we get there, the Darkness will open it as soon as he senses you," Sebastian asserted with a dismissive hand wave. He tilted his head back, the can of strawberry *Toro* he'd brought with him at his lips.

"And then we...What? Door travel into a free fall? Uh-uh. I'm not seeing how I'll survive the entry into the Below. You wouldn't have lived the first time if you hadn't been found." *And turned into a demon*, I finished inside my head.

"I'll hold onto you," he assured me as he tossed the empty can into the garbage bin. "I'll land on the ground in the Below and gently set the precious Light on her delicate feet."

"You joking isn't helping," I told him.

"I want you alive and well as much as you want to stay alive and well."

It was my turn to make a face.

"Think what you want, but you dying doesn't help me out. I need you to come to the Below of your free will and being alive is a part of that." Sebastian turned serious, dipping his head and making sure I met his gaze. "I promise I won't let anything hurt you, Lucie. Ever."

I didn't acknowledge his pledge. "Once we're in

the Below, then what? We head straight to the door to the Above?"

"We can try, but I'm thinking we'll have to deal with the Darkness first," he said. "I don't know what that'll entail, but you have free will. You can leave the Below at any time. He knows this. But some things we'll have to play by ear."

"Great."

"You taking the book?" Sebastian motioned toward the tome sitting on the counter.

"No, I'm not taking anything connected to magic into the Below." I spun in a slow circle, appraising my kitchen. I guessed everything was as it should be.

"Except yourself."

I lifted a shoulder. "Okay, I guess I'm as ready as I'm ever going to be." Resigned to following through on the insane mission, I pulled open a kitchen drawer and retrieved a sealed envelope. On it, I'd written Flame's name. I set it on the counter.

"What's that?" Sebastian raised an eyebrow.

"For my next of kin," I mumbled. "Alright, let's get going."

An orange tabby cat curved around the edge of the open pantry door.

Oh, for fuck's sake.

Flame sauntered by Sebastian with his tail held high before turning and eyeballing him.

"You have a cat?"

"Yeah. I have a cat." My eyes narrowed at Flame. "A cat who stayed out all night and should probably take a nap upstairs." I tried to nudge him along with the toe of my sneaker.

The feline instead meowed loudly, holding the note of the second syllable until it became a growl. I caught a barely perceptible headshake before he pivoted and dashed through the doorway into the hall. Seconds later, he padded back into the kitchen in all his bare-assed, 20-year-old glory. He'd shifted rapidly in the hallway – and returned with the usual accompanying half-erection. I slapped my forehead.

"What the fuck?" Sebastian barked, automatically advancing toward the younger man.

I cut him off, stepping in front of him, my hands lifted. "It's fine! This is Marcus. He's my... my...*boarder*."

Sebastian shook his head. "No."

"Yes." I frowned over my shoulder at Flame.

"Great timing, *Marcus*."

"Why is your 'boarder' naked?" Sebastian scanned Flame's body.

Flame put his fists on his hips.

I cringed. "He's naked because…that's how he came."

Sebastian continued to size up Flame, trying to make what he saw before him fit into the life he assumed I had. "That's 'how he came'? I don't get it."

I wasn't about to tell Sebastian that Flame was a shapeshifter. "You don't need to get it, but we need to go."

"Who's your friend, Lucie?" Flame chose that moment to join the conversation. He lifted his chin and sniffed the air. "I smell demon…No, no wait. That's the smell of an aging wannabe's cologne."

I realized up to then I'd been getting more Sebastian than demon, but that was about to change.

"You little fucker," he swore, shoving me aside.

"Sebastian, I compel you to be still," I blurted out as I stumbled, catching myself on the counter. "No moving until I give you permission."

Immediately, Sebastian stopped advancing on Flame. He wasn't completely frozen, but he wasn't going anywhere. His head rolled on his neck, his eyes seeking me. He slung a vicious look my way. His arms appeared heavy at his sides as he tried to lift them. His hands formed loose fists as he worked to resist the compulsion I leveled against him. When he opened his mouth to speak, I stepped forward and covered it with my hand. My palm pressed firmly over his lips, and Sebastian's eyes grew wide.

"Don't say a word. If you say anything when I remove my hand, I'll gag you. I'm not kidding – I have duct tape in a kitchen drawer." I watched the red haze drift inside his irises. He hesitated, then blinked slowly. Cautiously, I dropped my hand.

"Nicely done, Luscious," Flame grinned.

"And you! Living room – *now*." I snatched Flame by the arm, dragging him out of the kitchen, away from Sebastian, and into the modest room at the front of the house. I shut the door behind us.

"What's going on?" Flame searched my face. "You're not going through with it, are you? You're not going with this demon to whatever hole he lives in, are you?"

Reluctantly, I nodded.

"Lucie, you can't go." His face contorted in worry. He made as if to reach for me. "You'll be at his mercy. I don't like the vibe I'm getting off him."

I waved a hand in the general direction of my kitchen and tried to make light of the situation. "I'll be okay. As you can see, I do have a couple of tricks up my sleeve."

"You promised you were going to tell me if you were leaving," he said. His pupils fluctuated between round and slitted. I noted his fingertips kept wiggling. I realized he was struggling not to shift.

"I left a note on the counter letting you know," I told him softly. "I know, not the greatest, but you weren't here. We have to go now."

"When will you be back?" His pupils stopped their wild wavering between human and feline.

I threaded my fingers through my hair. "Hopefully by tomorrow at the latest."

His youthful face scrunched up. "You have no idea, do you?"

"Not a clue," I admitted. "But I'm going to do everything in my power to get back here – with

Templeton in tow."

"And the demon?"

"I can handle him." There was no reason to tell Flame that Sebastian was the least of my worries – and that was saying something.

Flame pulled me into a hug, pinning my arms at my sides. "Please be safe."

I flinched, my hands curling away from him so I didn't touch any private body parts by accident. "Don't worry. I'll be fine."

He squeezed me again.

"Flame?"

"Yeah?"

"Put some clothes on."

∞∞∞

I sent Flame upstairs to dress and returned to a seething Sebastian in the kitchen. I released him from his position after gaining a promise he'd not instigate anything or react if he thought he was being baited by Flame…er, Marcus.

I knew his promise was a lie, but what could I do? Frankly, I didn't trust either of them to keep their mouths shut.

Flame returned wearing only a pair of

basketball shorts. Sebastian ran his angry eyes up and down the shirtless younger man before making a derisive sound in the back of his throat.

I handed the envelope to Flame. "You can read this after I go. Take care of my house, okay?" I attempted to lessen the awkwardness filling the room with a weak joke. "And behave yourself. Don't set anything on fire."

"Don't turn your back on him." Flame gave a slow cat-like blink. "It's not just his cologne that smells off." The two glowered at one another from under their brows – one fair and one dark. They were similar in build, I realized then, with Sebastian having a couple of additional inches in height over Flame.

"Why don't you run along, junior?" Sebastian's upper lip peeled back. "Go work on your tan."

"Alright then." I zipped up the front of my sweatshirt. "We're all done with this conversation. Sebastian, I've only ever door traveled once. How do you want to do this?"

Sebastian continued to look daggers at Flame but held his hand out to me. "Come here."

Gritting my teeth, I put my hand in his. His long fingers covered mine, and he pulled me to him, my back to his chest. Sebastian finally ripped his stare away from Flame, wrapping his left arm around me and tucking me securely against him. I made a deliberate effort to relax as he angled our bodies toward the pantry door.

His lips touched my temple, then they were at my ear. "Think about the compound. Pick any warehouse. They're all the same." His hot breath tickled my cheek as he reached for the doorknob. "Keep picturing it, Lucie. I won't let you go."

The muscles in Sebastian's arm tensed, and I felt his door travel energy rising around us – so different from Templeton's. I pushed thoughts of my lost knight out of my mind.

Instead, I envisioned the compound, the warehouses, the quad. Against the wall of my brain, I saw the door I'd stepped through right before seeing the devil dog with Rabbit hanging from his jaws.

I shivered as Sebastian's energy ignited the air around us and we were swept out of my kitchen, through my pantry door, and into the Walled Zone.

∞∞∞

When I door traveled with Templeton, we'd fled the Congress of Empire Witches building with my feet skimming the floor but stepped into his penthouse as if we were casually walking into a room. He'd guided me from one place to the other with ease.

Sebastian's door travel energy was as powerful as Templeton's, but his felt reckless, chaotic, and furious. Although our travel time was short, I felt as though my bones had rattled hard enough to shed the tendons gripping them. I clung to Sebastian's arm, and he cradled me snugly into his chest. When we arrived, I fell forward, but Sebastian's grip kept me on my feet. I pulled away from him as soon as I regained my balance. The whole experience was jarring.

"You okay?" He peered down his straight nose. "You seem rattled."

"I'm fine," I lied. "I'm not used to door travel."

"You take it for granted when you're a Salesman," he said. "I can't imagine not doing it. It's second nature."

I paused. "What's it feel like to you?"

"Walking from one room to another." Sebastian looked past me.

I nodded, my eyes scanning the large square in the middle of the compound. We were surrounded by four large warehouses. The property, once owned by Ivanov Transport and used by the Fringe, was empty. It had been a battleground I'd fought on more than once.

Sebastian gestured forward. "Let's go."

The snow covering the ground on that wretched day in February was long gone. Grass grew weakly in clumps. Even nature knew nothing good ever happened here.

The place was still and quiet. Not even a tittering bird or a newly awakened bee disturbed the air. We approached the spot where the fifth and sixth doors had appeared. Nothing indicated the presence of either.

"Do we need to do something?" I kept my voice low.

"We wait." Sebastian kicked at the loose stone peppering the ground. A second later, he swept his hand low and scooped up a small rock. Effortlessly, he whipped it at one of the warehouse windows running under the edge of the building's roof. It shattered a pane.

"Do you have to do that?" I shook my head at him.

"I have no more love for this place than you do," he answered. "I couldn't give a shit if it fell to the ground."

Annoyed and anxious knowing that we had to wait for the Darkness to open the sixth door, I snapped at him. "You know what, Sebastian? If you weren't such an evil, selfish bastard, none of us would've faced the hell that's played out on this quad more than once."

He picked up another stone, rocketing it toward a different warehouse. I heard it smash through another window. The demon-enhanced Sebastian didn't even exert himself as he vandalized the buildings around us.

Another rock was gathered, and he speared me with a black look. "That night last year, you and your friends were trespassing. My men defended the compound –"

"And lost," I interrupted.

The rock soared through the air. Another crash. "Can't always win every battle in a war, Lucie."

"A war? You think you've been at war?"

"Yup. The Empire made its choices, and we were the result. Then they had to contend with us. Consequences." He lifted his arm to throw yet another stone.

"Stop it." I crossed to him, reaching up and trying to block the next throw.

Sebastian stretched, the stone lifted high above my head and out of reach. He laughed.

I stepped backward. No, I wouldn't let him bait me. "I compel you to put the stone down."

It fell from his hand. "You don't get it, do you?"

"Enlighten me," I challenged. My temper was controlled, but the fire under my skin reacted to his cockiness.

"The Empire is the enemy. The Salesman Court is the enemy. Those defending the Empire are the enemy."

I poked the inside of my cheek with my tongue. "Defending the Empire? People like Emily Swift?"

He sneered. "Enemy."

I wiped a hand across my mouth. Maybe we shouldn't be having this conversation now. "Do you regret attacking her?"

Sebastian's gaze never wavered from mine. He shook his head slowly.

No.

My eyes dropped to the ground. I honestly didn't expect a different answer, but I was...I was disappointed.

"She's the enemy," Sebastian said bluntly. "She stepped into this war, Lucie. She chose her side."

I lifted my gaze. "Emily's my friend. I love her very much. And I'm on *her* side."

He nodded. "Well, she's the lucky one then." Sebastian motioned to a strip of bare dirt. "I can hear him. He's coming."

I was grateful for the diversion – even though it meant I was getting ever closer to facing the Darkness. "I can't hear anything."

"You wouldn't be able to," he replied. "Step back. The door's about to open."

Under our feet, the ground shuddered, and then I *could* hear a rumbling noise coming from deep inside the earth. We retreated as blades of grass quivered and larger stones pushed up through the packed soil. A ripple persisted under our feet, and I backtracked even farther, fearful of the ground splitting open and dragging me below the surface. The swells crashed into one another, coughing up more jagged rocks as a deep gap formed. As the ground ripped open, the entrance to the sixth door was created – the passage leading into the Below.

The odor escaping the hole was vile, and I turned away, gagging.

"Ah, the fresh stench of rotting meat," Sebastian grumbled.

"Does it stink like that down there?" I'd forgotten about the smell. *How could I forget such foul air?*

"Pretty much, but less intense." He brushed off my concern. "Or maybe I got used to it."

"Great," I pulled my sweatshirt sleeve down over my hand and held it over my nose.

"Give it a minute," he said.

"And the Darkness?"

"Knows you're coming."

I examined the gash in the ground. It was easily about 12 feet long. The width left plenty of room for diving in and plunging to one's own death. I blanched.

"Let's go." Sebastian closed the distance between us. Before I could register what was happening, he bent and wrapped his arms around my thighs, rising quickly as I tumbled over his right shoulder.

"What the hell are you doing?" I huffed. The position I was in – and the rancid air – made me dizzy.

"Taking you into the Below," he said. "I need to land on my feet, and this is the best way to carry you."

"I doubt that," I blustered, fighting him as I hung upside down. "Let me go!"

Sebastian had the gall to slap my backside with his hand. "Settle down. I'm getting ready to door travel." He lifted his hand, and I sensed the energy beginning to swirl around us.

"Sebastian," I argued, squirming. "This isn't funny. Put me down – now!"

"You're right. It isn't funny at all." His right arm remained wrapped around my upper thighs in a vice-like grip. "Hold on, wayward witch."

Before I could get another word out, he jumped, and our bodies stabbed the center of the gaping hole, plummeting into the bleak world below. I yelped once but had no time to make any other noise. Within seconds, we hit the bottom, Sebastian's feet slamming into the ground, his body absorbing most of the impact as he crouched. His left hand steadied us as it slapped against the ground. The landing jarred me as well – the pressure of his shoulder driving into my lower stomach forced the wind out of me. As he straightened and set my feet on the ground, I tumbled backward, coughing. Every time I sucked in a gasp of air, the horrible stink of the Below invaded my nostrils, and I gagged. Sebastian snagged my arm as I fell and yanked me back up. I shook off his grasp.

I continued to wheeze and heave, my hands on my knees. Sebastian stood with his hands on his hips.

Wiping the wetness from my eyes, I grimaced. The stench was awful. I doubted I'd get used to it. Still bent over, I spit. The smell of decay was already coating my tongue. This did not bode well.

Straightening my shoulders, I absorbed our grim surroundings, first looking up toward the sixth door we'd traveled through. Nothing but a pitch-black sky overhead. The gap in the ground Sebastian leapt into was nowhere to be found in the space above us. Was it too far away? Had it already sealed itself shut?

The space we landed in was murky, not completely black as I expected. And yet, I could see no source of light. Around us, I could make out shapes – maybe some bare trees, maybe broken...*things*. I squinted, stepping toward one object. It was an old tricycle, its front wheel and triangle seat missing. Beyond the tricycle, I saw a crib on its side, one end crushed in. The mattress had been pulled out and shredded.

"Is it like a landfill here?" I shook my head, wondering at the dim landscape.

"Some parts," he answered. He spread his arms wide, a grotesque smile splitting his face. "Welcome to the Below. Don't bother to wipe your feet."

"Yeah, thanks." I pushed my hands into the pockets of my sweatshirt and shivered. I recognized the feeling crawling up my back. Something was watching us. The Darkness? Other creatures? "Which way do we go?"

Sebastian motioned off to the right. "This way. My house is on the way to the door with the symbol. It's kind of a hike from here. I'm hoping the case of water I left at my family's estate in the Empire will be here."

Puzzled, I shook my head. "I'm not following. What do you mean?"

Sebastian gave me a sideways glance. "Oh, you'll see." Before I could stop him, he grabbed my wrist. "Come on. Let's get going before anything takes an interest in you."

"Besides the Darkness?" I asked, allowing him to lead me.

"Yeah."

"Like what?"

"You don't want to know." He pulled me along. "Now shut up. Let's get out of the open and into someplace more hidden."

∞∞∞

The Below's landscape, what I could make out as I hurried after Sebastian, was bleak. The ground was often uneven, and I slowed several times to step more deliberately. Now was not the time to sprain an ankle. Sebastian was impatient, but I didn't blame him. He knew what was beyond the shadows surrounding us. His eyes took on a reddish cast overall, and they flitted back and forth over the desolate space in front of us.

It was as if Mother Nature abandoned the Below. Although I could make out the shapes of trees along the way, they were leafless and long dead. We never got a break from the rotten air, and when we navigated through a wet patch, the pools of water smelled of filth. The urge to gag returned, but I didn't dare stop. A buzzing sound stirring behind us drove me forward. Ahead I could make out an imposing mass. We seemed to be heading for the base of a towering cliff.

"Sebastian," I whispered. "What is that?"

"There's a path cutting through the rock. It's the fastest way to go," he answered.

"Is it safe?" Claustrophobia flirted with my senses in troubling anticipation.

"Nothing down here is safe," Sebastian replied as we stopped. "Here."

We stood in front of the narrow passage disappearing into the clammy stone. Visions of getting stuck in the cramped space – or worse, being trapped with *something* other than Sebastian assaulted my imagination. I stepped back. "I don't think I can do this."

Sebastian was quiet as he contemplated the opening. When he spoke, he was uncharacteristically honest. "I know, Lucie. I hate confined spaces like this, too. I'm terrified of the walls crumbling over me or getting caught up on something and trapped. I'm scared of not being able to get out." He turned to me. "But you need to understand that going this way is hundreds of times easier and less dangerous than any other way we can go." He held out a hand. "You can hold onto me. I won't let you get lost."

I put my hand in his, feeling small and helpless in this dreadful world. "How much longer until we get to wherever it is we're going?"

"It's not far," he said. I trailed him as he stepped sideways into the unyielding space leading deeper between the giant rocks. "Time doesn't matter anyway. We might walk for days or five minutes. It'll feel the same either way."

His words did little to reassure me, and I had no choice but to follow. I could see nothing. Sebastian's hand held mine firmly, and I didn't intend to let go.

I practiced my breathing as we snaked through the gloomy passageway, the smell of the Below not making it easy. The tiny path we traversed through the stone served as my meditation space. The breathwork helped me to feel more calm. When I was strong enough to share a slip of my peace with Sebastian, I sent a wisp of gentle energy into his hand. I heard his gasp. Several beats later, he gave my hand a squeeze.

More time passed. Sebastian was right. I

realized I had no concept of how long we'd been scooting along the passage. Did we come to the Below a day ago? Was it longer? I blinked several times, my vision mostly limited to Sebastian's shoulder in front of me. No, it wasn't that long. Maybe a minute? That's it. We'd only been inside the enclosed space for a minute. Maybe two.

"Fucking hell," Sebastian exhaled from the inkiness in front of me.

"What? What's wrong?" My efforts to remain calm flew out the window. I dug my fingernails into his hand and pulled on him to stop.

Then I heard it.

Light, light, light!

"Don't freak out, Lucie," Sebastian warned.

"What do you mean, don't freak out?" I hissed, trying to pull away as the sound grew louder.

Light, light, light!

He refused to loosen his grip. "The thin shadows are coming – it's okay. They don't hurt you. They just crawl on you. It's going to be alright. Come on, keep coming with me."

Light, light, light!

"They crawl on you?" I shrieked. All bets were off. I threw myself in the opposite direction, repeatedly trying to jerk my hand from

Sebastian's. I had to go back! I had to go back! I had to get away from these –

Light! Light! Light!

The sound was above my head, and I cast my eyes upward in time to see the constricting walls above and around us teeming with skinny, foot-long shadows. I panicked, trying to tear myself free before the wiggling, writhing... *Silverfish!* They were giant, black silverfish!

"Knock it off!" Sebastian yelled as he dragged me through the nightmare tunnel. "They won't hurt you!"

"Silverfish!" I freaked out, spasming in the confined space, banging my body back and forth between the rock walls. "No!"

"Shadows – they're only shadows," Sebastian gritted out. His fingers held me in a death grip. "Calm down."

LIGHT! LIGHT! LIGHT!

I screamed as the frightening shadows converged around me, my head whipping around and slapping into the stone. My cheek scraped over the rough surface as Sebastian ripped me through the last leg of the suffocating space. The thin shadows coasted off the walls, crawling up my arms and slithering over my stomach and chest. They spun up my legs and slipped under my hair across the back of my neck.

LIGHT! LIGHT! LIGHT!

The sound was deafening. I opened my mouth to beg Sebastian to help me get away from these desperate creatures, but the sparks snapping around me halted my voice.

Pop! Pop! Pop!

As each thin shadow crawled over me, the sensation erupted off my body in a bright pop. I'd turned into a human pack of firecrackers.

Abruptly, I was wrenched through the exit leading out of the enormous rocks and into an open space. We'd reached the other side. Sebastian took one look at me and backed away, his lips parted, his eyes blazing red and wide.

A multitude of thin shadows raced toward me from all directions.

LIGHT! LIGHT! LIGHT!

Pop! Pop! Pop!

The sparks flew off my body, and the air lit up around us in a mini fireworks display. Sebastian's horrified face revealed itself in the light swirling around me as each thin shadow burst into the air and disappeared. Not one thin shadow wavered in its course.

They targeted me.

They raced toward me and onto me.

Seconds later, they ignited and shot off my body.

I felt nothing. There was no pain.

Mystified, I watched the writhing mass glide over my body. A sense of peace descended over me as the sound dwindled.

Light, light, light.

The number of thin shadows seemed to lessen. The remaining ones approached more slowly before meeting their fate in a surge of light.

Sebastian moved to my side, his expression as confused as mine. "Are you okay?"

"I...I am. I'm fine," I stammered.

Light, light, light. The crying grew faint.

When all but one thin shadow had disappeared, I squatted and held out my hand. It drew near, then pulled away. I sensed its hesitation but also its desire to come closer. I lowered my hand to the ground, palm up.

The thin shadow approached, then gingerly slid against my skin. I stood as it traveled up my arm, spiraling on my shoulder and crossing my chest. It paused over my heart, and I heard its hushed cry inside my brain: *light, light, light.*

A moment later, it flashed and ceased to exist.

"What are you doing to them?" Sebastian asked, peering into the empty space surrounding us.

I pondered the feeling resting inside me, recognizing it with a dumbfounded revelation.

"I'm setting them free."

Chapter 15

"Well," Sebastian ran a hand over his forehead and into his hair, where he gripped a fistful. He held onto his sooty locks and tugged on them. "That was unexpected."

"The book of fairy tales talks about the thin shadows," I said. "I don't remember everything off hand, but the thin shadows come into the Below – they're not from here. I think the bird in the book tells the little girl he brings them into the Below."

Sebastian dropped his hand and squeezed his eyes shut. "I can't remember the details. So much I can't remember when I'm here." He reopened his eyes and motioned to an unknown destination. "Come on. My house is on the other side of this hill."

"Your house? You mean where you've been staying?" I followed as we picked our way over the scorched ground. "Was there a fire?"

"Huh?" His head swung back and forth as he scanned the ground. "Maybe. I don't remember."

Warily, I watched Sebastian as he wandered ahead of me, his pace less hurried. "Are you doing alright?"

"Yeah, why?" Sebastian suddenly stopped, glaring into the gloom. "I see you."

I shuffled to his side, trying to determine what he thought he saw. The thin shadows were upsetting, yes, but I had a feeling they were the least of my worries in the Below. "What do you see?"

"Him." Sebastian pointed.

"I don't see anything," I replied.

"In the shadows. He's always watching me." Sebastian flipped off the invisible being.

I could see nothing. "Are you sure?"

"He's right fucking there, Lucie!" Sebastian grabbed me by the arm, shaking me and pointing. "He's right there, watching so he can run back to the Darkness and tell him what I'm doing. He's always spying on me," he snapped.

I worked my fingertips under Sebastian's fingers and pried his hand off my arm. "Okay, I believe you. But let's keep going. Let's not stop.

Will we be safer in your home?"

"No." Sebastian continued to peer into the obscurity of the shadows ebbing and flowing around us. His chest rose and fell in shallow pants.

I reached up and pulled his chin, forcing him to look at me. "We need to go."

It took a moment for him to come back from wherever he'd been in his brain, but eventually, he nodded. "Yeah, let's get out of here." He resumed his dogged march uphill, and I followed him once more, the procession seeming to take much longer than it should. Sebastian was right. The Below warped your sense of time.

We crested the hill, and I gaped at the wretched structure greeting us on the other side. I'd never seen Sebastian's family estate to the north of Matar, but I had an idea of what to expect. The home in front of me was exactly what I would picture – except this was the horror movie version. The three-story, once-white brick house, with its broad staircase leading up to the set of double doors on the front of the expansive building, was in ruins. The clay-tiled roof was caved in at the right, and masses of black vines crawled up the sides, covering many arched windows. Still others bore smashed panes, and pieces of ripped drapery hung limply along the jagged glass. One banister leading up a flight of stairs to the raised front porch had crumbled. A chimney had collapsed on the ground in a ragged mass of bricks stretching out in a road to nowhere. Something bulky, with a furry appearance, scurried into a hole leading under the dilapidated building. Dead clumps of grass surrounded the place.

"Home sweet home," Sebastian mocked. "It's even better on the inside." He took off down the worn path leading to the terrible version of his childhood home. "We need to go in through the back. I don't trust the porch on the front. I think something's living underneath it."

We circled to the left, picking our way through the detritus populating the yard. Broken dishes, smashed furniture, and a selection of rusted yard equipment dotted the terrain. I gaped at the baby grand piano that had crashed into the ground with such force a full third of it was submerged. Above us, a mammoth hole in the wall indicated where the piano once lived. Did someone – or something – throw it through the wall? How did this happen?

"Coming?" Sebastian stood at the corner of the house.

I nodded, catching up with him as he turned. He ducked inside another hole in the wall. He reached a hand out to me, guiding me over the bricks as he helped me into the ruined estate. We had entered what was once the kitchen, but the destroyed appliances proved it was no longer in use.

"Watch your step," Sebastian directed. The rooms were gloomy, but again, there was enough ambient...*light*? No, there was no light, but the space around us could only be described as dim. We weren't blindly fumbling through in complete blackness.

When we reached what appeared to be a dining room, Sebastian crossed to a lone standing chair with a case of water sitting on it. It was covered with dust. He ripped the plastic covering on one end and pulled out a bottle, handing it to me. He took one for himself, turning the cap and smelling it. "I think it's still okay to drink."

I opened my bottle and sniffed. There was

nothing to dissuade me from taking a careful sip. "Mine is fine."

"It'll eventually turn brackish," he said. "I can go without drinking because of the demon part of me, but you won't be able to go without water for long. Drink up while you can."

"There won't be any clean water?" I asked.

Sebastian nodded somberly. "No food either. These will go bad." He showed me the boxes of energy bars he'd also transferred from his cabin to his family's abandoned home in the Empire. "Eat one now."

"What about you?" I took one of the fruit-flavored bars he offered. I wasn't a fan, but he was right. I should eat while I could.

"I don't eat down here," he answered.

"Don't you get hungry?" Even as I ate, the energy bar seemed to become stale. I crammed another bite into my mouth.

"I'm always starving," he said. "And thirsty. That's the worst. There've been times when I'd kill for a *Toro*."

I stopped chewing at his choice of words. "Yeah, I bet." I crumpled the wrapper and looked for a wastebasket. Finding none, I pushed the wrapper back into the box of energy bars. "What do we do now?"

Sebastian seemed lost for a moment. I touched his arm, and he jolted. "We can go to the door to the Above. Did you get enough water?"

"I did." I screwed the cap back on the bottle but assumed it wouldn't be fresh for long because it had been opened. I picked up a second unopened one and shoved it into my sweatshirt pocket. "I'm ready."

Sebastian reached for me as I turned. "Lucie, if something happens, or you get lost, or we get separated, this is where you come back to, you got it? Here. You can go upstairs and hide – but be careful of the hallway on the second floor. Boards are missing. You'll find a room where I try to sleep sometimes. It's got a lock on the inside."

A part of me wondered what creature in the Below I could lock out of a room. But instead of arguing or asking, I simply nodded. "Got it."

He wiped a hand over his face. "Alright, let's do it."

We wound our way back through the rooms and climbed out the hole in the kitchen into the dreary backyard. A path traced along the edge of an overgrown, then dead, garden. I kept on his heels as we crept silently away from the replica of his family's confiscated home.

Occasionally, I'd hear a soft bleating of 'light, light, light,' and a thin shadow would appear, racing over the ground toward me. Some hurried up my leg, shooting off in a spark moments after they touched me. Still others vacillated along my footsteps before gaining the courage to climb my body and cease to be. I marveled over how quickly this didn't seem to trouble me. It felt natural in this unnatural place.

Sebastian slowed and motioned into the thickening fog. "It's up here." He leaned in, his mouth at my ear. "But we're not alone. The Dancing Shadow is back. He says the Darkness isn't going to wait any longer. He wants me to bring you to him. If I don't, he'll send the dogs."

"He'll send the dogs?" My fear returned. "Wait, I have free will and –"

"You do," he cut me off. "But I don't." Sebastian lowered his head, turning it to the side while he rubbed the back of his neck with a hand. "The last time they chased me for hours, days, weeks – I don't know how long. I can't do it again. Look, you're the Light. You have free will, but I don't.

And I need to bring you to him if I'm going to fulfill my end of the deal and be freed."

"Are you going to make me go to him, Sebastian?" I asked softly.

He lifted his head. "No. I won't. But I'm going to ask you to come with me. If you say no, I'll still take you to the door to the Above. I'll fight off whatever I need to keep away from you while you do your...I don't know. This light thing, your witch thing. When the door is opened, the light from the Above will pour in, and everything dark here will cease to exist. And you'll be able to get into the Above."

"Will you cease to exist?" My mouth felt dry again, and I resisted the urge to open the bottle of water I carried with me.

He offered a half-hearted smirk, a shade of the smartass I knew so well showing through. "I guess. I'm part of the dark stuff here, aren't I?"

I studied his tired face before turning and calling into the fog drifting around us. "Show yourself."

The Dancing Shadow came forward immediately. It was as tall as Sebastian, and although it didn't have a clear shape like a person, I could imagine a lost figure occupying the space the shadow now filled. It towered over me but didn't seem to be a menacing creature. I reached toward it, and it backed away.

"You won't let me touch you?" I called after it.

"He doesn't want you to," Sebastian said, watching it glide through the fog. "I think he's... Well, maybe not afraid of you, but he's wary. He saw what you did to the thin shadows."

"I don't think I did a bad thing," I told him.

"I don't think you did either," he agreed, returning his attention to me. "What do you want to do, Lucie?"

"I want you to take me to the Darkness."

∞∞∞

As Sebastian led me through the fog, I realized the Dancing Shadow traveled beside us. He was always a step beyond my vision, but I could sense him. Sebastian claimed the being spoke to him inside his head, and I had no reason to doubt him. I'd kept my magic under wraps in the Below, afraid to draw attention to myself, but I let a tendril of my energy push out to learn more about this strange entity willing to serve as a messenger for the Darkness.

Focusing on the Dancing Shadow, I evaluated the impressions I could draw from it much like I would with a Tarot client. If it had emotions, what was there?

Curiosity. Fascination. Regret. Hopefulness.

Amazed, my head turned in the direction I believed the being inhabited. These were all human feelings I sensed.

No. Stop.

The connection I tried to establish ended unexpectedly.

"What did you do to him?" Sebastian's voice startled me.

"What do you mean?" I took an extra step, walking beside him instead of trailing him.

"The Dancing Shadow. He told me to tell you to stop."

"I was only trying to get a sense of what he was, that's all."

"He's a pain in the ass." Sebastian stopped. "I think we're here."

"Is he the only one of his kind?" Wherever 'here' was looked exactly like where we were when we first entered the fog – and where we were every step thereafter.

"No, there are others. But he's always up my

ass." Sebastian put his hands on his hips, his head swinging left, then right. "Yeah, this is the place."

"Maybe he's assigned to you?"

"Maybe. You see anything?"

"I see nothing. This is your world, not mine. Everything looks the same in the fog." I licked my lips. "Are we lost?"

"Nothing is lost in the Below, Lucie," a deep baritone voice reverberated in the air around us. "Nothing is lost because I know where everything is at all times. Nothing in the Below is hidden from me, and nothing in the Below lacks my consideration. Nothing in the Below is without the Darkness."

"Sebastian?" I hesitated as the hair on the back of my neck rose. "I think we've found the place."

The air around us seemed less dense, and I sensed a persistent scrutiny. Sebastian had already turned, his face registering surprise. Pivoting, I met the source of the disembodied voice.

A man stood about 15 feet away, his posture relaxed, his thumbs hooked in the front pockets of his jeans. His blazer was pushed open because of his stance, and his ruby red dress shirt was unbuttoned at the top. His right eyebrow was lifted in a recognizable arch, and his ash brown hair was brushed back in perfect waves. Caramel-colored eyes roamed over me with a familiarity that gave me the chills. His sensual mouth turned up at the corners under his aquiline nose.

"Guillaume?" Confusion mixed with my instant anxiety as I faced my former teacher.

"He's not who you think he is," Sebastian said. "He takes on the likenesses of people you know."

"Oh, I get it." I regarded the man warily. "Guillaume is an interesting choice."

The Darkness laughed, shaking a finger at me – mimicking one of my cruel teacher's mannerisms. "I was curious as to your reaction. I was right. Beneath your hatred for him, you are *deathly* afraid you'll be subjected to his tutelage again. I hear the fear banging inside your ribcage."

"I *was* afraid of him," I challenged. "I've dealt with much worse since I returned from France."

"Care to tell your teacher about the psychological pain you've experienced?" The Darkness moved, and as he did, around the three of us – four if you counted the Dancing

Shadow standing in the inkiest corner he could find – a room appeared. It was tastefully furnished, with a cozy fireplace casting a warm glow over us. Astounded, I recognized it immediately. It was Guillaume's study.

"I asked you a question, Lucie," the Darkness in Guillaume's form broke into my thoughts.

"You're not Guillaume, and I'm not playing this game with you."

"I've found others are more receptive to my presence if I adapt the likenesses of those they've known," he countered. "Although, some might recognize me as Asmodeus."

Asmodeus? I tried to pull the name from my general knowledge of demons. I came up empty. "I do not know who you are."

"I am King of the Below, a demon of lust. As Asmoday, another one of my names, my seal is pressed in gold. Despite the beliefs of some, I cannot be conjured unwillingly. My true faces are seldom revealed."

"And those would be?"

"The bull, the ram, and the face of mankind. I govern 72 legions of lesser beings including the one this demon –" he gestured to Sebastian, "– belongs to here in the Below."

I reached for Sebastian, grabbing his hand and pulling him to my side. "Sebastian fulfilled his end of the deal he made with you. He led the Light into the Below, *to the Darkness*, and I came willingly. Now, because the Light also has free will, I will be leaving. And so will Sebastian."

"Of course," the Darkness answered. "You are free to leave whenever you choose. The Light may come and go from the Below as it pleases. As for Sebastian, he has, as you pointed out, fulfilled his end of the agreement. Although, I wonder how the other man will feel about it?"

"Here we go," Sebastian mumbled.

I glanced at him before questioning the Darkness. "What do you mean? What are you talking about?"

"This man." Even more smoothly than the shapeshifter now living in my home, Asmodeus dropped Guillaume's visage and morphed into another man. His broader body narrowed slightly and lengthened. His jeans switched to a pair of perfectly tailored black trousers, and the button-down shirt turned to a crisp white. Faded blue eyes stabbed me through the heart. His gaze flicked once to Sebastian, then returned to me.

"Templeton?" Forgetting myself, I let go of Sebastian's hand and took a step forward.

"No, Lucie," Sebastian whispered. "It's still Asmodeus."

The fake Templeton reached out. "Wouldn't you like to touch him one more time? To have him hold you again – even just for a few minutes? I can do that for you, Lucie. I can make the hurting stop for a while. Would you like that?"

My hand landed on my chest, covering my heart. I drank in every inch of the man standing only steps away. He turned blurry when my eyes grew wet. "I..."

No. Find. Lost. A new voice entered my brain from the corner where the Dancing Shadow waited.

"Lucie, come to me." The Darkness still held out his hand. As I watched, his eyes turned bluer.

My hands balled into fists as I forced my arms to my sides. "You have no idea who that man is – *what* he is. You are nothing compared to him."

The imitation of Templeton sniffed disdainfully, then morphed again. This time the man standing in front of me was unrecognizable. He was tall, with jet-black hair graying at the temples. His sharp eyes were a deep brown set over a thin nose, his skin olive toned. The arrogant expression on his face switched to disgust as he looked me up and down. "Really, Sebastian? This is what you've been mooning over like a lost puppy? You defile our family name by fooling around with a witch? You disgust me."

I glared at the man. Who was this?

Sebastian lowered his head. "You're not real."

"Oh, I'm very real," the man continued. "And you continue to be such a fucking disappointment. The best part of you slid down your mother's leg."

Horrified, I watched as Sebastian ripped out a fistful of his hair. "You're not real! I don't have to listen to you!"

"Even now, you stand there *spineless* in front of this...This *witch*." He spit out the word. "You're nothing but weak. That's what you are – and that's what she sees. She feels nothing for you but pity. You thought she'd love you, didn't you? But no one wants you, Sebastian. You're worth nothing. Pathetic. Unlovable. You –"

"Enough!" I shouted, raising my hand and

pressing out an intense blast of the fire that surfaced right below my skin with his words. The white-hot energy coursed over Asmodeus, and he stepped backward. My power might not be the equivalent of the Darkness, but I could make him shut up.

Laughter rumbled up from his chest as Asmodeus morphed through several other likenesses: Rabbit, Loren, and the Congress elder, Timothy Richardson. The image of Timothy wavered, then disappeared. His first choice, Guillaume, returned.

"The Light has matured in her power, but not in her judgment," Asmodeus-as-Guillaume chastised me. "You waste your fire on defending a 'lowly' demon?"

"He's not a full demon," I spat back. "And we're through here. I'm going to use that free-will option now." I reached for Sebastian. "Come on, you did what you agreed to do. We're getting out of here." *If we can get that freakin' door to the Above open.*

But he stepped away from my grasp and refused to look at me.

"Sebastian," the Darkness began. "You can leave – of course. But would you deny your Lucie access to knowledge that would help her build back her witchline for good?"

My head snapped toward the fake Guillaume. He smiled benevolently at the silent man at my side.

Sebastian raised his head. "Witchline? What do you mean?"

"Witches have a special vein of power running through them," the Darkness replied. In a blink, he was standing before Sebastian, one hand on the demon's slumped shoulder. "Lucie's witchline is sick but there are books here that can help her learn how to heal it – without doing very bad things to herself in the process." With those words, we stood in a vast library. He gave Sebastian's shoulder a gentle shake. "You want to help her, don't you? You want to do something good for her for once, right? Not be so selfish?"

I'd wandered forward, my eyes devouring the rows of shelves teeming with books. I reached out to touch a spine, expecting the illusion to disappear on contact. It didn't. But Asmodeus' words stopped me. I remembered what I'd said to Sebastian in my backyard after conjuring him: *You have the opportunity to do something good for me. How about breaking the mold and being selfless for once in your damned life?*

"No." I dropped my hand. "We're leaving."

Asmodeus ignored me. "Show her you care about her. Give her some time to find the answers she needs, then you both can leave."

Sebastian nodded, his hand sliding down his face and pulling at his cheek. "Yeah, I want to do something right."

"Go. Go home, and when Lucie's done reading, she'll come to you. I'll make sure she gets there safely. Then maybe, who knows?" The phony Guillaume lifted a palm. "She might love you a little for what you've made possible for her."

This was not good. "Sebastian, I want you to listen carefully to me. You're being manipulated by the Darkness. Don't leave. Don't go anywhere alone –"

"No, it's okay, Lucie," he interrupted. "I can do this for you." He pursed his lips. "Fuck it. A couple more hours won't make a difference. I've made it this far in the Below. What? I've been here…a week? It's nothing."

A week? *Shit*. "Sebastian, don't –"

"I'd start with this one." The Darkness stood beside me. In his hand, he held a book. He turned the spine so I could read it. The title trailed down the worn red cloth.

The Bellerose Witchline.

I looked up into my former teacher's face. "There are books here on all the witchlines, Lucie. You can save them all," he explained gently. "You're my best student. Only you can do this. Only you can change the fate of all the witchlines."

My shaking hands took the offering. Guillaume – *no, Asmodeus* – was not to be trusted, but the book in my hands was real. I sought out Sebastian, but he was gone. "Where'd he go?" My voice sounded lonely in the silent library.

"The Dancing Shadow took him back home. You'll see him later." He guided me to a table by the elbow and pulled out a chair.

I sat down, staring at the book of promise in my hand. "I can see him later?"

"He's not going anywhere," Guillaume replied, stroking my hair. He bent and spoke softly into my ear. "Take your time. You have much to learn."

Chapter 16

The origin of witchlines is almost as murky as the history of the Empire itself. Young witchlines are still centuries old. The Bellerose Witchline is viewed as young with only 600-700 years – something I knew when the Darkness handed me the book. And yet, I read for hours, reading histories I'd never encountered before and understanding languages I'd never learned. Information poured into my brain in a continuous flow. I couldn't get enough.

A new witchline is formed when two equally matched witches come together, and their offspring carries a new vein of power that's singularly their own. Then, as the child grows and has children, the witchline is carried through the genes and is considered established. That's when it's added to the Book of Witchlines, kept under spelled lock and key in the Congress of Empire Witches. The name of the witchline is generally a hybrid of the first set of parents' surnames, but it might instead be named after the name of the child carrying the first trace of the new witchline.

A new witchline is easy to determine – parent and child do not draw from the same vein of power, which is the first clue. The child further proves the case when they have a child of their own, and they are the only ones drawing power from the same witchline.

And yet, new witchlines are rare. It had been at least five centuries since the last was named. Typically, the biological parent with the stronger witchline will determine the witchline of the child. It's tradition for witches to use the name of their witchline as their surname. My father carried the stronger witchline – which I inherited – and thus, my surname became Bellerose. However, my Aunt Lettie told me my mother was the more powerful witch. I had no real memories of her. She died when I was young, as did my father.

All these witchline facts were common knowledge, but the books I now opened told broader stories – tales of witches weaving in and out of the Empire, producing offspring with other magical beings much earlier than purported by the Congress. An unofficial but dangerous thread of 'witch purity' slithered through the body governing witches. I avoided those who were proponents of such vile dogma.

Each book in this enchanted library was in pristine condition regardless of age. I didn't worry about harming the old pages as I read for hours. I stuffed my brain with more information than I could hold and became greedy. But Guillaume – *that is, Asmodeus, the Darkness himself* – had laid the trap well. He knew about the thinning witchlines we all suffered from. He understood that the driving force behind every decision I'd made for over two decades was to make possible the strengthening of mine as it atrophied. And he knew I'd strengthened it under the mean hands of Guillaume.

He'd told Sebastian I could learn of a better way of healing my witchline without doing 'very bad things' to myself. Asmodeus knew I'd been feeding my witchline with pain. His casual words to Sebastian were for my ears.

I wouldn't have to call upon pain anymore.

And I could learn how to fix all the witchlines. This was the information I'd sought. On a shelf in this immense library sat all the answers – I only needed to find them. I didn't rely on luck, using my magic to choose each new book, letting tendrils guide me up and down aisles as I followed the trail of how the witchlines became at risk, how they became sick. With each fresh passage under my fingertips, I felt closer to the answer. I piled book after book on the table until I found two obscure lines of text in an untitled book buried deep in an archive with tomes counting two millennia since they'd been penned.

"The seed of poison is planted at the root of all the witchlines. Its dormancy ends when the heel of the enemy crushes it deep into the ground." I read the translation aloud. This reference to a poisonous seed was nowhere to be found in the history I'd learned. I turned back and forth through the pages leading up to and following these lines, but nothing seemed to fit. It was as though the writer picked a random page and wrote the words without thought to context.

And yet, the energy racing under my skin grew excited. It latched onto the secret and urged me to look for more. *More!* I had to learn who planted the seed and who owned the heel pushing it underground so it would grow. Who was the enemy? The answer was in *this* library. The Below contained all the information I'd ever need.

I licked parched lips as I searched the stacks. I ignored the bottle of water in my sweatshirt pocket. Drinking would only interrupt my quest, and nothing else was as important as finding this answer. I could save all our witchlines. I was Guillaume's best student, after all. Oh, he was proud of me when he handed me the first book – I could see the approval on his face. Maybe he'd bring me more? Yes. Maybe he'd help me. Guillaume wanted the witchlines strengthened as badly as I did. I'd do whatever he wanted if it meant we'd find the answer.

Movement in a dreary corner drew my attention, and the Dancing Shadow from earlier hovered. I ignored it, intent on my search.

Stop. Lost. Hurt. You. Help.

The words leaked into my brain. I didn't have time for this. "Go away," I told it.

Stop. Lost. You. Need. Help.

"Who needs help?" I asked absently as my fingertips touched a weathered spine, and the jolt of pleasure told me I'd found another book to guide me to the answers.

Demon. Help. Demon.

"I don't help demons," I answered. "I help witches."

You. Help. Demon.

My eyes flitted to the Dancing Shadow. The words in my head were no longer sounds but images. Sebastian recoiled, screaming in terror, blood covering his arms, his face, his bare chest. Something grabbed him from behind, dragging him backward. The next flash was Templeton, his limp body suspended in mid-air, held aloft by a vicious Beam of Light.

Lost. Templeton. Lost.

"He's lost, but he's still alive." The faint echo of my voice pulled me back to the present.

Hurt. Demon. Help.

I left the book on the shelf and turned. We appeared to be the only ones in the library. I rubbed my bottom lip while my gaze drifted back and forth. Sebastian. How long had he been gone? He was so upset.

So thirsty. I dug the water bottle out of my sweatshirt pocket and unscrewed the cap. Mindful of Sebastian's warning from earlier, I sniffed at it. Nothing. I took a sip, then a longer drink. I drained the bottle, the water soothing my throat as I gulped it down.

The Dancing Shadow followed me as I returned to the table where I'd sat reading for... hours? Days? Maybe it had only been minutes. I set the empty plastic bottle down on the table. Right. That was it. Besides, Sebastian lived in the Below. He could handle himself. And he deserved to be here, right?

Hurt. Blood. Demon.

The Dancing Shadow wouldn't let me be. Another vision of Sebastian assaulted my brain – but this time, I could hear him.

"Light!" Sebastian screeched as he tried to contort his body into a ball on the ground, covering his head with his arms. "Light! Light!"

"What's going on?" I asked the Dancing Shadow. It grew agitated, wavering back and forth in the inkiness at the end of one of the stacks.

"Lucie!" Sebastian howled again.

I backed away from the table. I'd been here too

long. Something wasn't right. "How do I get out of here?"

Follow.

The Dancing Shadow dipped farther into the gloomy stacks. I hurried after him, breaking into a run as the shelves and the library walls fell away. We raced through the blackening air, the fog growing steadily around us. I stumbled as I followed but kept my eyes on the Dancing Shadow. Its legs moved faster than mine, and I could make out its arms pumping up and down as it ran.

It had legs. It had arms. It felt...*human*.

There. Demon. Hurt. There.

The fog parted enough to reveal more of the burnt landscape under our feet. Putrid air assaulted my lungs as I sprinted forward. I spun in a circle and wheezed, looking for Sebastian. "Where is he? I don't see him!"

Ground. Demon. Hurt.

I heard growling. Images of devil dogs mauling Sebastian filled my thoughts, and I cried out before slapping my hand over my mouth. My heart hammered my breastbone as I remembered Sebastian's words: *A heartbeat stands out in the Below.*

"Sebastian?"

Here. Demon. Here.

I followed the snuffling sounds and found him, covered in blood and cowering against the side of a rusted-out truck bed. The tire was flat, and he clung to the wheel. His shirt was gone, and the muscles in his back and shoulders twitched as though electric shocks danced through him.

I approached him warily. "Sebastian?"

More growling interspersed with sounds of sniveling.

I crouched down, my hand hovering over his bloody arm. There was no part of him not slick with sticky crimson. "Where are you hurt?" I asked softly.

He wouldn't answer but pressed his face against the rubber of the tire, whimpering.

I had to get him back to the house – to the ruined building he called home. We'd have to be safer there than out here. Reluctantly, my hand covered his, cringing at the wet warmth coating it. I tugged at him. "Come with me. We need to get out of here."

Sebastian hissed at me, his eyes a solid red. I jolted when he suddenly choked – the wet sound warning me before his lips pulled back. Blood gushed from his mouth, over his chin, and down his neck.

"Listen to me," I ordered, holding my ground when all I wanted to do was run. "I compel you to do what I say. You're bound to *me*."

Lost in whatever torment raged inside his brain, Sebastian's eyes rolled back, and he gurgled as he spoke through a mouthful of blood. "Don't make me do it anymore."

Even though I gagged when my hand slid through the slippery blood, I grasped his upper arm and stood, pulling him to his feet by his grisly limb.

His hands dripped with blood, but I couldn't see any wounds on his chest or arms.

But something horrific had happened to him. I wrapped my hand around his wrist as he tried to rip himself away, his strength growing. He'd pop my shoulder from its socket if he kept it up.

"Sebastian, I'll raise my fire until your hand melts into mine if you don't stop it. Even your demon self won't be able to handle this heat." I zapped him with a miniature taste of what I'd unleash.

His head swung toward me, and he bared his

teeth, snarling. "You won't hurt me."

"I will if you don't come with me." I turned, yanking on him again and forcing him to follow.

Hurry. More. The Dancing Shadow pressed words into my head again. *Demons. Searching.*

"Oh, I'm sure *that's* not a bad thing," I grumbled.

"You hear him?" Sebastian asked through clenched teeth. He tried to twist out of my grasp, but I held onto him for all I was worth. I kept us stumbling forward, dividing his attention. Eventually, he stopped fighting me.

"Yes, and I don't like the sound of more demons. You're about all I can handle."

If time had any meaning in the Below, I would've thought we broke a land speed record when returning to the hellhole Sebastian called home. We circled to the back of the monstrous house, climbing over more trash to get to the hole in the wall. In the distance, I heard something reminiscent of thunder.

Panting, we stood in the relative silence of the house, listening for any unwanted sounds coming from the other rooms. Several creaking noises simply seemed as though the building was settling. I watched as Sebastian rubbed his bloody hands through his hair, causing it to stick up in perverse spikes. Bile rushed up into my throat, and I forcefully swallowed the burning taste. "The blood. Is any of it yours?"

Sebastian's haunted eyes raised to mine. He shook his head no.

"Okay," I replied warily. Blood had poured from his mouth – I didn't want to know how it couldn't be his. "Are you hurt anywhere?"

He shrugged.

This was getting us nowhere. "You have to help me out here. You need to cooperate. Tell me, is there a working shower in this house? Someplace where we can get you cleaned up?"

"Second floor. Back stairs."

"Show me." I followed as he reluctantly turned, sliding a rickety pocket door into the wall and revealing a narrow staircase leading from the kitchen to the second floor. Sebastian ducked into the passage, leaving bloody handprints on the wooden railing as we climbed the stairs. The door at the top had been ripped off its hinges, and we stepped over it.

"Watch your step," he warned as we edged around several large holes in the hallway floor. His voice was returning to normal – the gravelly inflections lessening.

Exposed floorboards under our feet groaned, and he paused, hovering by an open doorway. It was dingy, but I could make out the shape of a toilet and a shower. The separate bathtub was missing – the floor had given out under it. Propping his bloody body against the door jamb, Sebastian unbuttoned the top of his pants. His fingers fumbled at the zipper before he stopped, suddenly uncomfortable. "Two doors down on the right. There's a bedroom there." His voice trailed off when he turned his head away. "Don't look at me."

"It's okay, I'll go. Can I rinse my hands off first?" I held up my blood-coated hands.

"Yeah, use the shower. The sink doesn't work." Sebastian straightened so I could slide past. I maneuvered around the hole left in the floor by the missing tub. When I turned on the shower, an odor of sulfur overpowered me. Gagging yet again, I hurriedly rubbed my hands together under the hard water, driving the dried sludge off my fingers and onto the slanted floor of the shower. The blood drying on my sweatshirt was a different story. I doubted I'd find a place to wash it, but I couldn't wear it like this. I couldn't wait to get it off.

"Alright," I said, shaking the water from my hands, then wiping them on the front of my jeans. "It's all yours."

Sebastian waited until I exited the bathroom before disappearing inside. I heard his zipper lower and the rustle of clothing. I kept walking, choosing the second door he directed me to, and found myself in one of the bedrooms.

It was like the rest of the house, with broken furniture, a cracked mirror, ripped-up carpet, and shredded filthy curtains hanging in the window. I unzipped my hoodie and draped it over the back of a three-legged chair. A dresser missing its drawers was shoved into a corner, a line of tarnished trophies on top. They were athletic awards for basketball, the nameplates indicating they belonged to Sebastian St. Michel. Despite the nightmare surrounding us, I cracked a wry smile. High school. A smaller trophy sat behind the others, and I picked it up, examining the little plaque on the front. I shook my head. It was another one of Sebastian's, but this one was for a debate team victory. Sebastian was listed as captain. "Wonders never cease," I exhaled, returning the trophy to its position on the dresser before crossing to the window. I couldn't make out much on the other side of the glass because of the unending night, but I imagined creatures were wandering the shadows beyond what I could see. Speaking of... The Dancing Shadow was no longer with me. Perhaps it stayed with Sebastian?

I pushed the destroyed curtain aside, perching on the edge of the windowsill. I had to get us out of this world. Asmodeus most likely knew I'd fled the library and its tempting secrets. He had to know I was with Sebastian in this pile of rubble he called home. There was nothing I could do about any of that, though. We would still go for the door to the Above. We would still open it. I would still bring Templeton home.

I wiped away a solitary tear. He'd been gone for so long. Three months for certain, but how long had I been in the Below? It had only added more lost time to his life.

Stop it! I reprimanded myself. Focus on what you're going to do. Focus on the good that's coming. Focus on Templeton...You *will* find him. And now you have new information about the witchlines!

Frowning, I tried to remember exactly what I'd

read in the library. The origin of the witchlines. There was a seed. Was that it? A seed? Yes, it was planted, and that's how the witchlines grew. Right? No, that's not it. *Dammit!* I wiped my hand across my forehead. I needed to remember. There was a seed, and there was...*an enemy*. This enemy of witches did something to us? Why couldn't I remember? Maybe I was too tired to think about it.

The door behind me opened, the sound of the lock causing me to turn and face the room. Sebastian entered, holding a stained towel around his waist with one hand. Two bottles of water dangled from the other. He padded over to the dresser and set them by the trophies.

"You went downstairs wrapped in a towel?" I tried to ease us back into a normal conversation. Ugh. The thought of anything in this world as being normal was bone-shaking.

He lifted his head and blinked once, pausing before answering. "No, I went naked."

I chuckled, turning my head and allowing him some privacy to find a pair of jeans in a pile of clothes spilling from a doorless wardrobe.

When he was done pulling on his pants, I gazed at the shirtless demon standing barefoot in this lonely space we shared. He was a beaten man.

"Are you feeling better?" I asked softly.

"I'm numb," he replied. "It's the only way to deal with it after...After it happens."

Sebastian spoke again before I could ask him what he meant. "Lucie, I want to be with you tonight." He stepped forward, and I was troubled by the age marking his face.

Maybe we'd been in the Below for years.

"Just, please. Give me something good to hold onto. I need you. I need to have something good." His voice wavered, and I watched as his body tensed angrily at his weakness. Both hands twitched at his sides, and he formed two fists. His fingers relaxed when he let out a shaky breath.

I shook my head. "No, Sebastian. That's not going to happen. But there *is* something I want to do for you." Standing, I surveyed the depressing room, spotting a trunk pushed against a wall. Ignoring the scurrying I heard when I grasped the handle, I dragged the furniture to the middle of the room.

"What are you doing?" Exasperation crawled into his tone.

"Sit." I pointed toward the trunk.

Sebastian looked at the bed, lifting his hand and motioning. "I can sit there."

"Don't argue with me." Again, I pointed at the trunk.

After another dramatic sigh, he obeyed. He plonked down on the lid, his legs spread and his shoulders rounded. With his forearms resting above his knees, he peered up at me from under his brow, his eyes still shimmering occasionally with red. He watched me through a mass of long lashes. "Now what?"

I stepped closer. "I want to try something with you." Standing directly in front of him, I placed my hands on the sides of his face. I tilted his head back, lifting his chin as he straightened. I saw the curiosity ripple over his features as we stared at each other, conflicting emotions filling my heart. I gave my head a shake before sliding my hands higher and skimming my thumbs over his eyelids, closing them. I ran my fingers over his forehead and into his hair, tangling them in his damp black locks, pausing only when my thumbs passed over two small hard nubs under his skin.

"Horns," he muttered but kept his eyes closed.

"The longer I'm down here, the more likely they are to grow. I could feel them throbbing under my skin while you were gone...When you were in the library."

I bit the corner of my lip, nodding. "I see." I kept running my hands over his scalp, my fingernails drawing lazy circles as I concentrated on what I hoped to be able to do.

A ghost of a smile appeared on Sebastian's lips, and a slip of the man I knew surfaced. "I think this might be counterproductive to how you want me to behave. This feels really good." To emphasize his point, he pressed the insides of his thighs against my legs for a beat, drawing a long breath in through his nose.

I didn't acknowledge his comment or his touch but saw when the tension left his face. I watched him closely, allowing the good feelings that flowed through me last fall when we were together to resurface. I'd come to understand why I glowed when I was with him. I was happy in our chaos, in his unpredictability, his spontaneity. We had fun together, and I laughed a lot. I let myself tumble back into those perfect moments when I was beginning to fall in love with him. I thought of nothing else but how my heart raced when I knew I was going to see him, how the powerful current coursing through him attracted the fire living under my skin. Anything bad that happened after our last night making love, I pushed far from my thoughts. I didn't allow myself to think about how he'd lied to me, how he'd shattered my fragile heart, how he'd hurt people I loved.

Instead, I submerged myself in feelings of the wild abandon I experienced when we were together. How crazy good he made me feel before I learned who he was and about the violence he was responsible for – by his own hands and through others.

My eyelids drifted shut as these emotions washed over me. I let my head drop back, shivering as gooseflesh rose on my skin. I surrendered, allowing my unapologetic love to grow inside me, the sensation coasting over my body, chasing away the chills I'd given myself. In the deepest corner of my heart, I turned the clock back to find what I needed – what I needed to tap into for this broken man before me. I pushed more of my power into the love I once gave to him and realized I felt…*whole*. I wanted to help Sebastian experience the same. I opened the secret locked space in my heart and let my love pour out of me. It swelled in my chest and spread warmth throughout my body. It cascaded over my shoulders and down my arms. The energy pulsed through my hands and into Sebastian. Every single piece of hair on my body vibrated, my long tresses floating upward off my shoulders.

"Lucie," Sebastian whispered. "You're glowing for me."

I didn't answer but allowed him to pull me close. The side of his face pressed against the center of my chest while his arms wrapped around my waist. He held onto me as if I were his last lifeline – and maybe I was. I felt him shudder as the coiled fear and anger living inside his body unwound. He sagged heavily against me.

I stroked his head, opening my eyes. I watched as the illumination flowing from my skin surrounded Sebastian, caressing his aching body. It was sinking into him, filling him with light. I rested my cheek on the top of his head. "Sebastian," I said softly, my fingers still tenderly combing through his hair at the nape of his neck. "You don't have to stay in the Below anymore. I'm giving you permission to leave this horrible world behind."

His head lifted. "But the Darkness didn't say I could –"

"I don't care what Asmodeus did or didn't do," I told him. "He said you met your end of the deal. I have free will, and I am not leaving you here. You're bound to me now. *Me*. Not him."

Sebastian weighed my words. "Maybe."

"No maybes." The glow was fading from my skin, and the remaining light finished settling into his. The room grew dim again. Sebastian looked better, but a heavy tiredness crept up on me. The bones inside my body felt like bars of lead.

"Listen," Sebastian began, his hands still on my hips. He pushed me back a step before letting them fall away and standing. "You need to sleep before we go anywhere or do anything. Take the bed. I rarely sleep anymore – I'll keep watch. Nothing will disturb you." Before I could argue, he lifted a hand and continued. "Seriously, it's a demon thing. I hardly ever sleep. And since I guess I'm still part demon..." His bitter voice trailed off, and he ran a hand over the top of his head. He paused where horns waited to sprout, his fingertips rubbing at the bumps. "Drink some of the bottled water before it gets any worse. I think the case might be turning brackish."

Nodding, I retrieved a bottle of water from the top of the dresser. I sipped at it, wrinkling my nose at the taste. He was right; it *was* turning. I wouldn't be able to stay much longer in the Below without water.

Sebastian stood alongside the bed, pulling the blankets back. "Huh. It worked."

"What worked?" I watched him run his hand over the sheet.

"I put clean sheets on the bed when I was back at the estate."

"You did? Why? *Oh*." I pressed my lips together.

He looked up. "You know what people forget about me, Lucie?"

"What is that?" I grimaced as the second drink of water passed through my lips.

"I'm an optimist." One corner of his mouth lifted.

I shook my head at him, crossing the room and kicking my sneakers off. I'd sleep in my clothes, but the shoes needed to go. Sebastian held the blankets as I climbed past him into the sagging bed, a strange sense of calm coming over me.

Sebastian pulled the covers up to my shoulder as I turned onto my side, his body another dark shadow in the dingy room. I couldn't see his face, but I knew for the next few hours I could trust him to let me rest undisturbed.

When I woke, we'd face the sealed door into the Above.

Then I'd leave the Below behind.

And no matter what, I was taking Sebastian with me.

Chapter 17

He really did spend the night watching over everything while I slept – but truth be told, I slept so hard in such a dreamless state I wouldn't have known if he'd snuck out. I awoke to a vague arrival of the new 'day' with Sebastian leaning against the wall by the window, staring at the nothingness on the other side. He'd put on a tee shirt and pulled on a pair of unlaced boots. I raised up on one elbow, sliding my gaze down his profile. In a different time and place, I would've called him back to bed. I wondered what he spent the 'night' thinking about, but I also suspected I didn't want to know.

He turned as I sat up and slipped out from under the covers. I swung my legs over the side of the bed.

"Sleep okay?" Sebastian pushed off the wall,

leaving the window behind.

"Yeah, I guess I did." I stretched my arms upward. "I was exhausted. I'm still tired, but I feel better."

"Good." He brought me the last bottle of water, unscrewing the cap. "Give it a try."

I took a cautious taste before shaking my head and handing it back. "Nope. I don't dare drink it."

He screwed the top back on. "I figured."

I dropped to the floor, bending and grabbing my red sneakers. Sitting on the trunk where Sebastian had sat earlier, I pulled on my shoes and tied them. "We can't wait any longer."

Sebastian hunkered down and laced up his boots. "Now or never."

"You think you should wear boots? Do you have sneakers in case we have to run?" I picked up my sweatshirt, eyeballing the dried blood on the sleeves. Yuck. This I would leave behind in the Below.

"You ever try to kick something in sneakers?" Sebastian asked. He rose, the boots adding an inch or two to his height.

"Um, a ball?" Puzzled, I lifted a palm.

Sebastian laughed, the tip of his tongue doing

a fast swipe across his front teeth. "Alright, wayward witch. Let's go." He slung an arm around my neck and walked me to the door.

I pushed him off, scowling. "I suppose I prefer this Sebastian to the other one, but knock it off."

"Whatever you say," he held the door. "Watch your step."

We made our way cautiously around the dangerous holes in the hallway floor and down the narrow stairs leading into the destroyed kitchen. Nothing had changed since the night before, but now I noted splashes of blood dotting the floor and along the wall. I still didn't know what had happened to Sebastian before I found him, and as much as I didn't want to, I wondered if I should ask. If there was something out there waiting to pick up where it left off, he needed to tell me.

"Hey, what happened to you last night?" I motioned beyond the crumbling walls. "Out there."

His cheek twitched. "Leave it, Lucie."

"Honestly, I'm only asking because I want to know if we're going to be facing the same thing as we head to the door to the Above."

Sebastian passed a hand across his mouth. "It's

nothing for you to worry about. It's stuff I deal with as a demon. Stuff the other ones make me suffer through when they find me. I told you before, you don't want to know about it, why they do it to me. It'll make you...You already hate me."

"You've met your end of the bargain, Sebastian. You're not subject to any further... *demon participation activities*," I finished, turning away. "And I don't hate you. I hate the things you've done. There's a difference."

I could feel his eyes on me as I climbed through the hole in the wall, passing from the depressing kitchen into the unhappy backyard.

He followed, his head swinging right and left as he considered what might be hiding deeper in the shadows around his wretched estate house. "Do you need to go to the bathroom?"

I thought about it. "That's weird. I don't think I do." I paused again. When was the last time I'd gone? Definitely before we door traveled out of my home and into the Walled Zone. Even if that was only a handful of hours ago, it was plausible I'd have to pee by now. This was strange. I didn't even have the urge to go after he put the thought into my head.

Sebastian watched the silent questions flit across my face with a smug smile. "Trust me, you need to go. You only think you don't have to. If you don't, you'll piss yourself the first time you travel back into the Empire."

"What are you talking about?" I shot him a dirty look. What new game was he playing at?

"I did it the first time the Darkness sent me back through the sixth door. I was down here for months and never even thought about going. Then I hit the quad in the middle of the compound, and my dick exploded."

I pulled a face. "Nice visual, Sebastian. You're telling me now that when we leave the Below, I'm going to wet myself?"

"Probably not when we travel into the Above – but I'm not positive since I've never traveled from the Below to there. But yeah, if you don't go now, by the time you make it back to the Between..." Sebastian grabbed his crotch and pressed his knees together.

"Don't be childish," I admonished.

"Go now and you'll be less likely to have an issue. No guarantees, but hey, I thought I'd warn you. You feel like taking the chance, have at it. Not my problem," he finished.

"There's a working bathroom in there?" Incredulous, I pointed to the house. "One that's not disgusting and likely to give me some ghastly disease?"

"There's a big bathroom." He grinned, pointing in the opposite direction at the not-so-great outdoors. "Bust a squat, Lucie."

My mouth dropped open when he told me where to go...To *literally* go. I snapped it shut. "Are you messing with me? Because I've got to tell you, your timing sucks."

"You might need this." He tossed me an old dishcloth he'd fished out from one of the kitchen drawers piled on the floor. It was dusty but otherwise relatively clean. "Want me to stand guard?"

"No!" I could not believe I was doing this, but I spun around and picked my way through the junk in the backyard, heading behind the hulking shadow of yet another dead tree. I dropped my jeans to my ankles and heard him call for me to hurry up. Asshole.

"It's just like camping," I grumbled, relieving myself. "Camping in a fucking endless nightmare." I finished the necessary business and flung the used rag into the shadowy surroundings. *Gah!* When I got back home, I would shower for a week.

I returned to the house to find Sebastian zipping up his fly. "Ready?"

"Beyond ready. Let's get out of this miserable hellhole."

∞∞∞

Sebastian led me along a narrow path through the pervasive fog. How he could ever tell where we were going, I'd never know. Maybe the longer you were down here, the more everything made sense and the easier it was to find your way. The thought alarmed me.

As we traveled over the rocky ground, I pondered the square symbol Sebastian said we'd find on the door, with halves representing the light and the dark. If it was, in fact, how he drew it for me the first time, wouldn't the door be open? Or at least ready to be opened?

"Some things you need to explain to me," I said. "The symbol on the door to the Above. You drew it as a square equally split by light and dark. But that's not how it looks now, is it?"

Sebastian ducked under a dead tree branch

hanging across the path. It was crawling with bugs. "Nope. But that's how it's got to be."

"It needs to be balanced, doesn't it?" I asked. "How did you know this?"

Sebastian motioned to the dead landscape we crossed. "This is what happens when there is too much darkness. Everything dies. Too much light, and everything here is destroyed. I personally wouldn't shed a tear if that happened."

"And if there is balance?"

"We'll be able to open the door."

"What does the symbol look like now?"

"You'll see." Sebastian watched as a dozen thin shadows slipped over the ground in front of us, targeting me. They zipped up my legs and zapped off into sparks. He shrank back. "Do you still feel that?"

I lifted a shoulder. "Somewhat. It doesn't bother me anymore."

"I think I know what they are," he said, surveying the path in front of us.

"What?"

"Dead people. People who chose to come to the Below."

"Why would they ever choose –"

"Because they thought they deserved it."

∞∞∞

Sebastian's observation was intriguing, but there was no way of confirming it. I tried to recall what I could from *Empire Tales for Children*. What did the book of fairy tales say about the thin shadows? They led the young girl to a sealed door in the Below. Well, we were on our way to such a door. What else? The colorful bird. It said it took the thin shadows into the Below because they weren't ready for the light... Or something like that.

We hiked for hours – or maybe it was only minutes? Sometimes I could hear echoes leaking out of the lightless surroundings as if many people – *or things* – were whispering, and those low notes were bouncing off cavernous walls. It was unnerving. Asmodeus surely knew what we intended. The fact we hadn't been confronted yet told me we were heading in the direction where he waited. Yes, the Darkness was waiting for us. But would he be waiting alone?

"Where is the Dancing Shadow?" I asked

Sebastian.

"I don't know. I haven't seen it."

"Is that strange?"

Sebastian turned his head side to side, lifting his chin and stretching his neck. "I guess."

"I think it's human – the shadow." I pictured it running in front of me. "Yesterday, I could almost make out arms and legs."

"Shadow man," Sebastian replied. "Who knows?"

"He brought me to you." I hesitated. "That library, the one Asmodeus showed me. I could have stayed there for days on end studying. I wasn't even thinking of leaving. You were gone, and honestly..." My voice trailed off.

"You weren't thinking about me either, were you?" Sebastian asked. His cheek twitched. "No big deal."

"It was a very big deal," I corrected him. "For both of us. But the Dancing Shadow kept hounding me. I realized you were gone and that I'd almost forgotten why I'd come to the Below in the first place. The Dancing Shadow told me you were hurt and told me to follow." I tried to remember the details. "He mentioned Templeton, too."

"Are you sure it wasn't wishful thinking?" Sebastian's tone developed an edge. "How would a stupid shadow down here know anything about pencil dick?"

I gritted my teeth at the insult but decided to save my energy for bigger battles. "I don't know. But he referenced Templeton as being lost."

Sebastian slowed, peering into the black fog. I noticed it was lightening to the left of us. "I still wouldn't trust it. It's a spy for the Darkness." He reached for me, his hand wrapping around my upper arm. He pulled me to his side. "Up ahead. You can almost make out the door from here."

I didn't see what Sebastian supposedly could, but I trailed him as he cut to the left. I searched for shapes in the fog, looking for anything other than us. As we neared the metal door, the fog thinned. Here the blackness of the Below was not as dense. Perhaps it was because on the other side of this portal into the Above, there was true light.

We stood before the massive door. Taller than Sebastian and 5 feet wide, it was missing a handle. Sebastian brushed his hands over the top half of the door, wiping away dirt and soot. I uncovered the square symbol. As I'd imagined, the light and dark parts of the square were not evenly balanced. The bottom half, the solid portion, was greater than the upper lighter part of the symbol. The line separating them was positioned at an incline, stretching diagonally upward from left to right.

"The dark here in the Below is greater than the light," I said, reaching up to touch the symbol.

"You have to make it even out," Sebastian said, rolling his shoulders. "Then I'll pull it open."

"I'm not sure how to do it." I traced the lines of the symbol, trying to get a feel for it. It was about 20 inches long and 20 inches high – not terribly big. I touched the line bifurcating the square, withdrawing when it quivered. The line moved upward, increasing the mass of dark in the lower half. Beside me, Sebastian snarled, his body tensing. I turned to see what set him off.

Within the fog, I saw a bulkier shape moving toward us. At first, I thought it was the Dancing Shadow returning, but as it stepped out of the fog, the colored air stretched, reaching into the open space where we stood. The inky air swirled as it solidified and took shape. Asmodeus, in his Guillaume form, appeared.

"Lucie," he shook his head. "I'm not surprised,

but I am disappointed. I believed your witchline meant more to you."

This was a trap, and I would not discuss my witchline with him. If I allowed him to continue, I'd be caught up in his temptations again. "I am the Light, Asmodeus, and I'm exercising my free will. I'm leaving the Below."

The demon king smiled, curving Guillaume's generous mouth. "As the Light, you may leave, of course. But that door will remain closed."

"I will be leaving through this door," I countered, my hand drifting behind me and making contact with the cool metal. The door vibrated. "I will be traveling into the Above."

"You would disobey your teacher?" Asmodeus sauntered Guillaume's body closer. "Maybe you seek correction. This body believes you enjoy feeling his punishment."

Sebastian stepped forward, his head lowering as he watched the Darkness draw near. "You're not touching her." His voice hit that gravelly deep demon register.

Asmodeus laughed, abruptly turning toward Sebastian. "Did you enjoy playing with your brothers? They had fun playing with you. They like making you choke on your depravity when you relive your crimes. Your suffering gives them such pleasure."

My skin crawled as Asmodeus spoke. I remembered the river of blood pouring from Sebastian's mouth when I found him cowering and hiding from the other demons.

A shiver rippled across Sebastian's shoulders, but he held his ground. "Lucie's leaving this fucking wasteland, and so am I. I kept my end of the deal we made. I owe you nothing."

Asmodeus shifted forms, and once again, the man I believed to be Sebastian's father stood sneering at us. "No one wants you, Sebastian. Not even this witch. You have nowhere to go. This is where you belong. You're worthless. A failure. I'm embarrassed to call you my son."

The last time this image appeared, the life drained out of Sebastian, and I expected the same. Before he could reply, I yanked on his arm and his eyes cut to me. "It's not your father. I compel you to listen to only me. Don't look at him."

The red floating in Sebastian's eyes increased, but he heard me. "I'm bound to you?"

"Only to me," I told him. "Now start pulling on the door. When I get the symbol balanced, I want you to rip it wide open – then we're going through."

"Fill the fucking thing with light, Lucie. It'll blow the door off the hinges. The light from the Above will destroy everything." Sebastian was already obeying me, ignoring Asmodeus' attempts to control him by wearing the elder St. Michel meat suit. He dug his fingers into the rock where the door to the Above was embedded. The stone crumbled like dust around his fingertips. His demon-sized strength hadn't left him.

"And then what?" Asmodeus' face morphed into Templeton's. "You believe a world should be without a measure of darkness? How would light be recognized without knowing the dark?"

A part of me understood, not because he was tricking me with Templeton's likeness, but because the duality did provide a degree of balance. "Why do you want me to stay here, Asmodeus? What's the point of all this?"

"Possession," he answered without hesitation. The fake Templeton frowned. "The Darkness should possess the Light. In the Below, there are many truths. The Darkness hides them, and the Light reveals them."

Continuing the conversation was risky, but I had to know. "And the Above? Do they not want – as you say – a measure of darkness?"

Asmodeus morphed again, this time wearing the face of Congress elder Timothy Richardson. "This body means little to you," he said. "But he takes a keen interest in the witch with the stronger witchline. The Light should be wary. For him, there is only one way."

His observation of Timothy tripped me up for a moment, but I pressed on. "I asked you a question about the Above." I caught a glimpse of a shadow within the fog at Asmodeus' right. The Dancing Shadow had returned. He hovered at the edge of the blackness.

Beasties. Dog. Coming.

Sebastian must've heard him, too, because a cry exploded from his mouth. "Light that symbol up, Lucie! What the fuck are you waiting for?"

Asmodeus – the Darkness, himself – was impassive. He contemplated my question. "The Above embraces only One Truth. They choose only Light." The bland blue eyes of Timothy's likeness turned beady. "And when there is only One Truth, all others cease to be, burning away into nothingness. It is a worse fate than the Below."

"You're going to have a hard time convincing me of that last bit," I replied. The Dancing Shadow kept pressing against his boundaries.

"The Between," Asmodeus continued as he transformed again, this time shocking me with the otherworldly beauty of Nisha. "Is all that separates the absolute from the chaos. The Between is the balance. It is up to the Between to maintain it."

"But you want the Light here, with you," I shook my head.

"Because of the many truths." The figure of Nisha drifted forward, her hand lifting. "I want to see the pretty demon's face. I want him to stay with me."

Sebastian looked over his shoulder, his eyes widening and flitting over Nisha. His fingers, still working the stone surrounding the door, froze. "Do I want to know what this shit is about?"

"You do not." I cut in between Sebastian and Asmodeus-as-Nisha. "Okay, enough of this. We're –"

"Does your demon know what you've done?"

purred Nisha.

Sebastian's hands pulled free from the rock. "What's she talking about? What *is* she?"

"Again, you don't want to know," I told him, my concern abandoning Nisha and turning instead toward the fog. "And I think we have bigger problems right now."

Sebastian saw the same stirring I'd spotted, hissing and launching himself forward as a fast-moving spindly-limbed creature leapt out of the murky air. A piercing screech shot from its hideous mouth.

Beasties! The Dancing Shadow put the word inside my head.

Sebastian caught the Beastie before it reached me, swinging it by the arm and bashing it into the ground repeatedly as it squealed. He slammed his boot against its head, crushing the creature's skull and silencing it. Blackened blood poured out over a slippery tongue. I stepped back, the nauseating sound of bone snapping under Sebastian's heel making me gag.

"Now would be a fucking good time to do some witch thing, Lucie!" Sebastian thundered as three more Beasties sprung forward, crossing the desolate space in seconds. Two jumped on the half-demon, biting his arms as they tried to wrestle him to the ground.

The third Beastie circled me, its gray skin sagging away from the ragged hole where its mouth should've been. Pointed teeth protruded haphazardly from its ulcerated gums. A slobbering tongue lolled out the side of its mouth, and its blind eyes spun in its head. The creature's long arms and legs were no bigger around than my own slender wrists, its knees and elbows swollen into large knots. The Beastie was hairless and naked. It smelled of feces.

Advancing, it shrieked. "Eat the Light!"

I'd retreated as far as I could, my back against the door to the Above. The Beastie howled as more of its gruesome brethren emerged from the shadows, followed by a hollow-eyed devil dog. Staring into the deep empty sockets of the monstrous animal paralyzed me – the fear surging uncontrolled through my body. Ghastly memories filled my brain as I pictured Rabbit's bloody, lifeless body dropping from the dog's jaws. In my ears, I heard Sebastian cry out to me once, then a second time.

"No!" I threw up my hand, using the terror

coursing through my body to stir the fire within me. I pressed out the hottest, purest shockwave I could call up, forcing it to roll over the creatures surrounding us. The Beastie closest to me lit up in a fit of flames, screeching and twisting as the blazing heat ripped through its dreadful body. It crashed into a line of Beasties slipping out of the shadows, spreading the fire. More wailing filled the air, followed by the foulest stench. The devil dog sprang forward, its tailless body clearing a writhing mass of burning Beasties. A low thunder resonated up from its throat as the dog's head lowered. Heavy drool hung from its mouth, stretching low, with whitish globules dangling inches from the ground. The monster stalked nearer as I worked up my fire a second time. The first blast, birthed by fear, depleted a lot of my energy.

I heard Sebastian's bone-shaking roar as he tackled the dog, and the two tumbled out of sight. The black fog swallowed them.

"Sebastian!" I shouted before my attention was suddenly – and silently – diverted. Standing quietly at my side was my late father. Pain stabbed through the middle of my chest, and I swayed on my feet. "Daddy?"

"Lucie, sweetie." He held out his arms. "I'm sorry you had to go through this. But it's over now. Come to me. Let's get you out of here to where it's safe."

He looked exactly as I remembered before he died. I pictured the last moments of his life, convulsing in the air as the cord around his neck strangled him.

Not. Real.

The Dancing Shadow was still nearby.

The fake version of my father took my hand. "They told me you were working on making our witchline strong again. Oh, Lucie. I am so proud of you!"

Daddy squeezed my hand and pulled me to him. He smelled like home. Like being safe. Like being loved no matter what. I rested my head against his shoulder, a sob bubbling up from my aching chest. I wanted my family back. I'd been alone for so long. He touched my hair, murmuring how everything would be okay, that by staying with him now, I would remember how to save the Bellerose Witchline. I could save *all* the witchlines. He would help me. I pulled back, rubbing at the snot leaking from my nose with the back of my hand.

The Dancing Shadow tried again.

Not. Real.

But he feels real. My father was dead. Maybe this *is* him...here in the Below.

"It pains me to watch my daughter cry," Daddy continued, reaching out to wipe a tear away.

Not. Real. Bad. No. Father.

The words from the Dancing Shadow bounced around urgently inside my brain.

But, my Daddy...

No.

I shuddered, helplessly heartbroken for all I'd lost. But the Dancing Shadow was right.

I pushed the imposter away, stumbling as I did. The heartache filled my chest, my sadness overflowing as I realized how much love I'd lost in my life – over and over and over. I couldn't do it anymore. I couldn't keep losing people I loved.

I couldn't keep losing love.

Sebastian told me if I filled the square symbol with light, it would fill the Below with 'Light from the Above.' This world would be destroyed. The light it was desperate for would tear through it, causing everything dwelling in this nightmare to cease to be.

And that was precisely what I was going to do.

Instead of calling upon my fire, instead of pulling up the burning energy living in my body, I dug down into the core of my being. I reached out to my witchline, searching for the brightest light of purity I could find in the powerful vein. I pulled it through my body, my skin first glowing, then slipping into a blinding white as the light streamed out of me in every direction. Around me, the remaining Beasties shrieked and convulsed as their bodies filled with this cleansing light and shattered into pieces. I watched as the line of purity stretched farther, driving additional shadows back. Sebastian was revealed, crawling across the ground toward me, one arm held awkwardly to his chest as he inched along. From deep within his body, the love-light I'd pushed into his skin earlier radiated outward in response, protecting him as the force barreled over him. Unlike the other creatures living in the Below, he was spared.

Asmodeus watched as I drove the Beasties and the devil dog away. His likeness had switched from my father to that of another man. This visage I didn't recognize, and the new face was drawn to the symbol now shining in the door to the Above. I peered up at it. The square was almost full of absolute white light. A thin sliver of the solid portion remained.

Sebastian managed to climb to his feet. The battle with the devil dog had left its vicious mark, but like a man possessed, nothing was stopping him from ripping the door open now. "More, Lucie! More light!"

No. Much. Light.

The Dancing Shadow struggled out of the fog, coasting in my direction across the expanse of light, its shape a dusky smudge in the air.

Too. Much.

I maintained my power, but my resolve wavered.

Light. Much. Hurt. Demon.

Hurt demon? What did he – *oh!* My eyes cut to Sebastian. He was gripping the edge of the door, pulling at it with all his might. Down his back, a crack in the protective glow surrounding his body appeared. The intensity of my witchline's power was cutting into him.

And once Sebastian wrenched the door open, the Light from Above would destroy all that existed in the Below – including him.

"I can't do that," I whispered, letting some of

the power charging the light streaming from my body wane. The light in the symbol also lessened.

Yes. Balance. Both. Need.

The Dancing Shadow was nearby. I tore my gaze from the symbol, seeking the strange being who spoke directly inside my head. With light forced upon it, I could see the being was definitely humanoid. I judged it to be a man and held my glowing hand out to him. "I can give you freedom."

It – *he* – avoided my touch.

Above. Balance. Go.

Asmodeus used the opportunity of my diverted attention to drive more darkness into the symbol. The line inside the square retreated, closing in on the center.

It was becoming balanced.

"It's almost there, Sebastian!" I cried. "Pull! Raise your door travel energy!"

Not. Needed.

The Dancing Shadow hovered near Sebastian.

Worried we'd lose our window of opportunity, I crowded Sebastian, my eyes glued to the symbol. Asmodeus was only a stone's throw away from us. I risked a glance. His appearance was still that of a man unknown to me. As the perfect balance of light and dark filled the square imprinted in the door to the Above, a deafening crack – much like a bolt of lightning striking – pierced the air. Sebastian yanked the door wide open, and a burning light poured out.

My demon spun and laughed, the sound echoing between the rays of light. "Fuck you, Asmodeus!"

I felt it – the balance was shifting in a great movement in the Below, in a wave far stronger than what I'd pressed out of my body. I might've pulled back my power, but with the blinding light from the Above pouring in, we hung on the edge of catastrophic destruction.

It was now or never. I threw myself against Sebastian's chest and drove him backward through the door leading from the Below directly into the Above.

The Dancing Shadow came with us.

Chapter 18

As the door slammed shut behind us, we crashed onto the solid floor of the Above.

I say floor because it seemed as though we landed in an endless white room – floor, ceiling, faraway walls. The place was painfully bright, and I squinted under my hand while I shielded my eyes.

Unconscious, Sebastian remained on the floor in a heap. Carefully, I turned him over. I lifted one of his eyelids, and the unfocused orb underneath rolled to the side. I examined his arms and chest. His body was clearly roughed up, but his breathing seemed normal. There was a gash in his right arm, but it appeared to be shrinking. Scratches and bites covered his skin, but no blood ran from his body. As I watched, the bruises and cuts were replaced by unblemished skin.

Well, that was interesting. Was he healing because he was in the Above or because he escaped the Below?

Demon. Okay.

I raised my head. The Dancing Shadow glimmered next to me. Curiously, I inspected him. I could make out a trace of his face if I looked hard enough. Placing a hand on my knee, I pushed myself to my feet. The Dancing Shadow stayed.

I leaned toward him, searching the ghostly shadow that was made brighter in the Above. Yes, I could see the shapes of his features.

"You seem sort of familiar to me…Isn't that strange?" I whispered, detecting a slight change where his mouth might be. Did a corner of it just quirk up?

No.

Then.

Find. Him. Lost.

"Find Templeton, right?" I asked, still examining the figure. "He's here, isn't he? He's alive, right?"

Alive. Lost. Find.

"I will find him." I gave a half laugh. "I'd go through hell to find him."

Yes.

And that was it. The Dancing Shadow brightened and drifted away. It seemed our strange time together had come to an end. But the being helped us more than once, and I was grateful. If it now wanted to wander the Above, who was I to stop it?

I turned, startling when I realized a row of doors lined the wall behind us, stretching as far as the eye could see. This had to be the row of doors described in the book of fairy tales. However, unlike the young girl in the story, I could see the individual doors, each bearing a symbol. The door we'd traveled through, the one connecting the Above and the Below, was the only one made of brushed metal and missing a doorknob. The square symbol appeared on the Above's side of the door as well.

However, the symbol here had more light than dark filling it.

The rest of the doors were similar to one another, each glowing softly with a unique symbol carved into it.

"I'd give anything for a strawberry *Toro*," moaned a voice next to my feet.

I squatted next to Sebastian. "We did it. We

made it into the Above."

He sat up with effort, rubbing his bleary eyes. "I knew we would. Never a doubt."

"Oh, sure," I replied, raising an eyebrow. "Walk in the park."

"Did we leave the Below before we could blow everything up?" Sebastian winced as he pressed his hand against the floor. He pushed up onto his knees.

I stood, holding out a hand to him. "We did."

"Are you kidding me?" He let me pull him to his feet. "After all that –"

"Sebastian, if we would've let the full light of the Above in, you would have been destroyed, too." Uncomfortable, I looked past him. "That was never an option for me."

He was quiet for a moment. "I see."

"Anyhow, balance and all." I turned in the other direction and began to put one foot in front of the other. "I'm not sure which way we should go."

Sebastian followed, taking an extra step so he could walk beside me. He gestured in the direction we were headed. "The fifth door isn't far from here."

I stopped. "What?"

"Uh huh. I was here before, remember?" He hooked a thumb over his shoulder. "The door we just came through wasn't far from the fifth door. I didn't know what it was back then, but I remember it. The fifth door will have a square on it with two lines through it."

"What do you mean?"

"It'll make sense when you see it," he replied.

"I guess," I said. The abrupt end to our battle in the Below left me somewhat shell-shocked. I was on autopilot. *But there are monsters here, too,* I thought. "What about the 'beautiful beasts'? The Beams of Light?"

Sebastian scrunched up his nose. "It's a possibility we'll see one. If we do, don't argue with it. Do what it says."

His casual answer brought me to a halt. "You're not making any sense. Do what it 'says'? The Beams aren't exactly chatty – or open to reason. Have you forgotten?"

Sebastian stopped and turned back around to face me. "I came to the Above before all the shit went down – before I was pushed into the Below. When I was here, I had two of my men with me. We wandered until we were noticed by a couple of Beams of Light."

"Why didn't you tell me this before?" I asked.

"What, over dinner in the Below?" he scoffed. "Now shut up and listen to me. The last time, the Beams were...curious, I guess. They kind of floated near us. We didn't know what to do. We kept following this line of doors. Then I could hear this singing – kind of high-pitched."

"Was it them?" I remembered the shrill, metallic sound the Beams of Light had made back in the compound in the Walled Zone.

"Yeah. It drove the one guy nuts. He flipped out, screaming at one of the Beams and kicking at it."

"Wait, it was solid?" I tried to remember how the Beams appeared in the quad. The last thing I wanted to do was touch them. They were white hot. I touched my cheek where the ghost of a scar remained.

"No, not really – but he'd gone off the deep end. He wouldn't calm down."

"What happened?"

"He ran at it. Well, into it. Then his body – *poofed*." Sebastian waved a hand before combing his fingers through his hair. He paused, pouting as his fingertips felt for the horns threatening to erupt.

"Poofed?" I prompted.

"Evaporated, I guess." He continued to explore his scalp. "Ceased to be."

"And the other guy?"

"Freaked out and took off running. Never saw him again." Sebastian puffed out his cheeks before dropping his arm. "Could still be here for all I know."

"But you made it back," I argued. "How?"

"I listened. They wanted to know where I was from and why I was in the Above. It was another one of those 'inside my head' conversations – like the Dancing Shadow."

I'd already decided not to tell Sebastian about the Dancing Shadow hitching a ride with us into the Above. "You're telling me you chatted with the Beams, and then you returned to the Walled Zone through the fifth door?"

"Sort of, yeah. I agreed to respect their laws and leave through one of the doors."

"Do you know their laws?"

"Listen. Protect the One Truth. There are no other truths."

I halted yet again. "You know the One Truth from the Beams of Light from Above? The one referenced in the book of fairy tales?"

"I have no idea what they meant, Lucie. I agreed, left, and lived to tell the story." He motioned for us to keep moving before stretching his arms up into the air. "Fuck, I hurt."

I wasn't done. "Did you ever come back to the Above after that? Before now?"

We trekked farther through the stark world. He was reluctant to answer at first, but finally, he nodded. "I wanted to check out some of these other doors. Look," Sebastian pointed. "There's the fifth door. This is the one leading into the compound in the Walled Zone."

As we approached, I noted the square symbol. It was divided into horizontal thirds. The top third was bright white, the middle third was empty, and the bottom third was solid black. This door would lead into the Between – and back home.

"Alright, good." I popped my lips several times, considering my options. "I'll come back here when it's time. It's a one-way door back into the Empire, so…" I lifted a hand. "It'll be fine."

Sebastian fidgeted with the collar of his shirt. "Do you want me to stay in the Above with you?"

"No," I shook my head. "I don't think that's a good idea."

He didn't answer, but his long fingers continued to rub along the neckline. When he'd lifted his chin, I realized I could see the thin scar extending across his throat and winding back around his neck. While many of the wounds inflicted on his body had faded or disappeared altogether, the reminder of his last run-in with a Beam of Light remained. I wondered why.

I found myself reaching for Sebastian's arm. "Hey, are you feeling okay? Any different?"

"I'm fine." He cocked his head to the side. "Wait, are you asking if I'm still a demon?"

"Well, are you?" I had a feeling I knew the answer.

Sebastian's gaze drifted past me. "Yeah. But I feel a little less demony if that makes you feel better."

"Less demony?" I repeated.

"Not as empty." He swallowed once, before returning his attention to me. "I feel better, especially after last night. Being with you like that. When you were good to me."

"Oh." I rubbed the toe of my sneaker against the glossy floor. We hadn't talked about what'd happened, and I didn't think it was a smart idea to go into it now – *or ever.* "If you're still a demon, then you're still bound to me, correct?"

"Looks that way." He pursed his lips. "I can feel it. It's still there. Are you going to break the binding, warden?"

I hesitated. If Sebastian remained a demon – even in a demon-lite version – if I released him, Nisha could probably conjure him and bind him to her. I lowered my eyes. No, I wouldn't do that to him. It wasn't fair. I had no right to trade his blood away like I did – even if I was desperate. What I did was wrong. I shook my head.

"Hey, what's going on?" Sebastian's fingers tucked under my chin, turning my face upward. The concern I found in his eyes was genuine.

His tenderness was too much to take, and I pulled away. "Here's the thing. If I release you, it's possible that..."

Sebastian searched my face. "What? What's the matter?"

"Asmodeus might be able to call you back to the Below." I had no idea if that could or would happen, but I figured it was entirely in the realm of possibility.

He rubbed the sharp end of his right canine

with the tip of his tongue. "Good point."

I clapped my hands together. "Here's the deal, Sebastian. I'm giving you permission to go off on your own to...*wherever*. But you're not allowed to pick up where you left off before you were thrown into the Below. You're not allowed to resurrect the Fringe or engage in any of those types of criminal activities. I'm keeping you bound to me for the foreseeable future. I call, you come."

A wicked smirk lifted a corner of his mouth. He made to speak, and I quickly reached up and covered his lips with my hand.

"I'm not done. I compel you to behave only in ways I would approve." Sebastian's tongue licked my palm, and I jerked my hand back. "Dammit, I'm serious, Sebastian! I compel you to stay out of trouble, stay away from your old Fringe-related contacts, and just...just don't be an asshole."

"You're asking a lot of me," he grinned.

"I'm sure I'll have more rules in the future, but this is the best I can do for now. Do me a favor, don't search for loopholes for at least a week." I rubbed the back of my neck. "And yeah, if I call you, you better hustle. I promise I won't abuse the power, but if I think you're in trouble – or more to the point, *causing trouble* – I will demand your presence."

Smug satisfaction spread across Sebastian's face. "Whatever you say, warden."

"And don't call me that." I peered into the distance, looking for a sign of anything in the endless white. I needed to start my search for Templeton.

"Lighten up, Lucie." Catching me off guard, Sebastian snagged my arm, pulling me to him and planting a loud kiss on the top of my head.

I shoved him toward the line of doors. "Go."

He paused in front of the fifth door, the door that would take him back to the compound, back into the Empire where he would now have free reign – at least within the boundaries I tried to set. "You honestly think you're going to find him alive, don't you?"

I nodded. "I have to."

"I'd wish you luck, but…" Sebastian shrugged. "But he's a dick. And he doesn't deserve you any more than I do."

"Bye, Sebastian." I pointed toward the fifth door.

"Later, wayward witch." He lifted his hand to

raise his door travel energy. Stunned, I realized I could see it growing around him. I watched as the gray – no, *purple* tendrils – swirled around his legs and feathered through the air toward the line of doors.

I turned away, feeling a fresh pang of guilt at the vision. I couldn't even see Emily's door travel energy. Until now, I'd only ever seen Templeton's royal blue waves. And yet, I could make out the colored bands of Sebastian's – the seductive hues reminding me of the purple and lavender you'd find in the sky when the sun finally set. I kept marching forward, heading farther into the bright white of the Above, putting distance between us. I checked over my shoulder to see if he'd left. Yes, my demon was gone.

My eyes darted to the vibrating shimmer to the right of the fifth door.

Son of a bitch!

His purple door travel energy left a trail around another door's edges. He'd chosen a destination other than the Empire.

∞∞∞

I wondered if the strange vagaries of time existed in the Above, too. I put one foot in front of the other, traveling in what I hoped was a straight line away from the row of doors. If I couldn't find anything after searching for a bit, my brilliant plan was to turn back around and attempt to follow the straight line back. I'd walk down the row of doors, pick a new starting point, and do it again.

It was not a good plan, but I didn't know what else to do – except maybe risk sending out a tendril of my energy to see if I could connect to Templeton. I decided it was worth a try. As I wandered, I allowed a thread of energy to press out into the bright white surrounding me. Because it was Templeton I sought, I attempted to make my energy receptive instead of seeking. It was easier to pull him to me than to chase him.

The silence wasn't as stark as I would've imagined. My ears didn't ring because of a lack of noise. I was remarkably unafraid. Mostly, I was disoriented. The world of light was endless in all directions, save for the wall of doors I'd left behind. I kept going.

Out of the corner of my left eye, I caught a

slight quiver of something in the air. I turned, at first believing that off in the distance, a light shone. As I leaned forward, squinting to determine the source, I realized I wasn't seeing something far away. I was peering through a thin Beam of Light right at my side. I jerked backward.

The Beam swayed, and I detected a presence slipping inside my head – not quite in the same way Templeton had stood in front of my mind's eye in the past. This was more of an attempt to link up with me in some manner. I raised my hands, my fingers touching my temples. Inside, I felt a tickling sensation.

Unlike the Dancing Shadow, words weren't put into my head. It was more of a series of distinct feelings – emotions injected into me. I waited, my confusion conveying my uncertainty. A corresponding wave rushed over me. Curiosity.

"You want to know why I'm here?" I said aloud, twitching at the sound of my voice. "I'm looking for someone." I pressed my hands to my chest, picturing Templeton in as much detail as possible. The related longing running through me was genuine. "He's lost here."

The Beam rippled in the air, and immediately I was hopeful. The sensation I experienced was not organic, and I quickly recognized it as coming from the Beam. "Does that mean you understand me?"

Sebastian had implied his communication with the Beams was similar to how the Dancing Shadows talked to him. But it was not going to be the same for me. I needed to provide a feeling to the Beam to communicate my question. I scrambled to think of something.

Reluctance. My body tensed when the word popped into my head. Would that be sufficient?

I waited, trying to remain open. And then I sensed it – reassurance, like an arm around my shoulders.

The Beam glided away. I identified a new emotion pressing into me – desire. I wanted very much to follow it.

As soon as I stepped toward it, the Beam was on the move again, only this time, it didn't pause. It kept going forward into the brightness surrounding us. The new feeling growing inside me was filled with confidence.

In the distance, I could see a black speck in the middle of the white. It remained tiny, and for a while, I believed it was moving away from us. Eventually, the speck took shape.

Various images floated through my mind as I tried to better understand what I saw. Was it a piece of furniture? I struggled to make a connection between what I moved toward and the flashes of possibilities my brain suggested.

Then I felt it – a tug on the thread of energy I'd sent out.

I recognized it. Goosebumps spread across my skin.

I covered my mouth with both hands, stilling. The pull on my energy grew stronger.

"Please…please…" I begged as I began to run across the bare white floors. "Please let it be…"

What began as a distant black dot in the infinite light was now fully fleshed out. A man sat at a table writing a note as his long, elegant fingers skimmed the page of an open book.

Oh.

Oh.

Oh.

Templeton.

∞∞∞

My heart pounded so hard inside my chest that I was sure it was trying to launch itself out of my body and into Templeton's hands. I couldn't tear my eyes away from him as I slowed my approach, my throat constricting as I tried to squeak out his name.

He didn't seem to know I was there.

The Beam waved gently in the air beside me.

"Templeton?" I croaked again. "Templeton? Can you hear me?"

The pencil lifted, and he raised his chin. He looked...*fine*. Nothing was different. The light that had poured through his body months ago, rendering him helpless, left no sign of injury. He wore the same clothes I'd last seen him wearing. I watched as he tilted his head to the side and blinked. Not a trace of color remained in his irises, and his pupils were minuscule.

I tried again. "Templeton? Do you know who I am?"

"Of course I do." His lips pressed together, dismissing my question.

I gave a quiet laugh as I wrung my hands. He sounded perfectly normal. He sounded irritated. "You've been here a long time."

"Not long," he replied. He went back to taking

notes. "What do you need?"

Anxious, I edged around the corner of the table, drawn to his side. "Where do you think you are?"

"The library," he answered, waving a hand absently as he kept reading.

I turned to seek assistance from the Beam and realized we were smack-dab in the middle of a monumental library. The Beam had disappeared. Shimmering windows arched high above our heads. The rows of books around us traveled in all directions, towering stacks of tomes stretching as far as I could see. Glorious light cascaded down over us as if a golden sun peeked in through a window. White marble columns rose from the floor to the sky itself – if there was such a thing in the Above. It was a cathedral built for the gods of knowledge. I turned to Templeton. Piles of books surrounded him.

"What..." I rubbed my lips together, attempting to moisten them. "What are you researching?"

A corner of his mouth lifted, and his eyes flicked up to mine. "Everything. It's all here. Everything I need to know to become more than what I am."

"A Sorcerer?" My voice was barely a whisper.

"Yes. The answers to everything are here." Triumph curved his lips.

"Templeton, listen to me. You've been in the Above for months. That's where you are right now." I gestured to the library surrounding us. "This is not real."

He snorted. "Lucie, don't be ridiculous."

"I'm not making this up." I tried again.

"Then you're delusional."

That pissed me off. Apparently, even a brain-addled Templeton wasn't above casually insulting someone. *Fine.* New approach.

"Okay, then prove it to me." I held out a hand. "Show me where I'll find a section on the history of the Empire. Or archaic languages. Better yet, if this library has everything in it, show me where the section on witchlines is located." Angry, I flapped my hand in front of his face. "Take my hand. Show me."

He batted it away at first but then grabbed my wrist and stood, knocking his chair backward and abruptly pulling me toward him. "What is wrong with you?" Templeton gave me a shake.

"None of this is real. Look at me, dammit!"

I reached up and rested my free hand on his cool cheek. I searched his colorless eyes. "When is the last time you remember seeing me, Templeton?" I demanded. "Where were we?"

The grip on my wrist tightened, and he clenched his teeth. I watched his pupils dart back and forth as he scanned my face. The rise and fall of his chest became noticeable. "I don't remember."

"We were in the Walled Zone, in the Fringe's old compound." I allowed my hand to slip down to his shoulder and gave it a tender squeeze. "You were...They took you through the fifth door into the Above."

"Who?" His face grew hard, and the fingers around my wrist twitched.

"The Beams of Light." I didn't dare check to see if the thin Beam that had led me to Templeton was still present.

"I don't remember that. Why are you saying this?" He reached up and pulled my hand from his shoulder.

"Do you trust me?" I forced my voice to remain calm while I fought to keep from panicking on the inside. How could I get through to him?

"I don't know." He hadn't blinked in at least a

minute.

"Will you take a chance and trust me now? Let me show you where you are?" I hoped what we were experiencing in the Above would work much like it had for me in the Below. Once we started walking, I hoped the walls of this book-lined prison would fall away.

It was hard to know what was going on behind those unique eyes. He still held onto my wrist. I reached up and slowly pried his fingers open. Then I took his hand and tugged gingerly. He didn't resist. I turned down the first aisle of books, leading him from the table where he'd been reading.

"I want to show you something important," I said to fill the silence between us. "There's a row of doors. They lead in and out of the Above. One of them is the fifth door. That's how you came to be here. Do you remember? Maybe you can't. I don't even know if you were conscious then." A sharp sob escaped my lips before I could stop it.

Templeton pulled my hand and forced me to stop. "Why are you crying?"

"Because I lost you." How could I get through to him? How could I break this...library spell?

"I'm right here," he huffed.

"But you're not where you think you are," I argued, letting go of his hand and pulling books from the shelves at random. I let them slam to the floor, the sound echoing up into the air above our heads.

Templeton made as if to grab me, but I sidestepped his reach, then lurched forward against him, catching him off guard. I threw all my energy – physical and metaphysical – into pushing him into the stacks. The shelves swayed, and Templeton struggled, shouting for me to stop. I fought, lunging forward a second time, forcing both of us against the shelves. He cried out, but it was too late. We were falling along with the tower of books, texts raining down, beating against us. Shelves, books, and the two of us crashed to the floor. The chain reaction of destruction raised clouds of sparkling dust in the air. Templeton rolled, wrapping his arms around me, cradling me to his chest as he covered my body with his. Everything collapsed on top of us.

And then it was silent.

The side of my face pressed against Templeton's shirt. His heartbeat thundered under his skin. His embrace relaxed as he sat up, but his hands remained on my upper arms, holding me still. I turned my head, seeing nothing but white stretching endlessly in every direction.

The library storing all the secrets Templeton sought was gone.

∞∞∞

He didn't speak as I led him a second time, my hand holding his firmly as I picked a direction and pulled him along after me. The Beam that led me to Templeton was no longer in sight, so I was winging it. I didn't dare call out, and I was worried if I alerted Templeton to my ignorance, he'd fight me – and we'd be stuck in this desolate place.

Wary, I snuck a peek at him every once in a while. He said nothing, his eyes wandering over the empty landscape as we trudged onward. A hint of pale blue had returned to his irises.

In front of us, I saw a twinkle, a whitish shadow in the light. Templeton noticed, too, but said nothing. It was far enough away that I couldn't see anything definitive, but I knew it was the Dancing Shadow. It – *he* – had returned.

Found.

Yes, I thought.

Good. Follow. Home.

"You got it, buddy," I said low.

A wordless Templeton seemed content to let me lead. As much as I wanted to know what he was thinking, it seemed prudent to let him come around more naturally. I understood how time was different beyond the fifth and sixth doors. No matter how intelligent or magically adept he might be, logic was a casualty here.

Again, with the warped sense of time, we could've walked for hours or minutes, but eventually, I made out the row of doors stretching the length of the Above, separating it from the Between.

We were almost home. The Dancing Shadow, in its new form, hesitated.

Wait. Message. Him.

My gaze landed on three Beams of Light gliding steadily toward us. My instinct was to run, but the Dancing Shadow anticipated my impulse.

Wait. Calm.

They were calm, or I should be calm? I checked on Templeton. If he noted the Beams advancing on us, he gave no indication. He stared blankly at the row of doors. When the Beams were less than a dozen paces away, I heard it.

At first, it was a high-pitched melody. I concentrated on it, realizing I could make out an odd word here and there. Then I heard a voice sing with clarity: *One Truth.*

I would agree to anything they said if it meant we could safely leave. I waited. When nothing else came through, the Dancing Shadow pressed more words inside my head.

Time. Go.

He drifted toward the row of doors. Leaving the lingering Beams behind, we approached the door with the square divided into three parts: the white Above, the colorless Between, and the black Below. This was the fifth door. We were going home.

"Are you ready?" I asked my quiet companion. The Dancing Shadow had moved close to Templeton's side, and I watched as his vacant expression sharpened. He studied the twinkling being.

Home. Go.

"You don't have to tell me twice." I glanced at Templeton.

Reluctantly, Templeton pulled his scrutiny away from the Dancing Shadow at our side. "So familiar," he sighed, then raised his hand.

I felt the charge of his door travel energy beginning to surround us and wrapped an arm around his waist. I reached forward, my fingers grasping and turning the doorknob. The fifth door swung open and sucked us out of the Above.

Chapter 19

We tumbled out of the fifth door onto the unforgiving ground in the center of the old compound. I shrieked when hands grabbed at my body from the left and the right, immediately separating me from Templeton.

"No!" I wrenched away from unwanted grasps and launched myself at the unconscious man. Templeton's limp body was bundled in a blanket, and men shouted as a board was shuffled through the crowd.

"No, not again! Not this time!" I raged, raising my fire inside my body. I smacked down the first unsmiling Rabbit I saw. They would *not* take another piece of my heart away from me. I'd kill them all first. *Every. Last. Fucking. Rabbit.*

The burly Rabbit I'd targeted yelped as my heat knocked him to the ground. I heard another holler to get a blanket around me, and I spun, swinging my arm violently and clocking someone's cheekbone with my elbow. The crack vibrated up to my shoulder, and the Rabbit cried out. Unrelenting hands pulled at me for a second time.

"Templeton!" I struggled, my eyes locked on his covered body as Rabbits hustled him away. Calls of *'he's alive!'* and *'move it!'* echoed across the quad. "Templeton! No!"

"Pin her arms down!" A man ordered. Another voice instructed someone to *'secure her legs.'* I was lifted. Twisting, I arched my back and called upon my deepest fire, my witchline opening. I'd light this whole fucking place up like a Roman candle.

"Lucie!" A familiar voice barked. "Lucie, stop it! Now! It's okay. Dammit! Put her down. Let her go before she goes nuclear and kills someone!"

I hung onto those words, my vision clearing as I rolled my head back and forth, seeking the man directing the others to release me. My witchline quivered and closed as my fury backed down. Hands still held loosely onto my arms, but this time they only sought to steady me as I stumbled, my feet trying to find purchase on the stony ground. "Rabbit? *Rabbit!*"

"It's okay," Rabbit said again, appearing and pulling me against his chest into the safety of his arms. He balanced carefully, a crutch under one arm. Big Rabbit hovered behind him, his massive hand steadying my old friend. I turned my face into Rabbit's shirt, inhaling his comforting scent – laundry soap and a damp night spent outdoors. He cupped the back of my head. "I got you. It's okay. You're okay."

"Don't let them take him away from me like they took you," I blurted out. "Please help me stop them."

"Shh, they're not taking him away from you," Rabbit promised. "But he needs medical attention. We've got a nurse in the van. We'll get him back to his estate. We've already sent a message to Mr. Archie. He'll get a doctor there to look at him."

"Yes," I nodded, rubbing the snot away from my nose. A feeling of dread weighed on my heart, and I shook my head. "No! Take him to my house. I'm not letting him out of my sight."

Confusion flitted across Rabbit's face. "Mr. Archie will let you –"

"But his mother might not," I countered before Rabbit could finish. "No. My house. And I'm going in the van. You can't keep me from him."

Rabbit's cheeks puffed up. His eyes flicked to Big Rabbit. "We're all going in the van."

The other man nodded. "I'll drive." He called across the way. "Hold up! Change of plans!"

"How did you…?" My voice faltered as Rabbit led me toward the waiting vehicle. He used only one crutch and was slower than he probably wanted to be, but he looked 10 times better than when I last saw him at the cabin.

"I'll fill you in once we're on our way," he said as another Rabbit helped me into the back of the van where Templeton was strapped to a board. They'd attached it to the floor to keep it from sliding. A female Rabbit, presumably the nurse Rabbit referenced, ignored me as she checked the IV attached to his bare arm.

I sat on the floor next to him, my hand stroking through the longish hair framing his pallid face. A scraggly beard appeared along his jawline and across his chin. Shocked, I touched the wiry bristles.

The van was running, and Big Rabbit sat in the driver's seat. Rabbit pulled himself up into the passenger seat and stashed the lone crutch along the floor. "You sure you don't want to sit up here instead? We've got at least two hours before we're back in Matar."

"I'm fine," I said, refocusing on Templeton's gaunt face. Leaning down, I kissed his forehead. His skin was cool under my lips. "You're going to be okay." I glanced up at the female Rabbit. "Right?"

She watched me with glittering black eyes. "Let's get some fluids into him. He needs to be kept warm. His temperature is low, but his pulse is stronger than I'd expect. He'll need to rest, and we'll have to watch to make sure everything is functioning properly in the next day or so. Everything else will be up to him."

"He'll be okay," I reassured myself. I felt Rabbit's gaze and turned to face him. The words were out of my mouth before I could think twice. "You were here when I needed you."

"I couldn't let you down again," he answered, his eyes a solid, shiny black. His admission, although ultimately untrue, surprised me.

"You've never let me down," I told him.

Rabbit's attention strayed to Templeton. "We sent a follow-up message to Mr. Archie. He'll meet us at your house. A doctor's on standby."

"Good, good." My hand was back at

Templeton's cheek. I smiled. The knight to my light was no longer lost. And we were going home.

Together.

∞∞∞

After the initial shock of landing in the hands of a crew of Rabbits had lessened, I listened to Rabbit's explanation of how everyone came to be waiting on the other side of the fifth door.

It seems a man – some young 'blond guy' – showed up at the building Big Rabbit had been working out of in downtown Matar. He didn't give his name, but he said I was in trouble – that I'd 'conjured a cologne-drenched demon' and was headed for 'the hole he lived in' as part of a plan to 'get the other guy back.' Big Rabbit wasn't sure what to make of this story, but the younger man was beside himself, skittishly pacing back and forth in the workshop. Eventually, Big Rabbit calmed him down enough to learn I'd door traveled 'with the stupid demon' to a place in the Walled Zone. Big Rabbit realized a demon with door traveling abilities had to be Sebastian and blew up the network calling in reinforcements. Before he could get more information out of the man who'd come to him, he was gone. Big Rabbit said the only thing he saw outside was an orange cat 'like Flame' zipping across the street.

Rabbits living in the Walled Zone made it to the compound first, reporting nothing in the quad. No doors were open, but the ground looked recently disturbed. Big Rabbit raced in with his crew from Matar.

Another man picked up my Rabbit from his secluded cabin outside of Becket, stopping only for gas as they tore up the road heading for the Walled Zone. He was the last one to arrive. They set up camp and waited.

"I'm guessing the blond messenger was the guy staying with you," Rabbit finished.

"Sounds like Marcus." I took a drink from the bottle of water he'd handed me.

"He got lucky. Big Rabbit was getting ready to take off for Templeton's estate." He lifted his head and nodded toward our driver. "He still has the wooden box you gave him. He won't need to take it to Mr. Archie now."

The Crimson Stone. "I'll hang onto it and ask Templeton what he wants to do with it when he wakes up." I reached down and brushed Templeton's hair from his forehead for the hundredth time. I didn't want to stop touching him.

"You're not going to keep it?" Rabbit asked.

"I don't know. I learned it doesn't open the fifth and sixth doors – it just closes them." I shrugged. "We've got time to make these decisions." I paused. "What day is it?"

"Sunday. It's late in the afternoon." Fatigue lined his face.

"It felt like I was gone for so long," I told him. "Time feels way different in the Below. At one point, I thought weeks had passed."

Rabbit's attention returned to me. "You conjured Sebastian. What were you thinking?"

I lifted a hand and laughed weakly. "At which point?"

"Yeah." Rabbit rubbed a hand back and forth over his face. "Exactly."

"I was desperate." I sent a sideways glance toward the female Rabbit still monitoring Templeton. "Sebastian wasn't a part of my original plan, but…" My voice trailed off. "What's done is done. And Templeton is back where he belongs. It worked out."

"But Lucie, going with Sebastian – into the Below..." Rabbit searched my face. "Did he hurt you?"

"He did not." I didn't want to talk about Sebastian. "He helped me. We made a deal, and he helped me get into the Above. That's it. There's nothing more to say on the matter. It's over."

Rabbit considered my answer. "There's more to this story."

"Do you tell me everything?" I challenged softly.

"Point taken." He gave a small cough. "Are you sure you're okay?"

After taking a moment to assess myself, I nodded. "I am. I'm exhausted, and I do have a weird feeling it's not the right time of day, but I'm fine."

"What do you mean, feeling it's 'not the right time of day'?"

"Like when you take a nap in the afternoon and wake up thinking it's the next day when it's not," I replied. "Confused as to what time it is, but without the grogginess."

"We should have the doctor look you over, too," Rabbit said.

"No. Really, I'm okay." I arched my back, fidgeting and trying to find a more comfortable position. "The fifth door, when it appeared...Did anyone – or anything – come through it before we did?"

"Like a Beam? Or a demon?" Rabbit's rich brown eyes hovered on the edge of turning black.

I hesitated. Now wasn't the time. "I wondered if we were the only ones, that's all. What's on the other side is so unpredictable. I think the doors are used by more beings than we know."

He shifted in his seat, a trace of pain zipping across his face. The van wasn't the comfiest of rides. "Only you two. The fifth door shimmered and opened. We surrounded it – keeping our distance – and waited. Seconds later, you and Templeton dropped out. It shrank almost immediately afterward."

Rabbit's answer confirmed for me that Sebastian had door traveled from the Above to someplace other than the Empire. The more I thought about it, the more I believed it was a good thing. Had he traveled through the fifth door into the compound, he would've found himself surrounded by deadly enemies.

And frankly, with Sebastian's leftover demon abilities – whatever they were – Rabbits would've been hurt, too. No, it was better he'd left for parts unknown.

I sat back, again letting my eyes fall on an unconscious Templeton. *This* was the man I wanted to build a life with. Sebastian was on his own now. Hopefully, he would heed my words and do no harm.

∞∞∞

It took us a couple of hours to get back to Matar. The weather turned overcast, and evening seemed to come earlier than usual. It was the first of May. A year ago, I'd celebrated the fire festival with witches from the method coven I occasionally joined. Today's celebration was Templeton's homecoming – even if he wasn't out of the woods yet.

We took advantage of the gloomy weather, carrying the makeshift stretcher from the beat-up van double-parked in front of my brownstone into my house without a sidewalk audience. Mr. Archie had arrived shortly before us with the doctor. Our strange hodgepodge of people marched up the front steps and into my home. The Rabbits carrying Templeton followed me upstairs where he was transferred from the board to my bed.

Rabbit hobbled after us and pulled Mr. Archie aside. He motioned to the doctor and then to the Rabbit who'd served as Templeton's nurse in the van. Mr. Archie nodded. Rabbit then beckoned to me. Reluctantly, I left Templeton's side.

"Let's go downstairs," Rabbit said, putting his hand on my elbow as the remaining Rabbits shuffled out of the bedroom.

"No," I said. "I'm not –"

"Lucie." Rabbit's hand slid up from my elbow to my shoulder. "We've got a doctor, a nurse, and Mr. Archie – who's cared for him since he was a toddler. What he needs now is privacy while they tend to him. You can come back but give him the space you know he'd want while the doctor examines him."

I looked at the helpless man on my bed. Rabbit was right. This was not about me. I nodded. "Okay, yeah. You're right."

"You want to shower?" Rabbit inclined his head toward the door leading out of the bedroom. I noted a familiar sparkle in his eye.

"Let me rephrase that. You *want* to shower."

Realization swept over my unwashed self. "Do I smell?"

"You stink to high heaven." He grinned.

I sniffed my arm, my nose wrinkling. "It's the Below. It reeks. I didn't realize I carried the stench on me. I must've gotten used to it or something. But you can smell it?"

"Why do you think Big Rabbit was driving with the heater blasting and the window down?" Rabbit escorted me out of the bedroom. "Go get in the shower. I'll bring you clean pajamas."

I didn't resist Rabbit's handling. I welcomed it. *This* was the Rabbit I knew. *This* was the friend I'd missed. He left me to strip down and climb under the blessedly clean water of my shower. I heard the door open and shut as he delivered a set of pajamas and a robe. I didn't ask if he'd be waiting downstairs when I finished showering. I was counting on it.

∞∞∞

As much as I wanted to hurry back to Templeton, I lingered under the hot water pouring over my skin. I lathered, rinsed, repeated. And repeated. And repeated. I scrubbed my skin with the bodywash Flame left in the bathroom. It smelled like sugar cookies. I hoped my efforts would get rid of the stink I'd brought back from the Below.

I combed through my wet hair, pulling it up off my shoulders and holding it in place with a clip. Mouthwash followed a vigorous teeth-brushing, and I put on the clothing Rabbit had left for me. It felt good to be home.

I tapped on the door to my bedroom, and the female Rabbit answered. She told me the doctor was finishing, then Mr. Archie would bathe Templeton. She'd help with the sponge bath and also assist in dressing Templeton in the nightclothes Mr. Archie had brought with him.

Having this weird people barrier between us felt strange, but I knew Templeton was safe and getting good care. I didn't argue. I thanked her.

Rabbit and Big Rabbit stood in my kitchen talking quietly. All the other Rabbits had gone, and I was grateful. As much as I knew I owed everyone, I needed time alone. More to the point, I needed time alone with Rabbit.

"Hey," I said, padding into the kitchen.

Big Rabbit's face lit up. "I have something for you." He retrieved the wooden box containing the Crimson Stone from a backpack.

"Thank you for taking care of this," I said, accepting the offering. I unlatched the lid and peered at the three pieces. They lit up and blinked contentedly back at me. "How will I ever repay the kindness you've always shown me?"

The sweet giant put his hand on top of my head. "We're friends, Lucie. That's enough for me."

I smiled as his hand dropped away. "Well, I'm glad," I answered, closing the lid.

Big Rabbit motioned to Rabbit. "Staying here tonight, right?"

Rabbit's focus flipped to me. "I'm staying."

"Then I'm off." Big Rabbit stretched. "I'm heading to bed. These bones feel old. But I'll be back in the morning. Text me if you need anything before then."

I nodded, squeezing him gratefully as he hugged me. He clapped Rabbit on his shoulder – an unspoken connection between the two told me Big Rabbit was back on Rabbit's crew.

The universe was righting itself.

When it was only Rabbit and me, I inclined my

head toward the pantry. "A snort?"

That beautiful grin I'd missed for months lit up his face. "One. But let's sit in the living room. I can't take these barstools."

I nodded, retrieving the vodka and pouring a shot for each of us. We touched glasses, then tossed the silky liquid back. Comforting warmth spread throughout my chest. "Would you like wine?"

"Nah, but I'll have some water." He maneuvered on his one crutch and waited by the door. I poured myself wine and grabbed a glass of water before following him to the front of the house. In the living room, I set both glasses on the coffee table between us. Rabbit eased himself into a chair.

"You look better, and it's only been a few days since I was at your cabin," I said, sitting on the couch across from him.

Rabbit ducked his head, an unusually shy expression crossing his face. "Yeah. I dunno. Seeing you…I wanted…" He lifted a hand. "I'm trying to make do with one crutch. It's not easy, but…Anyhow, it hurts like a sonofabitch."

"Where?" I whispered. We were in such delicate territory. I didn't want to spook him.

"My hips. Legs. In addition to two broken legs, I had three fractures in my pelvis." His gaze landed on the glass of water. I pitched forward, picking it up and handing it to him. Two frustrated bursts of red appeared on his cheeks as he accepted the glass. Rabbit took a sip and nodded. "Thanks."

"I'm sorry you're going through this," I said softly.

"Yeah." His voice was gruff. "Rabbits heal quickly – I think you know that. But I had problems...The legs healed up okay, but the bones in my pelvis didn't heal after the surgeries like expected."

Surgeries. *Plural.* I winced.

He saw my expression, and his jaw tensed.

"Is it because you're also sick?" Would he open up to me?"

He nodded. "I'm having trouble healing."

"Will you tell me your diagnosis? Maybe I can help." I sat on the edge of the couch, picking up my wine and wrapping my hands around the glass.

"No, you can't. I know you want to, and I appreciate it, but it's not something you can fix." He took another drink of water before continuing. "It's a disease that sometimes develops in Rabbits as they age. It's called *withering* – because the illness slowly drains your energy and strength and ultimately affects your musculature. It weakens your bones – they can become brittle. Cognitive ability is affected in the worst cases, usually in later stages. Withering isn't common, and Rabbits can have periods of relief – a remission of sorts. I'm in the early stages of the disease. It was an annoyance before the..." Rabbit cleared his throat. "Before the attack in the Walled Zone. Being injured ramped up my symptoms. The disease impacts my healing. Vicious cycle."

"Is there a cure?" I feared I knew the answer.

Rabbit shook his head. "No cure, but it's possible for the disease to slow its progress, almost to the point of stopping altogether. That's when it becomes more of a chronic illness than a terminal one. A Rabbit can still live a long life. But right now, my body's too weak to do any better than it is."

"I know you don't want me to say this, but I'm sorry." I knew my eyes appeared watery, and I didn't want to upset Rabbit by letting tears leak out. He did not want my pity.

"You're right," he replied. "I don't want you to say that."

"As long as I'm saying things you don't want to hear..." I began, setting my wine back down.

Rabbit huffed out a short laugh. "Maybe I should have a second shot."

I ignored him. "I'm sorry to have dragged you back to the compound. It couldn't have been easy. I'm sorry you had to go back to where..." I put my fingers to my lips.

His expression was grim. "I needed to be there for my crew. It was Big Rabbit who called in reinforcements, but my crew still reports to me. I wasn't going to abandon them. I wasn't going to not be there for you. My demons come last."

I left the couch, pulling the ottoman behind me. I sat as close to Rabbit as I could, my hand resting on his knee. "Please tell me you won't stay away again – no matter what. I can't go through losing you a second time any more than I can handle losing Templeton again. I love you, Rabbit."

Rabbit's big hand cupped my cheek, his face revealing something both loving and sad. "I'll do my best to stay." His rough thumb stroked my skin.

I pressed my lips together. I understood what he was not saying.

Mr. Archie tapped the door jamb. Rabbit made to get up, but the other man held up a hand. "Please, Mr. Rabbit. Stay seated. I'm only stopping to let you know I'm leaving. I have a car waiting. I'm staying at Mr. Templeton's penthouse and will be back tomorrow morning to check on him."

I nodded. "You are welcome here at any time. What's going on upstairs?"

"The physician is packing up. The nurse will stay the night to monitor him. They want to keep him on the IV."

"Oh, of course." My brow furrowed. I hadn't thought of the nurse spending the night.

Mr. Archie was one step ahead of me. "Mr. Rabbit, in light of this development, why don't you come with me to the penthouse? There are several spare bedrooms. You'll get a good night's sleep, and we can return as early as you'd like in the morning."

Rabbit turned to me. "You'll be okay?"

"It's all good," I told him. "The nurse can sleep in the spare. I'll sleep in my bedroom – I planned to anyway." I looked at Mr. Archie. "I won't disturb him."

"I think you sleeping near Mr. Templeton can only help him come around. His body is simply tired – weak. I have no doubt he'll be fine." Mr. Archie sought to reassure me. "I'll return tomorrow with some hearty broth. Assuming he'll regain consciousness soon, you'll want to have something at the ready."

"Thank you." I stood up. "I'm grateful to you. What about Templeton's mother? Have you told her of his return?"

Mr. Archie seemed to consider his response before replying. "I believe it's to the benefit of all if we give it a day or two. When Templeton wakes up, we'll ask him his wishes."

That certainly worked for me. I had a feeling Gavina might swoop in and demand her son be removed from my home. Could I stop her? Doubtful. "Well, if you think Templeton would be okay with that, I'm for it."

"Mr. Templeton and his mother have a rather unique relationship. This would be in line with the norm." Mr. Archie turned as the doctor came down the stairs.

The physician was a pleasant man with clay-colored skin and snow-white hair. "His vitals are improving, and I can't detect any injuries. He needs fluids and rest. When he wakes, give him a liquid diet for two days, then a soft one for several more. Regular foods should be introduced slowly. Make sure he gets plenty of water." The doctor paused. "He might not want to talk when he regains consciousness – even if he can. From what Mr. Archie has told me, he's been missing for a long time. Sometimes interacting comfortably with others takes a bit longer."

Ugh. Templeton rarely 'interacted comfortably' with others before he vanished. "Got it. Thank you, doctor."

"We should go," Mr. Archie said, motioning to the door.

Rabbit used his crutch to stand. My hand automatically reached for him, but he shook his head. I nodded, drawing it back.

"We'll return in the morning," Mr. Archie stated again as the three men made to leave.

"Oh, wait," I said, tugging on Rabbit's long shirtsleeve. "Emily. Can you send her a message?"

"Already notified," Rabbit replied. "Big Rabbit messaged her the good news but also told her to wait until tomorrow before door traveling in."

"Good, good." I gave him a hug. "I'll see you tomorrow then."

"You will." He hesitated, then leaned over and kissed my forehead. "I'll be back."

"I'm counting on it."

Rabbit started to leave through the door when an orange tabby cat darted past his feet. Flame spun in his routine circle before sitting in the middle of the hall, his amber eyes watchful.

"Is this the cat Big Rabbit foisted upon you?" Rabbit asked. "Kind of scrawny, isn't he?"

Flame's cat eyes narrowed.

"We're working at fattening him up," I said, tossing a smirk at my shapeshifter.

"He needs it," Rabbit said before ducking out my front door. "See you tomorrow, Lucie."

"Tomorrow," I repeated, shutting the door behind him before turning to Flame. "How much do you know?"

Flame lifted a paw and licked it several times. I waited. Nothing.

"Are you going to shift?" I asked.

The licking paused. He blinked. The licking resumed.

I squatted down. "I want you to know I'm not

mad. I'm glad you went and told Big Rabbit I'd left to go get Templeton. But here's the thing. Templeton is in my bed, and there's a nurse upstairs who's planning on spending the night in the spare bedroom. I'm going to sleep by Templeton. You're more than welcome to stay here in your most beautiful feline form, or you can shift and sleep on the couch as my boarder Marcus. What'll it be?"

Flame sat quietly, mulling over my words before standing and rubbing his furry cat face on my knee. I scratched the top of his head, listening to the steady purr rising in his chest. When I stood, he scooted to the front door where he meowed.

"Really?" I asked. "Okay." I opened the door and watched as he disappeared into the night. I called out after him. "Be safe!"

∞∞∞

The female Rabbit caring for Templeton was an efficient nurse. He was tucked in comfortably under the covers. The nightlight cast a soft glow over his face. I stroked the top of his head, marveling at how black his eyelashes were atop his pale cheeks, like tiny little raven's wings.

"I think he'll be fine for the night," the nurse told me. "I appreciate you letting me take the spare bed, but I'd be happy to stay on the couch if you'd rather."

"No," I said. My fingers threaded themselves through his hair. It was long for him – this length would drive him nuts. "There's no place I'd rather be tonight."

"I do understand," she replied kindly. "Come get me if you need anything."

"I will." The Rabbit left the room, shutting the door silently behind her.

Removing my robe, I draped it over the chair near my bed before circling to the other side. I lifted the covers, slipping into the bed beside Templeton. I laid my head on the pillow and watched his face. He looked peaceful.

My hand traveled under the covers until it found a place to rest on top of his chest. I felt the steady rise and fall of his breathing. As my eyelids drifted shut, I let my energy caress his, but I didn't attempt to press any deeper. For now, this was perfect.

For now, I couldn't ask for anything more.

Chapter 20

I slept deeply and dreamlessly, my eyes only opening when I heard a rustle of covers. The nurse had pulled the blanket down, and the end of her stethoscope disappeared inside Templeton's unbuttoned pajama top. My body was pressed against his side, and I rolled away to let her work more easily. She checked the IV next.

Leaving the bed, I retrieved my robe. "Everything good?"

She nodded. "As I'd expect. My sister is coming to relieve me. She's also a nurse."

I was surprised but happy for the care they'd arranged. "You will be compensated for the –"

She held up a slender hand. "Mr. Archie took care of everything. My sister and I have worked as private duty nurses for the better part of 30 years. He's one of our easier patients, I assure you."

And she doesn't look a day over 20, I thought. Rabbits. "Thank you. I don't know what I'd do without the help."

The nurse finished checking Templeton's arm where the needle was attached. "It's no problem. The doctor ordered another IV, and it's being sent with my sister." She pulled up the covers to Templeton's chin. I watched as she ran a hand across his forehead. "When he wakes and can take in fluids on his own, he won't need an IV."

"Do you think he'll wake up today?" I knew it was silly to ask, but I couldn't help myself. I was eager to hear his voice.

The woman smiled, tenderly stroking his forehead like a mother leaning over her own precious child. She pushed the unusually unruly locks aside. "Perhaps. But don't be disappointed if he doesn't. It won't mean anything bad. He's recovering."

I nodded once. "I understand."

∞∞∞

Mr. Archie and Rabbit arrived shortly after 8 o'clock. Big Rabbit was on their heels, delivering the day nurse – another youthful-looking Rabbit with a kind face. Effortlessly, Big Rabbit carried in a compact refrigerated unit housing several IV bags. He placed it upstairs in my bedroom.

After an offer of coffee or tea – which Mr. Archie politely declined – I accompanied him upstairs to Templeton's side.

"His color has improved," Mr. Archie noted.

"It has." I rubbed Templeton's blanket-covered leg. "I'm trying to be patient – to be satisfied with him being home – but I'm going crazy."

Mr. Archie turned toward the round travel case he'd brought. I watched as he pulled out a pair of clippers and a razor. Shaving lotion and a ceramic basin followed. A white washcloth and a matching hand towel were draped over the open lid of the case. "Mr. Templeton would feel the same if the roles were reversed." Mr. Archie raised his head and suppressed a smile. "But his impatience would be unbearable."

A quiet laugh escaped through my lips. "I could not agree more." I gestured toward the items he'd unpacked. "Are you going to give him a cut and a shave?"

"Shave, yes. Cut his hair? Oh, no, no, no. He

is quite particular." Mr. Archie's eyes twinkled. "Mr. Templeton does allow himself some guilty pleasures. Weekly, a stylist meets him at his penthouse where she cuts his hair."

My eyebrows raised.

Mr. Archie put a finger to his lips. "Let's keep it a secret that you know."

"You got it." So many things to learn about the enigmatic man.

And we had all the time in the world.

∞∞∞

I left Mr. Archie to the private task of shaving Templeton. The day nurse was on deck to assist with another quick sponge bath before Mr. Archie left his side. From there, the female Rabbit would relieve me whenever I needed a break.

Big Rabbit demanded I get fresh air, dragging me off to *Coffee Cove*, where we picked up unnecessary coffees for everyone. Rabbit stayed at the house in case anyone arrived while we were gone. A shadow of frustration crossed his face when Big Rabbit said he'd take me to the coffee shop. I understood. It used to be Rabbit and me strolling side by side.

Emily Swift door traveled in through my pantry door – her cheerful energy following her into my kitchen. After hugging me, she grabbed Rabbit in a death grip and refused to let him go. Words spilled out of her mouth in a never-ending stream: *never again; missed you so much; why didn't you text me; walk me down the aisle;* and ending with, *glad you're here, Rabbit. Don't leave us ever again.*

I understood exactly what she meant. Rabbit grinned over the top of her head as he patted her back. He told her he missed her, too.

Upstairs, Emily was more somber. She snuffled at the side of the bed and babbled a bunch of incoherent words before unexpectedly bending and kissing Templeton's forehead. She turned away, briefly meeting my eyes with her wet ones before scurrying out the bedroom door.

The next day was more of the same. He remained unconscious. Again, I'd slept at Templeton's side at night, my hand resting over the comforting beat of his heart.

As the day nurse took his morning vitals on Wednesday, Templeton's eyelids fluttered open. I stood at the end of the bed, both hands covering my mouth. The nurse noticed immediately and set about with gentle murmurings – who she was, where he was, and that he was okay and should keep resting. He blinked at her, then turned his head slightly. Our eyes met, his displaying the faint blue they typically held. Afraid I'd break the moment by speaking, I remained silent, watching as a tired sigh pushed past his lips. His eyes closed again.

We let him rest. That night, I slept on the couch, thankful he'd regained consciousness and wanting to make sure I didn't disturb him as he slept.

Thursday morning, as she helped Templeton sit up against the pillows stacked behind his back, the nurse told him if he'd let her feed him some broth, he might be able to say goodbye to the IV soon. He still hadn't spoken but seemed interested in the bowl she'd set on the nightstand.

"Or I could?" I whispered.

He gave his head a tiny shake, but his eyes stayed trained on the broth.

"I think –" the nurse turned and gave me an apologetic look, "– it might be better if you let me. That's what I'm here for, after all. Maybe come back in an hour?"

Swallowing, I nodded. *It's okay,* I soothed myself. The doctor said it would take time before he'd find his way.

I slept on the couch that night, too, but this time I tossed and turned, worrying the blanket between my fingers. Troubled thoughts filled my brain – a mix of anxiety and fear. What if Templeton could talk but didn't want to talk to *me*?

Friday afternoon, I tapped on my bedroom door. Templeton was sitting up in bed, and the nurse removed his IV as he watched. The doctor had packed up his bag and nodded to me as he passed. The nurse finished her task, then followed. She offered an encouraging smile as she left.

Templeton had yet to speak a word. My concern grew each day, but I purposely hid my nervous energy from others, using conversations about nothing with Rabbit and trips to *Coffee Cove* with Big Rabbit to keep myself distracted.

I joined him at his bedside, pulling a chair behind me and picking up the book Mr. Archie brought for me to read aloud to Templeton when he was still unconscious. It was one of Templeton's favorites – a classic sci-fi novel. I turned to the page where I'd left off and started to read. Like the day before, Templeton simply looked at me, the color in his irises fluctuating from faint blue to almost white. He didn't speak. After an hour, I closed the book, resting it on my thigh and sitting in silence. Hesitantly, I reached over and smoothed the blanket at his side with my fingertips. I was afraid to touch him. Something fragile was hanging in the balance, but I didn't know what it was or how to keep it from shattering.

After a minute, I nodded and turned to set the book back on the nightstand.

"No." The word was so soft I barely heard it.

My head swung back around. "No? You want me to keep reading?"

Templeton's brow dipped. He shook his head. "No."

I waited, but he said nothing else. Reluctantly, I stood. "I'll let you rest."

"No."

I studied his face as I sat back down. "I'm not sure what you need, Templeton. I'm sorry."

Wiggling fingers caught my attention.

Cautiously, I reached for his hand. He didn't try to draw away.

"Is this okay?" I asked, my fingers gently wrapping around his.

Templeton gazed down at our joined hands. He nodded.

We sat that way for another 30 minutes until we were interrupted by the nurse. Templeton never looked back up, but I believed something had changed. Maybe simply being quiet together kept something from breaking. Maybe he *was* coming around.

That evening, Mr. Archie came by to bring Templeton fresh clothes. He spent time alone with the man who was once his young charge. Before Mr. Archie left, he pulled me aside.

"I know this has been difficult for you," he said. "But Templeton responded to a couple of my questions. He seemed to process what I asked more readily. I think he's returning to us. Let's see what the morning brings."

Mr. Archie's news gave me hope.

∞∞∞

Saturday morning, I said goodbye to the nurse.

Rabbit and Big Rabbit reported for what I'd grouchily called 'Lucie duty' inside my head. I didn't want to appear ungrateful, but I told both men they didn't have to keep up their babysitting. Rabbit told me he had nothing better to do these days, and Big Rabbit said it was good to be back to normal.

This he said while holding a blaze-orange tabby cat in his arms. Flame rubbed the top of his head against the bottom of Big Rabbit's chin. His front paws kneaded the large man's sizeable arm, and Flame's purring filled the kitchen. I glared at him.

"He's a good little fella, aren't cha?" Big Rabbit cooed over my naughty shapeshifter. Flame rubbed his head back and forth along Big Rabbit's strong jawline. I swore I could see a satisfied smile gracing his thin kitty lips. He'd been in and out all week but remained in his feline form, hiding his other identity. Rabbit wondered where my 'blond boarder' had gone. I told him *Marcus* was staying with a friend. I guessed he was. I hoped it was David and not some random person.

I'd confided in Rabbit about Templeton's behavior and his reluctance to speak. My friend assured me it made sense. Although his experience was different from Templeton's, he understood what it was like to have your entire world flipped upside down and to be at the mercy of others caring for you. He said it was hard for him to talk in the beginning, too.

He told me Templeton was probably angry – not at anyone in particular, but angry in general. *Give him time,* Rabbit told me before promising to come back in the evening. Earlier in the week, my friend added his direct line back into the network phone I used to text Big Rabbit. He reminded me if I needed anything, he was only a text away.

So many good things were happening after months of hurt, anger, and loneliness.

Upstairs, I checked in on Templeton. His eyes opened as I poked my head around the door. He was still sitting up, so I entered the room. I hesitated, foregoing the chair and choosing instead to sit beside him on the bed. I took his hand in mine.

"Feeling better today?" I tried to ask him mostly yes or no questions.

He waited, then nodded.

"Good. Can I get anything for you?"

He shook his head.

I waited. "I'll let you rest."

"No." His fingers tightened.

My heart racing, I squeezed back. "Okay. I can stay as long as you want me to."

Again, a nod, then he produced a frown. "Can't remember."

"What can't you remember?"

Templeton's cheek twitched. "Everything."

I aimed for a calm expression on my face while a knot formed in my stomach. Was he experiencing memory loss? I chose my next words carefully. "Do you know how you came to be here?"

His eyes lifted to mine. "Yes."

"Do you remember where you were before coming here? Do you remember being in the Above?"

"Yes."

"Okay," I replied. I was on uncertain ground. "Do you remember how you ended up in the Above?"

He hesitated, then nodded.

"You were gone a long time," I told him, stroking his arm. I worried this information would be detrimental to his recovery, but I could see the anxiety lining his face. "What is it you think you can't remember?"

He seemed to struggle but finally uttered more than two words. "What I learned."

∞∞∞

Templeton's revelation was unexpected, but I glossed over it, not fully understanding what he meant but eager to reassure him that he was recovering. Whatever was troubling him would be okay. He needed to regain his strength and the rest would follow.

He accepted my explanation – or rather, he didn't have the energy to fight it.

Rabbit returned Saturday evening and spent time upstairs alone with Templeton. I let the two men have their space. Although they had many differences, I knew Rabbit cared deeply for Templeton – and Templeton needed Rabbit whether he admitted it or not. Maybe he felt affection for him, too. Whatever was said would remain between them. When I brought Templeton his dinner of mashed potatoes and gravy with a side of cottage cheese – a soft-diet combination questioned by the convalescing man – I saw more of the Templeton I knew. Seeing Rabbit did him good.

Before I left him for the night, he told me he was feeling better. He still didn't talk much, but he spoke in full sentences now.

This was such a good sign.

∞∞∞

Sunday morning, as I brought him pulp-free orange juice and toast smeared with avocado, an orange kitty zipped past me and leapt up on the end of the bed. There he sat, his front paws pressed firmly together while his tail flipped back and forth behind him.

"You have a cat?" Templeton scowled.

"A 'gift' from Big Rabbit," I said, setting the tray down on the nightstand. I gave the unpredictable feline a tiny shove. "Get down, Flame."

"Flame?"

"That's what I named him. He has a tongue of fire in his fur over his brow." I gave Flame a second push. He made as if to leave, but when I turned away to retrieve Templeton's tray, he spun around, sat down again, and lifted his back leg. He stroked his pink tongue over his balls.

Templeton grimaced. "Is it neutered?"

Flame's head shot up. He growled.

"He's going to be if he doesn't skedaddle back downstairs," I said meaningfully. I pointed toward the bedroom door. "Go. Now."

Flame stood and turned. Before he jumped from the bed, he gave me a butt flicker. We watched as he pranced off, the tip of his tail bobbing in time to his steps. I rolled my eyes. I'd tell Templeton about Flame eventually, but it was a story we didn't need to get into right now.

On the other side of the room, I noticed the curtain was pulled aside and the window raised. A warm morning breeze blew in. "Did you open the window?"

He nodded, taking a bite of the toast. "I needed fresh air."

"You're getting restless," I grinned. "It's a good thing."

He lifted his chin. "Is it?"

"I think so," I told him. "You look better, too."

Self-consciously he passed a hand through his hair. "It's too long."

"Well, it's not Big Rabbit-long," I replied, squinting and evaluating him. "But we can't all have his manly curly locks of love."

Templeton closed his eyes and pressed his lips together.

"You want to smile at me," I teased.

He shrugged, reopening his eyes. "Maybe."

"You should be nice to the lady who's playing nurse to you right now," I told him. "Or you –" I affected a low, monotone accent, "– do not get fruit cup."

The corners of his mouth quirked upward. "Mel Brooks."

"A genius," I told him. "But seriously, if you don't behave, no banana for you with lunch."

∞∞∞

Mr. Archie stopped by an hour later. He was leaving the city and heading for Templeton's estate. I left them to their conversation but caught up with Mr. Archie before he left.

"How do you think he's doing?" I asked.

"I'd say very well. I wouldn't be surprised if he got out of bed today to get some exercise," the older man replied. "He's thinking about routine decisions. He told me he'd like to have roasted lamb this week."

"Really?" I pulled on my bottom lip. "Well, I suppose it's a good sign his appetite is coming back."

"He also had questions about the estate – basic ones, of course. Mostly confirming that everything has been running smoothly while he was away."

I twisted my mouth to the side. "I think he's more talkative with you – and maybe Rabbit. I'm trying not to push him, but he seems uncertain when we talk."

Kindness lined Mr. Archie's face. "He probably *is* uncertain. You know he feels deeply for you. He sees his role as your protector. And now you've seen him at his weakest. This past week turned the tables on him. He is embarrassed on top of trying to physically recover from his ordeal."

"But he doesn't need to be," I argued. "He's gone through…so much. He doesn't even know. But I know. I understand."

Mr. Archie took my hand. "I agree he has not yet fully grasped where he's been and how it affected him. But I can tell you most assuredly, Mr. Templeton does not like to be coddled. He never has. And I think he's feeling…Well, perhaps that it's time for him to get out of bed and back to his life."

"But…But he's still…" I paused. "You don't think it's too early?"

"I think he needs to decide for himself." Mr. Archie patted my hand before letting it go. "He asked about the estate and gave his dinner preferences. He asked after his mother and directed me to schedule a brunch date with her for next weekend. I believe he's ready to return to some normalcy. I guarantee he wants you to do the same."

I lifted a shoulder. "I understand. I'm simply not ready to let him out of my sight yet."

"He won't go far," Mr. Archie promised.

∞∞∞

The afternoon brought Rabbit and Big Rabbit by – each man checking in to see if I needed anything. Emily returned with a bright bouquet of yellow flowers from a shop called *Petaling*. The owners, Bernie and Trudy Bloom, specialized in magical botanicals, as well as more mundane plants.

"These are Butter Huffs," she explained as I led

her upstairs. "Throughout the day they puff out teeny blasts of butter-scented air – you know, like warm butter when you're making cookies? You can't help but feel great when you have a bunch nearby."

"I'm sure Templeton will love them," I lied.

"Oh, he won't," Emily laughed. "But you will."

The door to my bedroom was cracked open, and I gave it a push, peeking around the edge. "You have a visitor."

Templeton was sitting in the chair, reading the sci-fi book. He sighed.

Emily swept past me and swung her arm through the air. "Ta-dah! Flowers." Suddenly overwhelmed, she froze, her grin slipping off her face, her lower lip wobbling.

Templeton's horrified eyes cut to mine.

Be nice, I mouthed.

Another sigh.

"I'm sorry." Emily's voice quavered. She set the bouquet on the bed.

Templeton slowly rose from the chair, and before he could stop her, Emily jumped forward and wrapped her arms around his torso. She rested her head against his chest and cried.

I waved my hands at him.

On the third sigh, he lifted his arms and awkwardly hugged her back, the corners of his mouth tugging down.

Emily sniffled against his robe, then nodded, pulling away. "I know that sucked for you. But I'm really glad you're..." The younger Salesman wiped snot away from her nose with the back of her hand. "I'm just glad."

Templeton continued to be largely uncomfortable. It was time to rescue him. "Hey, Em. How about you go put the Butter Huffs in a vase downstairs? Rabbit will show you where they're kept."

"Right, yeah." Emily worked up a smile. "Oh, wait." Fishing a folded envelope from her back pocket, she handed it to Templeton. "It's your wedding invitation. I knew you'd come back in time. I told Lucie you would – she's a bridesmaid, but I figure you can be each other's plus one."

Templeton looked at the envelope, then at Emily, then at me.

"I'll make sure the date is in his calendar," I assured her.

"Good." She reached out again and tapped Templeton lightly on the arm. "I'll save you a dance." Retrieving the Butter Huffs, Emily left the bedroom, giving a rattled Templeton a wave as she disappeared into the hall.

Templeton's expression pleaded with me.

"How about no more visitors today?" I suggested.

He nodded. "But you can come in whenever you want."

∞∞∞

After eating a portion of pasta and sauce for dinner, Templeton told me he wanted to shower. I couldn't blame him. Sponge baths and wash-ups in the bathroom sink got old fast. I left him to it, remembering Mr. Archie's words. The man didn't want to be babied. And truthfully, I *could* see he was much better – at least physically. Sometimes he'd get a faraway look in his eye, which worried me, but I didn't press him about it.

I tapped on the door to my bedroom, opening it a crack. "Hey," I called softly. "May I come in? Are you decent?"

Upon hearing Templeton's muffled acknowledgment, I pushed the door open, stepping inside and closing it silently behind me. He stood by the bed, his hair combed back and still damp from the shower, the wetness making it appear black. Now that it was two or three inches longer, it curled boyishly over his ears and at the nape of his neck. He'd taken the time to shave again, and although his face was thinner, the familiar angular lines of his handsome face made my heart soar. The latest robe Mr. Archie brought was wrapped around his body, the thick cloth belt tied at his waist. On the bottom of the bed, he'd laid out a pair of black trousers and a neatly folded dress shirt. A bright white undershirt sat next to the outfit. The modest suitcase from Mr. Archie's visit sat open on the chair, and Templeton held a pair of dress socks in his hand.

"Wait, are you going somewhere?" I asked, glancing from the clothing to Templeton. "It's getting late. I mean, it's after 8 o'clock."

Templeton gestured to the closet door. "I've been thinking about this all day. I'm well enough to door travel to the estate. I'm sure Mr. Archie is eager to return to a routine."

"Mr. Archie or you?"

Guilt flickered over his face. "Probably both.

But you haven't even slept in your own bed since I've been back."

I laughed lightly, realizing he didn't know how I'd slept curled at his side the first two nights he was home. *Home.* I shortened the distance between us, standing only inches away. "It's only been a week. You don't have to leave. Everyone else is gone. No one is downstairs. We're alone. I know you feel better, but you shouldn't overdo it. Door travel requires precise energy, and...Well, it's only us now." I reached forward, letting my fingers brush one of his hands.

His strange eyes shimmered. "It does require precision – which comes easily to me." He lifted the same hand I'd touched to my face, the back of his fingers barely making contact with my skin. He paused where the faint burn scar appeared on my cheek, a shadow crossing his face when he touched it with a fingertip.

My eyes slid shut, and I allowed myself a moment to savor the intimacy. "The thing is, we keep finding ways to mess things up." My hands drifted upward, my eyes reopening when my palms landed on his chest. I stroked the front of his robe. "And it's cost us. I almost lost...I almost lost you forever. I know it seems silly to you, but I don't want you to leave tonight – even if you are well enough, even if it makes sense." I paused. "And I do want to sleep in my bed tonight."

Slowly, Templeton's head tilted to the side. He tossed the socks back into the suitcase. The corners of his mouth rose the tiniest bit. "You want me to stay tonight. With you."

I nodded, guiding him backward until he sat down on the bed. My hands cupped his face as I brushed my lips against his mouth. I could smell the birchwood soap wafting up from his body. It about did me in – the earthy scent richer when mixed with the oil of his skin. I straightened but kept his face cradled between my palms. An excited trembling grew in my belly. I was finally going to tell him what I wanted. "If you feel well enough, yes, I want you to spend the night with me. Do you...Do you want to be with me, too?"

Templeton responded by moving backward, pushing a pillow behind him as he rested against the headboard. His hand caught mine, and he guided me onto the bed, my knees pressing into the bedspread as I straddled his lap. When his hands landed on my hips, I kissed him a second time. I pressed his mouth open with my lips, pushing my tongue inside to tease his. Inching my body forward, my hands returned to the sides of his face as our kiss deepened.

I felt rather than heard a sharp grunt against my mouth as he twitched. I edged backward slightly, putting space between us. He pulled a pained face and repositioned himself against the pillow.

"Are you okay?" His expression alarmed me. "Maybe we *should* wait. I'm sorry. I...I shouldn't have pushed –"

"No, I'm fine," he interrupted. "I'm just stiff."

I covered my mouth with a hand to stifle the happy-but-nervous giggle bubbling up. It was even funnier when he seemed confused by my reaction. The front of his robe above the belt gaped open, and I caressed his chest. "Um, think about it."

A beat later, realization flittered across his face. He shook his head. "I meant I'm still a little stiff from staying in bed this past week."

My hand slipped down to the belt of his robe, my index finger drawing a circle on the knot.

"As much as I want to be with you tonight, I also don't want to hurt you."

"I don't think you need to worry," he replied. "But I'm not exactly at my most energetic. I had a different vision of the first time we'd be together."

My fingers pulled at the knot. "You've thought about us? The first time?"

"Many times." Templeton's voice dropped lower. I shivered as I finished untying the belt.

I didn't pull the robe open but walked my fingers lower, skimming my fingertips over the erection rising under the fine fabric. I pursed my lips, my eyebrows shooting upward. My fingers were walking a longer trail than expected.

"Second thoughts?" A particularly wicked smile appeared on his lips. Another sign he was feeling better.

"My, we think a lot of ourselves, don't we?" I teased, still tracing the shape of him through the robe.

The naughty expression remained.

I kissed him again, this time letting my hand wander under his robe while our lips sought to please each other. His skin felt hot and tight yet silky smooth. I stroked him. "Forget any plans you had," I said against his mouth. "Let me lead for once."

I straightened then, rising and pulling my tee shirt off over my head. Templeton's attention snapped to the three gemstones of the Crimson Stone nestled between my breasts. They hung from a silver chain, and the flames inside each piece swayed. Long fingers glided up from my hips, sweeping over the white lace covering the underside of my breasts, and lifted the three gemstones. "They're activated."

"They are." There would be time to explain everything to him later. "But I couldn't reunite the pieces without your spell."

Templeton contemplated the gemstones. "But how did you –?"

"Later," I said, arching my body as I reached behind my back with both hands to unhook my bra. I pulled the straps down my arms, and the garment fell away.

Templeton abandoned the gemstones, his question forgotten. Instead, both of his hands palmed the curves of my breasts.

I relished the feeling of his graceful fingers sweeping over my skin. Lifting up onto my knees, I pushed the robe off his shoulders before stilling.

"Lucie?" Templeton asked against my skin. He'd begun to kiss the sensitive spot by my collarbone but stopped when he felt me hesitate.

"I'm trying to think of a sexy way to shimmy off these shorts," I admitted with a faint laugh.

"Everything you do is sexy." He resumed kissing me, but his hands left my breasts to pull at the waistband of my cotton shorts, his thumbs hooking inside my clothing.

Taking the cue from him, I twisted, lifting off his lap and bringing my knees together. Templeton sat forward, lowering my shorts – along with my underwear – and I quickly pulled them the rest of the way off, sending everything over the side of the bed. Naked, I knelt beside him. His gaze roamed over my body while he peeled away the rest of his robe. It joined my clothing on the floor.

For a few seconds, neither one of us moved. This was the one time in our lives we'd have this first moment together – it was unplanned, but it was the *right* time. Templeton swiped his tongue back and forth over his lower lip. His left hand reached for my right, and lacing his fingers through mine, he pulled me onto his lap. I straddled his thighs again, my knees on either side of him.

"Closer," he whispered.

I chuckled. We could hardly be any closer. Bowing my head, I kissed him, shuddering as his hand wrapped around the nape of my neck and his tongue slid into my mouth. I let him take control, savoring the kiss until I couldn't go another second without feeling him inside me.

Pulling my mouth away from his, I reached between us, positioning him between my thighs. Templeton's barely blue eyes never left mine as I sank down, enveloping him. I placed my hands on his shoulders.

Oh.

He felt wonderful. I rocked my hips, controlling how I wanted to experience this pleasure with him during our first time. My eyelids lowered, and my head dropped back. I'd waited too long for this. I let myself leave my head – forgetting all my worries – and concentrated solely on how he felt inside me, how his mouth felt on my skin. The rhythm coursing through my hips came naturally, and I rose to again experience the sensation of taking him deep inside me.

Templeton's expression was amused but affectionate as he gripped my hips and steered me down onto him. He held me in place. "Don't move."

Lifting the three pieces of the Crimson Stone, Templeton attached them to each other, forming the one magical object. He muttered the spell – *the one I could never find* – used to reunite the three gemstones. The Crimson Stone came to life, sending a blazing red flash through the room. Templeton nestled it between my breasts, where it hummed and pulsed.

Fascinated, I looked down, watching the flames dance inside the one Stone.

"Lucie." Templeton's hand pushed my hair back away from my face. "The Stone has never been more beautiful than right now."

His words stirred a shyness inside me. Instead of speaking, I leaned forward and kissed him.

He nosed his way to my ear. "Sit up and keep your eyes closed."

Smiling, I did as he directed. "Can I also do this?" I swiveled my hips. He gripped them.

"No. Be still," he gritted out. "Behave yourself,

witch."

I raised an eyebrow, but obeyed.

His palm covered the Crimson Stone, and he pushed it gently against my flesh. A few quiet words passed through his lips. Another spell. The temperature of the Stone grew.

"Now, slowly and gently raise your fire," Templeton directed. "Not too much. Don't burn me. I only want you to connect with the Stone's fire."

Again, I did as he said, meticulously lifting the fire coursing under my skin. I let it roll over me like warm bathwater. "Like this?"

"Yes," he answered, his voice hushed. "I can feel it. Don't open your eyes. Focus on me now. Let me in, Lucie."

Like so long ago, Templeton let his magic drift around me, pressing his energy into mine. I opened to him completely, my lips parting. Inside my mind, I watched as the shadows swirled before brightening with gold stars populating a blue-black sky. "Where are you, Magician?"

"Right here." And he was. He was inside my mind with me. His hand took mine, and he drew me forward. He pulled me into the night, waving his other hand against the velvet sky we passed through. "Watch."

A shower of shooting stars filled the endless ceiling inside my brain, mesmerizing me. "I've never experienced anything like this," I told him, overwhelmed by his magic. "It's beautiful."

The stars continued to streak across the universe he created inside my mind as Templeton released the Crimson Stone. His hands returned to my hips, and he guided me back and forth, urging me to ride him. The Stone swung away from my body, then tapped my breastbone with a comforting thud in time to my rhythm. "Don't stop. Keep your eyes closed. Watch the stars," he instructed softly. A moan followed his words.

As the flickering swirled around us, filling the blackness with glittery light, my fire grew inside me. Pitching forward, I blindly reached for my headboard, one hand gripping the wood while the other landed on his shoulder for balance. My fingers splayed over his warm skin. I soared through the magnificent night, riding the celestial wave he'd created. Somewhere outside myself, I heard Templeton's voice shake when he said my name. As my fire grew, I left his exhalation behind, my body shuddering through an exquisite explosion of its own, filled with shooting stars.

Chapter 21

Early in the morning, with dawn peeking in through the curtains, I awakened to Templeton's mouth moving over mine. My last memory of the night was sliding toward sleep under his arm, my cheek against his chest. His heartbeat soothed me into slumber while his graceful fingers caressed my hair, my arm, my face.

He'd since eased me onto my back, urging my thighs apart with his knee while I slept. Now he balanced above me, his hands on either side of my shoulders. As I became aware of my surroundings, he pushed his tongue into my mouth before retreating and catching my lower lip between his teeth. He gently tugged. The corners of my lips curved upward.

"Good morning," I lisped.

Releasing me, he nosed my face to the side and

purred into my ear. "It's about to be."

"Oh, is it?" I replied, lifting my chin so he could kiss his way down my neck. "I guess you're no longer feeling too stiff to be on top?"

"Be quiet," he admonished before nibbling his way to a shoulder. His hand caught mine, lifting it and threading our fingers together. He pressed it into the pillow, sliding it toward the headboard. My back arched when he lowered his head and swept his tongue over a hardening nipple.

My free hand was captured, and he lifted it to join the other. "Keep them there," he instructed as he released his grip. He returned to my breasts, his mouth warm and wet on my sleepy skin. He blessed each nipple with equal parts nipping and nursing. I shivered as the gooseflesh rose across my chest. This *was* good. Oh, *so* good!

Templeton kissed a path down the full underside of my left breast, before rubbing his face against the soft flesh of my stomach. He pushed his tongue into my belly button, making me jump. He snickered against my midsection when I let out a squeak.

My hand floated down and touched the side of

his face. "I'm ticklish."

"You shouldn't reveal a weakness I can exploit," he teased as his naughty digits dug into my sides. He grinned wickedly when I wriggled and shrieked. When he paused, I quieted but stiffened in anticipation. He did it again, and I struggled, my laughter laced with pain.

"Stop it, Templeton," I panted as I tried to pry his hands off my sides.

"Put your hands back where I left them and I'll stop," he taunted.

"Please!" I begged as he forced several more cries out of me with his evil fingers.

"Put your hands up," he needled me. "Then. I'll. Stop."

"Bastard!" I swore as I tore my hands away from his and threw them upward. I could feel the flush spreading over my skin alongside the fire coursing impatiently under it. My eyes screwed shut. "You are such a bastard," I sighed as the tickling stopped and turned into soothing touches and squeezes.

"Such a mouth," he mumbled against the curve of my belly. His hands skimmed my hips as he backed his body down the bed. Gliding his palms over my skin, he pressed them against the insides of my thighs.

I felt his warm breath, then his mouth grazing over my most intimate parts, his pointed tongue probing. He found his target, and I hissed. Sliding a hand under my knee, he lifted and pressed my bent leg to the side, leaving me fully exposed.

Templeton's right hand gripped my thigh; his left flattened against my lower belly, pinning me to the bed. I looked down to find Templeton watching me. I turned my head.

His skilled tongue was relentless. I didn't want him to stop – I didn't want to stop what was coming. I could feel it building deep inside, the heat spreading up my back as my hips bucked upward.

The thought of Templeton, so controlled as he watched my body's reaction, pushed me over the edge. I shook, my back forming a curve as I came. He didn't pull away when I cried out, an orgasm reverberating through me in a blast of sharp pleasure. It lingered as I relaxed into the bed, easing down from such a blissful high.

He kissed a trail upward over my hip before sliding higher, nipping the rounded side of my breast. His body covered mine as his kisses returned to my lips. This time I pressed my tongue into his mouth.

His hands reached up, clasping mine as the solid muscle of his thighs nestled against my softer counterparts. Templeton shifted, his erection nudging against the heat between my legs. As I opened to him, he burrowed inside, filling my body with bliss and my heart with joy.

The world melted away. I drifted on the buzz leftover from my orgasm and the deliberate fluidity of Templeton's lovemaking. His hips rose and lowered, rocking my body along with the bed. I met each downward stroke until he overpowered me, his pace increasing as he drove me into the mattress.

"Lucie, I'm…" Templeton's words sounded hoarse against my mouth as his last three thrusts forced the headboard to slap the wall. His cheek slid along mine, and he buried his face against my neck. My eyes widened at his sudden intensity, my vision unfocused in those last seconds. My hands were squeezed against the pillow. His hips lifted once more before he sank himself deep inside me and trembled.

Templeton gasped against the skin of my neck under my ear. Drunk on the sensation of him coming inside me, I stared blindly at my ceiling.

When his grasp on my hands loosened, I coasted my fingers down both of his arms, one hand coming to rest on his hip. The other sought the base of his neck, my fingers playing in his hair while I memorized the feel of his hips cradled between my thighs. His weight rested on my body as the last tremors flitted through him. Fascinated, I listened to his breath moving deeply in and out of his lungs as he recovered. Curving my fingers, I drew my fingernails over his scalp, causing him to shiver.

Templeton eased back up onto his elbows, our bodies remaining intimately joined. He brushed a stray hair from my face as I peered up into his eyes. They had turned such a brilliant royal blue.

"Templeton," I whispered. "Your eyes, they're so blue."

"Are they?" He blinked several times as though he might be able to sense the change.

"I've never seen them like this. They're beautiful." My hand drifted to the side of his face.

He turned and kissed my palm, but his expression grew wary. He dropped his gaze to the vicinity of my chin. "Does it bother you when they change? When the color completely drains away?"

I frowned as I smiled up at him. He seemed painfully anxious – almost shy. "Of course not," I assured him. "I love everything about you."

Astonished, Templeton raised his bright eyes again. My words hung in the air, and I realized what I'd said, the words that flowed so easily from my lips.

I love everything about you.

A corner of Templeton's mouth lifted in a half-smile, and he lowered his head, tenderly pressing his lips to mine. He kissed me.

And kissed me.

And kissed me again.

∞∞∞

Eventually, I pulled myself from our warm love nest, scooping up a discarded satin robe and wrapping it around me. My room smelled of burnt vanilla – a somewhat unusual manifestation that occasionally happened after I'd…Well, after I was *satisfied*.

No one's ever complained.

Templeton watched me dress from the bed. He rested on his stomach, his arms raised and wrapped around a pillow. The blanket only covered him from the waist down, and I admired the smooth curve of his lower back. He had lost weight, yes, but he'd not lost his appeal. His cheek was pressed into the pillow, and one eye tracked my movements while the other remained hidden. Even with his arms lifted and the lower half of his face partially hidden, I could see he was smiling.

Or smirking. He looked very pleased with himself.

I couldn't hide the satisfaction on my face either, so I didn't hold his smugness against him. "I'm going downstairs to make coffee."

"You don't have to," he said, lifting his head an inch to speak. "Come back to bed. Be with me."

I shook my head at the temptation he presented. "I need coffee. Do you think you're up to coming downstairs, or do you want me to bring you a cup?"

"Are you really asking if I'm well enough to get out of this bed?" Templeton rolled onto his back, tucking his hands behind his head. The covers slipped lower, the edge barely touching the bottom of his hip bones. There were random moments when Templeton appeared incredibly boyish. This was one of them.

"Point taken." If I stayed a second longer, I *was* climbing back into bed. "Come downstairs. I'll have coffee. There's orange juice for you, too."

He said nothing, and I finished tying the robe's belt around my waist before stepping out into the hall. In the spare room, the bed was made, and Flame was nowhere to be seen. I fished out a clean nightshirt from the laundry before stopping in the bathroom and freshening up. Shirt and robe rearranged, I tossed the washcloth into the hamper and headed downstairs.

Flame seemed to be out. Either he hadn't come home at all last night, or he'd left early in the morning. My money was on the former since the spare bed was still made. Maybe the intimacy I shared with Templeton would remain between us.

I pulled the bag of ground coffee from the pantry, placing a filter inside the coffee pot, and setting the glass carafe on the warming plate.

Drawing a short glass from the cupboard, I set it on the counter before retrieving the orange juice. I chewed on my lip while I evaluated the fridge shelves. Templeton had once made me a perfect French omelet. I, however, was not as skilled in the omelet department. I wondered if he would like scrambled eggs and toast. I hummed while I pulled out a carton of fresh eggs and some milk.

I whisper-sung a line from a favorite song as I set a mixing bowl on the counter.

As I was getting two coffee mugs from the cupboard, a barefoot Templeton wandered into the kitchen. He'd pulled on a pair of trousers and a button-down shirt with the sleeves pushed up. It remained untucked. Pressing against my back, he wrapped his arms around me, nuzzling the side of my neck.

"Orange juice is on the counter," I told him after a moment of surrendering to this unusual domesticity.

He reluctantly released me, helping himself to the juice. He chose a barstool and took a sip from the glass. "Would you like help?"

This type of everyday exchange was new for us but welcome. "I've got this."

I watched as Templeton reached for the newspaper I'd left on the counter, experiencing a disturbing flashback of Sebastian also sitting barefoot on the same barstool one week prior. I pushed the thought away. No, I would not let memories of Sebastian into this space. This morning was too precious.

Templeton read the top headlines. "I'll need to catch up on what's been happening in the city."

"I'm sure some things will be new to you." I sliced bread for toast. My voice became strained. "You were gone for such a long time."

"I didn't know how much time was passing," he replied. "When I was in the Above, I didn't even consider my absence would be noticed. I never thought about anything except the books the library offered. I didn't realize you were trying to get into the Above to find me."

I paused and read the curious expression forming on his face. "But you're home safe. We don't have to talk about everything right now. We have time." I turned away and cracked an egg into the mixing bowl. My growing anxiety pulled open a sour pit in my stomach. How upset would he be when I told him what I had to do to get him back? When I admitted I'd cut a deal with Sebastian, accompanying him to the Below so I could get into the Above? *Please don't make me tell you anything right now,* I pleaded silently. *We need some time together without the outside world tearing us apart.*

But then it happened. Templeton asked the questions I dreaded.

"Something's been on my mind. How were you able to travel through the fifth door? If you didn't use the Crimson Stone, how did you open it? How did you get into the Above?"

"Let's eat first," I stalled, pressing my lips together as the tension drew across my shoulders. "Then we can talk." I pulled a whisk from a drawer and began to beat the eggs. For a moment, the only sound in the kitchen was the tinny clang of metal on metal as I scrambled our breakfast.

I could feel Templeton's energy bumping up against mine, seeking. I jolted, pushing the mixing bowl farther back on the counter. "Don't do that."

"What are you hiding from me?" Templeton's voice remained calm, but his question revealed his suspicion. The relaxed demeanor he'd worn into the kitchen drained away.

I'd left the pantry door cracked open, and Flame strolled into the kitchen in his cat form.

He paused, sizing up Templeton as he sat on the floor, his tail wrapping around his furry body. Its tip rested on top of his two front paws, flicking up and down.

Templeton registered Flame's arrival before redirecting his attention back to me. Again, his energy nudged mine, causing me to step to the side as if I could avoid it. "I can sense it, Lucie. You're not telling me something."

"It's a lot to go through. It's a long story." I snuck a peek at Flame. He remained laser-focused on Templeton. "Please, let's have breakfast and coffee, then we can talk about the past three months."

"It's a simple question. How did you get into the Above?" Templeton's voice lowered.

Flame rose to his feet, taking a couple of steps toward the Salesman. The claws on his two front paws extended and flexed.

"Flame, time to go back outside," I said, crossing to him and bending. The 'cat' easily avoided my grasp, skittering sideways. He changed direction and launched himself onto a counter before leaping to the top of my refrigerator. He sat out of reach and resumed staring at Templeton.

"Lucie, did you go through the fifth door? Yes or no? This is not a difficult question." The color in Templeton's irises faded dramatically – radically – and in that second, my heart crumpled.

There was no way I could answer his question without undoing much of what we'd built while making love. Maybe everything we'd built. I swallowed. "No. I didn't get into the Above through the fifth door. I had no way to open it after the Beam took you." My voice thinned when I referenced the monster that stole Templeton from me.

Templeton's fingers bent around his glass as he contemplated my answer. He lifted it and drained the last of the juice. Setting it back on the countertop, he raised his eyes. "How did you enter the Above?"

His energy hovered around me, a hair's breadth beyond mine. I could feel the unseen force. It felt controlled but angry. I chose my words carefully. "I found another way, another door. Then, I found you."

I knew my short answers were not going to appease him, but I was hopeful he would stop. That we could have this one day before everything exploded. My eyes grew hot and wet.

He noticed, but there was no sympathy in his expression when he rose from the barstool. His eyes never left mine when he pushed the seat under the lip of the counter. I saw his chest rise and fall. He anticipated the storm coming on the heels of my answers. "Where is this other door located?"

"It's in the Below," I said quietly.

"The Below," he repeated. I watched as Templeton's jaw clenched. "You went into the Below?"

"Yes." I felt dizzy. Panic bloomed in my chest.

"Through the sixth door?" Templeton stopped looking directly at me. Instead, he stared past me, unblinking. The controlled energy he'd wrapped around mine morphed into furious waves and constricted. I suppressed my instinct to fight against it – now was not the time to do battle with him.

"I made a deal to get to a door located in the Below. It leads straight into the Above. I couldn't make the fifth door open. I didn't know what else to do. You'd been gone for three months, Templeton. Three months! I didn't know if you'd still be alive. I was running out of time

– *you* were running out of time. I couldn't wait any longer." The words rushed out of my mouth. I swayed, lightheaded. "I did what I had to do."

"This deal..." Templeton's voice turned menacing. "Who made it with you?"

Out of the corner of my eye, I saw Flame rising from where he'd been sitting on his haunches.

"Templeton..." I faltered.

"Tell me, Lucie." His voice grew tight. His fingertips touched his empty glass.

"Sebastian." The name passing through my lips was said so quietly I wasn't sure if I'd actually made a sound or simply mouthed the answer.

Templeton snagged the juice glass from the counter and hurled it across the room. It hit the wall and shattered.

Flame hissed from his perch on top of the refrigerator before jumping back to the counter and bouncing to the floor. He raced past Templeton and disappeared through the doorway into the hall.

Templeton's eyes, with their pupils barely pinpricks, tracked Flame as he fled the kitchen. They ricocheted back to me. "What the hell is going on?"

I lifted my hands, my palms facing him in surrender. "I didn't know what else to do, Templeton. I couldn't get to you, but I could conjure Sebastian. We knew he'd been through the fifth door. I needed to find out how he opened it. He was my only hope."

"Your cat." He gnashed his teeth.

My mouth hung open. What was he talking about? He was upset over the hissing? "I don't know what you mean. Flame? I think you scared him."

"Your cat just door traveled out of this kitchen." Templeton's head snapped back toward the hall as Flame returned.

The shapeshifter was in his human form. He breezed in from the hallway wearing nothing but a pair of basketball shorts. I had the presence of mind to give thanks for the small things – at least he wasn't naked during yet another hellish confrontation in my kitchen.

Flame positioned himself directly in front of me and faced Templeton. His long arms hung relaxed at his sides, but I wasn't fooled. I saw the rippling of agile muscle under the skin on his back. "I know things haven't been good for you, man, but I think it's time for you to go."

Templeton laughed. "You're out of your league."

"Flame," I tried to cut in.

"Look, I don't care who you are or what you think, but this is not how you behave in Lucie's home," Flame continued calmly.

Well, at least there was another win – Flame didn't say 'our home.' But when I tried to step around him, he angled himself in front of me again, pushing me backward with one hand. I ducked out from under his rangy arm. "Flame, enough."

Templeton stepped forward, his door travel energy rising as he zeroed in on Flame. I jockeyed between the two men, my fingers brushing against the front of Templeton's shirt as I tried to defuse the escalation. He jerked back as if I'd called my fire into my hands. "Don't touch me."

I swallowed the ball of hurt swelling in my throat. This was crazy! "Templeton, please listen to me."

"I don't want to hear a word from you," he snarled, taking another step and increasing the distance between us. He raised a hand, gesturing toward Flame. "And this? I don't even want to know what you're playing at with… With *this*."

"Let him go," Flame said, putting his hand on my shoulder. I shrugged it off, following Templeton as he started to turn away.

I reached for him again when I realized he was raising his door travel energy. "Templeton, please don't leave. Not now. Not after this morning…"

"Fuck you, Lucie." His face turned to stone.

His words hit me hard – staccato blows slamming against my heart. Frantic, I blurted out the only thing I believed would make him stay. "He set fire to the Stone."

Templeton's hand remained suspended in the air, but the royal blue waves of his door travel energy dropped instantly. "What do you mean?"

"The Stone was dormant. He touched a piece, and it lit up. Flame 'fired up' the Crimson Stone." I raised a shaking hand. "Please stay here. I will tell you what happened. Please don't run away from me." My heart was clay spinning on a potter's wheel. Abandoned by Templeton's hands, it beat itself into a desperate, ugly shape.

Templeton glared at me. "You have three minutes."

I turned to Flame. "Go wait in the backyard. Now."

"Lucie, I don't think..." The shapeshifter was ready to argue.

"Now Flame! For fuck's sake, please listen to me for once!" My temper fully flared, and the toaster popped and blew on the counter by the stove. The three of us startled at the noise.

Flame lifted his hands in submission. "Easy. It's okay. I'm going to be right outside. If you need me, yell." His focus bounced to Templeton and back to me. "Got it? He's not worth it if this is how he behaves after what you risked for him."

"Outside, Flame." I pointed to the pantry. He shot one last look of warning at Templeton before leaving the kitchen.

Templeton snorted.

I slowly spun to face him. "I didn't know Flame was a shapeshifter until he'd been here for a few weeks. No one knew. Almost three weeks ago, I was on the couch with the Stone, alone except for Flame. I was reading through one of your books of magic and thinking out loud." I stopped, my arms lifting and falling helplessly. "You were all I could think about."

"Please," he sneered.

"No!" I hollered. He couldn't dismiss my pain. "No, you have no idea what I was going through. Every fucking moment of the day I thought about you. I dreamt about you every night. My heart was dying."

Disgusted, he shook his head at me. He opened his mouth and made as if to answer.

"No." I pointed at him. I was angry, yes, but I was more afraid of Templeton walking out. "You want to know about Flame and the Stone, you listen. You don't speak."

Templeton glowered at me but remained silent.

"I had the Stone and Flame jumped into my lap. I had no reason to think he was anything but a cat." I ran both hands through my hair, remembering the pivotal moment when Flame touched the Crimson Stone. "He touched one of the pieces of the Stone with a claw, and it immediately lit up."

"Then what happened?" Templeton asked coolly.

I shook my head. "Then he shapeshifted into the young man you saw."

Templeton crossed his arms. "Does he know

about the prophecy?"

"I didn't tell him. When I asked him about using magic, he told me sometimes he can do 'things' when he's a cat." My adrenaline high plummeted. I turned, pulling out a barstool and sitting. I rested my elbows on the counter. "His mother is a shifter, too. Nothing magical happening there. He doesn't know his father, though. I'm going on the assumption that's the connection to any magical ability he might have. Obviously, there was a magical being in his ancestral line."

Templeton eyed me guardedly. "One of his parents is a Salesman. I could see his door travel energy as he left the kitchen. I saw it again when he came back."

"It would have to be the father." My shoulders hopped up again. "But I didn't know he could door travel until now. I didn't even realize that's what happened until you told me."

"You're a wealth of great decisions, aren't you?" Templeton derided me. "You're letting a stranger live with you. Someone who has misled you more than once. Someone who has some sort of magical ability *on top of* being a Salesman if he's door traveling. And how old is he? Salesmen don't fully develop their power to door travel until they're 30. By the looks of him, he's not even close. This means there's much more than meets the eye with this shifter. You don't know the type of magical being you've allowed into your home. Unbelievable."

"If he's truly our successor and linked to the prophecy, I thought it would be wise to keep him here." I rubbed my face. I'd run out of steam.

"Are you sleeping with him, too?" His words were sharp and cold, like thin shards of ice pressed into tender skin.

I knew this question was coming – and I knew Templeton really didn't think I was. But it would be another angry swipe he could take at me. Still, I was disappointed he'd stooped to it. "I am not." I looked Templeton square in the eye. "I've not slept with anyone – no one – since you've been gone. Until last night, I hadn't been with anyone since last fall, long before you were taken by the Beam of Light."

"Since last fall," he scoffed. "Since Sebastian, you mean."

I nodded, lifting my hand and letting it fall to the countertop. What could I say? It was true.

"Yes."

"And then you conjured him. And you...What? Went to the Below? With Sebastian?" A muscle in Templeton's cheek twitched.

"Yes."

"And he helped you out of the goodness of his black heart?" Templeton mocked me. "Why doesn't that sound like the Sebastian I know?"

"I compelled him to help me." I drew my hand over my forehead.

"So, you conjured him and made him take you to the Below, then what? You just happened to know about this door and –"

"Sebastian told me about it," I interrupted. "I conjured him specifically to ask how to open the fifth door. He couldn't tell me. It was open when he found it last year – when someone from Ivanov Transport found it. Then he went through it like we already knew. But he told me about a different door in the Below leading straight into the Above. I told him I wanted to go to it."

"How did you get into the Below?" Templeton still hadn't moved away from the doorway.

I flinched. "Sebastian door traveled with me as his passenger."

Templeton's tone turned condescending. "Stupid. You're lucky you made it. He's incompetent."

"Clearly not," I snapped. "Because we made it there without issue."

Templeton reacted as if I'd slapped him. "I suppose in a pinch, any Salesman will do – for door traveling or otherwise."

"Okay, I've had enough." I slid off the kitchen barstool. I crossed to the sink, wearily staring out the window as I struggled to hold my anger in check. Outside, Flame relaxed in the morning sun, his long legs stretching out from the garden chair to the matching table where he balanced his oversized feet. His arms were crossed over his bare chest, and his eyes remained closed. The sunshine kissed his face as he lifted his chin.

Déjà vu.

I turned back toward Templeton and finally lost it. "Here's the deal. Yes, I conjured Sebastian. Yes, I went into the Below. Oh, by the way, it's a fucking nightmare down there – in case you were interested. I'm thankful I made it back in one piece because guess what? While in the Below, I met the Darkness. Remember the

Darkness from the book of fairy tales? Yes, *that* Darkness. Turns out he's the – *get this* – the King of the Below, a demon called Asmodeus! Oh, and funnily enough, he was overjoyed to see me. Why, you ask? Because I'm the Light. Sound familiar? Why, yes! Lucie's the fucking Light, and the Darkness was so very happy to have her around. Asmodeus wanted me to stay in the Below, Templeton. He made it hard for me to leave. But no matter the temptation he put before me – and there was *real* temptation – I was not giving up on finding you, on bringing you back. Then, because I haven't had enough of them in my life, there was a lovely bloody fight to get back out of the Below – but we still got through the door and made it into the Above. I made it to *you*. I found *you*. I want *you*." My voice cracked. I'd balled my hands into fists during my diatribe, and I shook with the effort to keep my fire inside me.

Templeton's lips parted. The soft blue flowed back to his irises.

For a moment, I had hope.

He dropped his gaze to the floor. "You said 'we.'"

"What do you mean?" Breathless, I studied his

reaction.

"You said 'we still got through the door.' You mean you and Sebastian. He was with you when you went into the Above." He raised his head.

My lips formed an 'O' and I nodded. "Yes."

"You didn't leave Sebastian in the Below?" It was Templeton's turn to sound defeated.

I shook my head.

Seconds passed as he seemed to search for the words he wanted to say. Finally, he spoke, his expression resigned. "I'm going upstairs to get my things. Please do not follow me. I'm leaving."

"Templeton, wait! Please, not after everything —"

He stopped, but the pained expression on his face halted my speech. "I'm going to let you in on a little secret, Lucie. You're not the only one with a heart that can be broken. You're not the only one who feels things. The world was supposed to stop when you were hurt by... *Basha*." He spit out Sebastian's nickname. "But here's the difference between us. I'm not going to expect everyone to put their lives on hold for me no matter how much I've been hurt by *you*. The world can keep on turning. Even after last night." His voice grew somber. "Even after this morning."

Before I could reply, he door traveled out of the kitchen. Like Flame did earlier, Templeton simply traveled upstairs. I resisted the urge to chase after him. Instead, I returned to the barstool, sitting and folding my arms on the surface of the counter. I laid my head down.

I was too empty to even cry.

Chapter 22

Flame returned, his eyes wide as they swept through the kitchen.

"He's gone." I'd remained where Templeton had left me, my fingers stroking the Crimson Stone pulsing gently under my nightshirt. "He left. He's gone."

Flame stood on the other side of the counter. "What happened, Lucie? What went wrong?"

"He's angry I conjured Sebastian," I told him. "I get it, I really do. He hates Sebastian – and with good reason."

"Do you hate the demon?" Flame asked.

I shook my head. "No. But we're not…We're not friends, either. We're nothing."

Flame raised his eyebrows. "And your Templeton doesn't believe you?"

I lifted my palm. "What do you think? He doesn't trust me. He doesn't understand I did what I had to do to get him back. I conjured Sebastian as a last resort. Everything else was failing me. The Stone, the piece of magic I hoped to use to translate Templeton's book...My Congress membership is suspended...Nothing could help me. Even Rabbit abandoned me." As soon as I said the last sentence, I slapped my hand over my mouth, my eyes screwing shut. No. I didn't mean that.

"Oh, Luscious," Flame tutted, rounding the counter. He stood by my barstool and hugged me as I struggled to get control of myself.

"I've had no one to help me," I said through one lone, pathetic sob.

"Except for the demon," Flame mused.

"Yeah," I answered, angrily rubbing an eye. "Not that Sebastian's Mr. Altruism, but yeah. He was the only one. We made a deal, but he also did everything he could to help me. He hates Templeton, but he did whatever it took to help me get to him because that's what I wanted. He did it for me."

"What did you do for him in return?" Flame released me so he could retrieve a paper towel.

"I agreed to go into the Below with him." I took the offering and blew my nose. "My presence was supposed to earn his freedom."

"Going there wasn't the best idea." Flame leaned against the counter. "But I understand why you did it."

"You're the only one." I rested my elbow on the countertop and lowered my forehead to my palm. I hoped the pressure would lessen the headache developing behind my eyes. Again, I touched the Crimson Stone through my clothing.

"The Stone you wear," Flame began. "Did Templeton give it to you?"

"What? No. I only held onto it after he was taken from us. He'd dropped it in the Walled Zone, and I picked it up and used it – until it was knocked out of my hand. That's when it split." I pulled the necklace out from under my shirt and examined the Stone. "He reunited the three pieces last night when we…When…Um, we talked."

"I get it," Flame replied. "I figured you could use some privacy once he was better."

I made a face. "I guess it didn't matter."

"Oh, it matters." Flame's blond eyebrows bounced up and down once. He pointed. "He left the Stone with you. He doesn't strike me as a man who leaves loose ends. Now he has an excuse to return."

"Ha. Maybe."

"No maybes," Flame said. "I know men. I know drama. And I know men aren't above it."

"Templeton's not like that," I argued.

"No? That's not what I witnessed, Lucie. Look, he's probably not fully in his right mind since he was trapped in the Above place. But this guy has some pretty big energy going on, and that means drama." Flame crossed his arms.

"Hmm." I eyeballed Flame. "Can you see Templeton's energy?"

He shrugged, his arms still in front of his chest. "I can feel it."

"And what about your energy?" I asked.

"Oh, it's big," he laughed. "But my ego is nothing like your Templeton's – or the demon's, for that matter. I could feel his, too."

"I see." I continued to give him the hairy eye. Was the energy he sensed Salesman-related? "And when were you going to tell me you could door travel from place to place?"

He winced and grinned at the same time, ducking his head. "Is that what you call it?"

"Yes, and I think you know that already. You

told me your mother is a shapeshifter but is she also a Salesman?" I knew the answer, but I decided we'd have this conversation in steps.

"Nope. Only a shapeshifter."

"So that means your father must've been a Salesman," I said.

"I guess." Flame turned away and rooted through the refrigerator. "Ooh, did you buy strawberry *Toro*?"

"Um, no." Sebastian must've stashed a can in my fridge. "Back to your father."

"I already told you, I have no idea who he was. Mom doesn't either. She was young, she met a guy at a concert or a party...Something like that. They hooked up, she got knocked up." He opened a can of *Toro*.

I wrinkled my nose. "But there's more, isn't there? Flame, I wasn't planning on having this conversation now, but I need you to be open with me. You've been keeping secrets, like the door traveling ability. I've seen you engage in magic, too. And not only in your feline form."

Flame sipped his drink. "Honestly, I don't know how I do what I do. Sometimes I want something to happen, and it does. Little things, nothing big. Like making a window rise when

I'm in cat mode or turning on a light by thinking about it."

"Or setting fire to the Crimson Stone," I said.

He nodded. "I didn't try to do what ended up happening. I simply wanted the nice lady who took me in to feel happy."

My laugh was reduced to one short huff. "Well, it worked."

"Then I did a good thing."

"An extremely good thing. But by doing what you did, I think you proved you are part of a larger legacy."

He tilted his head. "What do you mean?"

I'd wanted to discuss this with Templeton before talking to Flame, but Templeton's reaction to what I had to do to bring him home safely blew everything apart. I'd written the prophecy down on a piece of paper and tucked it inside the book of fairy tales. I lifted the newspaper Templeton had browsed and pulled the book out from under it.

I showed Flame the paper. "Have you ever seen or heard these lines before?"

A traveler is born.
The knight protects the light.

Their successor sets fire to the stone.
A shadow is cast out.

Flame read the words silently. "No. Should I have?"

"Not necessarily, but my friend Emily, Templeton, and I all knew only a line or two of the prophecy. Emily is the traveler, Templeton is the knight, and I'm the light." I tapped the third line. "And I think you might be the successor."

Flame seemed nonplussed over his potential role in the prophecy. "Who's the shadow?"

"We don't know who – or what – the shadow represents. Rabbit took us to meet with an old Rabbit called the Tortoise. He thought perhaps it meant evil might be cast out of the Empire as a whole," I said.

Flame sipped his drink. "But you don't know for sure."

"No. But I do think it's likely you're the successor. The fact you can do magic adds weight to my belief."

His questioning cat eyes blinked slowly. "Am I supposed to use the Stone for something?"

"Maybe. I don't know. I wanted to go over this with Templeton, but…" I shook my head. "Now I don't know what to do."

"Nothing, that's what you're going to do," Flame instructed. "Well, after you shower. You smell, you know...*musky*."

My face ran through 10 shades of embarrassment.

Flame lifted an eyebrow. "I'm half cat. I can smell these things. And I know what naughtiness you were up to last night."

"I want to die now," I groaned.

"Don't rush it, Luscious," Flame laughed, tossing his can into the recyclable bin as the Empire service line phone rang in its cupboard. Without missing a beat, Flame popped open the door and answered it. "Hello? Yes, this is the Bellerose residence. Yes, I'll take the message." Flame held out a hand, wiggling his fingers. I pointed toward the kitchen drawer holding a notepad and pencils. "Hang on, Empire Operator Person, I need to...What? Yes, well, hang on."

I watched as he wrote.

"Uh huh, got it. Yup. I'll tell her. Thanks." Flame hung up the phone before reading the message aloud. "You're expected at the Congress of Empire Witches tomorrow at 11 o'clock in the morning for your membership review. A Congress elder will meet you in the lobby and escort you to the panel. If you don't attend, your membership will be completely revoked. You'll also be held liable for damages the Congress incurred as a result of your non-compliance."

I gaped. "What? What does that mean?"

Flame pulled a face. "That's all the operator said, but it doesn't sound good."

"It certainly doesn't." I threw up my hands before hopping off the barstool. "Like I need this right now." Son of a bitch! "I need to get a message to Loren. I need to find out what's going on."

I reengaged the Empire service line. "This is Lucie Bellerose. I need to send an urgent message to one Mr. Loren Heatherworth."

∞∞∞

I certainly wasn't in the mood to schedule a lunch date, and I didn't want to intrude on Loren at home, so I sent a message explaining I'd meet him at a park in the eastern portion of the city. It would be close to Loren's home but still outside the part of Matar where the majority of witch business was conducted. I asked to meet at noon. If he wasn't available, he would contact me.

Word of the CEW's review, although not the most joyous of news, was enough to help break up my concentration so I didn't sit around stupidly aching for Templeton. It also gave me something to do – whether I wanted to or not.

The weather was beautiful, a perfect warm and sunny May day. It didn't match my spirits, but I went through the motions of showering and dressing, slipping a spring green button-down blouse over my shoulders. As I pulled up the denim skirt I'd paired with my top, I stared at the bed I'd shared with Templeton only hours before. I didn't have to be a cat to smell 'us' in the room. The air was thick with memories of our lovemaking. I shook my head. How could he so easily walk away from me?

I was angry, but to be honest, I was more hurt than anything.

As I pulled my hair up into a twist, I wondered if he'd door traveled to his estate in the countryside or downtown to his penthouse. A part of me wanted to go after him. A bigger part of me knew it was a bad idea.

And the more I thought about it, I needed the space, too. I was not up for dealing with his judgment after the hell I went through to find him. His words had cut me to the quick. Maybe he'd finally pushed me to my limit.

I swiped mascara over my eyelashes and called it good.

Loren received my message and sent one back immediately, agreeing to meet. For me, it was a 20-minute drive across town. As I prepared to leave, Flame swept up the broken glass in my kitchen. He asked what he should do if Templeton returned. Should he tell him to wait for me?

No. I wasn't ready for round two – that is, if there would be a second chance to defend my choices. I asked Flame to hang around the house, though. We needed to talk more about the magic he seemed to be able to do. I also wanted to test his abilities if he was willing.

As I drove, I pondered Flame's observations about Templeton. Would he return? Had he purposely left the Crimson Stone behind? Or had he simply forgotten, caught up in the betrayal he accused me of committing? I believed it to be the latter. Either way, he would be back for the Stone. It was only a matter of time.

And I would give it to him. It was his.

As for the prophecy, perhaps my role was completed with Flame's appearance. Perhaps I was no longer needed – like Emily and the part she played.

Templeton would take his Stone back.

We'd have no reason to see each other anymore.

My chest felt so hollow, it made my throat ache.

Gripping the steering wheel, I turned right at the sign pointing toward Lilac Hill Park, where I'd meet Loren and find out what I could expect at the review I was facing.

∞∞∞

This time of year, Lilac Hill Park was a kaleidoscope of purples, pinks, and even creamy whites. The multitudes of lilac bushes would be in full flower mode mid-month, but there were still many branches already blooming and pushing their glorious scent into the early afternoon air. The park counted amongst its floral beauty tulip beds, azalea bushes, and the delicate perfection of a handful of flowering cherry trees.

As I maneuvered into a narrow parking spot, I was struck by how fast loss happened in life, how everything could change in a finger snap: my father's death, the brutal way Rabbit was pulled from my life, Templeton's abduction into the Above...Even my relationship with Sebastian had turned in an instant prior to his first descent into the Below. And now, in less than 24 hours, Templeton and I had gone from lovers to...whatever this was.

My stomach churned.

Damn him.

I'd told Loren I'd meet him by the gazebo. I sat on a bench waiting for my friend, hoping he could fill me in on everything I'd need to know to prepare for the review panel. The sun bounced off the white pavement of the trails winding through the park, and I squinted. As I stroked the Stone through my blouse, I contemplated what I might need to do.

"Lucie," Loren greeted me as he approached from the left. "How are you?"

Blinking against the afternoon brightness, I

stood so we could hug. I held onto the older man a tad longer than planned, seeking comfort. He patted my back.

"Thank you for coming on such short notice." I motioned to the bench, inviting him to sit beside me.

"Of course," he replied. "But frankly, I was dismayed to learn from you about the review panel convening. As soon as I got your message, I hurried to the Congress. I was told a notification was sent to me last week, but Lucie, I received no such message."

This I did not want to hear. "Do you think there was a mix-up? Someone dropped the ball, and you weren't told?"

He sighed. "I don't know. But it troubles me."

"Me, too." My hands gripped the edge of the bench where I sat. "And you know nothing about the review itself?"

"Not a word. I expected to be presented with their 'findings' before the actual convening of the panel. When I brought this up at the Oversight Office this morning, I was told the 'findings' would be outlined at the panel on Tuesday." Every time Loren said 'findings,' he used air quotes. He looked as perturbed as I felt.

"Do you think my membership will be reinstated?"

"I do. But I have a feeling it will come with strict stipulations," he replied.

"Well, there's not much I can do about it." For a hot minute, I wondered if I should reach out to Timothy Richardson but pushed the thought out of my mind. It'd be better for me to limit my time with the man. I didn't feel good about the things he'd said.

"No, we'll both have to wait and see." Loren was miffed about not knowing what was going on. He sighed a second time before changing the conversation. "There's been a lot of activity at your house."

I contemplated the purple and pink landscape. "Spying on my house seems to be a popular pastime."

"Rabbits have been noticed coming and going. Rumor has it a physician was called." Loren's shrewd eyes bored into my profile.

"There was a...*development*." I chewed on my lip. It didn't matter, I supposed. Templeton's return wouldn't remain a secret forever. "Templeton is back. He stayed at my house. A physician performed a routine physical.

Everything's fine."

"Then why do you seem sad?" Loren asked. He seemed unsurprised at the news about Templeton, but Loren was good at not letting his guard down.

"Because it didn't work out between us in the end." Again, my fingertips touched the Stone under my blouse. "He's made it clear he's not interested in pursuing anything with me."

In my peripheral vision, I could see Loren's head shaking. "I don't believe it, Lucie. Passionate couples argue."

"Oh, this wasn't an argument," I replied. A soft breeze drew several errant stray hairs across my forehead, and I lifted a hand to brush them away. "This was quite the blowup." I considered telling Loren about conjuring Sebastian. In the end, I decided not to go down that road.

"Give him time," Loren advised. "Whatever it is, he'll come around."

"Sure." It wasn't worth arguing with Loren over Templeton's behavior. "I should let you go. I just wanted to find out if you knew what was happening – what I was up against."

Loren stood, holding out a hand to escort me to my feet. "I do need to go. But I will see what

I can learn before tomorrow's panel. I sent a message to Timothy Richardson."

I made a face. "I don't need any more favors from him."

"I don't plan to ask him for help on your behalf," Loren said before planting a peck on my cheek. "I'm only curious to see what he knows. I will plan on meeting you in the lobby tomorrow morning."

"Sounds good," I said. "I appreciate it."

Loren gestured to the lush environment surrounding us. "Take some time for yourself, Lucie. Clear your thoughts. Listen to the bees hum. Follow a butterfly. Let go and relax. It will be okay."

I squeezed his hand. "I might do that. I'm not sure if it will improve my headspace, but it's good to be outside. Thanks again for meeting me on such short notice. I'll see you tomorrow morning."

Loren gave a wave as he turned and headed back in the direction he'd come. I chose the opposite path, inhaling the perfumed air before straying deeper into the sea of lilacs.

∞∞∞

I spent an hour strolling through the park, dodging joggers and the occasional bicyclist. The sunshine drew everyone out, and the park was a popular destination. I did follow a butterfly off the beaten path, ducking under low tree branches. A shadow crossed overhead, dragging a black shape over the ground. I lifted my eyes, expecting a bird. Nothing.

After scaring a bunny and giving a wide berth to a young couple necking rather enthusiastically on an outstretched blanket, I decided it was time to go. I couldn't stay in this peaceful place no matter how much I hated returning to the ugly memories of the morning. I rounded a large lilac bush to locate a paved trail and came face to face with the last being I expected to see on a sunshiny afternoon in the park.

Nisha.

"Bellerose Witch," she greeted me.

Crazy bitch, I thought in reply. Out loud, I simply said her name. "Nisha. I was just leaving."

"The demon," she began, ignoring my intention. "I am unable to conjure him. He is still bound to someone. He is bound to you."

I kept moving, circling to the right. "I can't help you."

"You were to unbind him after you were finished questioning him," she continued.

"Maybe I'm not done," I answered. She spun as I passed. Although I didn't want to turn my back on her, because who knows what kind of terrifying magic she'd unleash against me, I was not going to keep engaging with the woman.

"You were to unbind him. He is mine. I want him at my feet during the Full Moon." Nisha's voice lowered, her sensual mouth sliding into a frightening, broad smile. "I will consider lending him out to you if pleasure is the reason behind your hesitation."

I stopped in my tracks, shaking my head. I'd had about enough of this creature. "Here's the thing. I never agreed to unbind him. I simply offered his blood in trade for the page. That deal is done. And he's *my* demon, Nisha, because he is bound to *me*. He's not *your* demon. Go find another to play with you. Sebastian's not an option." Again, I started to leave.

"There's been a significant shift of magic in the Empire, witch. I sensed it over a week ago – it's been getting stronger as the days pass." Nisha's voice trailed after me. "You must be pleased Templeton has returned."

Keep walking, the voice inside my brain encouraged. Instead, I stopped, pirouetted, and lifted a hand. "Your point?"

Nisha strolled across the grass, her bare feet leaving soft imprints. "The John Templeton I know is a possessive man. But perhaps he's changed? Perhaps he doesn't mind if his witch keeps a demon to satisfy her needs?"

She's baiting you, the voice spoke up again. *Don't get rattled.* I let my gaze flick down and up, then dismissed her. "Nisha. I'm no one's witch. I belong to no one. As for the demon, it's none of your business why he remains bound to me. Frankly, I don't care what you think. I'll keep him bound to me for as long as I choose. And this –" I pointed to my chest, then to Nisha, then back to myself, "– is done. *Done.*" This time when I turned my back to her, I didn't stop walking.

Nisha's words carried on the breeze, hissing into my ear as I followed the curving trail, disappearing from her line of sight.

"I'll look forward to learning Templeton's thoughts on your bound demon the next time he comes to me."

Chapter 23

By the time I'd returned home, my mood was so foul that poor Flame shifted into his cat form and ran out of the house before I could grab him. He slipped over the backyard fence and scurried off for parts unknown.

I'd not felt this angry in months. After Templeton's cruel behavior and the Congress' actions against me, the confrontation with Nisha was a firehose filled with gasoline hitting the fire raging through my core. The static electricity popping off my skin felt out of control.

The Crimson Stone burned bright underneath my blouse.

I drew the necklace out from underneath my clothes. The Stone throbbed against my palm, my fury making it hard for me to breathe. I'd felt this way before.

I felt it last year when I used the Stone in the faceoff with the Fringe.

I gritted my teeth. The remaining rational part of my brain told me to stop, to not follow the thought leading me to strip off my clothing in the kitchen before retrieving the basement keys.

I was going to do something I'd never done. I would feed my witchline with the raw energy growing in my body in response to the power radiating from the Crimson Stone.

Naked except for the necklace hanging from my neck, I descended into the dark. I didn't bother to turn on a light.

Alone, with plenty of new pain to use, I cupped the glowing Stone in my hands and knelt, my knees complaining against the hard basement floor. Bowing my head, I concentrated on the pain filling my heart, the despair that returned. It grew, amplified by the power of the Stone. I reached out to my witchline, the Bellerose Witchline, and fed it. Awakened by the Stone, it drew upon the pain I raised, pulling at me even before I was ready to release my energy. The force was so great that I shook, gripping the Stone and crying out. My ears were filled with ringing and the room blurred in a red haze. Dizzy, I clung to the Stone with one hand, pressing the other to the floor in front of me as I tried to remain upright.

My witchline gurgled like an engorged vein, its power steadily growing while I fought to regain control. Over and over, the witchline pulled energy from me. Lightheaded, I clutched the Stone to my chest and collapsed onto my side, the point of my hip bone coming in hard contact with the cement floor. My body weakened, I surrendered to my witchline, fuzzy-headed as the blackness filled my vision. I passed out.

∞∞∞

"Lucie!" Flame shook me. "Lucie, wake up!"

"What's going on?" Groggy, I blinked up into Flame's worried face. "Why are you here?"

"I could ask you the same," he said, helping me sit up.

Flame had placed a blanket over me, and I drew it around my shoulders. "My head is killing me." I licked my lips. "And I'm really thirsty."

"Let's get you upstairs." Flame guided me to my feet. When I was steady enough, he shuffled me up the stairs, carefully supporting me.

When we got into the kitchen, it was clear it had become late. "What time is it?"

"After midnight," he replied. "Are you okay to stand there while I get you water?"

I fluttered my hand at him. "I'm fine."

"You look like shit." Flame grabbed a glass and filled it as he assessed me. He handed me the water. "What in the name of the Empire were you doing?"

"I was feeding my witchline," I mumbled before taking a long drink.

"I don't know what that means." Flame became anxious. "Are you sick? Do we need to call someone?"

"No, I'm not sick. I'm fine. I just...*wow*." I dug under the blanket and pulled out the Crimson Stone. "I'd never used it before – I never *had* it to use for this. My witchline went crazy. I couldn't control it. It nearly sucked the life out of me." With those words, I realized it wasn't hyperbole. My witchline became a danger to *me* when it sensed the Stone's power mixed with my energy while I fed it.

"You sure you're alright?" Flame's brow wrinkled. Before I could figure out what he was doing, he'd set his big hand on the top of my head. His thumb reached down and pulled up on my left eyelid. "Lucie, your eyes are all bloodshot."

"Great." I pulled away from his grasp. "Whatever." I downed the rest of my water.

"I came home and found your clothes on the floor." He gestured to the garments I'd left behind hours earlier. "Then you passed out in the basement. How long were you down there?"

"Too long."

"You need to go to bed," he continued. "You have that thing tomorrow. Wait, did you even eat?"

"No." I paused, reflecting on my poor diet. I wasn't even hungry. "I'm going to bed."

"Fine. But let me help you." Flame herded me out of the kitchen and upstairs to my bedroom, mumbling the whole time about how I'd become a hot mess and he didn't know what to do with me.

I hesitated, my gaze falling on the bed where I'd curled up inside Templeton's arms. I pulled the blanket I was wearing more tightly around myself. "Tomorrow I'll change the sheets."

Flame stroked my back. "Tomorrow," he said

softly. "But for now, get some real rest."

I climbed into bed, nestling my face into the pillow.

The earthy scent of Templeton's birchwood soap was my companion as I waited for sleep to claim me.

∞∞∞

Maybe I'd finally crashed. After months of struggling, and fighting, and putting the broken pieces of my life back together, my mind and body gave out. I slept like the dead.

I slept through my alarm.

Right before 10 o'clock, I woke, groggily squinting at the time. *Shit!*

Flying from bed, I grabbed a sky blue summer dress and a sunshine yellow cardigan. One look at my unshaven legs meant I was wearing pantyhose.

I hate pantyhose.

I slipped on a pair of tan flats and pulled my hair up in a slapdash twist, attempting to secure it with several pins. I had 20 minutes to wash my face, use the bathroom, and put a piece of toast into my empty stomach.

But I'd ruined my toaster yesterday. It wasn't the first one I'd fried, and I knew it wouldn't be the last.

Ten minutes later, I stood pouring a glass of orange juice while I chomped on a piece of stale bread.

I hate orange juice.

My hair was falling out of the pins I'd haphazardly pushed through my locks. I surrendered to the lost cause, pulling them from my hair and flinging them across the counter in frustration. I turned to put the container of juice back into the fridge.

Templeton stood silently brooding.

"Oh, for fuck's sake." I shook my head, ignoring him and returning the juice to the refrigerator.

"You don't like orange juice," he stated.

"No, no I don't." I returned to my glass, took a big gulp, and made a face.

"Walk me through this again," Templeton demanded. "You conjured Sebastian, and then what? Had a chat, then door traveled into the Below?"

"Yeah, that's exactly it." I ripped off another piece of old bread and crammed it into my mouth.

His faded eyes narrowed.

I chewed, my eyes darting to the clock on my stove. I had five minutes. I'd have to run to the garage where my car was parked and break all kinds of motor vehicle laws to get to the CEW remotely on time. Damn, I should've called for a car. "It wasn't part of the original plan. I thought I'd use the page Guillaume had given me to translate the text in one of your books. I was convinced the spell needed to reunite the Stone was in it."

"Do you still have my book?" He interrupted.

"Yes. It's in the living room," I said. "I –"

"How did you get the page from Guillaume back?" Templeton cut me off again.

"I traded something and got it back." I checked the clock. It would take me 30 minutes to get to the CEW. "Let me finish. I don't have much time."

He opened his mouth to speak.

"Stop it! Stop interrupting me, Templeton!" I pressed my lips together, my palms raised and facing him. I regained control. "I got the page back. I was going to use it, then at the last minute, it hit me: I was planning to write your words – *your spells* – on a page that came from Guillaume. It was a horrible idea. Instead, I conjured Sebastian because he got into the Above *without* the Crimson Stone. I conjured him to compel him to answer my questions. That's when I learned the fifth door leading into the Above was open when it was found. He didn't open it. Then he told me the Stone only closes the doors. I never opened the sixth door in the Walled Zone, Templeton. The Darkness – Asmodeus – sensed me at the mouth of the entrance to the Below. He opened the door, not me." My shoulders lifted and dropped. "The little girl in the book of fairy tales never uses the Stone to open the doors. She only closes them. We assumed I opened the sixth door. I didn't."

"Then what?" Templeton's face remained impassive.

"Then Sebastian told me about the door in the Below leading straight into the Above. He was right. That's how I got into the Above." I checked the clock. One minute. "Listen, I have to –"

"And Sebastian did this because –"

It was my turn to interrupt. "Because he owed me."

Templeton frowned.

"I need to go. I was notified yesterday that my

hearing at the Congress is scheduled for today." I pointed to the clock. "In a half hour. I'm going to be late, and I still have to get my car." I grabbed my oversized purse with the library book I'd stolen buried deep inside. At the kitchen door, I turned. "The Crimson Stone is upstairs. It's yours, and I wouldn't want to keep it from you. I'm leaving. You can let yourself out."

Templeton nodded, his lips pursing. His head lowered, and I watched as a familiar compulsion appeared. The fingers of his left hand plucked at an imaginary piece of lint on his right shirt cuff.

I hesitated, my heart and head warring with each other. "I can't stay here. This panel convening now is unexpected. Even Loren doesn't know what's going on. The message I received said if I don't show, not only will I lose my membership, I'll be held responsible for damages the Congress 'incurred as a result of non-compliance.'"

He lifted his chin. "What does that mean?"

"I don't know, but I've got to go." I turned, this time being the one to leave my house after a confrontation with Templeton.

∞∞∞

I arrived at the CEW at precisely 11 o'clock. I double-parked on the street in front of the building, climbing out of my vehicle and waving at a young man wearing black skinny jeans, a skin-tight concert tee shirt, and a pair of work boots. I handed him two bills and my keys.

"I'm a friend of Rabbit's," I began. "I'm in a shitload of trouble, and I'm late for a stupid meeting at the CEW. I'm begging you...Would you find a parking spot for my car, and leave my keys at the security gate?"

"Will the guards let me get that close?" He laughed.

I cringed. "Good point. Leave the door unlocked and hide the keys under my seat."

"Nah, we can handle it." He motioned to a girl who looked about 10 years old. "I'll send my sister over with the keys. They won't give her much of a hard time."

I bit my lower lip. The prejudice in the Empire overwhelmed me sometimes. "I'm sorry."

"No worries," he grinned. He handed back the money I'd foisted upon him. "And any friend of

Rabbit is a friend of mine."

"Thank you. I'm Lucie. Stop by 1106 Autumn Avenue sometime for a sandwich. Bring your sister." I touched his arm.

"You got it. Good luck with your meeting," he added.

"Thanks." I made a mad dash, clenching my teeth at the gate while the guard searched for my name on the appointment list. After being let inside, I pressed through the ward – which felt unfriendly – and entered the building. I stopped.

The blind being – the woman who performed the ritual of recognition – was gone. In her place, another guard sat. He asked to see my Empire ID, then my Congress membership card.

"I don't have a Congress membership card," I told him. "What…What is that?"

"New thing, hold on," the man answered. He made a call on one of the internal phone lines. He provided my name and nodded as he listened. After he hung up, he motioned to the set of doors at the side. "You can go in. They've confirmed you don't have a card yet."

"Um, thanks." I hesitated. "The woman who used to sit here and perform the ritual of recognition, where is she?"

Again, the guard pointed toward the set of doors. "You can go in now."

I didn't know what to make of this. "Yeah, thanks."

In the lobby, Loren was waiting. He swayed from foot to foot. "You're late, Lucie. This is not good."

"I know," I said. "I'm sorry. It couldn't be helped."

"We're not going downstairs this time," he said, pulling me as he hurried down a hall to our right. "There are several rooms they use for panel reviews. We're in 'A' – the first one. I'll be on the panel with the other elders. When we get there, take your place at the podium. They might want to ask you questions."

"Did you find out anything? Do you know what I should expect?" I worked to calm my energy. Entering the room flustered would put me at a disadvantage.

"Nothing," he spat. "I don't like it."

Loren's reaction added to my anxiety. The voice inside my head sought to relieve my concerns. *What's the worst that can happen? You are booted out of the Congress for good, and the 'incurred damages' you must pay leave you penniless.*

The voice inside my head was due for a day off.

"Who will be there?" I asked. "I mean, on the panel."

"Nine elders, like before. The Acton matriarch is presiding. The Waverton patriarch. Timothy Richards, of course, and several others you do not know by name." We stopped outside a door labeled 'Review Room A.'

"Let's do this," I said.

Loren squeezed my arm. "It'll be okay."

In my heart, I knew Loren really didn't know if it would or wouldn't be alright. Looking at the dear man, the family friend who had shown me such kindness over the years, I knew Loren's star was fading. Loren no longer carried enough influence to affect an outcome in my favor.

He held the door for me, and I stepped inside. The room reminded me of a courtroom with a raised panel for the elders. Eight of them were already seated and scowling. The Acton matriarch sat in the middle of the others. I approached the podium, folding my hands on the top and glancing to the right, where two rows of benches were placed.

Involuntarily, I gasped, recoiling. *Guillaume.*

My reaction amused him. Sitting in the center of the closest bench, Guillaume's left arm perched comfortably along the back. His legs were crossed, and his right hand rested on his knee. His body was angled toward the podium, and his trademark raised eyebrow mocked me.

He'd dressed for the occasion, wearing a single-breasted jacket in black. It draped open, revealing a red silk shirt. He'd skipped the tie. While Guillaume favored jeans – even with a suit coat – he'd made the sacrifice for the panel review. He wore black trousers in a lightweight summer wool. His dress shoes were polished to a high shine.

My attention flicked back to the panel.

The Acton matriarch glared down at me. "One would think with your future at stake, you would endeavor to be on time for this panel."

"I'm sorry, madam. It couldn't be avoided." I said no more. Whether I told the truth or lied, offered a good reason or not, it didn't matter. Begging for mercy wouldn't help, either. I surveyed the length of the raised panel. Loren was as taken aback by Guillaume's presence as I was. The Waverton patriarch stared a hole through me. Next to him was an elder I recognized from the demonstration months ago. He stroked his well-groomed beard nervously, his eyes meeting mine once before he turned away. Another man filled the spot next to him, and on the end sat Timothy Richardson. His bland expression gave me chills. After Guillaume, Timothy was the most dangerous person in the room.

To the other side of the Acton matriarch, two older men and one significantly aged woman sat, their faces grim. Loren had taken a seat next to the woman. Off to the side, an assistant readied to take notes.

As the matriarch read from a document describing why the panel was formed, my eyes wandered back to Guillaume. Perhaps he was there to provide 'evidence' of my transgressions. He studied me – his cruel, patient smile unwavering. Guillaume was a powerful witch, and although today he would not risk using his magic inside the building without permission, our student-teacher relationship had formed a bond he seemed to be able to tap into effortlessly when we were near one another. Maybe it's because he handled my witchline as I worked to strengthen it. It was an intimacy not shared before I'd met him.

Although I'd awakened late and run myself ragged to get to the Congress, I couldn't ignore how my witchline was at its healthiest. It had never felt as strong as it did now. Using the Crimson Stone to boost my power when feeding it must've delivered a supernova-sized amount of energy. In the light of day, I was brave enough to seriously consider if I should risk using it again.

Guillaume's perusal of my person drifted up and down, from my shoes to the crown of my head, his brow dipping in concentration. I could see he knew my witchline was more powerful than ever. He pursed his lips and nodded. I saw the satisfaction in his expression. Our eyes met. He was pleased with me.

I might hate Guillaume, and he might get off on hurting me, but he definitely wanted to see me succeed. After all, it made him look good, too.

But my time under Guillaume's control was over. I would never submit to him again.

"Ms. Bellerose, do you understand the reason for this panel?" The Acton matriarch's question cut into my thoughts, and I returned my attention to the elders.

"Understand why it was formed? Yes. Agree with your reasoning and your decision to conduct a formal inquiry? No." Again, it didn't matter what I said – but I wanted it on record that I wasn't complying because I thought I did something wrong. I was complying because I was forced.

"Following our investigation, Ms. Bellerose, we've determined the lifestyle you embraced after your year with Guillaume is not in line with our expectations. We have decided to take corrective action. Your membership in the Congress will be reinstated, but we require strict supervision for the next six months. At the end of the period, the panel will reconvene to discuss if more time is required to realign your interests with those of the Congress," the horrible woman finished.

"Absolutely not," I interjected. "I do not have to submit to this panel. I will not."

"Oh, you will, Ms. Bellerose," the Acton matriarch threatened.

"Then I no longer seek membership," I shrugged. I sensed Guillaume's silent chuckle and refused to look in his direction.

"We are not giving you a choice," she retorted. "However, this panel is not in agreement as to who should provide this supervision, this instruction to return you to the fold of your own kind. Today, we will vote. You will either return to France for six months for additional instruction under Guillaume, or you will be assigned an elder to oversee your activities, moving into their family home."

Loren spoke before I had a chance. "If these are the options for Lucie, then she will move into *my* home, and *I* will provide the oversight this panel believes she needs." His face was red, but he soldiered on. "I have known Lucie since she was a child and –"

"Loren, your relationship with this woman is one of the reasons you will not be serving as her mentor," the Acton matriarch barked across the three elders separating her from my friend.

"I'm leaving," I announced. "This shitshow is over."

"Lucie." Timothy's voice cut smoothly through the elders' grumbling. "A word in private first." Without waiting for an answer, he stepped down from the panel, passed a suspicious

Guillaume, and placed a hand on my elbow, steering me toward the door.

"Mr. Richardson," the Acton woman's voice followed us. "I did not –"

"Ten-minute recess," Timothy interrupted as he pushed me through the door and into the hallway.

I twisted out of his grasp. "I'm not staying here."

"Yes," he sighed. "You are. And you are going to listen to me. Let's go for a walk. I trust you have a library book to return?"

Wary, I nodded. "Yes. Then I'm leaving."

He was amused. "You are willful. I...I shouldn't like it, but sometimes I do. Let's take the book to the library. Then I'll tell you what you do not yet know."

"Fine." I needed to return the book before I left the Congress anyway. If he wanted to tag along and annoy me, there was not much I could do.

"Was the book useful?"

"Yes."

"Good. I'm glad to hear that, once again, the Congress was the resource you needed. Everything you need, Lucie, is held here inside these walls. And it's yours for the taking." We turned the corner. The library doors appeared ahead.

"The library is a resource I will miss," I said as we entered. "But I'm not submitting my freedom to the Congress. That it was even suggested is laughable."

"Hmm." Timothy paused at the circulation desk to speak to a clerk. I continued onward, pulling the book from my oversized purse. I chose a returns cart at random and slid the tome in between two others. There. My theft was officially undone. When I turned, Timothy was standing right behind me. I hoped he didn't see exactly which book I'd 'borrowed.'

"Loren told me Templeton returned from his extended traveling," Timothy stated.

"That's correct. Templeton is back."

"You must be happy." He watched my face carefully. "I'm guessing it was a sweet reunion."

I flinched. "My relationships are private, Mr. Richardson."

"Of course," he replied. "And now that he's back, I'm sure you'll want to stay in the Empire. I'd wager he's eager to spend as much time with you as he can."

"Yes," I sniffed, adjusting my purse before

fidgeting with the bottom of my cardigan. I smoothed out an imaginary wrinkle.

Timothy lifted his chin. "Or maybe not?"

I hesitated. "I beg your pardon?"

"You sniff and fidget when you lie, Lucie. It's not a wholly unique tell, but you're relatively consistent." Timothy grinned. "Most people never realize what they confess to someone with astute observation."

"You think everyone has a tell?" I shook my head. Did I really do that? I sniff?

"Yes, of course. The more self-aware people can suppress it, but sometimes it leaks through when emotions run high."

I pictured Templeton's odd habit. "Like invisible lint picking?" I wondered aloud.

He laughed, an abrasive noise echoing in the silent library. "I'd love to know the emotional trauma behind that peculiarity of Templeton's. But no, the searching for lint on his sleeve is not his tell when he's being deceptive."

"Oh." I nodded but said nothing more.

"You want to ask me what it is, don't you?" The expression dancing across Timothy's face wasn't a particularly pleasant one. His lower lip twitched while he waited. He wanted to tell me.

Why? To prove he had one up on Templeton?

"I'd be surprised if you truly knew," I answered.

"Oh, he controls it quite well, but as I said, in times of emotional distress..." He raised a hand. "Like the night he asked me for permission to join the elders and watch the demonstration you were forced into with Guillaume. He waited until after the poker game. He lost a lot of money that evening. Several bad hands and an utter lack of control. His tell told me every time he was bluffing."

"Okay, I'll play along." The man was exasperating. "What *is* Templeton's tell?"

Timothy's fingertips lingered over the spines of the books on the returns cart closest to him. "It's barely perceptible. You have to pay close attention, and if his chin is lowered, it's difficult to see." He looked up. "But before he bluffs – or misleads, lies, whatever – there is the tiniest flutter in his neck. He must be suppressing a swallow. What he doesn't realize – or maybe can't control when he's upset – is that it still creates a quick flutter to the left of his Adam's apple. You've never noticed?"

"I've never had a reason to." My patience was

long gone. "While this story's been fascinating, I'm ready to go home. Please convey my rejection of my Congress membership to the others on the panel. I will not be returning. Thank you for your past help. I'll be leaving now."

Pressing his lips into a mean line, his eyebrows pulled together, and he shook his head. "No. We're not done. Now you'll listen to the real terms of the agreement you will accept, Lucie. This is what's going to happen. We'll return to the room, and the panel will vote on how you'll spend your next six months. The vote will be split down the middle. Half will vote to send you back with Guillaume; the others will vote to keep you closer to home and away from your former teacher's hands."

"There are nine elders," I cut in.

"I will be the deciding vote. It's up to you as to which course I'll choose. If you accept my terms, my private agreement, I will vote for you to stay in the Empire. With me."

I didn't even hide my distaste. "I want nothing to do with you."

"I'm not finished," Timothy continued, nonplussed. "We will marry, and you will bear me a child combining our witchlines. I will make sure your health is monitored throughout the pregnancy since your age carries some risks. But you will have everything you need to bring a healthy baby into the world. You will agree to remain married to me until after the child's first birthday. We can then divorce, forming a 50%-50% custodial split regarding decisions affecting the child. I will ensure you are well-compensated, and we will raise the child with his or her interests placed over our own. I have no desire to turn a child into a pawn. I've seen it happen one too many times."

I stood rooted to the library floor. Never in a million years would I have expected to be presented with such a ludicrous offer. I opened my mouth to speak, but no words came out.

A glint of excitement formed in Timothy's eyes. "The Richardson Witchline is thinning at a high rate. I expect the Bellerose Witchline will easily transfer to our child. My heir will continue the strongest witchline in the Empire."

"No. There's no way I'd ever agree to any of this." I found my voice. "No."

He ignored me. "To put your mind at ease, I

do not seek a life with you. I have someone I care for already, but she's not a witch. Nor does she want children." He paused. "She's a lawyer at my firm. She'll support our agreement. Lisa will understand our coupling – however pleasurable it might be – is simply a means to an end."

"You're insane," I blurted out. Time to go. I turned away but only made it two steps before Timothy grabbed my upper arm, dragging me back.

"And this is why you will agree," he snapped. "No matter what, you will be compelled to submit to the panel's decision. It's already been discussed. Do you think we were stupid enough to believe you would willingly submit? Especially to returning to Guillaume's abuse? Arrangements have been made, Lucie. Unless you submit, once you leave the Congress building, a set of magical practitioners will come together every day of your life to bind your magic. *You. Will. Be. Powerless.* Every day spells will work against you. Every day you will have to fight to do the bare minimum of magic. Maybe some days you'll gain an inch. But more often than not, you'll lose a mile. And it won't be the same practitioners working against you every day. No, people will need time to recharge. But you, you will be on deck every single day of your life to fight to use your magic. You're strong, but eventually, we'll exhaust you. And then you'll eagerly submit. *To me.*"

Terrified, I wrenched away from his squeezing hand. "You can't do this – the Congress can't do this. I have free will."

"No," he hissed. "You don't. But you do have a choice. We're going to return to that room now, and the Acton bitch will call for a vote. How should I vote, Lucie? Do you want to go back to France and suffer under Guillaume's hands? Or do you want to come to me? Think about it. Let's go."

Again, he wrapped his hand around my elbow and pulled me after him. Stunned, I allowed him to lead me. My fire wanted to tear from my body and set him aflame, but the fear he called up in my gut kept me in check. No, I needed to make it out of the Congress building and away from this craziness before I fought back. I needed a plan.

How in the fuck was I going to fight this?

I've heard of such bindings – they were rare, but they happened. Usually, it was a method employed to control prisoners of the Salesman

Empire who were also practitioners of magic. As strong as I was, it's true. They could wear me down. It would be a constant battle. It would never stop. They'd siphon the magic out of me.

When we reentered the room, the murmuring from the bench halted. Concern flashed across Guillaume's face when he saw me. He stood and made as if to come to my side but was stopped by Timothy.

"Please take your seat, Guillaume. The panel is returning to its review immediately." Before he was even back in his chair, Timothy nodded to the Acton matriarch. "Madam."

The woman made a moue of distaste at Timothy's indirect order but picked up where she left off. "The panel is going to vote. Those in favor of Lucie Bellerose returning to study under Guillaume for the next six months, please say aye."

Four 'ayes' came from the bench, including the Acton matriarch, the Waverton patriarch, the man sitting next to Timothy, and the ancient woman sitting next to Loren. My focus flipped to Guillaume. Anger skittered over his features.

The Acton matriarch bared her teeth. "Those in favor of Lucie Bellerose remaining in the Empire and submitting to an elder for supervision for the next six months, please say aye."

Loren and three men called out their 'ayes.'

Timothy leered down at me from the panel. I held his gaze for a beat, then lowered my eyes to the floor. I nodded.

Timothy's voice dripped with victory. "Panel madam, I vote...*aye.*"

Chapter 24

It wasn't exactly chaos, but Guillaume had much to say to the panel after the vote. Whatever would happen next, I certainly wasn't invited to the discussion about my future. Timothy looked past Guillaume's rant, satisfaction bloating his face. When Loren appeared at my side, I asked him to escort me out.

Loren kept trying to reassure me that it would work out alright. He was unaware of the conversation I'd had with Timothy, though, and I didn't have the energy – or the heart – to tell him. It was clear information was being withheld from Loren, but I'd bet he wasn't the only one without a clue. No, the deal Timothy forced on me was his own. I doubted any of the other elders on the panel knew what he had planned. And now, he would convince the panel to select him as the elder to 'supervise' me.

I said goodbye to Loren in the lobby and fled the building. I needed time to think, to plan my next steps. At the gate, I picked up my keys, and he pointed me to the right. After I stepped outside to the curb, I saw a man waiting for me. He rested against my RAV4, a cane at his side.

Oh, Rabbit.

"I got a text saying some pretty witch in the 'middle of a meltdown' claimed to know me and was waving her car keys around like a madwoman outside the CEW." Rabbit's eyes turned glittery as he teased.

"That's not entirely true," I said. "It wasn't a meltdown. I was running late."

Rabbit's expression switched from mischievous to concerned. His nose twitched. "What's wrong? The Congress isn't letting you come back?"

"Oh, I'm allowed to come back," I said, unlocking my car doors. "I'm not allowed to leave."

"I don't like the sound of that." His lips formed a grim line.

"It's not good." I motioned to my vehicle. "Come home with me? I could use a true friend about now."

∞∞∞

On the way back to my townhouse, I told Rabbit everything. He kept shaking his head and muttering 'fucking witches.' I reminded him I was a witch. He told me I was different.

And that was my problem. I *was* different. I had strengthened my witchline. I'd done the impossible. But I didn't play in witch politics, and I didn't 'stick to my own kind.' I'd pulled the spotlight on myself and fought back, aligning myself more often with non-witches. Now I had to deal with the outcome of the entire mess. And I still didn't know what to do.

At home with Rabbit, I found I'd grown hungry and made egg and olive sandwiches for lunch. It was strange to go through such routine motions with the Congress' demands hanging over my head. I just kept putting one foot in front of the other. And yet, what else could I do?

"I'll do whatever it takes to help you," Rabbit told me. "The network is at your disposal. We'll find a way out of this without your magic being crushed by the Congress. You need to stay away from this Timothy Richardson. I'll see if the network can find anything out about him."

"Thanks." I cut our sandwiches in half. I couldn't see how Rabbit or the network could help, but it was good to have him by my side. I needed him.

"When are you going to tell Templeton?"

I lifted a shoulder. "Um, I don't know. He's not speaking to me."

Rabbit snorted. "Back in the Empire for a week, and he's already a pain in the ass. I know you love him, but Lucie, I don't know why."

I lifted my head at Rabbit's words. "You believe I love him?"

Rabbit took a bite of his sandwich. He pushed the bigger crumbs around his plate as he chewed. He raised his eyes after swallowing. "Don't you?"

"I think so," I whispered, suddenly reluctant to talk to Rabbit about how I felt. "It's complicated."

"It's always complicated with you, Lucie." Rabbit sighed. "But if I didn't think you loved him...I'd..." My friend shook his head.

"What? If you didn't think so...You'd what?" I ignored my sandwich.

"It's complicated." Rabbit gave me a half-smile before his eyes snapped to the pantry door behind me. His smile disappeared.

My head tilted back, and I blinked at my ceiling. I didn't believe in reincarnation or karma, but if I did, in a former life, I must've been the worst person ever. I turned toward Templeton. "Are you here for...Did you get the Stone? I have to get your book. Give me a minute."

"Rabbit, I need to speak with Lucie in private. Now." Templeton's voice dripped with anger.

Oh, for the love of all that's good and holy, I thought. *Now what?*

"You know what? No. You don't get to tear her apart today, Templeton. Go spread your misery someplace else." Rabbit took another bite of his sandwich.

Templeton's lips parted and his irises – already a translucent blue – drained of all color. "This has nothing to do with you."

"Does it have to deal with Lucie? If yes –" Rabbit met Templeton's steely gaze with one of his own, "– then it *is* my business."

I studied Templeton, remembering Timothy's description of his tell. I saw nothing out of the ordinary. I did notice he'd indulged himself with a haircut since the morning. Except for some missing pounds, he looked exactly like the old Templeton.

He dismissed Rabbit with a sneer. I could sense the rage he was trying to contain. "This morning, I paid someone a visit and learned something very interesting."

I lifted my hand and rolled my wrist so he'd get on with it. I wasn't in the mood for guessing games. "And?"

"I visited Nisha."

"What the fuck are you doing playing with her, Templeton?" Rabbit abruptly pushed back the barstool he'd been resting against and rounded the end of the counter. "Did the Above make you stupid? Why? Why would you go to that...*that vile bitch?*"

There was something in Rabbit's past involving Nisha. I didn't know what it was, but I knew he was almost afraid of the priestess. And Rabbit wasn't afraid of anyone.

Templeton's nostrils flared. "Before you pass judgment on me, why don't you start with the witch?"

Wait, what? Why would he...? Wincing, I

closed my eyes. *Oh, no.*

"What's he talking about, Lucie?"

I opened my eyes to see Rabbit's pinched face. "I had to, um, I had to go to Nisha. I needed the page from Guillaume's personal book of magic, and I went to her to see if I could get it back."

Rabbit paled. When he spoke, he sounded as if the air had left his lungs. "What did you give her in return?"

I glanced at Templeton. Contempt poured out of him, filling the room. "You know, don't you?" I began. "You know what I gave to her."

"Oh, Lucie. I know *so* much." Templeton wasn't even blinking at this point.

"What did you give to her?" Rabbit tried again.

"Sebastian's blood," I said softly. "I kept the bloody tissues he'd left behind after I hit him in the face earlier this year. I figured Nisha might be willing to make the trade. She was."

Rabbit's brow pulled down. "Dammit, Lucie. You are…You were foolish to go to her. Don't do it again. *Ever.* But it's a done deal. It's over."

"But it's not, is it?" Templeton continued. "Seems like that demon blood is useless to Nisha at this point."

Rabbit interjected again before I could get a

word out. "Alright, cut to the chase, Templeton. Now what's the fucking problem?"

Templeton finally moved. He stepped close, crowding me. I was forced to look up. "You kept him bound to you. He's *still* bound to you."

I held my ground. "Yes."

"Sever the connection," Templeton gritted out. "Now."

"I won't do that."

He glared at me, his menacing energy coiled against his body. The fury flowing through it was palpable. "Why?"

"Because…" I searched for an answer he'd understand and came up empty. I certainly couldn't say to keep him safe from Nisha. I rubbed the back of my neck and picked the other truth. "Because in the Below, the Darkness…I think he'll pull Sebastian back and punish him because he helped me leave. I can't…I wouldn't let that happen to anyone."

"Especially Sebastian," Templeton spat.

"No, anyone," I argued, noting Rabbit's expression was as incredulous as Templeton's. "You weren't there; you didn't see what I did. You can't even begin to know what it's like…The Below. The constant dark and the smell – the absolute loneliness. Evil permeated everything. There was no clean water, all the food was spoiled." I paused, shuddering as I pictured Sebastian's blood-covered body, huddled on the ground in fear. "The abuse the creatures deal out to one another. And the Darkness, he controls it all. He could send Beasties and devil dogs after you at any time."

Rabbit blanched when I mentioned the dogs.

I refocused on Templeton. "And he *did* send them after us. I've never been surrounded by such evil in my whole life. We fought for our lives. But it wasn't only the physical danger, Templeton. It was the mental games the Darkness played. It wrecks your head. The Below takes the worst things about a person's life and exploits them, and it does it in a place with no hope." I remembered the likeness of my father, asking me to stay. "The temptation to remain in the nightmare is real because you're seduced by…by…" I fumbled with my words. "The Darkness showed me his library. He told me I would find the answers to healing my witchline – *for good!* He said I could heal all the witchlines. I read passages from books proving I could do exactly what the Darkness promised.

And I *was* affected at first. I gave in to my desire. I didn't care about anything else. Only what I wanted to learn. And it was the most terrifying part of all of it – that I could leave everything behind and forget anything or anyone who meant something to me. That I would choose to stay in the Below to chase the answers I was desperate to find. That I would abandon my search for you, Templeton. But I didn't. I rejected it all. I left. And right or wrong, I wasn't going to leave Sebastian behind. I just couldn't do it."

Templeton didn't answer, his expression abruptly changing. The anger disappeared from his face, but it wasn't understanding or even pity left behind. No, it was something unexpected.

It was guilt.

I covered my mouth with my fingers. *The library.* He knew exactly what I was talking about. Slowly, I lowered my hand. "You were given a choice in the Above's library, weren't you? To stay there or to come back to...?"

And then I saw it.

The tiniest flutter to the left of his Adam's apple.

"I remember no such thing," he lied.

A piece of my heart broke free and crumbled in the increasingly hollow space inside my chest.

His words stole my breath. "Well, then there you have it." I blinked, my gaze lifting back to his eyes. "I can't deal with this right now, Templeton. I've already lost one battle today, and I can't do this. I can't keep up with all the fighting."

"You really suck as the prophecy's knight," Rabbit suddenly broke in. "You treated Emily better – hell, you protected Emily better – and you don't even like her!"

"This has nothing to do with you," Templeton snapped. "Why are you even here?"

"Because I give a shit that the Congress is going to force Lucie into marriage and breed her like a fucking animal." The muscles in Rabbit's shoulders grew taut. "Because I care more about Lucie than you ever will."

The two men were headed toward blows – I'd seen this show before. "Rabbit, it's okay."

"The fuck it is!" Rabbit slammed his fist against the counter.

Templeton contemplated Rabbit in silence. "What is he talking about?"

"The conditions of my membership." I rubbed the back of my neck. "The panel demanded I submit to six months of supervision. They threatened to send me back to Guillaume. But one of the elders...He was the deciding vote. If I agreed to his terms, he would vote for me to stay in the Empire."

Templeton's jaw worked. "Which elder?"

"Timothy Richardson."

"His terms?"

"Marriage and a child, to be followed by a divorce after the baby turns a year old. Custody shared. My witchline added to his family tree. This would give him an heir with a powerful witchline." Templeton was still standing close, and I could feel the rage he worked to control.

"And you agreed to this?" His cheek twitched.

"Under duress," I told him. "I said what I needed to say so I could escape the building with my magic intact."

Templeton's icy eyes narrowed. "What do you mean?"

"If I don't agree to follow the panel's ruling – and Timothy's terms – they will bind my magic daily until I capitulate." I felt trapped between the counter at my back and Templeton in front of me. Rabbit stood to my side, steadily watching Templeton. "Can I have some space?"

Rabbit stepped back. Templeton reluctantly inched to the side, leaving me only enough room to squeeze past him. My shoulder grazed his chest. I gave my uneaten sandwich the once-over, picking it up and considering it for a beat. Shaking my head, I dropped it right back on the plate. I fixed the two men with a long hard look. "I'm tired of fighting everyone. I'm never allowed to stop fighting. Can someone tell me why?"

Nobody said anything. For once, I wished Flame would come sauntering in, his pretty feline form sizing everyone up before shapeshifting and adding his youthful optimism to the mix. He was such a pain in the ass, but he was such a comfort, too. He believed things always worked out. I spit out a bitter laugh. Give him 20 years.

"You okay?" Rabbit asked. He grunted as he moved, reaching around the counter for his cane. "You want to go out for some fresh air?"

Templeton tracked Rabbit's movements, his focus bouncing to the cane, then away.

"Is that the answer to everything? Fresh air?" I

shook my head.

"That's what they keep telling me." Rabbit limped to the door. "C'mon. Let's go to *Coffee Cove*." He disappeared into the hall.

This would be a long walk. I didn't follow right away, instead resting my gaze on Templeton. "I want to be with you. That hasn't changed. But it's not good for me if I constantly need to defend myself to you. I will fight the Congress. I will do everything I can to keep Timothy Richardson away from me. And, yes, I will keep Sebastian bound to me for as long as I see fit – not because I want him, but because he's my burden to bear. If you can't accept my troubles and my choices, if the only thing you can bring me is more pain, then I don't want you in my life. I can't keep my head above water if you keep pulling me under."

He didn't answer, and he wouldn't look me in the eye. I waited, and when still no answer came, I turned and left.

∞∞∞

The trip to the coffee shop took us a while, but Rabbit was moving better these days. He admitted to improving, but he also said his hips gave him trouble. Mostly, he was frustrated. He hated using the cane, but crutches made his armpits ache.

Coffee Cove was next to a park, and I bought us each a coffee, joining Rabbit on the bench. I sat close, resting my head against his shoulder. For a moment, I could pretend it was last summer, and Rabbit and I were getting to know each other before I met Sebastian and started to date the Basha version of him.

"What did you mean before Templeton arrived? You said something about if you didn't think I loved Templeton. What did you mean?" I played with the lid of my cup.

He sighed. "I just want you to be happy. If Templeton makes you happy, then I'm glad."

"He makes everything hard," I said. "Has he ever had a meaningful relationship? I mean, I'm not talking about a date here and there – or even a lover. I mean an honest-to-god relationship where he's…I don't know. *Normal.* Committed. Not making demands all the time. Not a huge pain in the ass."

"He's always a pain, but I only know of one 'committed' relationship. Not that it was typical." Rabbit sipped from his cup. I waited, but he didn't elaborate.

"I'm guessing it didn't end well," I said.

"Nope."

"Who dumped whom?"

"She dumped him."

"For another man?"

"Yup." This time Rabbit's sigh was more pronounced.

"I feel like I'm pulling teeth here," I teased. "Who was the other guy?"

Rabbit coughed. "Me."

I sat up. "You're kidding?"

"You find it hard to believe?" He gave me the side-eye, a corner of his mouth lifting.

"No, not that someone wouldn't want you, but that you would've gotten involved in a love triangle in the first place." I shook my head. "Messy. I just can't see you doing that."

Rabbit's brow lowered, giving his strange smile a dark quality as he resumed staring across the park. "Yeah. Imagine that."

I decided not to press him on what he meant. I wasn't ready to have that conversation. Instead, I turned and watched a teenager throw a ball for an enthusiastic chocolate lab. "I don't suppose

I've met the woman you stole away from him."

Rabbit didn't answer.

I whipped my head around. "Seriously? I've met the woman? Who? Who is she?"

Rabbit pulled an unhappy face. "Nisha."

My mouth popped open. He tucked two of his fingers under my chin and pushed up, closing it. "Don't be so shocked. Nisha was beautiful and seductive. Templeton was young and hungry for her attention. And me? I was younger and way more stupid."

"I don't know what to say."

"I don't advertise it," he replied. "After Emily's father died, Templeton was drawn to a darker magic. Losing Daniel was hard on him, although he'll never admit it. The warped power he was building gave him something to throw himself into, to hide inside. Nisha was drawn to the force behind Templeton's magic and offered to teach him more. She seduced him. They became lovers."

I took a sip of my coffee, then hesitated. "Was she his first?"

I felt Rabbit's shoulder lift and lower. "He'd never share anything that private, but if I had to take a guess, yeah. Then again, I don't know.

Maybe some awkward fumbling as a teenager took care of his virginity."

"I'm not seeing that," I huffed, holding the coffee cup to my lips. I paused. I couldn't help myself. I had to know more. "Then what happened?"

"He ended up falling hard for her. And it wasn't just physical – they had powerful magic in common," Rabbit continued. "I met Nisha through him, and she ended up taking an interest in me, too. Several times she appeared when I was walking home late at night, inviting me to her penthouse. Eventually, I gave in and went to her and...Yeah. I slept with her. A lot. Like Templeton, I couldn't get enough. I wasn't the same man either. My friends finally helped me figure out that Templeton and I were both spellbound. She compelled us to want her, building off our original attraction. To gain our freedom, I had to give something up. Something I regret losing."

"Will you tell me what?" I asked. As he spoke, I turned sideways on the bench. I reached up and touched his face.

"No," he answered, turning his head and pressing against my palm for a beat. "But maybe someday."

"Okay." And it was. He'd bared enough of himself to me. Rabbit reached up and pulled my hand away but held onto it as he resumed watching the dog racing back and forth after the ball. The comfortable silence was a balm on my soul. Once again, I leaned on his shoulder. I'd be going through hell soon enough with the Congress, but right now, I could be quiet and sit with my dearest friend.

∞∞∞

Rabbit walked me home, refusing my offer to order takeout like in the old days. He suggested I get a good night's rest and we'd catch up the next day. In the meantime, he'd see if the network could come up with anything on Timothy Richardson. I wasn't sure of the point, but Rabbit felt if he was rotten enough to impose his will on me, perhaps he was also dirty in other ways. It was a long shot, but it gave Rabbit a way to be helpful. Templeton was gone when I returned, of course. The Crimson Stone remained upstairs in its box, sitting on my bedside nightstand. As I affixed the silver chain around my neck, I wondered why he kept leaving it.

Empire Tales for Children – the book of fairy tales – still sat on my kitchen counter. The book from Templeton's library remained on a shelf in my living room. To find it, he only needed to let a slip of his magic out to explore. It would connect with the magic in the pages of his book. And yet, it sat undisturbed.

On a whim, I checked the jewelry armoire holding the remaining pieces of tissue stained with Sebastian's blood. I kept them in a drawer protected by my magic. Immediately I sensed Templeton's signature pressed against the spell I'd cast. He could've dismantled it to see what I'd hidden, but he must've decided to let it be.

Flame still hadn't returned, and I tried not to be annoyed. We had a lot to talk about, and frankly, I needed to bring him up to speed on what I'd be battling soon enough.

Ugh.

There was leftover egg and olive salad, and this time I ate the sandwich. Afterward, I pulled out the bottle of Pinot Noir Sebastian had brought and poured myself a glass. I raised it. "Wherever you are, I hope you're safe, staying out of trouble, and not being an asshole." Then I took a sip.

Damn him. It *was* my favorite vintage.

As the sun set, I gazed out my kitchen window. I mused on how even with the shit coming from the Congress, and even with the mess with Templeton, things were maybe better than they were only a couple of weeks ago.

Rabbit was back in my life, Templeton wasn't lost in the Above, and my witchline was at its strongest. While my witchline made me an attractive target, perhaps I could turn it into a dangerous weapon. I smiled evilly into my glass. With the Crimson Stone, it was possible.

Maybe it was time to bring out the bad witch.

Cackle cackle.

Later that night, as I readied for bed, I also changed my sheets. There was no point in subjecting myself to the subtle scent of Templeton's body and our lovemaking embedded in the cotton. The new sheets were crisp and smelled of clean laundry.

The network phone sat charging on my nightstand. Rabbit said he'd text if he had any news to share. I knew he'd still touch base either way.

I checked the alarm and snuggled into the covers, letting a wisp of melancholy flow over me. I'd rather rest my cheek on Templeton's chest instead of my pillow, but that wasn't the way it was going to be. Maybe we'd get it right someday, but I couldn't force it to happen. He'd have to meet me halfway.

My eyes blinked, then closed to chase sleep.

After midnight, my house shook violently.

"What the hell?" Jerked from a deep slumber, I scurried up onto my knees, my hands out at my sides as I called up my fire to my fingertips. The Crimson Stone swung from the chain around my neck, waking as my fire came to the surface.

The air felt heavy with tension – like something was about to give. I waited, listening, straining alongside the thick air as something...*stretched*. Then...*Snap!* Something somewhere gave, and my home shuddered again. Outside, several car alarms sounded, and I could hear a few shouts. I stumbled out of bed and pulled the curtain aside. Lights were coming on in the townhouses across the street, and several front doors opened, casting bars of yellow down their front stairs. In the distance, I heard sirens – emergency vehicles were on the move.

"What's going on?" I asked. Instead of putting on my robe, I stopped to pull on a pair of jeans and a fitted gray tee shirt sporting the call to *Free Your Mind.*

The network phone from Rabbit grew warm, snagging my attention. The text read: *Are you home? Stay there. I'm coming.*

What's happening? I typed into the device.

Stay there, Rabbit texted back.

"What is going on?" I asked aloud for the second time, pocketing the phone. On my way downstairs, I checked the spare for Flame – he was still out. I'd have to talk to him about checking in more often so I didn't worry. In the kitchen, I padded across the floor barefoot. I switched on the radio and dialed in the Empire Public Radio station.

"...northeastern part of the city. Officials will not confirm if a bomb had been detonated, but speculation now includes a natural event, such as an earthquake."

"An earthquake?" I asked the radio.

Although when I thought about it, a bomb in the northeastern part of the city wouldn't be felt in my neighborhood. But an earthquake might send out aftershocks stretching for miles. Very strange. I turned to another station. Reports of massive destruction were coming in.

I skipped around to the other stations allowed in the Empire, but the news was the same. Mainly guesses and promises of more information to come. I poured myself a glass of wine and retrieved the bottle of vodka from the pantry shelf. Rabbit's text was puzzling. While on one hand, I could see him checking in to make sure I was fine – this was part of his caretaking nature – the sense of urgency I picked up from his text was curious.

I switched the station back to the Empire Public Radio.

"...reports coming in now of a massive sinkhole appearing in the northeastern quadrant of Matar..."

A sinkhole? Maybe the earthquake caused it. It certainly sounded more like a natural disaster than a bomb explosion.

"...it appears one whole city block has been destroyed..."

The network phone in my pocket grew warm.

Two minutes, the message from Rabbit read.

I shook my head. I was missing something.

I poured a shot of vodka for my friend and paced to the front of the house. Peeking out the side window, I turned on the porch light seconds before Rabbit came into view. He grimaced as he climbed the stairs. When I opened the door, he pushed me back inside.

"Lock it. Is the back door unlocked?" He lumbered toward the kitchen.

"No, I don't think so," I called after him. "I usually lock up tight for the night. What's going on?" I stepped into the kitchen as he returned from the pantry. He shut the door behind him.

"Are you okay?" He leaned on his cane and gripped my arm with the other hand.

"Yes, I'm fine. Tell me what's going on."

"Where have you been tonight?" Rabbit glanced at my shirt, reading the logo. The tips of his ears grew red when he realized I was braless. His eyes quickly raised.

"Home. I was sleeping." I pulled at my shirt's neckline. "I changed into this when the chaos erupted outside. Now tell me what's happening."

Rabbit pulled me to him and hugged me. "Okay," he said into my hair. "Let me catch my breath."

I waited. He gave me a squeeze before releasing me. I handed him the shot, and he tossed it back.

"Thanks," he nodded, squinting and giving his head an abrupt shake. "You've been home all night?"

"Yes. I've been here since you walked me home earlier." I motioned to the counter. "The radio's saying something happened in the northern part of the city. A natural disaster or something?"

"Yeah, *or something.*" Rabbit ran a large hand through his short hair. For a split second, I remembered his soft curls and hoped he'd grow his locks longer like before.

"I'm guessing the Empire's news is a step behind the network?"

"As usual," Rabbit replied. "What they are getting right is that it's a sinkhole. A massive hole in the ground opened up and swallowed an entire city block."

"You've got to be kidding me?"

"I'm not." He shook his head. "Lucie, it was the CEW."

I frowned. "What do you mean?"

"I mean the block where the Congress of

Empire Witches building sat is gone. That whole block. It's been sucked into the ground. Deep into the ground." Rabbit reached for the bottle of vodka.

I was flabbergasted. I didn't know what to say. Shaking my head, I found my voice. "Was anyone hurt?"

"Probably," he replied. "I'm guessing security guards inside the building – or even at the gate. If anyone else was in the building...It's late. Hopefully, the number of deaths will be small. But still."

"Unbelievable. There's speculation on the radio that it's an earthquake," I said.

"Lucie, listen to me. This was no natural disaster. There's already chatter. This is the result of some big fucking magic." A second shot was knocked back.

"You think someone was messing around in the building?" My nose scrunched up. Could a late-night magical working have gone horribly wrong?

Rabbit shook his head. "You're not getting it. It was an attack on the Congress."

"No way," I replied. "That's impossible. To overpower all the magic and wards protecting the Congress? Not even possible. Not in a million years."

"Not even by a powerful witch with the strongest witchline in the Empire? One who holds the Crimson Stone?" Rabbit's eyes flicked wildly over my face.

I laughed. "That's what you thought? No. As much as I would like to tell the CEW to fuck off, I don't have that kind of magic in me. I'm strong, but that's...Rabbit, that's huge magic at work. Not even with the Crimson Stone. No."

Then two things happened at the same time.

Rabbit dug into his pocket, pulling out his network phone and reading the screen as a new message came in.

Templeton door traveled silently into my kitchen behind Rabbit, the royal blue waves of his energy lit up with brilliant bands of silver. As the waves swirled lower, a ghost of a smile hovered on his lips. His eyes were solid white except for two tiny dots of black where his pupils remained.

Unaware, Rabbit did a double take as he gaped at the device in his hand. "Holy fuck. Lucie, there's a report of...The magic I was talking about. Someone is claiming it's the work of –"

"A Sorcerer," I finished softly.

Rabbit jolted at my words, turning and following my gaze. "Oh, fucking hell, Templeton. What did you do?"

Templeton ignored Rabbit, speaking instead to me. "I remembered. I remembered everything I read, everything I learned in the library. It was hidden inside my mind. I unlocked it."

I eased past Rabbit and stood in front of the transformed man. Only inches separated us. "You achieved it, didn't you?"

He didn't answer.

"Did you attack the Congress building?" I reached out a hand, touching his chest. Yes, the energy was profoundly different. The power coursing through him was unlike anything I'd known. It was so massive it frightened me.

"I took care of your problem," he replied.

"Yeah, that's not how I'd look at it," Rabbit scoffed behind me. "Templeton, you just started a war with the witches."

Templeton's strange eyes swept from me, to Rabbit, then back to me. "Not this one. I'm protecting her. They won't dare touch Lucie now."

Rabbit literally slapped his forehead. "This is

madness. Did the Above ruin your ability to reason?"

"Lucie needs to go away for a while. Take her south. Get her out of the city, but keep her in the Empire," Templeton directed Rabbit.

Here we go again, I thought. I fixed Templeton with a firm stare. "No. I'm not leaving my –"

Rabbit nabbed my arm, yanking me toward him. "Yes, you are. Pack a bag." He paused to text with one hand. "I told Big Rabbit to get his ass and his van over here. We're getting out of the city tonight. Go. Go pack a bag." He gave me a shove.

Reaching instead again for Templeton, I pressed both palms against his chest, opening myself to him, watching his eyes.

His energy flowed into my body – strong, confident, possessive…No. *Protective.* I heard his voice inside my head.

I will never let them touch you.

Are you still Templeton? I asked him.

Of course.

You feel different.

I am different.

Templeton touched my cheek, his fingertip gliding over the pale burn scar left by the Beam of Light months ago. A cool sensation stretched in a line over my skin. Without even needing to check, I knew the reminder of that horrific day was gone.

From there, he wrapped his elegant fingers around mine and pulled my hands from his chest. He touched the silver chain at my neck and drew the Crimson Stone out from under my shirt. His lips moved, and I heard multiple whispers inside my head as he spelled the Stone. When he finished, his voice became clear once more: *Do not take the Stone off. It will keep you hidden.*

Out loud, he spoke to Rabbit. "Take her now. They could come for her tonight."

The window slamming open over the kitchen sink caused me to jerk. Flame appeared on the sill. He pushed the screen in with an expert swipe and hopped inside. Perching on the counter, his tail twitched back and forth while his eyes bounced from Rabbit, to me, and then to Templeton.

Templeton smirked at Flame. "And take the stray cat with you. Don't let *it* stay here."

Flame hissed.

Rabbit pulled a second device from his jeans

pocket, tapped in two lines of code, and tossed it to Templeton. "I'll let you know where we end up. I've programmed it so you can text both Lucie and me."

Templeton pocketed the phone. He stepped backward, his hand touching the pantry doorknob. Our eyes met right before a silver light flashed through the kitchen. I blinked, and Templeton was gone.

"Subtle," Rabbit muttered. "Alright, let's get this show on the road."

In disbelief at all I'd learned, I turned to my Rabbit, my palms lifted, facing up. "Where are we going?"

Rabbit's thumbs were a blur on his phone. "We're going to hide you in plain sight."

Twenty minutes later, I was racing out of Matar toward a city called Vue in a beat-up van with two Rabbits, one orange cat, several suitcases crammed with clothes, a book of fairy tales, two personal books of spells – mine and Templeton's, the Crimson Stone, and one small wooden box holding the blood of a bound half-demon.

Chapter 25

On June 5, the Rabbit network snuck me out of the Empire and into Kincaid, New York, to serve as a bridesmaid at the wedding of one Ms. Emily Swift to one Mr. Jack Greene. The wedding was heavily 'watched over' by a modest contingent of Rabbits. No one expected any trouble, but Rabbit was unwilling to take any chances.

The day began with Emily puking her guts out in the bathroom, complaining about wedding day jitters. Several times she dashed back to the toilet before wiping her mouth and allowing her maid of honor to reapply her lipstick for the hundredth time. When the wedding march played, she looped her arm through Rabbit's, and he walked her down the aisle. The florist had wrapped a vine of flowers around his cane. Big Rabbit escorted Emily's mother to her seat, and I smiled in my not-so-bad bridesmaid dress as I scanned the pews for a familiar Salesman.

I hadn't seen Templeton since that insane night when I'd fled my home.

The ceremony was sweet and short, and at one point, I saw Emily's head suddenly lift. She glanced over her right shoulder. I felt it, too, but when I looked, no one was there.

Remnants of silver and blue waves drifted in the air. I caught Emily's eye. She winked.

After the ceremony, a female Rabbit approached the happy bride, handing her an envelope. I recognized the script-like handwriting on the outside. Emily opened it, pulling out a sheet of paper. Her mouth popped open as she gaped at the page. I tilted my head to the side and read the document.

A John Templeton established a sizeable trust fund for the first grandchild of Daniel Swift.

Emily announced she had to puke and ran for the bathroom.

The weather was perfect for the outdoor reception. In between dancing with the other bridesmaids, I sat with Rabbit, Big Rabbit, and Big Rabbit's girlfriend, laughing, eating, and feeling good.

I was amazed I could feel so happy with such

an uncertain future.

And I missed Templeton.

∞∞∞

The fallout from the attack on the CEW hadn't fully hit yet. Officially, the city of Matar – and therefore the Court of the Salesman Empire – ruled the destruction of the block holding the Congress building a natural disaster.

But magical beings across the city knew better.

The buzzing started. A Sorcerer was in the Empire.

A Sorcerer attacked the witches' seat of power.

A Sorcerer declared war on the witches.

Rabbits watched my townhouse around the clock. There had been several visitors, but no one attempted to enter. Rabbit made sure Loren Heatherworth received a discreet message. It was simple and to the point: *Lucie is safe. She has left the Empire.*

Of course, I had not. Truthfully, I was safer inside the Empire, where I had an army of Rabbits and a Sorcerer to protect me. I'd simply relocated for the summer – the 'for the summer' portion of my relocation was my claim. Rabbit grinned at me each time I said it. He was certainly kinder than Templeton but just as bossy.

We lived together in a tiny, rented house in Vue – a city in the southernmost part of the Empire. It was within walking distance of the dock where the ferry came in. Vue, known for its robust art scene, was alive with music, summer festivals, art shows, and city-wide artist celebrations. Rabbit took me on a tour. In the center of a park, I was introduced to a statue of Emily's father, Daniel Swift.

Templeton's mentor.

∞∞∞

Rabbit touched base with Templeton frequently, updating him on what the network was hearing regarding the attack on the CEW or simply reporting we were fine. I texted Templeton occasionally, mostly brief check-ins reiterating that everything was okay and how I hoped to see him soon. That I missed him. He never replied, but one day, while Rabbit and I were sitting by Sight Sea and watching the ferry arrive at the dock, he checked his phone and shook his head. He handed it to me.

Templeton: Is she doing well? Does she need anything?
Rabbit: She's good. She misses you.
~~Templeton: I miss her, too. Take care of her.~~
Templeton: Take care of her.

"I don't understand," I said, reading the message.

"Templeton doesn't realize it, but the phone records everything he types – even if he deletes it before sending. I see what he wants to say but still doesn't have the courage to admit, even after all this time." Rabbit huffed. "He's still the same old Templeton."

I lifted my face toward the sunshine and smiled.

∞∞∞

My remaining bank card was confiscated and shredded. The Rabbits didn't want me to leave a trail. I understood but fretted about money.

Templeton made sure cash was passed through the network to our place in Vue. We lived simply and wanted for nothing.

∞∞∞

My orange mackerel tabby cat, my pretty Flame, was a bit put out about being relocated back to Vue. After a heart-to-heart conversation, he agreed to shift and officially meet Rabbit.

Understandably, Rabbit was uneasy about Flame – he'd been hiding his true nature as a shapeshifter, after all. Still, Rabbit was fair and listened intently as I explained what I believed to be Flame's role in the prophecy. He agreed it was important to keep Flame close as events continued to unfold.

Flame, back in the bosom of his awfully large family, was thrilled to announce that David had rented an apartment in one of the trendier art districts. He would spend the summer in Vue with his boyfriend. David was becoming more devoted to Marcus, which made me feel better about their tumultuous relationship. As for Flame, I saw less of the cat and more of the sweet young man who promised me upon our first meeting that *'whatever it is, we can fix it.'*

∞∞∞

Unlike Templeton, I could not unlock the hidden place inside my mind holding all the secrets I'd learned in the library in the Below. For now, the information about the witchlines was lost. Still, I thought maybe, just maybe, someday Templeton would help me. Maybe if the Magician – I mean, *Sorcerer* – would slip inside my mind one more time, he could show me where to look.

∞∞∞

Rabbit and I talked a lot about the future – mostly in 'what ifs' related to the prophecy. We agreed Templeton's attainment of Sorcerer was meaningful, but we didn't know how it would play out.

We also talked about the secrets I'd kept – specifically Sebastian. I admitted we'd had a more significant relationship than I'd let people believe last fall. Rabbit told me he'd guessed as much. He also said something I didn't expect, that in a way, he understood why I kept Sebastian bound to me. How I was making the sacrifice to protect someone from a horrifying existence, even if he didn't deserve any mercy. Rabbit told me my 'big heart' was one of the things he loved the most about me – and that it was also my biggest flaw.

∞∞∞

Sebastian…I did not call him to me, and I had no idea where he was. I could feel it, though – the tether keeping him bound to me. After the frightening experience of feeding my witchline while wearing the Crimson Stone, I'd also become hyper-aware of the connection I allowed to continue between us. Whenever I paused to check on it, it was there. My sense was he had not been pulled back into the Below. That he remained free.

I was glad.

∞∞∞

Rabbit kept me informed about any news he

heard concerning the CEW. But as he once noted, witch secrets were hard to crack. A new Congress building would be established outside of Matar. The Salesman Court, the governing body of the Empire, took advantage of the misfortune that had befallen the witches and did not approve rebuilding. I feared this did not bode well for future relations between Salesmen and witches.

The worthless spot went up for sale.

In the beginning, Rabbit kept tabs on Timothy Richardson, too. Within a week of the Congress building's destruction, Timothy disappeared on an extended trip outside the Empire. Was he looking for me, or was he running from the attack on the CEW?

∞∞∞

The 'sinkhole' in the northeastern part of Matar was purchased by Lightworks, Inc. The Rabbit network spent weeks digging through digital paperwork to find its parent organization – a real estate company called Forefront Properties. The chair of the board? John Templeton.

Where the Congress of Empire Witches building once sat, a park would be established. The proposed name:

Victorum Square.

∞∞∞

As the summer progressed, I grew restless. I loved the oasis I'd built in Vue with Rabbit, but I missed my home. I missed Matar, the city where I'd spent my life.

I missed my 'real' life.

One morning, I sat cross-legged on a bench in the park next to the pier. It was another beautiful day in the lovely city, with the waves bumping into the shoreline and singing their watery song. I fingered the silver bracelet on my wrist, touching each charm. I paused on the tiny top hat with the word 'Hope' inscribed on it. I pulled out the network phone. It'd been two weeks since I'd last sent an update to Templeton.

I bit my lip, thinking.

Then I typed:

Do you remember the first time we met? You'd door traveled into my home looking for Emily. I walked into my kitchen to find a furious Salesman ranting on about how I 'let' Emily take off by herself. You were livid. Do you remember that night?

I hit send, then kept typing.

I had an idea of who you were based on Emily's description. I also thought you were being a jerk.

Send.

I made up the spell to give you the hiccups right on the spot. Totally pulled it from the ether.

Send.

It's still one of my favorite memories of us.

Send.

I grinned, picturing the serious and angry Salesman trying to lecture me through a wicked bout of hiccups.

As my friend Emily would say, it was epic.

The phone in my pocket grew warm. I pulled it out, expecting a message from Rabbit.

Instead, I saw the text from Templeton:

Mine, too.

(Go to the Epilogue.)

Epilogue

Flame – also known as Marcus – was originally from Vue. His whole family still lived there. Well, those on his shapeshifting mother's side.

It was the end of summer, and I'd been invited to a family picnic in one of the many large parks filling the seaside city. I sat by Ginger, Flame's mother, watching Flame – *er, Marcus* – play kickball with two dozen nieces and nephews. David tried to coach the opposing team. The result was noisy chaos.

Ginger was near my age – an attractive, petite-but-curvy woman with a sweet nature and a beautiful smile. She reminded me of a kitten. She giggled when I told her how Flame came to live with me in Matar, telling me 'that boy could charm a person out of his portrait.'

She was right.

When we got a moment to sit down without

an audience – an unusual break in a family of this size – I explained how I'd witnessed Flame performing magic, and that I was curious to know if there was a practitioner in her family line.

"Well," Ginger chewed on her lower lip while she studied her pointed and painted fingernails. "It's hard to say. My father didn't know who'd sired him, but a shapeshifting line came through his mother. My mother was also a shifter, and her parents were as well. Beyond that, I have no idea. If Flame has any magic in him, it could be through either of my parents' lines."

"Or, maybe Flame's father's?" I winced, hoping I didn't offend the kind woman who'd invited me to her table.

"Maybe," she said. "I don't know. Flame must've told you – he was conceived on a passionate night I had as a young woman." Ginger twirled a lock of curly strawberry blond hair around a finger as she gazed dreamily toward the kickball game. "Flame's my firstborn, my love child."

I nodded, watching Flame as he ran the bases, three laughing children trying to take him down. "He's a great young man. Very loving. You should be proud."

"I am," she dimpled. "He brought a tremendous amount of joy into my life."

"Um, his father," I cleared my throat. "Flame said you met him at a musical venue?"

Ginger tilted her head to the side. "I did. It was around the end of October when all the Witches Balls were being held. I was 19 and at one of those crazy warehouse parties with live music. I met a guy, and we ended up dancing all night. I think he was about a year younger than I was? Maybe? His name was kind of unusual. Anyhow, we did a couple of those sweet neon shots. Then we kissed…He got a little handy." She laughed. "I got a little handy."

I grinned. "It happens."

Ginger sat back in her chair. "I liked him right away. He was fun. He made me laugh. He definitely stood out in the crowd – tall and good-looking, with these intense dark eyes and oh-so-long eyelashes." Ginger made an appreciative sound. "Amazing kisser. And before you ask, it's true. I haven't seen him since. It's how it worked out. So, I can't answer your question. I have no way of knowing if there were any magical people in his family."

"It's okay," I told her. "The important thing is you have a wonderful son. I'd say that makes it all worth it."

"It was." She leaned over and snagged a drink from one of the open coolers. She snapped the can open, sticking a straw into the pop.

I absently reached for my bottle of water. "What was his name? You said it was unusual?"

"It was." She took a sip through her straw, her lips pursed. "I remember him telling me it was sort of a nickname, but everyone called him by it."

My eyes followed a rolling ball across the grass. Flame swept in, snatching it up in a long-fingered hand and palming it like a basketball before lobbing it toward home base. "And that was?"

"Basha."

The end.

Be on the lookout for
Walking a Fine Witchline, by T.L. Brown
– coming in 2023!

Resources

This book is a work of fiction. For portions regarding demons and demon conjurings, the author sought inspiration from the following resources:

Crowley, Aleister, and SL Macgregor Mathers. "Shemhamphorash (32.) ASMODAY." *The Lesser Key of Solomon*, Kindle ed., 2021.

Kramer, Heinrich, et al. "QUESTION IV By which Devils are the Operations of Incubus and Succubus Practised?" *The Malleus Maleficarum of Heinrich Kramer and James Sprenger*, Dover, New York, Kindle ed., 1971.

"Old Testament (1 Samuel 28:3 - 14)." *The Old and the New Testaments of the Holy Bible, Revised Standard Version: Translated from the Original*

Languages, Being the Version Set Forth A.D. 1611, Revised A.D. 1881-1885 and A.D. 1901, Compared with the Most Ancient Authorities and Revised A.D. 1946-1952, Second Edition of the New Testament A.D. 1971, T. Nelson, Nashville, 1972.

Acknowledgments

Dear Reader: I want YOU to know how grateful I am for your support. When you buy and read my books, YOU are helping me reach my dreams. When you recommend my work to other readers, YOU are helping me build my success. When you take the time to write a book review and share it on Amazon and Goodreads, YOU are not only telling others you liked it, YOU lift my spirits and inspire me to write more. YOUR words are important to me. *Thank you.*

I simply cannot imagine writing and publishing my stories without my husband Gordon at my side. I cannot imagine shaping worlds and characters without our deep discussions and passionate debates over character decisions and the consequences they'll face. I absolutely cannot imagine baring my soul to the world through these words without Gordon's hand resting on the small of my back. This book, like the others, was brought to life because of the loving support from my biggest fan, my own soul mate. Thank you, Mr. Gordon.

To my dear friend Jill Elizabeth Arent Franclemont: When our paths crossed at the writers "meet-up" in Rochester, I knew immediately that I'd met a kindred spirit. Thank you for your ongoing support, feedback, and critical eye throughout the writing process. I'm amazed at how you were able to give so much time to *Crossing the Witchline* – especially when your own schedule was already jampacked with a busy life and many responsibilities. Thank you from the bottom of my heart!

To fellow authors and awesome friends Jennifer Brasington-Crowley and Saffron Amatti: I'm so grateful for the time you made to serve as beta / ARC readers. As writers, you know the internal drama one wades through when getting the story "just right" while honoring your characters – even when you run them through hell. Thank you both for listening, offering advice, and making me laugh when I needed to pick myself up and smile. You ladies are beautiful.

And to those in the Instagram writing community who are true blue – *you know who you are* – thank you for connecting with me and becoming my InstaFriends!

Find the Author Online

Website and Updates

Visit WriterTracyBrown.com to learn more about her books and to connect with the author in all of her social media channels. There you can also sign-up for the T.L. Brown Newsletter (sent randomly and occasionally).

Social Media

Instagram: @WriterTracyBrown

T.L. Brown on Gooodreads:
www.Goodreads.com/TLBrown

T.L. Brown on Facebook:
Facebook.com/WriterTracyBrown

About the Author

Writer Tracy Brown lives in the beautiful Finger Lakes of New York State, dreaming up epic stories and quirky characters who definitely make her life much more interesting.

She believes magic still exists; you just need to look in the right places.

Tracy is the author of the Door to Door Paranormal Mystery Series, three books penned under the name T.L. Brown.

She's also the author of the adult dark fantasy Bellerose Witchline books. The Bellerose Witchline Series is a standalone one, but it shares some of Brown's most popular characters crossing over from the "Door to Door books" and revealing their darker sides.

Tracy's married to one damn amazing man. Together they talk about music for hours, cook up fabulous meals, and raise clever chickens.

Made in the USA
Middletown, DE
29 September 2022